High Seas:

The Cabin Boy

Michele L. Hinton

High Seas: The Cabin Boy

By: Michele L. Hinton

Copyright© Michele L. Hinton 2009, 2011, 2014
Published by: Seashell Books

Second Edition

Cover Art By:
SelfPubBookCovers.com/Shardel

SEASHELL
BOOKS
An On-Line Publishing Co.& Bookstore

www.myseashellbooks.com

Dedication:

This is dedicated to the first two people
to read and enjoy my rough manuscripts.

To Janet, one of my former Taekwondo students,
who said I was included among her favorite authors, and is
looking for me to publish her favorite of my works.

&

In memory of my aunt, Rose Marie Kuchenbrod.
If she didn't like it, she would tell me straight —
she loved everything I wrote.

Table of Contents

Introduction

Welcome to the adventure of *High Seas: The Cabin Boy*. The true author of these pages is the woman who lived them, and I'm about to tell you her story. To begin with, I need to explain to you how I came across it.

I went to an estate auction with my husband. I don't really care for them, but he does and we were looking for some nautical items for a room I was redecorating in my house. Among the items he won the bid on were a sextant, an old diver's helmet and a sea trunk. The trunk was pretty rough looking. The handles were broken, the latch was missing and it had a small hole in it. However, it had character and it went cheap. The trunk was also filled with old books. The auctioneer had put them in there earlier when no one bid on them. I assume the owner just wanted to be rid of them. So we ended up with a bonus.

When we got home, I started to unload the trunk so I could repair it. As I looked at the books more closely, I found they were actually journals. They were quite old. I read some of the pages and found them to be very entertaining, so I put them in order the best I could. The dates on these journals were faded with age, and it was difficult to make most of them out. Some of the pages were smeared where the paper had gotten wet. On other pages, there were no dates or the pages were torn. But as far as I could figure out, they began somewhere in the 1760's. The earliest journals were written by a child's hand. As they progressed, the handwriting improved.

The journals were written by Margaret Ann Wallingham, an English woman born on May 24, sometime in the 1750's, to the wealth and privilege of an aristocratic family. Her first journal was written when she was a child. The young girl wrote in one of her first entries that she hated keeping this journal. Writing down her thoughts, feelings and things she did was a requirement of her mother. She even wrote as one of her entries:

"Mother, if you want me to write things about myself, quit reading my journal!"

Her mother occasionally checked to make sure she was keeping it up. In later journals, she wrote that she was glad her mother encouraged her to keep one. They were a way to express her happy feelings, vent her frustrations as well as a way to remind herself not to repeat mistakes she'd made.

As I continued to read, I became more and more fascinated with the life she led. The journals were not only about her, but the history of her family. It was then I had a brainstorm. I wanted to write down her life — so here it is. I hope you enjoy her adventures as much as I did. I apologize to those people who like to read two page descriptions about women's clothing. Margaret only gave passing mention — so did I.

I'm picking up her story at age seventeen. Margaret had just received some upsetting news from her parents, Phillip and Clarice Wallingham. Therefore, without further comment, I present for your enjoyment, *High Seas: The Cabin Boy.*

CHAPTER 1
"Arrangements"

SLAM! The door closed with a bang. The vibration caused the sconces on the wall to shake, and a piece of porcelain went crashing to the floor. Margaret turned her head at the sound.

"Oh no," she sighed. It was one of her favorite pieces in the collection of porcelain cats that lounged in their places on the shelf in different poses.

"Just like my life!" She dumped the broken pieces into the wastebasket in her room. "Ruined!"

There was a slight rapping on the door, and then Scotty, a young maid of the household, entered the room. Margaret considered her more of a friend than a servant. She was the daughter of the cook and about a year older than Margaret. The petite, brown haired girl's real name was Heather Scott, but everyone called her Scotty — except for Margaret's mother, of course.

Their friendship had been a secret over the years. If it had been found out, her parents would have discharged the girl. According to them, friendship with someone below your station in life was not done.

When Margaret turned fifteen, Scotty became her attendant which made their friendly association easier. However, she was never able to get the girl to call her anything else but "Miss". The young maid was afraid she might make a slip of the tongue before her employers and feared being "sacked" as Scotty called it.

Margaret paced back and forth across the floor. "Scotty, they did it. They really did it! How could they do a thing like that to me? I'm their only daughter!"

"Now, now, settle yer'self, Miss, before ya' wear a hole in the rug," said Scotty.

Margaret sighed, walked to the window seat and sat down. "They signed my life away, Scotty. I am betrothed!"

***

It had started to be a wonderful morning for Margaret. She'd had an early morning ride on her horse, Shadow, and her dreaded piano lesson with Mrs. Albertson was canceled due to the woman's bout with the gout. Margaret thought the woman absolutely bathed herself in perfume to the point of nauseating a person.

It was while enjoying a fencing lesson in the recreation room of the family estate that the butler entered to issue Margaret a summons. He coughed slightly to make his presence known. "Excuse me, Miss."

"What is it — Charles?" Margaret replied in a breathless tone as she continued her swordplay.

"Your presence is requested in the library."

Margaret called her match to a halt and turned toward him. "By one or both?"

"Both, Miss."

Margaret removed her mask and rolled her eyes. "Lord, have mercy!" What have I done this time?"

There was a ritual with her parents when they requested her presence. If her mother called her to the sitting room, it was for a spot of tea with her boorish friends, or for needlepoint and general conversation. If she was called to the library by just her father, it was for a game of chess. However — if she was called to the library by both — she was in trouble. But this time, for the life of her, she couldn't think of what she'd done lately to irritate them.

Margaret turned to her instructor. "Thank you, Claude. The same time tomorrow?"

"As you wish." He bowed slightly. "You're much improved. I'd say you'd give Marcus a good challenge."

"Only in my dreams." She laughed as she tossed him her sword and mask.

Margaret loved fencing or just about any sporting activity for that matter. Her parents, especially her mother, disapproved of her 'boyish' activities as she called them. If it hadn't been for her brother's intervention on the issue of fencing lessons, she wouldn't be having them today.

Marcus was older than her by five years. He could talk their parents into anything, and just about everything he wanted he got. Anything Margaret wanted she had to go to Marcus for help — unless it was some sort of traditionally feminine pursuit.

Margaret changed out of her fencing attire in the dressing chamber inside the recreation room. Walking through the house in her knickers was strictly taboo. As she headed for the library, she racked her brain trying to figure out what she had done, but nothing came to mind.

Upon arriving, she opened the door and there they were. Her father, Phillip Wallingham, was leaning against the mantle with pipe in hand. His brown hair had just a touch of grey at the temples. He was a good father and provider for his family, but whenever she'd asked him for something, he would always say, "Go ask your mother."

Her mother, Clarice Wallingham, was sitting in the chair next to him. Margaret always considered her mother to be quite lovely and always wished she'd inherited her blonde hair and blue eyes.

Margaret gathered the butterflies fluttering inside her, entered the room and quickly stated before they had a chance to chastise her, "Whatever I've done this time, let me apologize in advance, and I promise not to do it again — or I'll do better the next time."

"Paranoia doesn't suit you, my dear." Her father kept his amusement in check. He raised his eyebrows an added, "Are you feeling guilty about something?"

Margaret shrugged. "No — not recently."

"Have a seat, Margaret. Your father and I have something important to discuss with you," said her mother.

Margaret was uneasy. This was the library and her parents were smiling. She knew this couldn't be good. The last time they summoned her like this was to convince her to attend the surprise birthday party for Aurora Sebastian, the daughter one of her father's friends. She didn't like associating with her. Aurora was selfish and probably the most spoiled girl in England — if not the whole of Europe.

"We want to talk to you about your future," her mother continued. "Your father and I feel that it's about time you take your place in society."

Margaret was rather perplexed. She was just introduced into society last year. It was one of the year's most lavish events. Her parents spared no expense. Since then, there was hardly a function that she hadn't attended; a ball here, a charity function there, boring teas with her mother's friends.

"How much more out in society can I be? If I'm not mistaken, you've only turned down one invitation this year," Margaret replied, "And that was only because it conflicted with Marcus's engagement party."

"Let me be blunt," her father answered. "It's high time you start to think about marriage for yourself. Your mother and I have made an arrangement…"

"Arrangement?" Margaret interrupted. She had this sinking feeling that she knew where this conversation was going. "What kind of an arrangement?"

"You know Nathanial Braxton," her father continued. "He's expressed a sincere interest in you."

"I don't think I like the direction of this conversation, Father!" Margaret folded her arm.

"Margaret, dear," her mother added, "You're beginning to be talked about. A daughter of ours is not going to be labeled…" Her mother could barely utter the word she was about to speak. She put a handkerchief to her eye to catch a tear and continued. "…Labeled a spinster!"

"Spinster!" Margaret laughed. "Please, Mother. I'm just seventeen."

"That's our point," her father said. "You should have started receiving gentlemen callers a year ago."

"I did, Father," Margaret replied.

"He doesn't count," her mother said in a huff. "Jeffrey Hawthorne is beneath you. He was just after you for your inheritance."

"You didn't know that! Just because his family isn't wealthy, that doesn't mean…"

"Don't argue! That is neither here nor there," interrupted her father. "The point is we've made an arrangement with Nathanial. He's had an eye on you for a while and approached me with a proposal."

"Nathanial Braxton — really, Father, he's double my age." Margaret's outrage was growing.

"Consider yourself fortunate, young lady," her mother replied. "He's from one of the most influential families in England. He's not only handsome, but one of the most eligible bachelors in London, and he's asked for your hand."

"But I don't love him!" Margaret insisted. "I've never even associated with him beyond a few dances and brief conversations."

By this time, Margaret had wished they'd called her into the library for something she'd done wrong. Now her whole life was going to be punished!

"Love has nothing to do with it. That will come in time," said her father. "You have to think about the respectable name you will want for your future children."

"Children!" Margaret couldn't believe her ears. Eventually she wanted a husband and children, but right now both were the furthest thing from her mind. True, she hadn't had any gentleman callers, and actually, Jeffrey Hawthorne was just a fencing partner. He was a friend of her brother's who came to call a few times and then for some reason, her father forbade him to visit unless it was to see Marcus.

"Needless to say, what is done — is done. I have accepted his proposal on your behalf. The two of you will need to be seen in public together. After a period of time, an engagement will be announced," replied her father. "That's our decision. Discussion closed."

Margaret was livid. Her face turned as red as her long, curly hair and her abundance of freckles disappeared beneath the color.

"May I be excused to my room? I want to contemplate my life — or should I say the ending of it!" She tried her best to keep her temper in check.

Her father gave his permission ignoring her dramatics as she left. It was all Margaret could do to keep from slamming the door behind her. When she got to her room that is exactly what she did.

✶✶✶

Scotty shook her head after hearing Margaret's account. "Tis' not fair, Miss, that they wed ya' to the likes of — him!"

Margaret thought Scotty's tone was somewhat coarse. The way she said "him" sounded like she knew something unsavory about Nathanial.

Nathanial Braxton was a well respected man of property and wealth. His generosity to the local orphanage was renown as well as his charity to the poor at Christmas time. He seemed to be a true gentleman. He was a fairly handsome man of thirty-four years and still had a youthful look about him. She might even have fancied him, if he'd come to call in the usual manor. But this way! An arranged marriage! It just went against her nature. If she made mistakes in her life for her decision, she could deal with that. However, having to live with decisions that someone else made for her, caused the hairs on the back of her neck tingle.

Margaret was curious about Scotty's disapproval. There was a look of hatred in her expression. She knew something about him that others didn't.

"What do you know, Scotty? Please tell me."

"I've been sworn ta' silence, Miss." She lowered her eyes to the floor.

"Scotty, this is my life we are discussing! If you care anything about me, you'll tell me," Margaret pleaded.

Scotty hesitated for a moment then sighed. "I do care, Miss. I'll tell ya', but this is ta' go no further than you and me. Do ya' swear on everything ya' count as holy?"

"Cross my heart. Not a word, I promise!" Margaret raised one hand and put the other on her heart.

"Very well, Miss," Scotty sighed. "Mr. Nathanial has two faces, he does. He looks and acts one way on the outside, but on the inside he's different. Me cousin worked for his family. A few bones rattle in his closet, don't cha' know! With his flowery words, he coaxed me cousin to his bed. He told her pretty words and gave her small gifts. Their relationship was a secret. No one knew 'bout it. One day, me cousin tells him she was with child. She was happy 'cause she thought he loved her as she loved him. But it weren't so. He called her such names! Then he told her he was sendin' her away. But he didn't do it quiet like. It was a public affair, it was! The Lady Braxton, God rest her soul, had a tradition ta' allow the servants of the house to throw a party for anyone of them that was gettin' married. So Mr. Nathanial had her lie. He had her tell everyone she was gettin' married and leavin' the county to be with her new husband. In return, he said he would make sure she and her child were taken care of. But if she ever come back to make claims on him or told a soul 'bout it, he would cut her off without a farthing! The boy is now goin' on three years. Surprisin' ta' say, the bugger has been true to his word. Me cousin has a small cottage in the country, and he's provided her with a story that her husband died as to keep her with a good name."

Margaret's anger was turned to sorrow, not only for herself, but for Scotty's cousin.

"If only my parents knew," Margaret sighed. "They would think twice about what they have done."

"Please, Miss, ya' promised!" Scotty pleaded. "For me cousin's sake!"

"Don't worry. I'll keep my word. I just need to think of something to get out of my situation. If only Marcus was here. He could help me."

Marcus was married about a month ago to a wonderful girl named Rochelle Dupré. They'd gone to Paris to spend time visiting with her relatives and wasn't due back for two or three more months.

Margaret walked to her vanity and sat down to take stock of her looks in the mirror. She wasn't one to spend much time in front of it. She hadn't thought much about it, but her parents were right about one point — she'd had no suitors. Was it the red hair and freckles that she'd inherited from her great grandmother? She knew some people were superstitious about redheads. She stood about five-foot, four-inches tall. She didn't believe herself to be a raving beauty, but neither did she think of herself as ugly either. Maybe it was her almost flat chest? Her mother had the bodices of her dresses stuffed to make her appear more enhanced in that area to disguise what wasn't there.

As Margaret ponder her situation, and how she could get out of it, her mother came through the door and looked at Scotty.

"Heather…" She addressed the maid by her given name, "…have a bath drawn for my daughter at once, and be quick about it."

"Yes, Ma'am!" She curtsied and left the room.

"Margaret, dear, you need to get ready," said her mother.

"Ready for what?" Margaret huffed.

"Don't take that tone with me, young lady! I'll not tolerate your disrespectful attitude."

"I apologize, Mother. I didn't realize my tone was ill. I'm just still upset."

"Be that as it may, what is done is done. Anyway, a messenger just delivered an invitation to dine at Braxton Manor tomorrow evening. Your husband-to-be wants us to join his other guests. So we have no time to dawdle. You need something appropriate to wear for the occasion."

She opened the doors to Margaret's wardrobe and scanned through her attire. "You've been seen in everything, and it wouldn't due for the future Mrs. Braxton to be seen in these old rags. We're going to the couturier."

"Oh, please, Mother," Margaret sighed, "I've got a headache. Besides, Gaston won't be able to create a dress to your specifications on such short notice."

Gaston's Modern Fashions was her mother's dress designer of choice.

"Nonsense! I'm his best customer. He makes a good income from my patronage. Besides, I commissioned three dresses two weeks ago for myself, and they are just about finished. I think one of them will be perfect for you. All he'll have to do is make a few adjustments here and there. So hurry on now."

"Very well, Mother."

Arguing would have been pointless. Her mother left and Margaret resigned herself to an afternoon of being dressed and adorned with all the trimmings just as a goose being served up for Christmas dinner.

CHAPTER 2
"The Braxtons"

The Braxton household was bustling with the task of getting the manor ready for the arrival of the guests that evening. Nathanial was in the smoking lounge with his older brother, Robert, discussing his upcoming nuptials.

"It's about time you get married, Nat. Maybe Mother will finally quit turning in her grave." Robert Braxton clipped the end of his cigar. "But why such a young woman? Why not pick someone able to run your social calendar? And why her? All that red hair!" Robert shivered. "You know what they say about redheads, they don't listen worth a damn. I have a feeling you, little brother, are going to have your hands full."

Nathanial puffed on his cigar and blew several smoke rings. "How about all that red hair. I can't wait to run my fingers through it," he said with a grin. "And I really don't give a tinker's damn whether she can run my social calendar or not. That's what I pay the household manager for. I'm just getting married for regular sex. Besides, it's about time I produce an heir to carry on the name."

"Dare I remind you, you've sired three little bastards already," Robert's disappointment in his brother's philandering rang in his voice. He cared about his brother, and basically Nathanial was a good man. However, he was somewhat of a whoremonger.

"And that's the point. They're bastards. What would it look like if I'd married one of those young harlots?"

"And who was it that took their virginities in the first place?" Robert shot back.

"Then answer me this. If they were such innocent lambs, why did they willingly go to the wolf's den? I never forced one of them. I guarantee you it was lust or hopes of upping their social status not love in their hearts."

"You don't know that for sure, Nat. I know how you operate. You could charm a turtle out of its shell."

"Be that as it may, it wouldn't do for our family image. I can see it now in the London Chronicle Headline: *Nathanial Braxton Weds Chamber Maid.*" He then laughed. "Mother wouldn't just turn in her grave; she'd climb out of it and paddle my ass!"

Robert couldn't help but laugh at that. "You're not wrong on that point."

"Besides, Robby, old boy. If I'm going to marry, you know I like them young, and Miss Margaret Wallingham foots the bill. She's just old enough for society to accept us as a proper couple, without me being labeled a lecherous cradle robber." Nathanial looked in the mirror over the mantle to make sure his blonde hair was still without any streaks of grey. "I still look good."

"But why her? Granted, she has a certain charm, but you could have your choice of London's most beautiful. They even to go out of their way to throw themselves at you."

"A couple of reasons," he replied. "She's not as pretentious as the others. I've only had brief conversations with her, but she still intrigues me. The second reason is her brother, Marcus."

"Marcus?" Robert laughed. "What in the world has he got to do with it?"

Nathanial puffed on his cigar. "I complimented him on his sister and asked him if she was seeing anyone. He told me to stay away from her. He's a protective bastard when it comes to his little sister. He said I wasn't good enough." He laughed. "Can you imagine that? Me!"

Robert just shook his head at his brother's conceit and Nathanial continued. "Unknowingly, Marcus has managed to put off just about every eligible young man in the city."

"How did he do that?"

Nathanial had a devilish grin on his face. "With my help. In conversations with others, I've found out that he's said the same thing to a couple of other men interested in pursuing her. So, for the past year, I've made it my mission to discourage anyone who's had an interest in her. I subtly had words put in inquiring ears that Marcus said they were not good enough for his sister."

"Why the hell did you do that?" Robert was aggravated by his brother's deed.

"Because no one tells me I can't have what I want," he huffed. "And I've decided I want Margaret. I've just made sure others lost interest."

"Nat, you're a cad!" Robert couldn't believe he made an important decision like this on such a silly premise. "Are you going to honor the vows you take once you have her?"

"You're always trying to be my conscience. And yes, I plan on keeping them. I'm tired of paying for my little mistakes. At least, if I beget any more little mistakes, they won't be bastards." He winked at his brother. "Who knows, maybe I'll be as good a father as you."

Robert chuckled. "When pigs grow wings!"

They both laughed and then changed the subject to other estate matters.

***

Margaret sat quietly in the coach as it approached Braxton Manor. It was a beautiful evening. The air was warm and a slight breeze blew through the trees as night birds were singing their songs. However, all Margaret could think of was rain. In her mood, it should have been pouring rain in buckets; the wind should be uprooting trees and lightning striking the ground. Bats should be flapping their wings in the night and getting tangled in her mother's hair!

Her parents just kept chattering away about the attributes of Nathanial Braxton, and what good fortune it was that he wanted their daughter. Margaret's mind, on the other hand, was cluttered with what Scotty had told her. All she wanted to do was blurt out what a philanderer he was. She also wondered if he would continue his flirtations with other women after their marriage — or even take a mistress!

"That would be too humiliating!" she mumbled.

"What would be humiliating, dear?" her mother asked.

Margaret just realized she'd spoken her thoughts aloud. "Oh, nothing."

As the coach pulled up to the door, it seemed they were the first to arrive. Usually her parents preferred to be fashionably late. The doorman greeted them cordially and announced their arrival.

"Welcome to my home," Nathanial said, as he shook her father's hand. "I'm glad you could come on such short notice, Phillip."

"Thank you for inviting us," Phillip replied.

Nathanial turned to her mother. "Clarice, you look absolutely lovely this evening. That is a Gaston original you're wearing, is it not?"

"As a matter of fact, it is! How did you know?" Clarice was pleased and impressed.

"What else would you be wearing? No one else could do justice to your natural beauty." He kissed her hand.

"You are too kind, sir." Clarice was now certain they were right in their choice of a husband for their daughter.

Margaret rolled her eyes. She hoped her mother wasn't so gullible as to fall for such obvious flattery.

Nathanial turned to her next, and she smiled at him politely.

"Margaret, my dear, I'm unworthy to stand in the light of your presence." He bowed gracefully and kissed her hand also.

"I hope that light doesn't blind you, sir," she replied, forcing a smile. However, internally she felt like throwing up. She also noticed her mother's disapproving glance at her sarcasm.

Nathanial just laughed. "Margaret, your wit is as charming as always." He extended his arm, and she reluctantly took it.

After the pleasantries were exchanged, the other guests were beginning to arrive. It was just a small gathering of about fifty. An orchestra was playing softly in the background, while servants offered champagne to the guests until it was time to dine.

Most of the people Margaret knew, and those she didn't, Nathanial introduced her as his special guest-of-honor. About twenty of his guests were relatives; an assortment of aunts, uncles and cousins. Those who live at the Manor were Nathanial's older brother, Robert, with his wife, Rose, and their younger brother, William, who was twelve years of age. Lord Albert Braxton, their father, was away visiting with friends in India.

The evening's conversation was as usual for this type of gathering. Margaret was relieved that nothing was said about the arrangement. She saw that Nathanial was cordial and witty with his guests and relations.

After a while, the chimes sounded that dinner was served. Throughout the meal, Margaret worried that the ball would drop and some sort of toast would be made on their behalf. To her relief, no announcement was made. When dinner ended, the men gathered in the billiard room to talk about affairs of state, and the women to the courtyard to enjoy the flora and fauna of the garden and the usual gossip.

Margaret was enjoying her conversations, when from the corner of her eye she saw two other eyes spying on her from the bushes. She excused herself from the woman she was talking with and approached the pair of eyes. They were attached to the smiling face of William, the younger brother. He was about her height and had the same blond hair and blue eyes as both his brothers.

"Are you playing hide and seek?" Margaret asked.

"Yes — and you found me!" He grinned. "Would you care to walk with me in the garden?"

"It would be my honor, young sir," Margaret said with a slight laugh.

She took his arm, and they walked down the lighted pathway of the garden.

"Is it true you're going to marry, Nat?" William asked.

His question caught her off guard. "What makes you think that?"

"I hear things," he replied.

"What kind of thing?" she inquired.

"I overheard bits and pieces when Nat was talking to Robert the other day. Your name and the word marry was all I heard before Rose caught me spying on them. So, is it true?"

Margaret was at a loss for words as how to answer the boy. However, before she could formulate an answer, he added, "I wish you wouldn't."

That statement caught her a little off guard and she couldn't help but giggle lightly. "And why not?"

William grinned. "Because I want you to marry me instead. I think you have pretty eyes."

Margaret laughed delightfully at the precocious young boy. "That's the nicest compliment I've ever had." She gave him a kiss on the forehead.

"Trying to steal her from me, Will?" Nathanial asked, as he came up behind them.

William tried to sound serious. "I asked her first."

"So, I leave it to you, Miss Wallingham. You have your choice. Will it be me, or young William?" Nathanial grinned.

"William, of course!" she replied, as she put her arm around the boy. "After all, he did actually ask me."

Nathanial sighed. "My heart is crushed! There's nothing left for me to do but satisfy my honor. William, I challenge you to a duel. Draw your sword!"

"Stand back, my love!" After saying that, William couldn't help but giggled and pushed Margaret behind him.

Nathanial pulled a wooden sword from behind his back, and William presented one from the scabbard at his side, and they began their mock battle for her affections. Margaret couldn't help but enjoy the spectacle, even though she tried hard not to. After a few moments, Nathanial thrust the wooden sword between William's side and his arm pit.

"I am vanquished!" William said as he fell to the ground pretending death.

"Alas, poor William, I shall miss him," Nathanial sighed. "But I must say, he was a lousy actor. Shakespeare would be appalled."

"I thought I was pretty good!" William exclaimed as he popped his head up.

"See what I mean? He's supposed to be dead," Nathanial laughed and extended his hand to help his brother up. "Off with you, scamp!"

William bid them a good evening and disappeared from sight.

"Care to walk with me?" Nathanial asked Margaret as he clasped his hands behind his back.

"Without a chaperon?" Margaret looked at him from the corner of her eye.

"Believe me, you may not see him, but rest assured William is there," he replied. "You seemed uneasy at dinner this evening. Were you afraid I was going to shout to the world our intentions?"

"You're very perceptive," she replied as they walked.

"Believe me, my dear. I wouldn't do that to you. I know you need time to get used to the idea of us being together."

"That was quite a production the two of you put on," she replied, avoiding the subject.

"I wanted you to feel more at ease before our talk. So I asked William to help me with this little play. Did it work?"

Margaret had to admit she was more relaxed. When Scotty said he had flowery words, she didn't understate it.

"Do you want the truth?" she asked seriously.

"Always. I want nothing but the truth between us. That's the best way to start a good relationship."

"Yes, I was nervous and still am. I don't really know you. Why me anyway?" she asked bluntly.

"Because you're real. You don't put on airs. For example, I watched you at dinner this evening. Most of the women took a small piece of prime roast, barely enough to satisfy the appetite of a small mouse. You, on the other hand, took a piece that was larger than mine. I looked at the expression on some of the other women's faces. You could see the jealousy in their eyes. They envied your plate though custom demanded that they deny their taste buds."

"I was hungry," she shrugged.

"So were they. Believe me. I know they'll satisfy their appetites when they get home. And as for my family, they'll gorge themselves when the rest of the guests are gone."

Margaret knew that to be a fact, for her mother had admonished her in private about her plate. It wasn't considered lady-like to eat more than a few morsels. One didn't want others to think you were piggish.

"I want someone by my side that will make a difference in my life. You have a vibrant personality. I'm sure in time love for me will grow in your heart. You've already begun to saturate mine just by your presence."

Margaret thought his words were smooth and buttery. "You present yourself well, Nathanial, but would you really want to marry someone who doesn't love you?"

"My parents had an arranged marriage that turned out well, until Mother passed on. My father was devoted to her, and she grew to love him. I'm sure our love will grow and develop as time goes on."

His words seemed sincere, and if she didn't keep her head about her, she could easily fall for this handsome devil's charm and wit. But, her resolve not to marry him was absolute. How could she marry a man who would ignore his own son, even if the child was a bastard?

"It's getting late. I think we should be going back." Margaret started to feel a bit nervous again.

"You're quite right, my dear." He then called out, "William! You can quit spying and join us."

The boy jumped out of bushes and walked beside them. They discussed William's play acting, and who was better at it, Nathanial or William.

"I wasn't acting when I said you had pretty eyes," William said. "Doesn't she, Nat?"

"Indeed she does," Nathanial replied. He took her hand and kissed it before they emerged into the courtyard.

Margaret shook her head. "The both of you could charm a zebra from its stripes!"

"Charm runs in the family." Nathanial laughed inwardly, for those were almost the same words that Robert had used earlier.

The evening was drawing to a close. The guests were leaving and the relatives that were spending the night excused themselves to retire to the apartments in the mansion that had been made ready. Nathanial bid the Wallingham's good evening, and Margaret was relieved that the festivities were finally over as their coach headed for home.

She'd wished that Nathanial had presented himself as the ogre that Scotty had painted for her. But to the contrary, he was charming, witty and the perfect gentleman. She remembered the gleam in her mother's eyes as she and the Braxton brothers emerged from the garden path together.

"Did you have a good time this evening, dear?" her mother asked.

"For the most part," Margaret answered honestly. She then decided to taunt her. "The meal was excellent."

"The less said about your behavior at dinner the better!" Clarice changed the subject. "I've received Nathanial's social schedule. We need to correlate it with our own."

"Do we have to discuss it this evening?" Margaret sighed.

"She's quite right, darling," her father agreed. "We've overwhelmed her enough for today."

"Oh, very well," her mother huffed. "Tomorrow at tea."

Margaret closed her eyes and listened to her parents talk about the evening's events. All she wanted to do was get home and go to bed. Tomorrow was going to come soon enough.

***

The next morning found Margaret with her fencing instructor. After disarming her a second time, he called a halt to their practice. Claude had been teaching both her and her brother years. Not only was he her instructor but her friend and confidant. Claude was about the same age as her father, born in France but raised in England. He lived with his wife, Renee, in a cottage not far away. Their son was recently honored to be assigned to the Queen's Guard.

After disarming her a second time, he called a halt to their practice. "Your head and your heart are not in this room today. Where did you put them? Yesterday there was anger in your foil. Today there is nothing."

Margaret walked over to a chair and flopped down. "My parents have arranged a marriage for me."

"I would offer you my most hearty congratulations, but by the tone of your voice, would condolences be in order?"

"I'll take the condolences." Margaret felt cheated. "My brother was allowed to pick his wife. Why can't I choose my own husband in my own time?"

"Such is the nature of the times and your status in the world."

"It's still not fair," she replied. "What would you do if you were forced to marry someone you didn't love?"

Claude grinned. "Is she rich?"

"I'm serious and you're laughing at me," Margaret huffed.

"I'm sorry. I was just trying to coax a smile."

"It didn't work."

Claude thought for a moment. "Join the army?"

"I'm not Joan of Arc! You're not helping."

Claude chuckled. "I'm sorry for your dilemma, Margaret. It's easy for me to consider what I would do. I'm a man. I could teach my craft anywhere. I could work anywhere I had a mind to. I could sign aboard a ship and work my way to another country and start over. But you, being a young woman, that's a different story. Do you have any relatives you could go to who would be sympathetic to your situation?"

"Unfortunately, no. Marcus is the last of the line. Mother and Father had no siblings."

"I'm afraid I'm not much help."

"Thanks anyway for listening. You're a good friend, as well as a fencing instructor, Claude."

"You wouldn't know it by today's lesson. Maybe you'll feel better by next week."

"I hope so," she sighed.

The chimes from the clock sounded that her lesson was over. Claude bid her ado, and Margaret entered her dressing chamber to change out of her fencing garments. She thought about what he had said:

He's right! What can I do? Where could I go? I have no real skills, and if I did, who would hire me around here? I can't book passage to some other country; I've no financial resources of my own. Father pays for everything.

Margaret sighed as she exited her dressing chamber. Escaping this eventual marriage seemed impossible.

My only hope is for Marcus to come home and intervene!

⋆⋆⋆

At noon, Margaret joined her mother in the sitting room. She poured the tea and they nibbled on their biscuits as they discussed the current gossip from last evening. Next it was down to the main topic — the itinerary. The list was three pages long and covered a span of about six weeks. Some of the functions were for her and her parents to attend, and others were just for her and Nathanial.

"Well, dear, your father went through Nathanial's schedule and compared it to his own before he left this morning. He marked the ones impossible for him to attend. Now we need to discuss a few conflicts of our own. I've marked them." Her mother handed her the papers.

Margaret scanned the list. "No opera — we're keeping the ballet." She continued scanning. "You and Father can attend the fox hunt."

"You! Don't want to go on a fox hunt?" Her mother was surprised. "You're giving up the chance to be on a horse?"

"Mother, the women's croquet tournament is next weekend. I'm sure to win top prize. I'm at the top of my game."

Her mother just shook her head. "You and your boyish sports!"

"I've heard the Queen even plays croquet," Margaret replied smugly.

"Why do you think I allow you to play?" her mother came back.

Margaret continued scanning the list. "The Seafarer's Ball is a must. Not the 25th anniversary party of Lord and Lady Huntington."

"Margaret, the Braxton's and the Huntington's are long time friends," her mother argued.

"Which is more important, Mother? A charitable function to raise funds for the widows and orphaned children of our naval seamen, or an anniversary party?"

"I agree." Clarice was disappointed at having to turn down that invitation. She was anxious to meet Lady Huntington. She had hoped with that event she would manage to be included in the woman's circle of friends.

The last statement on the list shocked Margaret, and she shot up out of her chair. "Oh, no! Mother, six weeks? I'm to be married in six weeks!" She crumpled the paper in her hand. "No! No! No! I refuse. That is too soon!"

"I know it's a short time to plan a wedding…"

"That's not the point!" Margaret interrupted as she paced the floor. "Marcus won't be home yet. He's not expected back for another two or three months yet."

"As it was explained to me, Nathanial booked passage to India to join his father. He wants you to go with him, and it wouldn't be proper for you to go unless you went as his wife," she explained.

"Then we'll just wait until he comes back! Believe me, I won't mind."

"Dear, he'll be gone for at least a year, if not longer."

"So! I don't care. I want to wait for Marcus to come home."

This time her mother came to her feet. "That's enough, Margaret! It's high time you quit depending on your brother. You need to put away your boyish toys and ways and start thinking about a family of your own to care for. Your brother has continued with his life, and you need to do the same. One would think I've been raising another son instead of a daughter. It's time to grow up!"

"But Mother!" Margaret pleaded.

"No buts!" Her mother was adamant. "Now go on about your day. Tomorrow we're going to be busy making plans, and I'll hear no more complaints. We have no time to waste. So anything you have planned for tomorrow — cancel!" Her mother left the room.

Margaret flopped down into the chair. A tear unexpectedly ran down her cheek, and she quickly wiped it away. "I'm not going to cry!" she said to herself. "It won't do any good."

Margaret thought about what her mother said, and she was right about one point. Depending on Marcus to come to her aid had become a habit. She had hoped to count on him with this situation, but he wasn't going to be here. She had to deal with this situation by herself. But what could she do? She stood and walked to the mirror in the corner of the drawing room and glared into it. "I'm doomed!"

***

Nathanial and Robert Braxton retired to the billiard room after dinner for a game of pocket billiards.

"Five ball in the corner pocket," called Nathanial. He made his shot.

"I don't know if I like this style of billiards," Robert said. "I like the traditional table without the pockets." He watched him sink another ball.

"Only because I beat your ass this way." He missed his next shot.

Robert took his shot, knocking in both his ball and the cue ball. "Damn!"

Nathanial laughed. "I rest my case!"

Just then the butler came into the room. "Excuse me sir, a messenger has just delivered this."

Nathanial opened the envelope.

"Who's it from?" Robert asked.

"The Wallingham's. It's the schedule changes." He looked down the list. "Hmmm — ballet instead of the opera."

Robert laughed. "Are you going?"

"I suppose."

"I thought you said you wouldn't be caught dead at the ballet?"

"I guess concessions have to be made — for now," Nathanial replied. "What about you and Rose joining us?"

"Oh, no! And don't you tell her either. She's been after me for years to attend the ballet with her."

Nathanial continued down the list. "Margaret's not coming to the fox hunt next weekend. She has a croquet tournament. However, her parents will attend. That spoils my plans."

"What kind of plans?"

"I was going to announce our intentions to be wed at that time," Nathanial replied.

"You're moving a little fast, are you not?"

"I have my reasons." Nathanial continued down the list. "Seafarer's Ball. It's the same night as the Huntington's anniversary party."

"Which are you attending?"

"The Seafarer's Ball," he sighed.

Robert smiled. "A harness around your neck already, brother?"

"As I said — concessions." As he continued to the end of the list, he smiled. "Good! No objections."

"Objections to what?"

"Robert, in six weeks time, you're going to have a sister-in-law."

"Six weeks! You're not in a hurry are you?"

"I want her wed and in my bed before her meddlesome brother comes home."

"So how did you convince them to prepare a wedding so quickly?"

"I told her mother that I was going to join Father in India in about six weeks, and I wanted Margaret to join me as my wife."

"When did you decide to go to India?"

"When I had the list prepared." Nathanial grinned. "I wanted to see what their reaction was before I did book passage."

"What if they'd said no?"

"I had faith in Clarice Wallingham. I know her type. She wants nothing but the best, so why settle for anything but the best for her daughter? If we didn't marry before I went to India, she would figure I would lose interest and marry someone else."

"And what about Margaret's father, Phillip?

"Now, he's a man with a harness around his neck! He follows where ever Clarice leads. The man may be wise in the ways of the world of business, but when it comes to his wife and household, she rules the roost."

"And what makes you think Margaret won't have the same control over you?"

"As I told you before, I just want a permanent bed partner and someone to bare my legitimate children. Other than that, I don't care one way or the other what she does."

"Nat, you may be my brother, but sometime you can be a real ass!"

"I don't think I'm being an ass. On the contrary, what other man would let his wife do what she wanted to do? I'll do what I want — she can do what she wants. What's wrong with that?"

"Nothing, I suppose. It just doesn't sound right. Something's missing in a relationship like that."

"If you're talking about love, to me it's overrated. I'll give her all the love she could ever want between the sheets." Nathanial took his next shot and missed. "It's your turn."

"I concede!" Robert hung up his stick.

"Why?"

"I've decided to ask my wife if she wants to attend the ballet with me." Nathanial was surprised.

"I thought you said you didn't want to go?"

"Because, brother, I *do* love my wife!"

Robert stormed out of the room. Nathanial shrugged and finished the table.

CHAPTER 3
"The Courtship"

The ballet had ended and three couples exited the theater. Margaret knew her parent enjoyed themselves. She also noticed Rose, Robert's wife, had a passion for the ballet. However, she saw no enthusiasm in Nathanial or Robert. She could tell they were bored.

"Wasn't the performance absolutely wonderful?" Margaret inquired. She wanted to see if he would tell her the truth about his feelings.

"Actually, the ballet is not my cup of tea," Nathanial replied.

"Why did you come then? You didn't have to," she shrugged.

"Because, my dear, you are passionate about it, and I take delight in seeing you enjoy yourself." Nathanial glanced at Robert and noticed he was rolling his eyes, but he said nothing.

Margaret was skeptical.

More flowery words?

"You know, Margaret, Robert surprised me by coming tonight. He hates the ballet," said Rose. "I've been after him for years to go, and then out of the blue he brings me flowers, and asks if I would like to accompany him. He's even arranged a private dinner for two at that new French restaurant, *Pierre's*. I don't know what's gotten in to him. He hasn't been this romantic in a long time."

Robert pulled out his pocket watch and looked at the time. "And we will just have enough time to make it." He bought a flower from the vendor. "A rose — for my Rose!"

Rose blushed. "Robert, have you been taking lessons from Nathanial?"

"As a matter of fact, he's taught me a thing or two." Robert shot him a glance.

Nathanial noted the sarcasm.

"You're the best thing in my life besides our children," Robert told his wife. He took her in his arms and kissed her.

"Robert!" Rose exclaimed as she blushed. "We're with company!"

"Shall we go?" Robert extended his arm and she took it. The two bid everyone good evening, and he escorted her to the carriage.

"Your brother is sweet," said Margaret. She could see true love in his eyes for his wife.

"Now I'm embarrassed," Nathanial said. "Actually, I was about to buy you a flower, but now, I don't know if I should or not. I'm afraid you might think I was copying his actions. Would you like one?"

"No thank you, it's not necessary," Margaret replied. "I'm not a flower type of girl, I imagine."

The two couples walked down the street to a café for a bite to eat.

"Margaret, your Father and I see some friends. Do the two of you mind dining alone?" her mother asked.

Margaret gave her a hard look. She really didn't want to be alone with Nathanial.

"We shall miss your company," Nathanial replied.

Phillip and Clarice excused themselves and joined another couple a few tables away. Nathanial and Margaret were seated at a secluded table in the corner.

"So, my dear, if you're not the flower type of girl, what type of girl are you?"

"I don't know really. I've never thought about it," she replied honestly.

"Would you care for some Champagne?"

"Just some tea, thank you." Champagne made her head swim, and she wanted to keep her wits about her.

The waiter came to the table and took their order. Nathanial ordered tea for two and a light repast for neither were very hungry.

"You're still not happy with our arrangement, are you?"

"As a matter of fact, I'm not," she said bluntly.

"Shall I tell you why?" Nathanial replied.

Margaret was curious. "Why?"

"Because I know what type of woman you are. You have an independent nature. You like to make your own decisions and don't want them made for you. You know what you like, and what you don't like. You're unhappy with me right now, because I'm being forced upon you. Am I correct?"

Margaret was surprised at how well he read her. "So, then why would you want to force a marriage on me that I don't want?"

Nathanial had prepared himself for that question. He reached across the table and took her hand gently in his. "I know you will find this hard to believe, but I do love you. Just being near you, I feel a ripple through my heart as a wave upon a pond. I've been seen with many women over the years. However, no one has ever made me feel this way. When I held you in my arms the first time we danced, I felt it then. It felt right for me, and I decided I wanted you with me for the rest of my life."

Margaret saw his eyes cloud as if tears were about to fall, but they held their ground. She thought to herself:

Are his words real? Or more play acting?

"I really don't know what to say," she replied.

"You don't have to say anything. Margaret, I can't be without you. I've hesitated for a year because of our age difference. But I could deny myself no longer. I know as time goes on you will grow to love me also."

Margaret listened to his words. If she wasn't on her guard, he could easily enter her heart — like a weed. She looked into his eyes to see if she felt that same ripple that he described. But there was nothing. She wasn't wise in the ways of men. She'd never had any experience.

Just then the waiter came with their order and conversation changed to something more comfortable to talk about — ballet verses opera. Soon dinner was over. The two couples rejoined each other and headed home.

The carriage stopped at the Wallingham home first. Margaret's parents bid Nathanial good evening and left their daughter alone with him to say their farewells.

Margaret dreaded this moment. Yet, she had also looked forward to it — just not with him.

"May I say good-night properly?" Nathanial asked softly.

She didn't say anything. She wanted to say no, but curiosity said, *What the hell!* She looked into his eyes, and there it came — her first kiss!

"Good-night, my love," he said quietly, as he held her in his arms. "This is where I want to keep you forever." After a moment longer, he got into the carriage and road off.

***

Nathanial sat back in his carriage and clipped the end of his cigar. "Home, Fredric."

"Very good, sir," replied the coachman.

A pleasant smile came over his face He thought to himself:

Shakespeare would be proud of your performance tonight!

He thought about her kiss. Her lips felt soft and sweet next to his, and he knew that he had been her first. He lit his cigar and blew a smoke ring:

She'll get better.

***

Margaret bid her parents good-night and went to her room. She thought about Nathanial's kiss. It was everything she thought a kiss might be. She enjoyed it, but something felt missing. Was it something missing from her — or from him?

***

Four weeks had passed and Margaret's life had been a flurry of activity. She'd won her croquet tournament, and that thrilled her. She also had the rest of that weekend to herself since her parents attended the fox hunt with the Braxton's.

After that, there were dinner parties almost every other night since then. People congratulated them on their engagement. Between her parents and Nathanial, they'd spread the word throughout London.

Some of Margaret's friends held a surprise party for her and showered her with gifts for her wedding night. She enjoyed this particular party. It was made up of just her friends, not her mother's. The girls that were married talked about the fun of the marriage bed after the first time. One of them even had a pamphlet that had very explicit behaviors. The girls laughed when Margaret's face turned bright red with embarrassment, as she looked at the drawings and read the articles. This went way beyond the birds and the bees! The girl didn't tell where she'd gotten it.

Margaret also attended a variety of sporting activities with Nathanial. And then there was the time spent with her mother to be fitted for her trousseau, invitations and other various arrangements necessary for a wedding.

Margaret's head was spinning. The upcoming weekend was the Seafarer's Ball, Nathanial's polo match and then dinner with his family afterward. Finally, she was able to talk her mother into one day for doing what she wanted to do, before she started pulling her hair out.

That next morning, Margaret got up early for a long exhilarating ride on Shadow, and then arranged to have Claude come for a fencing lesson.

"Ahhh! I was beginning to think you had quit on me," said Claude, seeing he his pupil exit her dressing chamber.

"Not by choice, believe me," she replied, adjusting the waistband of her knickers.

"Making wedding plans, I gather?"

"You gather right," she sighed.

"So, how are you and your intended getting along? Do you like him any better than you did the last time we talked?"

"He's been a real gentleman. He's been sweet and attentive — everything a girl could ask for in a husband and then some!" she exclaimed.

"Then why do I sense apprehension in your voice? You still have doubts?"

"I still don't love him. He professes his love for me every time he sees me. But there's something missing, and I can't quite put my finger on it."

Margaret went to retrieve her foil from its sheath hanging on the wall and thought about what Scotty had told her weeks ago.

"There's something else that's bothering you about him, isn't there?" Claude gave her a smile. "Come on — let's hear the rest."

Margaret gave a little laugh and folded her arms. "Aren't we a bundle of curiosity today? You know what curiosity did to the cat?"

Claude smiled. "Yes, but a cat has nine lives!" He flourished his foil. "I tell you what. You disarm me, you don't have to tell, I disarm you, and you tell me all."

"Sorry, Claude, what I know, I have been sworn to secrecy!" Then she took her stance. "En garde! Monsieur!"

"Ah ha! So I'm right! You've got something on him."

"Are you going to teach? Or talk?" she replied, twirling her foil.

"As you wish, Mademoiselle. En garde!"

Margaret was enjoying her time with Claude immensely. She had only just started when the butler came through the door. "Pardon me, Miss."

"I'm busy, Charles!" she replied, as she tried to concentrate on keeping her foil in hand.

"You have a gentleman caller," replied the butler.

She saw young William come through the door with his usual bright smile, and she halted her swordplay.

"Oh, no! William, I completely forgot." She had promised to go riding with him today.

"Margaret, is that you?" he asked, noticing her attire. "You look like a boy, except for your hair."

"Don't tell my mother that," she laughed. "Would you mind if I finished my lesson before we ride?"

"Oh, yes. I didn't know you fenced. This looks like so much more fun!" William exclaimed.

"Do you fence, young man?" Claude asked.

"A bit," he replied anxiously.

"Then choose a weapon and join us," Claude motioned to the wall. "The two of you against me."

Margaret had never enjoyed a fencing lesson so much. She watched William with delight. Toward the end of the lesson, the boy wanted to pretend that they were pirates. He took a handkerchief from his pocket and asked Margaret to tie it around her head to cover some of her hair. He said there was no such thing as a girl pirate.

"How do I look?" Margaret asked.

Claude laughed. "Like Marcus when he was thirteen — except for the red hair and freckles."

William gave them pirate names, set the scene, and gave them their parts for a great battle aboard the deck of his ship. At the end of their play, Margaret and Claude lay dead on the floor. William had saved his ship single handedly. After a moment of death, all three broke out into laughter.

"Well, as much fun as this was, it's time for me to go," said Claude.

"Thank you for coming on such short notice," replied Margaret. "I don't know when I'll be able to do this again."

"You know where to reach me. Let me know if I can do anything for you," he replied on a more serious note.

She knew he was talking about their earlier conversation. "I will."

Claude bid them good-bye and left.

Margaret turned to William. "I'll go change then we can go for a ride."

"Why? Just go as you are," he shrugged.

"Because my mother would swoon if she saw me like this," she laughed.

"So? Let's just climb out the window."

Margaret thought for a moment. Dare she? She gave William a big smile. "Let's go!"

It had been years since she'd climbed out a window. The gardener had seen them exit and put his hand on Margaret's shoulder.

"What were ya' doin' in there, boy?"

Margaret turned around. "It's me," she whispered.

"Miss?" The gardener was shocked at first and then laughed. "I didn't know ya."

She put a finger to her lips. "Don't tell!"

The man promised to keep her secret, and when they got to the stable, she had to swear the stablemen to silence also. They mounted their horses and speed off across the countryside. This was exactly what Margaret needed. She felt free and unfettered by the promise her parents made. It was as if she were a child again, only this time, a boy child. They raced, chased each other and climbed trees. She did everything she had seen Marcus do when he was young that she wasn't allowed to.

The time was getting late, so they headed back. With the help from a stableman and the gardener, to make sure they weren't seen, they returned through the window and Margaret quickly changed.

"I've never had so much fun," said William.

"Neither have I," Margaret replied. "Would you like to stay for dinner?"

"Thank you, but I had better be getting home. I told Rose I would be back by five o'clock and I'll just be on time."

They talked as she walked with him to the stables. It seemed to her that he had something on his mind to tell her, but he never did. William was the brighter part of entering the Braxton family.

When she returned to the house, she stopped to look in the mirror. She pulled her hair back and laughed. "I do look like a redheaded Marcus with freckles." She went upstairs to her room to change for dinner.

***

The night of the Seafarer's Ball arrived. It consisted of dinner, an auction of donated item and then dancing afterwards. The attendance was rather small this year, only about 150 couples due mostly to the Huntington's anniversary party. This was Margaret's third year attending the ball. She had a feeling that Nathanial would rather have gone to the Huntington's party. However, he agreed that helping widows and orphans was a worthy cause. He sounded convincing anyway.

Dinner had ended and Margaret looked over the items up for auction. There was a beautifully hand carved jewelry box and a quilt that she was interested in.

"If you wish to have them, they're yours," Nathanial said, noticing that she hovered over those two items.

"I'm still uncomfortable with you purchasing things for me," Margaret replied. She was used to her father buying the things she wanted.

"That's just one of the things you'll have to get used to." He gave her a smile.

Soon the auction started and just as he said, he won the bids on those items, plus a few other items for himself. When Nathanial left to settle accounts, Margaret turned around to examine her newly acquired jewelry box. As she did, she bumped into a gentleman carrying two glasses of Champagne and quickly jumped back.

"Oh! Please excuse me, sir, I didn't see you," Margaret apologized.

She looked up at the man. He was gorgeous! His hair was black as coal, and his dark brown eyes sparkled. His ruggedly handsome face was bronzed as if kissed by the sun.

"The fault is all mine," he replied. "My eyes were elsewhere. I didn't spill anything on you, did I?"

"Just a bit," she replied and gave him a smile. "But, I'll dry."

She found herself mentally comparing this stranger's features to Nathanial's blond hair, blue eyes and smooth creamy skin. She'd never done that before. She wondered:

Could there be muscles beneath his coat?

"Are you here with someone?" the man asked.

"Yes, I'm with my fiancé and parents."

"Then it is my loss." The man smiled at her warmly. "I was just about to ask you to join my sister and me, if you were alone."

"Thank you anyway. The thought is appreciated," she replied, but thought to herself:

Damn this engagement!

"Again, my apologies. I hope you enjoy the rest of the evening."

The man left her, and she suddenly felt a sense of loss, as she watched him walk away.

"Who was that, my dear?" Nathanial asked upon his return.

Margaret turned around and smiled. "I don't know. We accidentally collided."

"You're not hurt are you?" A look of concern came over his face.

"No, just damp. I'm fine and he apologized."

The music started to play in the other room, signaling everyone that dancing was about to begin. Margaret found herself nonchalantly looking around for the dark haired man, but he wasn't in the room, nor had she seen him the rest of the evening. She wondered why she was disappointed.

***

The man with the Champagne rejoined his sister, and he handed her a glass.

"Who were you talking to over there, Todd?"

"I don't know. I didn't ask her name. I was ogling the brunette over there, and bumped into a red head. I spilled half of my champagne on her dress."

"I hope you apologized!" she scolded him.

"Sarah, I'm not ten years old anymore." He laughed. "I have learned a few manners since then."

"You should have asked her to join us."

"I did." He sighed. "She's engaged."

"You sound disappointed."

"She had the most amazing green eyes." A mischievous grin crossed his face. "I'm afraid they're going to haunt me the rest of my life."

"Toddy! You're incorrigible!" She struck him playfully with the gloves she held in her hand.

"And you've been telling me that also since I was ten." He pulled out his watch and looked at the time. "Well, sister dear, I hate to leave you, but I have to get up early." He kissed his sister on the forehead and left.

***

Margaret was glad when her mother said she had a headache and wanted to leave. The night seemed to crumble after her brush with the dark haired man.

When they arrived home, Nathanial kissed her warmly and showered her with praises as he usually did. A stray thought entered her head while she was kissing Nathanial. What would the dark haired man's kisses be like? She also wondered why she was thinking about a man she'd only met for about two minutes and would more than likely never see again.

29

CHAPTER 4
"Revelations"

The day after the Seafarer's Ball, Margaret attended Nathanial's polo match. His team won and everyone returned to Braxton Manor for a celebratory dinner. Everyone laughed when Margaret said she wished there was a women's team. She said if they ever created one, she would be on it.

"Goodness me, Margaret! You are a daring thing." Rose laughed.

"And if my mother had heard me say that, she would scold me just as soon as we got into the carriage to go home," Margaret replied.

"Soon, my dear, you won't have to worry about your mother scolding you anymore for your eccentricities," Nathanial chuckled. "And if you like, I can help you start up a team. Rose, will you be the second member of our team?"

"Nathanial, don't be ridiculous! I might break a nail or mess up my hair." Rose tried to keep a straight face.

Margaret noticed that everyone was laughing and joking except William. He was being unusually quiet. Normally, he's the life of the table.

"Are you not feeling well today, William?" Margaret asked.

"Oh no, I'm fine," he replied. "I've just got something on my mind." He hesitated for a moment and then turned to his brother.

"Nat, would you mind if I play chess with Margaret this evening?"

"That's up to her," he replied and gave Margaret a wink. "You're not trying to steal her heart from me again, are you?"

"Too late, he already has," Margaret replied. She noticed that William's smile was more like a sneer when he looked at Nathanial.

"Then by all mean, your evening belongs to William." Nathanial looked to Robert. "Robby, how about a game of billiards?"

"Only if we play on the tradition table — not the one with pockets."

Everyone headed for different rooms. Robert and Nathanial to play billiards, Rose went to join her children in the nursery, and William and

Margaret went to the library to play chess. After a few moves, William sat there and stared at the pieces.

"You seem to be concentrating on something other than the chessboard," Margaret remarked.

He was quiet for a moment. "I have something very important to ask you, and I want you to be very honest with me."

"If I can. What is it?"

"Do you love my brother?"

It was Margaret's turn to hesitate. "We're getting married."

"But do you love him?" His voice was almost pleading.

She could see that he was bursting to tell her something, and only the answer that he wanted to hear would pry it from his lips. So she answered him honestly.

"No, I'm sorry, I don't." Her tone was low with a hint of sadness.

William breathed a sigh of relief. "I'm glad, because I need to tell you something."

Margaret watched as William got out of his chair and went to the library door. He looked out to see if anyone might be listening, and then he closed it and ran back to the table.

"Don't marry Nat! I beg you. You deserve better than my brother. He doesn't love you — I do!"

Margaret was touched. "I love you too, but as my young friend."

"I know that, and that's how I love you. But this is different. I told you before I hear things. I spy on my brothers all the time. This mansion is a playground of hidden passages and rooms, and I know them all."

He got up from the table and went to a panel on the wall. When he pushed in on two decorative carvings the wall slid back. Margaret's eyes widened as she got up from her chair.

"Come with me, but be quiet," he whispered. He grabbed a lighted candle.

Margaret's curiosity was aroused. "Where are we going?"

"Spying," he replied.

"Spying!" she repeated.

"Shhhh! Not so loud," he warned. "Robby and Nat talk about you almost all the time. If they say anything about you tonight, I want you to hear."

Margaret couldn't resist. She followed him through the opening then he pushed on the wall and it slid back into place.

"This passage way leads to the billiard room," he whispered.

The corridor was littered with cobwebs, and she could see tracks in the dust evidence of where William had roamed. After a few twists and turns, he stopped and put a finger to his lips. He knelt down on the floor and carefully slid back a panel covering a vent. He motioned her down on the floor with him and mouthed the word, "Listen."

Margaret could clearly hear the clack of the balls on the table and the voices from inside the room. They were in the middle of a conversation.

"…would steal her from you if he were older," she heard Robert's partial sentence.

"William's quite taken with her," Nathanial replied.

"It seems like Margaret is becoming more comfortable with you. I guess that she's come to the conclusion that marrying you is inevitable." Robert sighed, "Poor girl, having to put up with the likes of you for the rest of her life."

"How could she not become more comfortable? I ply her with phrases of my love and devotion. All women surrender their resolve to handsome men who flatter them."

"You've been with her for a little over four weeks now. Don't you have any more feelings for her than being a vessel for your lust? She's a wonderful person, and if you hadn't sabotaged her chances over the past year, she'd have suitors running out the ass."

"And she'll be a wonderful wife performing her duty nightly. I can hardly wait. My loins have been without for a while now. My hand is getting tired."

"Well, that surprises me. You're actually practicing celibacy?"

"I owe her something," he shrugged.

"If I didn't think that Margaret might do some good for you, I'd tell her, to tell you, to piss off!" Robert scolded.

Margaret motioned William to close the vent. She'd heard enough. She sat there a moment with her eyes closed. A stray tear escaped, and she quickly wiped it away. They both got up and headed back to the library; neither of them saying a word.

William pulled open a small hole in the wall and looked through it to make sure no one was there. He opened the panel and they went back to the chessboard.

There was a deathly silence for a moment until William broke it.

"Are you angry with me?"

"Not with you!" It was all Margaret could do to keep from screaming in anger. "Your brother is an — ass!" She may have thought vulgar words such as that, but that was the first time a curse word had ever exited her lips.

"I told you! You just can't marry him. You're too nice. We've got to think of something. Would your parents stop the wedding if they knew?"

Margaret got up and started to pace the floor. "No, he has them wrapped around his little finger. I've been trying to get out of this marriage from the very first day. They wouldn't believe me."

"What if I said something to them?" William asked.

"Nathanial told them that you have a crush on me. They wouldn't believe you either." She racked her brain to come up with an out of her situation. "What to do! What to do. I can't think right now."

"Margaret! Your face is as red as your hair. If anyone sees you, they'll know something's wrong."

She walked over to the mirror. Anger was written all over her face. "I've got to cool down. We can't let anyone know that anything is out of the ordinary."

She saw the glass of water by the chessboard and wiped some of it on her face to cool it down, but it didn't help much. At that moment, they heard laughing voices coming toward the room.

"Quickly! I have an idea. Back to the chessboard. Act like nothing has happened," Margaret whispered. She then arranged the pieces on the board to William's advantage. "As soon as they come through the door, move your rook to here, stand up and yell checkmate."

William nodded and watched the door intently with his hand on the piece. When Nathanial and Robert entered the room, William did exactly as instructed. "Checkmate! Ha! Ha! I won!" He then added the little dance he usually does whenever he beats one of his brothers at a game they're playing.

William's brothers laughed at his antics and then Nathanial looked over at Margaret. "What's your face doing so red?"

"Yours would be red too, if you were just defeated by a twelve year old," she replied and gave William a wink when Nathanial wasn't looking.

Nathanial stood behind Margaret's chair and put his arms around her. "Well, my dear, your parents will be worried. I'd better get you home."

It was all she could do to keep from slapping his hands away, as they walked out the door together. She turned back to William.

"Thank you for the game, William. I may have lost this time, but the next time I'll win."

William knew she wasn't talking about the chess game. "Anytime you want to play, let me know," he replied.

Nathanial walked Margaret to the coach.

"You don't have to accompany me this evening," Margaret said. "Fredric can take me home. I know you have an early day tomorrow. Just give me a proper good-bye here."

"Are you sure, my dear? I don't mind accompanying you. It will be a few days before we see each other again," he replied, but was glad he didn't have to go.

"I don't mind. I'm a little tired myself. I think I just want to close my eyes and enjoy the night air."

Normally, Margaret's kisses were gentle and reserved, but tonight would be different. She remembered the article she read in that pamphlet one of her friends showed her. Tonight, she would give him a kiss to haunt his dreams, for it would be the last one he would ever get!

Nathanial took Margaret in his arms. Even though she really wanted to give him a slap that he'd remember for life, she gave him a kiss that he'd not soon forget!

Margaret got into the carriage and shouted to him as it drove away. "Good-bye Nathanial!"

Nathanial stood there speechless as he watched Margaret wave good-bye.

Damn! Where the hell did that come from?

He didn't know what to think. She was all lips and tongue. Her hand even grabbed his ass and pushed it close to her body. He felt a surge in his groin that threatened to burst the seams in his breeches, and then she left him hot and unfulfilled. There was no way he could walk in the house as he looked at that moment.

***

Margaret leaned back in the carriage and closed her eyes, trying to formulate a plan.

I don't care what it takes, or what I have to do, I'm not marrying him!

CHAPTER 5
"The Plan"

When Margaret finally arrived home, she went straight up to her room. She motioned at Scotty to follow her when she saw her in the hallway.

"Yes, Miss? Ya' seem a bit ruffled." Scotty watched her mistress and friend pace the floor. Her arms were crossed, and she was chewing on her thumbnail.

"Ruffled, is not the word for what I am, Scotty. I'm not going through with this marriage, and I don't know how to do it!" She then told her what she'd overheard this evening.

"The ruddy bastard! I was worried 'bout ya' marryin' the bugger. But if ya' runs away, where are ya' ta' go?"

"That's the problem. It's on the edge of my brain. I've just got to formulate it." Margaret thought quietly for a moment. "Go to Father's study and get today's newspaper."

"Back in a jiff!"

While waiting for her maid to return, Margaret tried to think of who she could trust to help her with her getaway. Most of her friends were the worst gossips in town. If she'd told any of them, the whole of London would know an hour later. She knew she could trust Scotty, Claude might help her and William was a definite possibility.

When Scotty returned with the newspaper, Margaret quickly skimmed through it. "Look here — in the advertisement section."

Scotty picked up the paper. Margaret had taught her to read while they were growing up.

"Go to sea. Now hiring to man three ships, apply..."

"No, not that! The next one," Margaret interrupted.

"English Governess needed for two small children. Must be willing to relocate to America. Must pay for own transportation, inquiry at the London Chronicle for more information," Scotty read.

"The problem is — how am I going to get the money? I just can't ask Father for it. Passage is expensive. The second problem, if I just run away, it would cause my parents great embarrassment. I don't want to do that either."

Scotty thought for a moment. "Ya' can make it look like ya'd been murdered!"

"No, that wouldn't do, I might want to come back someday." Then the idea struck. "Not murdered but — kidnapped! Somehow we need to make it look like I've been kidnapped and have Father pay the ransom." Margaret walked to her writing table, composed two notes and then gave them to Scotty. "First thing in the morning, I want you to delivery one to Claude and the other to William Braxton."

"The boy?" she questioned with surprise.

"I'm developing a plan, and he can help."

It was getting late, so Margaret dismissed her maid for the evening. She also retired, though sleep was difficult. Her brain was running a marathon of thoughts, but eventually she drifted off.

***

Early the next morning Scotty returned with her mission accomplished. Margaret had until noon to do what she had to get done. After that, her day would be monopolized by her mother and the dreaded wedding plans.

William arrived at the stable where Margaret had asked him to meet her at nine o'clock.

"Did you have any problems being able to come here?" Margaret asked.

"I told Rose that I was going for a ride, and I might go fishing. I do that on occasion, and she knows not to expect me back for a couple of hours." William grinned. "You've come up with a plan, haven't you?"

"Follow me and I'll tell you about it when we get there."

Margaret had the surrey harnessed, for Scotty couldn't ride a horse. It wasn't long before they reached Claude's cottage and he invited them in.

"Your maid scared the wits out of my wife when she came knocking so early this morning," said Claude. "Your note said this was a matter of urgency. I assume this has something to do with your upcoming marriage?"

"More to the point, how I plan on getting out of it!" Margaret said excitedly.

Claude looked at William. "So you're bringing part of the enemy into your camp?"

"Not her enemy," William replied, in a mischievous tone. "Her spy!"

Margaret explained what William had done for her, and then she showed him the advertisement.

"Go to sea….."

"Not that one…" Margaret interrupted, "…the next one!"

After he read the advertisement, Margaret explained her idea and wanted him to help her formulate it.

"Have you gone daft?" Claude shouted, "It's madness!"

"What else can I do? If you have a better idea, I'd like to hear it!" she exclaimed. "I've got less than two weeks to carry out my plans, or I'm doomed to a loveless marriage. You said you would help," she replied, as she paced back and forth.

"Do you know how many years we would spend in prison if we are caught?" Claude shuttered. "I don't even want to think about it! Furthermore, if we do this, what if something goes wrong? What if this governess job doesn't pan out? Then you'll have stolen your father's money. Have you thought about how you're going to collect the ransom without being seen? What if the ransom isn't paid? Then you're pronounced kidnapped and nowhere to go. How are you going to explain your return?"

Claude fired one question after another at her. Each question was sound. The possibility of something going wrong didn't even enter her head. Her desire to escape this marriage was so intense her vision was narrowed.

"I don't know," she sighed. She flopped down in a chair at the table and lay her head down on her folded arms. "Maybe I'll just chop off my hair and go to sea!"

Claude knew she was just rambling, but that statement started the wheels in his head to turn. "Say that again?" he asked.

"Say what?" she replied in hopeless tones.

"What you just said?" It was Claude's turn to pace.

"She said chop off her hair and go to sea," William repeated for her.

William quickly sat down at the table across from her and stared at her intently. Claude joined him.

"It might work!" Claude said as he scrutinized her features. "She has one of those faces that could go either way if you wash away all the paint."

"Do you mind telling me what you are talking about?" Margaret asked feeling frustrated.

"I'm talking about going to sea! Signing aboard ship," Claude replied. It was his turn to get excited.

Margaret jumped up from the table. "Are you crazy? I'd never pass as a man!"

"I'm not talking about passing as a man, I'm talking about…."

Claude and William looked at each other and smiled. They looked back at Margaret and said simultaneously, "…Cabin Boy!"

"Me! Of all the hair brained schemes. And you thought mine was bad. It will never work!"

Margaret started pacing again, and then Claude stood up and put his hands on her shoulders.

"Sure it will!" Claude exclaimed. "Besides, you're always telling me you wish your life was more adventurous. If you're hired on, you can work your way across the water. If you're found out, they won't throw you off until you get to port. At least I don't think they will. Anyway, I even have a connection."

"I don't know anything about being a boy!" Margaret insisted.

"But I do!" William replied. "I know everything there is about being a boy. I can teach you. Remember a few days ago when we were playing pirates? If you cut off your hair, you look just like one."

Claude led Margaret back to the table, and they sat down. He laid out the plan that was developing in his brain. Margaret listened and couldn't believe she was even going to consider this. But the more he talked, the more sense he made. He was right about one thing. She would feel guilty about stealing money from her father. It was one thing to pretend to be kidnapped — it was another to ask for a ransom. She continued to listen as Claude put together a plan for her kidnapping and her transformation into a boy. The more he talked, the more she started to come to his way of thinking. It was either this or marriage!

After Claude finished explaining his plan, they all agreed to meet the same time the next day. In the meantime, he would go into town and find out more information and talk to his connection.

***

The next day the conspirators met. Claude found out the information they needed to know and relayed it to them.

"I've got good news and bad news. Which do you want first?" Claude said.

"I guess the good news," Margaret replied.

"They are hiring cabin boys, and I gave your name to a friend of mine."

"Speaking of names, I'm sure you didn't give him my real name. So who am I?" she asked a bit sarcastically.

"Actually, I almost had a slip of the tongue, and then the name Marcus came out. Marcus Allen to be exact. You're a young friend who lost 'his' parents."

"At least the name will be easy to remember." Margaret attempted a laugh. Allen was her brother's middle name. "So what is the bad news?"

"Registration is in three days, and they set sail within two to five days, depending on which ship you're hired on. So we need to have you kidnapped and transformed by tomorrow."

"I'm getting nervous." Margaret shivered. "I still can't believe I'm doing this."

"It's this or marriage," Claude reminded her.

Margaret sat in silence for a moment with her eyes closed. She thought to herself:

God help me!

"So when do we start?"

William jumped up with excitement. "You can do it! I know you can."

Margaret wished she could get that excited. Her stomach was in knots.

"We'll do it tomorrow," Claude replied. "Today, we need to rehearse our parts and gather a few items you'll need."

Claude then turned to William. "Will, my boy! We have work to do. You will be playing a major part, and you need to be as convincing as possible."

"I'm game," he replied.

While Claude and William practiced, the three women worked on how they were going to conceal Margaret breasts. She didn't have much, but if her shirt got wet, they'd be noticed. They also had to work on how they could create a bulge for her breeches. The absence of that particular male aspect might also be noticed. Scotty worked on making alterations to some old clothing that Claude's wife, Renee, had saved from when their son was younger.

Margaret returned home at noon, and spent the day with her mother, as she chattered away about the wedding plans. She hated that things had to be this way, but they gave her no choice. Going through with this wedding was out of the question. She hoped that one day her parents would forgive her for what she was about to do. When evening came, she played a last game of chess with her father and tickled the ivory keys of the hated piano for her mother, before she gave them a final good-night.

CHAPTER 6
"The Kidnapping"

Margaret felt anxious when she awoke the next morning. A wave of fear ran through her as she dressed:

What in God's name am I doing?

But the thought of being in a loveless marriage with Nathanial for the rest of her life was not an option. She sat down at her writing table and composed one letter for her brother, one to her parents and then she called for Scotty.

"This is the day," said Margaret in quiet tones.

"Yes, Miss. I'll be missin' ya," Scotty replied sadly. "I wish I could be helpin' ya' ta'day."

"I know." Margaret gave her a smile. "But it's best you stay here in plain sight. Questions will be asked when I disappear. This way you can answer honestly that you haven't seen me."

"Ta' be sure, Miss! I don't think I could lie convincingly," she replied.

"But I do have a task for you." She handed the girl the letters. "Give this one to Marcus upon his return. It tells him exactly why, and what I have done. If he asks you any questions, be honest with him." She then warned, "But not around my parents! Make sure you're alone with him." Margaret wanted to make sure they didn't terminate Scotty's employment. She was a hard worker and a good friend. She continued. "This other letter is to go to my parents in about three weeks when the dust settles from my disappearance."

"What does it say? If ya' don't mind me askin'?"

"Unfortunately, it's partly another lie," Margaret sighed. "It tells them I escaped my kidnappers and since they were forcing me to marry Nathanial, I wasn't going to come home for a while. It also assures them I'm safe and unharmed."

"Ya' want me ta' hand them it also?"

Margaret thought for a moment. "Best not. Slip it into Father's other correspondence. Make sure you're not seen. I don't want you sacked!"

"Oh no, Miss! I wouldn't want that either." Scotty was relieved, for it might not only affect her employment, it could affect her mother's employment also.

The two hugged good-bye, and then Margaret went downstairs to wait for William's arrival. She went through her normal routine and told her mother she was going for a ride.

"Margaret, dear, we have a lot to do today. You've been gallivanting about the countryside everyday this week," she said, while sipping her morning tea.

"Mother, I promised William. You wouldn't want me to go back on my word would you?" she asked.

Just then, William's smiling face came into the room, after being announced by the butler.

"Good morning, Margaret — Mrs. Wallingham," he said politely. "Isn't it a lovely morning for a ride?"

Clarice looked at the boy's anxious face and relented. "Very well, Margaret, you can go. But tomorrow we start early." "Yes, Mother." She kissed her on the cheek and they left the room.

"Your timing was perfect," whispered Margaret.

"That was a close one!" William let out a sigh of relief.

As they rode, William talked about the things a boy his age likes to do or might say. He also gave her a pair of his old boots. Margaret tried them on and surprisingly they fit.

As soon as they arrived at Claude's cottage, they set their plans in motion. It had rained lightly during the night, so the first order of business was to set the scene where the kidnapping was to take place. They went to a location where William normally fished and made it look like a scuffle had taken place. The three of them trampled the ground. Margaret ripped off a piece of her dress, along with a hair ribbon and put them in a conspicuous place.

Claude looked over the area, and then told them how they were next to proceed. "The ground is damp, so the horses' prints will make an impression on the ground. We need to make sure that your 'kidnappers' trail heads off toward the woods so their tracks will be lost. Then we'll double back, retrieve Margaret's horse and return to my house. That will be the first place they'll probably investigate."

Margaret tied up her horse then mounted up behind Claude. They wanted the impressions of one horse's prints to be deeper, as if she were being carried off. Then the three of them galloped off toward the woods to plant the tracks.

Stage one of their plan was completed. Now was time for stage two. Margaret had to be transformation from a seventeen year old girl to a thirteen year old boy.

Claude and William continued to rehearse outside to get his story right. He didn't want to over act or under act his part. Inside, it was time for the dreaded hair cut!

"Are you ready?" Renee asked with shears in hand.

"No," Margaret sighed. "I didn't think it would be this hard. I've never had more than an inch or two cut off at one time."

Margaret ran a brush through her long, waist length locks one last time. It may have been red, but she thought it her most redeeming feature.

"I'm ready." She closed her eyes.

"It will only hurt for a minute..." Renee chuckled, "...then you'll feel like a new person."

Margaret heard each snip of the shears and in a few moments her head felt a couple of pounds lighter. Renee continued to clip and snip. The short round woman had been cutting both her son's and her husband's hair for years, so she had an idea of the look she would need.

"All done!" Renee said. "Go and have a look."

Margaret walked over to the mirror. Her chin dropped and her eyes widened.

"That's me? I look like a red haired poodle!" she laughed.

With her weighty length gone, her hair twisted into a tight curl which covered her ears and exposed the back of her neck.

Renee laughed. "It's not that bad is it?"

"I didn't say it was bad," Margaret said, as she picked at her new hair style. "It's just —not me!"

"Well, that's what we were going for," replied Renee.

Margaret went to the basin and washed the 'paint', as Claude had called it, off her face and put on the shirt and breeches Renee and Scotty had altered for her the other day. With her transformation complete, she looked in the mirror again. All traces of Margaret were gone. No breasts on top, not that she had much to begin with, and when she pulled her loosely hanging breeches tight, she could see the make-shift bulge appear.

"How does it look?" Margaret grinned.

Renee laughed heartily. "Very convincing. How does it feel?"

"Uncomfortable." She then broke into laughter. "If only my mother could see me now! I guess she raised another boy after all."

Claude and William entered the house upon hearing all the laughter and stopped dead in their tracks.

"Unbelievable!" Claude remarked as he circled her.

"Margaret, is that you?" asked William.

Margaret looked around the room. "Margaret?" she questioned. "Who's Margaret?" She then smiled. "Let me introduce myself. The name is Marcus — Marcus Allen."

"Damned! If you don't look like a version of your brother when he was a boy, I'll eat my hat!" Claude replied. "If you had straight brown hair and lost the freckles, you'd be the spitting image."

"Do you think I'll get away with it?" Margaret asked, on a more serious note.

"You would have fooled me!" William exclaimed.

"You've got the look…" said Claude, "…now we need to work on the mannerisms. Everything your mother taught you about being lady-like throw out the window."

Claude looked at the clock on the mantle and turned to the boy. "Will, now it's up to you. Everything depends on how convincing you can be."

William turned to Margaret and gave her a hug. "I'm going to miss you. Will I ever see you again?"

"One day I'll come back. If I can, I'll write to you," she replied warmly.

"If only I were older…." William sighed.

Margaret gave him a kiss on the forehead and he left.

***

It was late afternoon at Braxton Manor. Rose paced back and forth looking at the clock. "Where is that boy? He should have been back hours ago!"

The clock on the wall chimed five times.

"Don't worry, dear, he's probably lost track of time with Margaret. You know how he feels about her." Robert gave her a reassuring smile then continued to read the newspaper.

"I know, but I just feel like something is wrong! He's never late," she replied.

"Would it make you feel better if I rode over to the Wallingham's and dragged him home?" Robert asked as he folded the paper.

"Would you please?" she sighed with relief.

Robert stood and gave his wife a kiss. "I'll be back shortly." He headed for the stable. Rose followed him out.

Just as he was about to mount, he saw William's horse approaching in the distance.

"There he is now," Robert said. However, as the horse drew nearer, he noticed that William wasn't on it.

"I knew something was wrong!" Rose cried.

"Now don't panic, he probably just got off and the horse ran away. I'll go look for him." Robert rode off in the direction that the horse had come from.

***

William went back to the pond leading Margaret's horse. After he dismounted, he smacked both animals on the rump and sent them running. Each horse went in the direction of its own stable.

Now it was time for phase three of their plan. He rolled around on the ground, got his clothes grass stained and dirty, then tore his shirt. The hardest part was to injury himself slightly. He picked up a jagged rock and made scrapes on his cheek and forehead to complete his look. It was painful, but he considered it a necessary touch. He took off running for home. He figured by the time he got there he would be a sight.

The whole time he ran, he told his himself that Margaret had really been kidnapped. It wasn't going to be too difficult to force real tears to stream down his dirty and scratched up face, for it was all he could do to keep from crying when he said good-bye to her.

***

Robert followed the trail of William's horse. He was beginning to worry himself, and then he saw a figure running toward him in the distance. It was William. Robert whipped his horse to a gallop until he reached the boy.

"William!" Robert yelled as he jumped off his horse and grabbed the boy into his arms. He had trickles of dried blood from scratches on his face and his clothes were torn and dirty.

"Oh, Robert! They took her!" William gasped, and then he passed out in his brother's arms.

Robert scooped up his tattered little brother, mounted and sped home as fast as he could.

45

"Oh God! I knew something was wrong!" Rose cried when she saw Robert carry in the boy. She turned to one of the servants. "Get some water! Quickly!"

They wiped off his face and the boy came around.

"What happened, William?" Robert asked concerned.

"They took her, Robert!" he cried, tears streaming down his face.

"Took who?"

"Two men came out of nowhere by the pond where Margaret and I were!" He cried real tears. "They grabbed her. We both fought as hard as we could. One of them hit her and knocked her out and then pushed me down and I hit my head on a rock. When I got up they were already riding off."

"What did they look like?" Robert asked.

"I don't know!" William started to cry harder as he put his arms around his brother's neck. "They wore hoods over their heads!"

"That's ok, Will," he said in a soothing tone.

"Thank God, you're alright," Rose sighed, as she also put her arms around him.

Just then Nathanial entered the room.

"What's going on? Did William fall off his horse?" he laughed.

"Shut up, you ass! William was ruffed up defending Margaret. She's been kidnapped! We need to inform the Wallingham's," Robert yelled.

Both men ran from the house to the stables. They'd also sent one of the servants go for the authorities to meet them at the Wallingham's.

Rose walked with William to his room and stayed with him until she thought he'd cried himself to sleep. When she left, he opened his eyes and rolled over with a smile, thinking to himself:

Hook, line, and sinker! Shakespeare smiles on me tonight! Don't tell me I'm a lousy actor, Nat!!!

CHAPTER 7
"Marc"

Margaret and Claude worked on her new identity the rest of the day. She had to have a new past and a new way of doing things, if she wanted to pull this thing off. He told her to try and keep as low a profile as possible and not to draw attention to herself.

Some of Claude's rules to remember were; if you break wind, laugh about it — don't apologize if someone comments about the smell; elbows *do* go on the table; spit, but never into the wind unless you want it back in your face.

"Swear out loud not just in your thoughts," Claude continued. "Vulgarity in the company of men is appropriate."

"So in other words, if I act like a pig, I'll be fine," Margaret laughed.

"Basically, yes," Claude replied. "And another thing — boys from around the area don't read or write well and some not at all. If you deem it necessary to be able to, make sure you read poorly, and when you sign aboard ship, your handwriting needs to look as if a chicken walked on the page."

"So, do I act like a moron also?"

Claude chuckled at her sarcasm. "No, not that far. Intelligence is a good thing. Being able to read and write well is not a show of intelligence. It could be taken as arrogance to some. Remember, you're not going to be with a high class group of people. It's how you present yourself that matters."

"There's a lot to remember," she sighed.

"No, not really. Just try not to standout."

"Well, I guess tomorrow's the big day. Do you really think I'll get hired?"

"If my friend, Pete Smithers, has anything to do with it, you will."

"And how do I find him?"

"You won't. He'll find you. With that red hair, you'll not be hard to spot."

It was getting late and everyone turned in for the evening. If she wanted to be sure of a position, she needed to be at the docks a few hours before dawn.

Morning came early for Margaret. Her nerves were on edge, so she sleep came with difficulty. She also felt a bit nauseated and her bowels were as loose as water. After stuffing her clothes in a cloth sack that Renee had made for her, Margaret thanked her for her hospitality and bid her farewell. She mounted up behind Claude and they were off.

"I wish I could stay with you, when we reach town," Claude said.

"Why can't you?" Margaret felt her bowels growl again.

"I have a fencing appointment with you this morning at your house. We can't let anything out of the ordinary *not* take place. Besides, it will more than likely save the authorities a trip to my house to question me."

"I'd forgotten about that," she sighed.

They'd talked about the possibility that he might be questioned. They'd burnt her clothing in the fireplace as well as her locks of hair and scattered the ashes in the wind. Renee baked some fresh rolls to cover any lingering smells of Margaret's perfume as well as providing her something to eat during the day, along with cheese, dried meat and fruit she'd packed.

Their long ride was finally over. Claude pointed out where she should go and wait. "Good luck, my friend," Claude said.

"I don't need luck — I need prayers," Margaret replied. "I appreciate everything you and Renee have done for me. I know I've put you to a lot of trouble."

"A little spice in life just adds to the flavor of it," he replied.

"I always said I wanted adventure. I guess a person had better be careful of what they wish for." Margaret tried to laugh even though she found nothing funny about her situation.

They bid each other farewell then Claude wheeled his horse around and sped off. Margaret turned her attention to the dock. She slung her sack over her shoulder and headed in that direction.

There wasn't much activity as of yet. It was four o'clock. She saw a few men waiting around, apparently for the same reason she was — a chance for work. There were also shop keepers and street venders preparing for the day's business.

Margaret looked out into the harbor and saw three great ships. One of those she hoped to be on. They didn't look too impressive without their great sails unfurled.

"Are ya' signin' on, lad?"

Margaret turned around and saw a big burly man behind her. He had a full beard and his graying hair was tied back. A scar ran down the side of his face.

"I'm planning to," she replied. She was surprised her voice was steady — unlike her stomach. She wondered:

Could this be Pete Smithers?

"Ever sailed before?" the man asked.

"No. Have any advice?"

The man spat out the juice from the tobacco he was chewing. "No, just makin' conversation." He walked off and sat down against a post by the pier.

Margaret figured that the man wasn't Pete or he would have introduced himself. However, she was relieved that her disguise had worked so far. But there was one thing she did need to find immediately — a public facility. She could deny her angry bowels no longer!

As the morning wore on, more men and a few boys started showing up. Men were starting to set up registration tables. When the clock tower struck six times, the dock was full. Some men were standing around by themselves and others were laughing and talking. She'd thought about joining some boys that were playing marbles, but thought it best to stay as close to the tables as possible for the best chance at getting a position.

When the clock struck seven, a man in a suit appeared and rang a bell on the dock and the men quieted.

"Registration will commence in five minutes. All men with seafaring skills to the first table, first timers to the middle table and those under the age of fourteen to the third table," he shouted.

Everyone went to line up at the appropriate station. Margaret was now glad she'd stayed close to the tables for she was third in line. As she looked back, she saw about fifteen boys, some smaller than her, and others about the same size. One boy looked to be about seven.

Suddenly, she heard a commotion behind her. One of the boys was pushing himself up to the front of the line. When one of the smaller boys objected, the bigger boy punched him in the stomach, and the others let the bully have his way.

One of the things that William had told her was if someone tried to push you around, you'd better fight back. If not, others would think they could push you around too. Finally, the boy was just behind her. They were about the same height and size. He could have been twelve or thirteen, she figured.

"Outa' my way, red," the boy said.

He tried to push her, but Margaret held her ground. She was determined to keep her place.

"Wait your turn. This is my spot!" she shouted.

The two of them started a scuffle in the line. She quickly realized that he wasn't that much stronger than she was. The harder he pushed, the more she stood fast.

One of the things that Claude had told her was not to call attention to herself. But this couldn't be helped. If she lost her place in line, she might not get the job.

Then POW! Her eye caught his fist, and she fell to the ground. Unfortunately, she hadn't seen that coming. She could feel the anger grow inside her towards this bully. He may have been just a young boy, but she couldn't afford let him get away with this. So she got up, pushed back and regained her spot. Suddenly, the boy pulled out a knife. The other boys backed away and surrounded them.

"Fight!" she heard someone shout

Even the men left their line to watch the spectacle. She looked around for something to defend herself with as he started to circle her. He made stabbing motions at her, and she was thankful for her fencing skills. Her reflexes were sharp, and she was able to avoid his thrusts. Finally she spotted a possible weapon of defense. A piece of broken board about two and a half foot long was lying by another boy's foot. She made her way to it and picked it up. It wasn't much, but it was better than nothing. She instinctively took her stance ready to block his next attack.

Everyone was shouting around her encouraging the fight. However, she was much too involved with her problem at hand to tell who they were cheering for. When the boy lunged toward her, she side-stepped and smacked his hand with the stick causing his weapon to fall to the ground. She heard cheers from the crowd — especially the young boys who had gotten pushed around. Then, before another move was made, two men in suits came out of the crowd and grabbed them.

"Enough!" shouted the man who held the bully. He addressed the others. "All of you — get back in line or go home!"

The crowd dispersed and things settled down.

"Now, both of you get the hell out of here before I have you arrested," said the man who held her.

The man who held the bully kicked him in the rear, and he ran off. The man who held her, pushed her, but she didn't run. She had nowhere to go.

"Sir, if I…"

"Did you hear me boy? I said…."

He raised his hand and was about to smack her, when the burly man who had spoken to her earlier stepped in.

"Easy there, Mr. Richards," he said. "I seen the whole thing. Weren't this lad's fault. He didn't start it." His voice was calm and matter of fact.

"Do you know this boy, Pete?" asked the man called, Mr. Richards.

"Maybe I do." Pete turned to Margaret. "Be yer' name Marcus?"

"Aye," she replied, using the jargon she'd been hearing all morning. She thought to herself:

So this is Pete!

"I know him," Pete replied.

"Then I leave him to you," said Mr. Richards

When the man name, Mr. Richards started to walk back toward the table, Pete shouted to him and he turned back around.

"Mr. Richards! Be puttin' Marc's name down in the ledger fer' Neptune's Daughter, if ya' please, sir. He'll be sailin' with us."

The man scowled at her for a moment. "His performance will be on your head, Pete."

"Aye, Mr. Richards, sir," Pete replied.

Mr. Richards turned back to Margaret. "Then get your scrawny ass over to the table and make your mark."

Margaret stood for a moment in shock as he walked away.

I made it! I got the job!

"Well? Move yer' arse, lad!" Pete shouted as he slapped her upside the back of the head.

She ran toward the table and watched as Mr. Richards wrote the name, Marcus Allen down in a book. He turned the book around to her.

"Make your mark," he said.

She scrawled her name where he indicated and then he turned the book around to look at her signature. "Well, at least you have a modicum of education," said Mr. Richards. "You can at least spell your name. Go over there with the rest of the crew for Neptune's Daughter."

Margaret thanked him and turned around to thank Pete, but he'd disappeared. She started to join the rest of the crew but realized she didn't have her sack. After an extensive search of the area, she gave up. "Just wonderful!" she huffed. It was gone. No blanket, no extra clothing and more importantly, no food or money to buy more.

"Now what am I going to do?" she mumbled, and wondered else was going to go wrong today. Again she headed to the area where she was told to go to and heard a voice call out behind her.

"Ay! Ay you! Red! Is this what yer' lookin' for?" A boy held up her sack.

Margaret walked toward him and he handed it to her.

"A couple of the little tikes pinched it, whilst ya' were fightin' with Butch," the boy said.

"Thanks for saving it for me. It's all I have." Margaret was relieved.

"All they wanted was food or money. I wouldn't have bothered, but I figured I owed ya'."

"How's that?" Margaret asked, as she opened her sack. Everything was there but the food.

"I was late gettin' here. When the fight started, I went to the table and sign aboard the Arrow Star, whilst the others was watchin' the fight," he replied.

The boy stuck out his hand and they shook. That was her first real handshake. Normally, in her former life, if she put out her hand, the gentleman would have kissed it. Those days were gone — for now.

"Jackson Evers is the name. Jax to me friends."

"Marcus Allen. They call me Marc," she replied. Actually, the only person to call her Marc was Pete — a few minutes ago.

"Glad ta' know ya'. Have ya' got a place ta' flop for the night?"

"Actually, I thought I was going to spend the night aboard ship." She had hoped anyway.

"Not tonight," said Jax. "I tell ya' what. Meet me here after the crew meetings, and come with me." He looked at the thinning lines at the tables. "We better head off. We don't want ta' be late."

Jax ran off in the direction of the Arrow Star's crew, and Margaret joined the crew of Neptune's Daughter.

Several men came up to her and told her she did well in the fight. One man advised her that she'd better start carrying a knife if she didn't want to be gutted like a fish.

Moments later, Mr. Richards got upon a box to address the men. Twelve in all were hired to add to the regular crew compliment of sixty to replace those who'd either died or quit. The man introduced himself as the pay master for the Neptune's Daughter. He looked to be in his fifties and was mostly bald except for patches of graying hair on the sides and around the back of his head. The spectacles he wore sat almost at the end his nose. He was the bean counter, as they say, in charge of making sure the inventory was accurate, collected the bill for shipped goods, as well as paying the hands.

He asked for a show of hands for all who'd sailed before with Captain Withers aboard the Neptune's Daughter, and three raised their hands. Those men he dismisses and told them to be back in two days to start work. The rest of the crew followed him out to a long boat.

"The Captain always wants new hires to have a complete tour of the ship before we sail. That way you have a better knowledge of where to put things when we start loading in two days," said Mr. Richards.

Margaret's stomach was churning as she took a seat. She'd never been in a boat much less rowed one.

The man behind her started to laugh. "If you puke, boy, make sure it's over the side."

She wondered if the look on her face was that obvious. She took one of the oars. "I've never done this before," she said.

"First time for everything," a man replied. "Just dip your oar in the water, put your back into it and stay in rhythm. But don't lose it, or they'll make you go in after it."

"That makes me feel better." Her sarcastic reply caused a couple of men to chuckle.

Rowing out to the ship was the most strenuous thing she'd ever done. In fact, it was the only thing she'd ever done that required strength. She watched the man in front of her to keep time and held onto the oar for dear life. She wasn't about to take a swim if she could help it.

"Ahoy the ship!" called Mr. Richards. "Permission to board?"

"Permission granted!" was the reply.

Margaret watched as they threw what looked like a rope net over the side. One by one each man stood and started to climb. Again, she was the last to go. Her hands felt sweaty and her legs wobbly as she started her assent. Her foot slipped a couple of times on the way up, but she managed to hang on. She was glad to see a hand come over the side to help her aboard.

"Gentlemen — and I use the word loosely, welcome to the Neptune's Daughter," said Mr. Richards. "She's a three masted, full-rigged ship just out of dry dock from a refit. She's fast and carries twenty-two guns for protection against marauders."

Mr. Richards showed them every aspect of the ship and explained where things were to go when they started to load up. When they got to the crews quarters he pointed out the bathing area.

"Each man will be issued a cake of soap," said he said. "You will be expected to use it."

"Does the Capt'n want us ta' smell fresh as daisies?" asked one of the men. The others laughed.

"As far as I am concerned, you can wallow in your own piss. Smell is not an issue — disease is. If any of you can read, which I doubt, you may have heard of The Portman. She was on a long haul to India with seventy-five crewmen plus passengers. Thirty of the crewmen died as well as half the passengers from the disease of being unclean." The men stopped laughing after that. Mr. Richards continued. "They say cleanliness is next to godliness. So I suggest you get closer to God. Use the soap. You'll be given a schedule when you're assigned your bunks."

The tour of the interior of the ship was done and Mr. Richards led them topside.

"One last spot," he said, stopping in front of the main mast. "When the Captain said to see all, he means all! The crow's nest is the last place to see."

Margaret looked up. More climbing!

"Just like climbing a tree, sonny!" said one of the men. "Up you go!"

As she climbed, she started to wonder what she had gotten herself into. A random thought came to her mind. Maybe she would have been better off marrying Nathanial. Then she thought:

Hell no! This was temporary and Nathanial would have been permanent!

With that thought, she quickened her pace and made it up to the top. A feeling of pride washed over her for her achievement. She thought she would have felt dizzy when she looked toward the dock then out to sea. She took a deep breath of the salty sea air.

I can do this!

"We ain't got all day, sonny! You've seen it, so get yer' arse down!" she heard a crewman call.

After the last man came down, they headed for shore. Mr. Richards had told them to be there in two days at five o'clock in the morning. Their quarters would be assigned at that time.

CHAPTER 8
"The Ale House Tavern"

With the tour of the ship complete, Margaret found Jax where he'd asked her to meet him.

"What a shiner!" Jax exclaimed. "Does it hurt much?"

At first she didn't know what he was talking about, until she noticed him looking at her eye. She hadn't really thought about the fight earlier. "Not much. Does it look bad?" she asked.

"It's turnin' blue. I bet it will be as black as the ace of spades in the mornin." Jax laughed.

Margaret thought to herself:

Just Lovely!

"By the way, where are we going?"

"To the Ale House Tavern," he replied. "Me mum works there. She can fix us up with somethin' ta' eat, and you can flop with us ta'night."

They got better acquainted as they walked. Margaret learned that he was fourteen, and he hired on a ship so his mother could retire from her line of work.

"What does she do?" Margaret asked.

"She's a whore — and pretty damn good at it too!" he replied.

Margaret was surprised that he was so casual about it. Jax laughed at her expression.

"As me mum says, ya' call a spade a spade. She's a good mum. I get plenty ta' eat, and she loves me. One of her regulars wants ta' marry her, and she likes him. But he doesn't want me around. So, now that I got steady work, she can marry him and have a proper house instead of just a room." He then asked, "What about you?"

"My parents drowned," Margaret sighed, as she told her fictional history. "They were crossing a bridge during a rainstorm trying to get

56

home. The rushing water caused the bridge to collapse and they fell in."

"Sorry 'bout that, Marc," he replied.

They swapped stories of their lives as they walked, his truth, for her fiction, until they arrived at the Ale House Tavern. Margaret thought it to be a fairly nice looking establishment in comparison to others they'd passed on the way. Inside was also neat and clean. It looked like a small hotel. The upstairs had twelve rooms for rent. They rented by the week, the day or the hour. In another section was the tavern where they served food and drink — but mostly drink.

"Hey, Joe, where's me mum?" Jax asked the barkeeper.

The man looked at the clock on the wall. "She should be down directly. She's with Harold, ya' know."

"A bit early ta'day ain't he? He usually don't come in till seven o'clock."

Joe laughed. "His mother-in-law is comin' for a visit ta'night. He said he wanted a toss in the sack to steady his nerves."

A voice called from behind them. "There's me handsome man. Come give yer' mum a squeeze!"

Margaret turned around and saw a beautiful woman standing with her arms spread wide as Jax went towards her. She didn't look anything like she thought a prostitute would look like. She was clean, wore a simple blue dress, and her long, brown hair was neatly tied back.

"Did ja' get it?" his mother asked.

"I got the Arrow Star," he replied.

"Yer' a good son, Jackson." She hugged him again and then she asked seriously, "Are ya' sure ya' really want ta' do this? I figure I still got a few good years on me back left."

"I'm sure," he replied. "I'm almost a man. What's a couple of years? I'd be out and about anyway by then. Ya' deserve someone ta' love ya' permanent besides me."

The woman then looked at Margaret. "Who's yer' friend?"

"This is Marc," he replied. "He sorta' helped me get the job." Jax explained what happened that morning. "Do ya' think he can stay with us a couple of nights and get a bite ta' eat?"

"I don't mind about him stayin', but he'll have ta' earn his supper. Ya' know how George is. He's not one for charity." She turned to Margaret. "I'm Shirley."

"Thank you for your hospitality, Miss." Margaret's stomach growled quite loudly. "I don't mind working for my supper."

Shirley laughed. "Come on then. Let's see about gettin' a piece of meat for that eye and then have George cook it afterward."

They headed for the kitchen, and after Shirley argued for about fifteen minutes with George, part owner of the establishment, he finally agreed. Margaret was to work with Jax cleaning dishes and scrubbing floors after the tavern closed for the evening to earn her meals.

While George was cooking, Jax went about his usual chores and Shirley took Margaret upstairs to show her where she could put her things. She closed the door behind them and folded her arms as she gave Margaret the eye. "Okay, deary. Out with it."

"What do you mean?" Margaret replied. Her face was starting to glow red. She had a feeling the woman knew her secret.

"Yer' no more a thirteen year old boy than I am!" She laughed.

"What gave me away?" Margaret felt embarrassed.

"Yer' disguise is a good one. It took me a few minutes ta' realize. But, I know men. It's my business. I wouldn't have said anything, but me curiosity got the better of me. Why are ya' doin' this?"

Margaret sighed and gave her the true story, except what she promised Scotty she'd keep secret.

"Really! Ya' don't say? Nat decided ta' finally tie the knot."

"You know him?" Margaret was surprised.

"Just as the bible says, I knew him," she replied. "He might even be Jackson's father, but I wouldn't swear to it. He quit comin' 'round after I told him I was in the family way and couldn't see him for a few months. Never saw him again — never looked for him."

"You see partly why I ran away. The man has no scruples!" Margaret said angrily.

"I don't know what scruples is, but if it has anything to do with the size of what's between his legs — yer' right. He ain't got much ta' brag about even though he thinks he does." She giggled. "I can understand why yer' runnin' away. Now, my man, Freddy, there's a man who knows how ta' put a smile on a woman's face!"

Margaret laughed so hard she could barely see, and her other eye was practically swollen shut.

"Will you keep my secret?" Margaret asked.

"Cross me heart. If ya' have a mind ta' do this crazy thing, who am I ta' give ya' away. Besides, ya' helped me son. I owe ya' that." She heard Margaret's stomach growl. "We better get downstairs before George changes his mind about feedin' ya.'"

***

For the next two days, Margaret washed dishes and scrubbed floors. She had a new appreciation for servants who worked for her family. The worst thing was cleaning out the spittoons. She threw up three times the first night she had to do them. The good thing about scrubbing the floors at night was she could keep any money she found on them, unless it was behind the bar. George also gave both she and Jax a coin from the purse strings of the drunks he rolled to keep their mouths shut when they caught him.

When they weren't working, Jax showed Margaret a few card games. She also had a few private moments with Shirley to indulge in a bit of female gossip when the woman wasn't with a customer.

Margaret and Jax finished cleaning the floor and retired for the night. Earlier in the day, she'd packed her duffle bag with some food. Shirley had also given her a leather money pouch that one of her customers had left behind to put her coins in. Margaret kept that on her person just in case her sack got stolen again.

The hours crept by as she lay on the floor trying to sleep. Nervous anticipation had a grip on her. About four hours of sleep was all she managed to get before she had to report for duty. Jax didn't have to report to his ship for another day. They said their good-byes and wished each other well before they'd retired for the evening. When the time came, Margaret got up and left as quietly as she could to begin of her new life.

CHAPTER 9
"Heave Ho!"

The Neptune's Daughter was ready and waiting at the dock for the crew to start loading her with supplies and trade goods. Before loading commenced, the new hands were taken to the crew's quarters to stow away their gear.

Margaret was nervous about having to share quarters with the men. She was sure that her disguise would be seen through much sooner than she wanted.

"Marc!" she heard a voice call. When she turned around she saw Pete.

"Come with me, lad, yer' bunk is this way," he said.

"I didn't have a chance to thank you for helping me," she said as they walked. "Why didn't you tell me you were Claude's friend when you first spoke to me the other day?"

"I told Claude I'd look out fer' ya', but it were up ta' you whether ya' got hired. I seen ya' got there early and was in front of the line. So I figured yer' chances were good. The way I figure it, if a man is worth his salt, he does things on his own and not let someone else do it fer' him. If ya' wanted it bad enough ya'd get it."

Actually, she thought he made a good point. She'd been waiting for him to make an appearance to intercede for her, just as her brother used to do.

"Then why did you help me?" she asked.

"Well, after yer' fight the other day, and by the way ya' did good..." he said interrupting his own thought. Then he gave her such a healthy slap on the back in congratulations, he'd almost knocked the wind out of her.

"I know Mr. Richards," he continued. "He don't hold ta' fightin'. I knew then ya' didn't have a chance. When I seen how ya' held yer' ground with that little bugger, Butch, and tried ta' speak up yer'self with Mr. Richards, I knew ya' had the makin's of a good lad in ya'. So, I kept my word ta' Claude. I looked out fer' ya'. And Pete Smithers always keeps his word," he finished pointing a thumb at himself.

"You know that bully?" Margaret asked when Pete named him.

"Aye. I knows him. Sailed with us a year back. Laziest little bastard that ever set foot on a deck. Even if he did get ta' the front of the line, he would'a never been hired on any ship. Mr. Richards would'a seen ta' that. The bugger hid his spectacles for a joke and Mr. Richards — he don't have a sense of humor."

"Well, I certainly didn't get off on the right foot with Mr. Richards."

"Ah, don't ya' worry 'bout 'em. The only thing 'e likes anyway is his ledgers and numbers."

Pete took her to a room that was near the passengers' quarters and that of the Captain and top hands. The Neptune's Daughter was primarily a merchant vessel, but occasionally they booked travelers when the regular passenger ships were unavailable. There were twelve special cabins built to accommodate them and their desire for comfort during the voyage.

"Well, here ya' be! Home sweet home." Pete said as he opened the door.

The cabin she looked into was smaller than her wardrobe cabinet at home. There was a bunk, a sea chest for her things and barely room for her to turn around. She also had a small round window, a porthole, is what she thought they called it. A feeling of relief washed over her. The room may have been small, but it was private and that's what she needed. However, she was curious about it.

"Why am I not bunking with the other men?"

"Couple of reasons," he replied. "Yer' closer to the Capt'n and the passengers' quarters when they need somethin'. They be yer' main responsibility — takin' care of them and 'specially the Capt'n."

"What's the other reason?" she asked. "You said there were two."

Pete scratched his head. "Well, I don't know if I should tell ya'. Yer' a might young ta' know 'bout such things."

Now her curiosity was really piqued. "Pete, I'm on a man's ship, going to be doing a man's job. So shouldn't I have a man's knowledge?"

Pete hesitated for a moment. "Ya' talk pretty smart fer' a lad of thirteen."

"My father told me once, speak well and it will open doors. If you think smart, you'll get somewhere and if you do your best, you'll succeed." She remembered that from a speech her father had given Marcus one time.

Pete nodded his head in agreement. "Smart man," He thought for a moment then asked. "Do ya' have a knife?"

"No, why?" she asked, looking at him out of the corner of her eye.

"Then here." He pulled a knife from his boot. "Keep this. It belonged ta' Butch. I picked it up when he dropped it."

"What would I need one for?" Now her curiosity turned to worry.

"'Bout three years back, we had a boy aboard named Jake. He was the best lad this ship had ever seen. He was an orphan who'd escaped from the workhouse and hired aboard." Pete eyed her for a moment. "'Bout yer' age I'm thinkin' — maybe younger. He didn't even know. The Capt'n took ta' 'im right off. Was gonna' make arrangement for him to become his ward. He bunked in the regular crew's quarters. One day, a couple of new hires caught him alone in his bunk. We'd been out ta' sea fer' a month. They raped the boy. Beat him terrible. Jake lived long enough ta' tell the Capt'n what happened ta' him when we found him. The men said that boy lied, but we saw evidence on one of them where Jake clawed his face. The boy's blood was on the other man's breeches. I'd never seen the Capt'n in such a rage. His face went white. He had them dragged topside and whipped with all hands present. The Capt'n gave them twenty lashes each himself and then threw the whip down and said, 'If any other man is offended by what these two bastards have done, feel free to express it!' He went to his quarters after that and each man took their turn — even after they were dead."

Margaret saw the expression on Pete's face. It was a combination of sorrow and rage.

"I had the pleasure of throwin' their carcasses overboard ta' rot in the belly of a shark. It were two days before the Capt'n came topside," Pete finished.

Margaret dropped down on the bunk. "How awful!" She hadn't thought about the possibility of a boy being raped. She looked at the knife in her hand. "I'm fairly capable with a sword — but not a knife."

Pete smiled. "Good! I haven't scared ya' off. I knew I was right 'bout havin' ya' aboard. I'll teach ya' when there's time after we sail. Right now, stow away yer' gear. We've got work ta' do."

Margaret shook off what she'd just heard. Being forewarned, she would make sure she was weary of her surroundings, especially when she was alone. She thought about what happened to that poor boy, Jake, and though there was no comparison, she couldn't help but wonder if Nathanial would have forced her if she'd said no.

She took an apple from her bag and locked her things in the sea chest along with her bag of coins. She looked at her knife again. Where was she going to put it?

"I know what yer' thinkin'," said Pete. "I have an extra sheath ya' can borrow till ya' get one. Just put it away. I don't think you'll need it ta'day."

She did as he said and followed him topside. Pete may have looked like a hard, brutish man on the outside, and he probably was if you crossed him, however, she also felt that if he liked you, he was a good friend to have on your side. She meant to keep him there.

***

The Neptune's Daughter was buzzing with activity. There were men working on the ship to make her ready to sail; checking lines, rigging, canvas and various other duties aboard.

Margaret and some of the others were put to the task of helping load ship's stores. Barrels upon barrels and sacks upon sacks of water, flour, lard, dried meat, beans, fresh fruit, dried fruit, sugar, tea, coffee and rum were a few of the items loaded — just to feed the crew. They hadn't even started on loading the cargo of trade goods.

Mr. Richards was there with his pen and ledger in hand checking in items on each wagon that was unloaded. Pete was one of the men in command on the dock telling the men where things were to be taken. Other men managed the storage of the items brought on board. Margaret thought the loading of the ship seemed very well organized.

After about four hours of pushing, pulling, lifting, carrying and hoisting, Margaret thought she was about to die! She'd never worked so hard in her life. Every muscle in her body wanted to declare mutiny. Her hands had blisters! Her blisters had blisters! The only breaks they had were waiting for supply wagons to arrive. But finally, Mr. Richards announced that loading was done for the next three hours. They had leave until then. Cargo was the next order of business. Some men headed for town and others went aboard.

The only place Margaret wanted to go was her bunk. She was exhausted from cleaning the floor late last night at the Ale House Tavern and then the major task she'd just finished. All she wanted to do was get something to eat and lie down.

She'd just pulled a piece of hard cheese and bread from her bag and collapsed on her bunk to eat it. It wasn't as comfortable as her bed at home, but at that moment, she would have laid down on a bed of nails. But just as she was about to fall asleep, she heard a knock at the door and a voice call her from outside.

"Marc! Cook needs ya' in the galley."

It took every ounce of strength she had to pull herself up to open the door. "I thought we had three hours?" she asked the man named Charlie.

Charlie was a little man, not much taller than her, but well muscled. She'd only spoken with him for a brief moment in passing when he introduced himself. He seemed to be a pleasant fellow. He'd been sailing with Captain Withers for about five years.

"That's for them that's loadin' cargo," Charlie replied. "If ya' want ta' eat, best be ya' get goin'. And mind ya', Orvil is one hell of a cook! Best food I ever ate on a ship." He turned and went about his business.

Margaret sighed and shook her head. Every step she took was agony. If she'd known she was going to have to get up so soon, she never would have laid down.

"There you are. It's about time! We've got a lot of men to feed and just a few hours to get it ready," said Orvil upon her arrival.

"I don't know how to cook," she replied with a yawn. She noticed he had a different accent. Though he spoke English, it was neither formal nor the cockney that most of the crew spoke.

"You prep, I cook. You start peeling the onions I've set aside. Then chop the potatoes and carrots and throw them in that pot of water on the stove."

She looked at the table of vegetables. It would take her the better part of an hour, if not more, to do all that peeling and chopping. But at least there was a bench that she could sit down on.

"You're not very talkative for a kid," said Orvil as they worked.

"Busy morning. I'm too tired and too sore to think of anything to say." Margaret yawned.

"Sorry about that. My regular assistant got drunk last night and just the sight of food makes him puke. I traded him for you."

"I was looking forward to three hours sleep," she replied.

Orvil grinned. "Well, it's your choice. You can either chop vegetables or in another two hours and thirty minutes you can go back to the loading dock. Which would you prefer?"

Margaret stopped peeling for a moment and though about what he just said. She wiped away the onion induced tears. "I think I'll just sit here and cry over my onions."

Orvil laughed. "I thought as much."

"You're not from here are you?" she asked.

"Nope! I hail from Virginia."

"And where is that? I've never heard of it."

"America, of course," he replied as he kneaded bread dough. "Don't they teach you anything here?"

Margaret's brain just engaged. "The Colonies!" That's how her father always referred to America. "I'd like to go there one day. How come you left?"

"There was this woman…" he started, but didn't finish. "Let's just say I stow away aboard this ship. When they found me, I told Captain Withers I knew my way around the kitchen. He kept me on after he tasted my cooking."

Margaret enjoyed talking to the ship's cook. Orvil Catrill was a fairly handsome man of forty-five year. At first, she didn't think she was going to like him, for his tone was harsh when she first came in. However, as they talked, he laughed and made jokes and she just chalked his earlier mood up to being angry at his assistant.

They worked on until it was time to serve the ship's first meal. He made a stew, fresh baked bread and stewed apples. Orvil went ahead and let her eat before she helped serve the men. His boast about being an excellent cook was no boast. The man could rival the best chef in England!

With the meal done and galley cleaned, she was finally dismissed and headed straight for her small cabin. The only prayer she could think of was:

God, please don't let anyone wake me until morning!

No sooner did she hit the bunk, she was out like the flame on a candle.

CHAPTER 10
"The Captain"

Margaret woke the next morning with her muscles screaming at her. She forced herself to sit up on the side of her bunk and look at her surroundings. There was no mirror, no wash stand, no towel, no combs or brushes. She sniffed the air in her cabin then realized the bad smell was coming from her. Running her fingers through her hair it was as if rats had nested in it.

She left her cabin and looked about. No one was around. It seemed too quiet.

Where is everyone?

She quickly ran topside. The crew was gathered on deck.

"Well, if it ain't his Lordship! I see ya' finally decided ta' grace us with yer' presence," said Charlie. "They rang the bells two hours ago. Too bad ya' missed breakfast."

"Why didn't anyone wake me?" Margaret asked.

"We would'a sent yer' valet, but we couldn't wake him up either!" laughed Sam.

Sam was a tall, skinny man with a face that reminded Margaret of a pigeon. She just rolled her eyes as they laughed at their own jokes.

"Pipe down, ya' swabs!" someone shouted.

"What's going on?" Margaret whispered.

"The ship is bein' searched," replied another.

"For what?" she asked.

"They're searching fer' some high society bitch that up and got herself kidnapped," said Charlie. "A certain Margaret Wallingham. They're offerin' a reward for her return. Wish I knew where she was. I'd quit this floatin' workhouse."

"Ahhh! Ya'd just spend the money on a whore and drink away the

66

rest," one of the men replied with a chuckle.

Charlie shrugged. "What's wrong with that?"

All Margaret wanted to do was go back to her cabin and hide, but she dared not move. After all she'd gone through, she wondered if her charade was finally going to be over. She'd worked so hard and still no one noticed she wasn't a boy.

She saw two men walking to the bridge. The first man was dressed in black. She couldn't see his face yet, but he was tall and broad shouldered. His almost coal black hair was tied back, and his form-fitted shirt defined muscular arms. She assumed that this must be Captain Withers. The second man wearing a uniform was the constable.

The men opened a pathway to allow them clear access to the bridge. When the two men turned around she couldn't believe her eyes. Her thoughts were spinning in her head:

It's him! The dark haired man at the Seafarers Ball! Surely he won't recognize me. We'd only spoken for a moment!

"Is he the Captain!" she exclaimed. She hadn't realized she'd said it allowed.

"Aye, that's Capt'n Todd Withers. If yer' makin' the sea a career, he's the man ta' sail with," replied one of the men.

"Men!" shouted Captain Withers. "A young woman was kidnapped a couple of days ago. There have been no ransom demands from her abductors. For those of you who can read…" some of the men chuckled at that statement, "…you may have read that there have been three other young women taken in the past eight weeks. The authorities believe that she may have been taken by white slavers."

There was a low grumble among the men with that last statement. Margaret vaguely remembered the story in the Chronicle. That may have unconsciously been the very thing that gave her the idea of a kidnapping in the first place.

"I have assured Constable Wilshire of our complete cooperation in the search of this vessel. If any man has any information, it would be appreciated," the Captain concluded.

The Constable came forward and gave a description of Margaret Wallingham. Margaret looked around to see if any eyes went to her. When he was done, the officer went about his search with his men. She then saw Charlie giving her the eye. Butterflies fluttered in her stomach.

She looked at him and frowned. "Why are you staring at me like that?"

"Hey, Sam," Charlie nudged him in the ribs and he turned. "What do ya' think? Maybe we could put Marc in a dress and collect the reward?"

Margaret scowled at him and thought:

He didn't just say that!

Sam looked Margaret over. "Hmmm." He folded his arms and cocked his head to the side. "Na, what self-respectin' woman would look like him?"

"It was just a thought," Charlie laughed.

Margaret didn't know whether to be insulted or relieved. "Have the two of you looked in a mirror lately?"

"What I don't have in looks, I make up in other areas." Sam grabbed his crotch. "I haven't had a woman complain yet. Can you say the same?"

Margaret grinned. "At least mine…" she grabbed her stuffed imitation, "…doesn't have crotch crickets!" She'd heard someone at the Ale House Tavern say that jokingly to another man. When she'd asked Shirley what it meant, the woman told her it was one of those diseases one doesn't speak about in polite company.

Charlie laughed and Sam frowned. Sam was about to come back with another remark, when Pete Smithers announced that all new hires were to stay and all regulars back to duty.

"Smart ass kid!" Sam mumbled.

As he walked away, Margaret was pleased that she'd gotten in the last word in the battle of witty come-backs.

***

The new hires were about to be introduced to the Captain and his commanding staff. Rules and regulations were also going to be read, as well as the punishment for the breaking of them.

"Welcome aboard, men! I'm the Captain Todd Withers. Follow the rules, do your work and you'll find me a fair man. Shirk your duties and ignore the rules — you only have yourself to blame for the consequences."

Margaret felt that same tingling sensation she'd felt before when he'd spoken to her at the Seafarer's Ball. She listened as he continued to introduce his staff. Mr. David Coruthers was his second in command. He looked about the same age as the Captain. He dressed well and his thin mustache and goatee were neatly trimmed.

She'd already met Mr. Ben Richards, the paymaster. She hoped that she could get on his good side during the trip.

Dr. Jonas Ridenhour was the ship's surgeon. He looked to be about fifty, if she was any judge of age. His bushy sideburns and the suit he wore reminded her of her own doctor. He'd been on the Neptune's Daughter since her first captain, Captain Michael Jacobson.

There were the watch commanders. Pete Smithers was in command of first watch. He didn't tolerate slackers. She saw him throw one of the new hires over the side when he caught the man leaning against the railing while the others were working.

Doug Taggart had the second watch. He was tall, blond and well spoken. She was told he was a very likable and fair man, however, if a rule was broken, he gave no quarter. Expect to be punished no matter how small the infraction.

Levi Dalton was in command of third watch. He was bald with a tattoo of a dragon's head — on his head. He also wore and ear ring. To her, he looked like a pirate — but looks were deceiving. He too was well spoken, had a sense of humor and was generally liked — but don't cross him. One of the men told her that he'd slit your throat in a bat-of-an-eye, if you did him wrong.

These men made sure orders were carried out and work was done. When all the rules were read and introductions made, it was back to the loading dock. Every step Margaret took was agony and then she heard her name.

"Marc!" called Pete. "Come here, lad."

Margaret stopped and a shiver went through her body. She'd seen Pete and the Captain talking while Mr. Coruthers was reading the rules. She turned around and just knew the jig was up.

"Capt'n, this be Marcus Allen. The new ship's boy," said Pete.

Margaret looked into the Captain's dark eyes and saw that same warmth she'd seen before.

"Welcome aboard, Marc," the Captain said. "Pete tells me you have the makings of a good seaman."

"I hope to do well, sir," she replied.

"How's that eye feel? I heard you held a good accounting of yourself a few days ago."

"It probably looks worse than it feels," she replied touching the puffy area. "And as for the fight, I would rather have avoided it."

"That's the choice we have to make in life. Knowing when to fight and when not to," he replied. He then changed the subject. "Anyway, I have a guest sailing with us. Her luggage will be arriving shortly. Have them put into the large passenger cabin. After that, see Doc about that eye."

"Aye, sir," She gave him a smile then turned to walk away. She breathed a sigh of relieve that he hadn't recognized her.

"Marc," the Captain called back.

Margaret turned around. "Aye, sir?"

"You wouldn't happen to have an older sister or a cousin would you?"

"No sir, why do you ask?"

"You have the same hair and eye color of someone I met briefly," he replied.

"Poor girl," Margaret said managing a grin.

"On the contrary, I found her most becoming." He stood thoughtfully for a moment. "Well, on about your business." He then turned to talk to Pete.

Margaret tried to hide her smile:

He did remember me!

It thrilled her that he thought she was attractive, but it also made her nervous. What if she looked at him in the wrong manor? His looks appealed to her at the ball and they still did. Now she was going to be at his beckon call. She prayed silently:

God help me!

CHAPTER 11
"First Day Out"

The next morning Margaret made sure she got up early. She double checked the passenger's cabin to make sure everything was neat and clean — or ship-shape and bristol fashion is how she was told to make it. Everything was ready — except for the passenger. Getting underway was delayed because she hadn't arrived yet. Margaret couldn't help but notice how irritated the Captain was becoming.

"If she doesn't hurry, we'll miss the tide, sir," said Mr. Coruthers.

Captain Withers paced the deck. "If she's not here in five minutes — cast off!" he exclaimed and checked his watch again. "She's never on time!"

Everyone aboard the ship was waiting at their stations for orders. Margaret knew from the luggage she'd carried aboard that it had to be a woman even if the captain hadn't told her. The woman had two large trunks that she had to have help with carrying. Their passenger even brought her own porcelain thrown. Margaret remembered her mother bringing hers along whenever they traveled a long distance. In addition to her luggage were two cages of pheasants which she was instructed to take to the cook.

"Pete," Margaret whispered. "Who's the woman we're waiting for?"

"Mrs. Laura Sarandon," he replied.

Margaret had heard the name from a few parties she'd attended but never met the woman.

"The Capt'n asked her ta' marry him 'bout four years back."

Margaret was surprised. "She said no?"

"Well, yes and no. They almost tied the knot. Her father offered the Capt'n a position in his shippin' company. When he turned the man down, she and the Capt'n had a big argument. The former Capt'n of the Neptune's Daughter, Capt'n Jacobson, had just turned over the command of this ship ta' Capt'n Withers 'bout a year or so earlier. She told the

Capt'n that she wouldn't become a widow to the sea, so they called off the engagement."

"How do you know all this?" Margaret asked. "Did the Captain tell you?"

"No. They had words in his quarters. A couple of us were standin' outside waitin' ta' get orders. We couldn't help but overhear the yellin'. 'Bout two month later, she married Willard Sarandon — a rich old bastard, he was. He had more money than the Bank of London. He died three months after they got married."

"How did he die?" Margaret started to feel sorry for the woman.

"Old age!" Pete laughed. "He were seventy-three, and she were twenty at the time. She just married him for the money. Her father made some bad business dealin's and was 'bout ta' lose his company. She bailed him out."

"At least she helped out her family."

Pete laughed again. "Don't be sorry for that one, lad! No love of family made her marry old Willard. It were pure greed that motivated that one. She only bailed out her old pappy to save the family reputation fer' her own sake."

Margaret chuckled. "And you know this because…" she asked waiting for him to finish her statement.

Pete grinned. "Her maid is sweet on me."

Then they heard the Captain shout, "That's it! Mr. Coruthers, cast off."

"Aye, sir!"

Just as they were about to pull away the gangplank, a carriage pulled up to the dock.

Margaret saw a beautiful woman get off. She was elegantly dressed in lavender with white lace and her brown hair was piled just so. She carried a little white Pomeranian and her maid followed behind.

The Captain stood there with his hands on his hips and shook his head. "It's about time you show up!"

"Todd, darling," she said in a pitiful way, "Please, don't scold me."

She extended her hand and the Captain helped her aboard.

"About thirty more seconds and you would have been waving good-bye to your luggage," he said, then kissed her hand.

"You wouldn't really have left me, would you Todd?" Her tone was honey-coated.

"The tide waits for no man," he replied. Then he gave her a smile. "Not even for rich widowed women. Now, if you will excuse me, my dear, Marc will show you to your quarters. I have a ship to get underway."

Margaret stepped forward and bowed slightly at the waist. "If you will follow me, my lady, it will be my honor to show you and your maid to your quarters."

"Well, Todd, you've finally hired a boy on this boat that has manners," she said. This time her tone was one of superiority.

The Captain just smiled, bowed slightly and then shouted orders to get underway.

Margaret was all too familiar with her type. She had her pegged the moment she opened her mouth; just slightly flirtatious and a better than thou attitude with anyone out of her class. This is the type of woman her mother had wished she'd become.

Margaret led the two women to their quarters and opened the door. "I'm sorry, my lady, this is the best cabin we have," Margaret said before the woman had a chance to complain.

"Pitiful!" The woman shook her head. "However, I am already familiar with the accommodations aboard this boat. I've taken this trip many times."

"Will your maid be sharing your cabin or shall I show her to another?" Margaret asked.

"Normally, I'd have her stay, but she gets seasick, and I don't want her retching in my presence throughout the trip." She turned to her maid. "Matilda, when you're settled come back and set out my things." She turned back to Margaret. "Boy, I'll have tea in an hour."

"I'm sorry to say, no cream, do you take sugar?" Margaret asked in an overly polite manner.

"If tea was meant to be sweet or white it would be. You may go." She waved her off without even looking in Margaret's direction.

"Very good, my lady." Margaret bowed and couldn't help but snicker as she left the room. The maid followed behind her.

"Aow! Ain't you the smarty breeches," the hefty little maid said after the door was closed. "You was makin' fun of me Mistress all the time."

Margaret grinned. "You know what the funny part is? She didn't know the difference."

The maid laughed. "Truth is — I don't get seasick. I just tell 'er that so she'll leave me alone for a day and night. Then I can have some quiet time to me self for a change."

Margaret went back on deck. The ship's sails were unfurled and they were pulling out of the harbor. The men were scurrying about the decks following the orders given. She stood out of the way watching, and then turned to look out over the railing as the shore was getting further and further away. The fears she'd felt earlier turned to thrill. The wind blew through her mop of hair, and she breathed deep the salty sea air.

"First time out?"

Margaret turned around to see the Captain behind her.

"Aye, sir. I thought I would be terrified. But I'm finding it to be quite exciting!"

The Captain leaned upon the rail and looked out over the water. "That's how I felt when I was your age." He was quiet for a moment and then asked, "Did you get Mrs. Sarandon settled?"

"She wants tea in a bit."

"Don't mind her, her bark is worse than her bite," he said with a smile.

"I know her type," Margaret said without thinking, as she watched the shoreline get further and further away.

"You do?" he laughed. "How would a thirteen year old boy know about women?"

Margaret had to think fast. "What I meant was my mother told me about society women. She used to work for one. The trick is, if you want a positive response you tell them the negative. Never try to convince a society woman about how good something is. You tell them how bad it is and then they'll tell you that it isn't that bad and accept whatever circumstance you put before them."

"How so? Give me a for instance." The Captain listened with interest.

Margaret laughed. "This is what my mother told me. Just like tea in an hour. Her maid told me she likes it strong enough to dissolve the barnacles off the ship. So, that is how I'll bring it, and it will be nice and hot. If I don't say anything when I bring it to her, it will either be too hot, too cold, too weak or too strong whether it or not. She'll then tell me to bring her another and insult me. Now, when I bring her the tea in an hour, I will apologize for not bringing it quick enough and it may have cooled off. I'll again apologize and say that it may not be strong enough. She'll taste it and tell me it will do."

"And how do you know she'll still accept it after you go through all that?"

"Because she'll be making a gracious gesture by accepting bad tea — even though it isn't. If I don't do it that way, I will be a hopeless idiot in her eyes and anything I do for her will not be right. Then I'll have to do it again. So I'll save myself steps and a few insults."

Margaret knew how to act because her mother would do the same thing with waiters or the hired help at different restaurants and business establishments.

The Captain laughed heartily and patted her gently on the back. "If you have any more pearls of wisdom about women, let me know."

"Well, sir, I'd better see to the tea," she replied.

"Off with you then. You won't have to put up with her for too long, Marc. She'll be getting off when we reach Dover tomorrow."

"Aye, sir," she replied and headed toward the galley.

Margaret felt a tingling sensation go through her body when he touched her. His laugh and smile made her feel warm. She wondered if this is what Nathanial tried to explain to her what love is. She thought to herself:

Surely, this isn't love. I don't even know the man! It's just an infatuation. After all he is handsome.

Todd Withers watched his new cabin boy walk away. He liked him. He seemed quite intelligent for a boy his age. He thought to himself:

There's something familiar about him. I can't put my finger on it. Is it his looks? His voice? Something!

Pete walked up beside Todd interrupting his thoughts.

"What da' ya' think, Capt'n? Will he do?"

"Smart boy. Like-able as well," the Captain replied.

"He's a might scrawny, but he done the work tasked ta' him without complaint."

"Like Jake?" the Captain added on a sad note.

"Comparable," Pete replied empathizing with him.

"Keep an eye on him, Pete."

"Aye, Capt'n — no worries!"

***

When Margaret entered the galley, she found Orvil cursing at the pheasants.

"Damn woman and her cockamamie birds! The least she could do is bring them already dead!" he exclaimed as they pecked at his fingers through the cage. "She does this to me twice a year! Once going to Dover and then again on the return trip to London."

"Why does she bring so many?" Margaret asked.

"The first time she only brought two; one for her and one for the Captain. The Captain and Mr. Coruthers always dine with the other commanders, Doc, and Mr. Richards. He told her that if she didn't bring enough for each of them — don't bring any. Now this is what I get!" he raved and then nodded toward the stove. "By the way, the water for Mrs. High-and-Mighty's tea is boiling over there."

"How did you know that is what I came for?"

"Trust me! I know this woman and not in the biblical sense either. I don't know what the hell the Captain ever saw in that bitch, and that's too polite a word for her," Orvil groaned.

Margaret watched as Orvil put on a pair of gloves. He picked up the cages and headed through the passageway.

"What are you going to do with the birds?"

"Tie a rope around the cages and throw the damn things over the side and drown them!"

Margaret couldn't help but laugh at Orvil's dilemma. She then turned her attention to the tea. She poured one for Mrs. High-and-Mighty, as Orvil called her, and one for her maid, Matilda.

Upon delivering the tea to Mrs. Sarandon, Margaret said exactly what she told the Captain she was going to say, and the woman responded as she predicted. She called the tea dreadful and made the remarked that the cook was incompetent and there was probably nothing that could be done about it anyway, and she accepted it.

Afterward, Margaret went to Matilda's cabin. She knocked on the door and entered without being asked.

"I thought you might like some…" she started to say, when she saw Matilda and Pete quickly releasing their embrace.

"Just makin' sure our guest is comfortable," Pete said then cleared his throat.

"I had something in me eye," Matilda said, "Mr. Smithers was kind enough to get it out."

Margaret knew both of them were lying through their teeth.

"Mr. Smithers is a good man to have around in a pinch." Margaret tried not to laugh.

"If yer' eye gets any worse, Matilda, Doc is just down the passageway," said Pete as he exited the room.

Margaret entered the rest of the way and shut the door. "Care for tea?"

she asked dismissing what she'd just seen.

"Now, ain't you a thoughtful boy. A maid bein' served! They'll never believe me when we get home." Matilda took a sip. "By the way, I didn't have anything in me eye," she whispered.

"I know," Margaret replied and gave her a wink.

After she left the maid, Margaret remembered that she was supposed to see Doc about her own eye. She also thought about asking if he had something for her sore muscles. Just as she reached Dr. Ridenhour's quarters, she stopped abruptly:

What am I thinking? The last thing I need is for a doctor to examine me!

If anyone could see she wasn't who she pretended to be, it was him! She turned around to go about her business, but ran into the person she wanted to avoid.

"There you are, boy," said Dr. Ridenhour. "I was expecting to see you yesterday. Why didn't you show up?"

"I got busy and forgot," she replied. "Anyway, my eye feels better. You don't have to bother yourself. I was just coming to see if you needed anything."

"Nonsense!" replied Doc. "When the Captain gives and order, he expects it to be carried out. Now go on down to sickbay, I'll be there directly."

"Really, Doc I'm…"

"That's an order, son," replied Doc firmly.

"Aye, sir," she sighed.

The closer she got to sickbay the more nervous she felt. When she got there, she waited in a chair and looked around the room. There were twelve beds sectioned off toward the back of the room. One side of the room had a large cabinet with thick glass doors containing his medical instruments. Some of them looked like carpenters tools, especially the saw. On the other side of the room were cabinets with jars of herbs, roots, powders and liquids strapped down in their places so they wouldn't move with the motion of the ship. In the middle of the room was a table. It was stained in places. Margaret figured it was blood that had soaked into the wood and darkened it.

A few moments later, Doc entered the room and closed the door. He'd forgotten his spectacles and had gone to his cabin to retrieve them. Thing at a distance he could see fine without them but for close work or reading he needed a little help.

"Jump up here, boy, let's have a look see at that eye."

Margaret sighed and did as ordered.

Doc laughed. "I'm not going to remove it, sonny, I'm just going to look at it."

That's not what she was worried about, but so far, so good.

"I heard about your little encounter," he said as he felt around her eye.

Margaret winced as he pushed on the area.

"Easy there! I'm just checking to see if there's anything broken. There doesn't seem to be any damage except for the bruising. It should clear up in about a week." Then the doctor stepped back and gave the boy a smile. But his smile suddenly changed. "What the bloody hell! You're no boy!"

"Shhhh! Please, Doc!" Margaret whispered.

"The Captain should know about this!" he exclaimed then headed for the door.

Margaret jumped off the table and barred his way. "Please, Doc, I beg you. You're the only one on this ship who knows I'm not what I pretend to be!"

"This is no place for a young woman!" he scolded. "How old are you? Fifteen? Sixteen?"

"I'll be eighteen next month," she replied. "But what does that matter? I've pulled my weight. I've done everything aboard this ship that was expected of a thirteen year old boy. And I have the sore muscles and blisters to prove it!" she held out her hands.

Doc took her hands in his and looked at them. They were hands of someone who'd never done a day of hard labor.

"But why would you do this?" he asked seriously. "I want the truth."

Margaret sighed. "You know that woman they were looking for before we left port? I'm that person."

"What! They said she was kidnapped — not a runaway."

"With the help of friends, I staged my own kidnapping."

"Why would you do that? You were going to be married to the son of Lord Braxton for heaven's sake!"

"That's why! He didn't love me, and I was being forced to marry him. My parents wouldn't listen."

"But still, a ship is no place for a young...."

"What about — Joan of Arc?" she interrupted. "She led an army a few centuries ago. Then what about those women —.Ahmm..." She racked her brain trying to remember the names she'd heard. "...Anne Bonney!"

"The pirate from back in the 1720s," he exclaimed.

"She's the one! I heard she had her own ship and was one of the most fearsome women that ever sail. Mary Read is another I heard of. Me, I'm just a servant aboard this ship. What make me any different from Mrs. Sarandon's maid, Matilda?"

"The difference is you'll be living with a bunch of men. If they find out…"

"So far they haven't," Margaret interrupted. Besides that, I have my own small cabin. No one knows except you. If you tell the Captain and he puts me off at Dover, then what am I going to do? I don't know anyone. I have no money to speak of. Then if you take me back to London, I still have nowhere to go. I refuse to go back and marry Nathanial. If you reveal my identity, my safety aboard this ship will decrease by half. The crew wouldn't hesitate to turn me in for the reward — or do worse."

Doc was quiet for a moment to think. "You put me in a bad place."

"Doesn't your Hippocratic Oath say something about doing no harm?" she asked. "All I ask is that you give me a chance."

"You have me over a barrel," he grumbled. "I'll say nothing — for the present. We'll see how things go."

"That's all I ask." She sighed and then added, "Do you have anything for sore muscles?"

Doc shook his head and retrieved a bottle from the cabinet. "Back on the table and lift the back of your shirt," he huffed. "If you put this on with those blisters, you'll probably scream like a — girl."

She did as he asked and found he was right. The liquid burned into her muscles. He rubbed it over her shoulders and back and then she rolled up her baggy breeches and he rubbed some more over her thighs and calves.

"You should feel a difference by morning," said Doc. Next he retrieved another jar from the cabinet. "Put this on your blisters tonight, and I suggest when we get to port you invest in a pair of gloves for heavy labor."

"Thanks, Doc, I own you," she said and headed for the door.

"Marc."

Margaret turned around.

"Coffee, three sugars, tomorrow morning at six," Doc ordered.

"Aye, sir," she replied.

She closed the door and breathed a sigh of relief. A feeling of satisfaction came over her. This was her first real victory. Her first battle won without her brother's influence.

Margaret headed back to her small quarters to put away the jar of cream. When she exited her cabin, their passenger opened the door and called to her.

"Boy!"

"Yes, my lady?"

"Where have you been!" she scolded.

"Carrying out Captain Withers' orders," she replied. "Can I be of service?"

The woman's scolding tone had eased when Margaret dropped the Captain's name.

"It's much too windy upon deck and Prince Algeanon of Babylonia needs to be walked."

The woman handed Margaret the little Pomeranian. Around its neck was a diamond studded collar and the leash was similarly adorned.

"I know exactly how many stones are in that collar and leash," she warned. "And there better not be any missing when you return."

"Oh, no, my lady," Margaret replied. "I was just admiring the breed. He's a champion, is he not?"

"Of course," the woman replied proudly. "Babby won top honors for his breeding at a special showing held by the Queen at the royal palace this year."

Margaret didn't know anything about dogs, but she did read in the paper about the special dog show the Queen had held. She just thought she would throw a bit of flattery her way.

"Twenty minutes should do. When you return, my shoes have scuffs and I need you to polish them."

Margaret acknowledged and took the dog topside. She hoped the animal would hurry up. Those sparkling stones would be too much of a temptation for poor men.

"Well, would ya' look at that cute pup," said Charlie, eyeing the dog's collar and leash. "I'll be glad ta' air the little fella fer' ya."

"I bet you would!" Margaret exclaimed.

Charlie went to pet the dog, and it growled and snapped at him. "The little bugger just about took off me finger!"

"Good boy!" Margaret laughed and bent to pet the dog. "If one of these stones comes up missing, I'm not the only one that will go down for it."

"Me! Would ya' really think I'd do a thing like that?" Charlie asked innocently.

"I think you'd sell your own grandmother for the right price," Margaret laughed.

"Na, I wouldn't have got a brass farthing for her. She was a bitch." He laughed and then went about his business.

Another crewman approached her and said the cook needed her. He also eyed the dog's jewelry very hard as he passed.

Margaret entered the galley just in time to see Orvil chop off the feet of one of the pheasants. She instinctively turned her head in disgust.

"There's some newsprint in that barrel over there. Put some down and tie Algy up in the corner," he pointed. "I need help getting dinner ready for tonight. You know the drill — onions and potatoes."

"Algy," Margaret laughed. "I thought she called him Babby?"

"If you were a male dog, what would you rather be called; Babby or Algy?" Orvil asked as he threw one of the bird's feet to the dog.

"Neither," she replied watching Orvil disembowel the bird.

Orvil saw the grimace on Marc's face as he prepared the pheasant for cooking. "Marc, I think you need a cooking lesson. I have one more bird left."

"No thanks, I'm fine with onions and potatoes," she replied.

"That's an order, boy," he replied.

Margaret got up reluctantly. Orvil placed the dead bird on the chopping block next to the cleaver.

"Just one good whack and they'll come off clean as a whistle!" Orvil grinned.

She picked up the cleaver. "I don't think I can do this."

"First time for everything. Get to it."

Orvil pointed out where she should chop, and she raised her blade. Then WHACK! Off came the feet. Margaret put down the cleaver and ran from the galley and up the steps. Her hand was over her mouth and the other was holding her stomach as Orvil's hysterical laughter rang in her ears. She made it to the rail just in time and the contents of her stomach came up.

Pete saw her and approached. "Are ya' seasick, Marc?"

"No!" she replied, "Cooking lesson!"

"Cooking!" he laughed.

"Orvil's idea of a joke. He had me chop the feet off of one of those birds." Just the thought of what she'd done made her turn her head back to the rail.

"Carry-on then," Pete cackled as he left.

When she'd finished, she leaned her head upon the rail and a thought ran through her head:

The Diamonds!

"Oh shit!" she exclaimed as she ran back down to the galley.

She stopped at the entry way and saw the dog doing its business.

"Don't worry — not one stud is missing," said Orvil, still laughing. "Do you want to finish your bird?"

Margaret frowned. "I think my cooking lesson is over. I have shoes to polish." She wrapped up the dogs business and started to leave.

"When you're done, I do need you back to finish the potatoes and onions. I have Hank doing other things."

Margaret threw the wadded up newsprint over the side and headed below to return the dog. But before she left the deck, Mr. Coruthers gave her orders to bring him coffee, two sugars, tomorrow morning at four o'clock. That was the fourth request she'd had today. Levi Dalton wanted black coffee at eleven tonight before his watch started. Doug Taggart wanted hot water for shaving and tea with honey after his shift was over. She knew she'd never remember everything told to her. The necessity of seeing Mr. Richards for a pen, ink and paper to write things down was inevitable.

After returning the dog, Mrs. Sarandon counted the diamond studs and then pointed out the shoes to be buffed. Margaret hadn't a clue what to use to polish shoes with. She'd always given hers to Scotty, so she decided to ask Matilda.

Margaret knocked on her door, but this time waited to be invited in.

"Come in," said Matilda.

"I have a problem. How do you clean shoes?" Margaret asked holding them up.

Matilda chuckled. "Don't bother yer'self with 'em. I'll have 'em buffed up in a jiffy," she said. "Least I can do."

Margaret watched what she did and what she used, just in case she had to do it again sometime.

"Can I bring you anything?" Margaret asked.

"Just some tea in a bit when ya' bring 'er's." Matilda nodded towards the other cabin. "If I know 'er, when ya' return the shoes she'll want more tea. She should buy a tea factory as much of it as she drinks."

When the shoes were done, Margaret returned them and just as Matilda predicted, she ordered more tea — but not before she ordered her porcelain throne to be emptied and cleaned.

With the tea delivered and the potatoes and onions peeled, Margaret figured that now was a good time to see if she could acquire the things she needed from Mr. Richards.

"Come in!" he shouted.

"Excuse me, sir," she said politely.

"What is it, boy, I'm busy," he said without looking up from his papers.

"I wonder if I might be able to have a writing tablet, pen and ink?"

He looked up. "What the devil for?"

"To write down things to remember," she replied.

He let out a disbelieving laugh. "You can actually do more than write your name?"

"Yes sir." She tried hard not to sound rude at his sarcasm toward her.

"Prove it. Write something for me." He turned around the pad and gave her the pen.

Margaret remembered what Claude had said about showing off. So she dipped the pen in the ink and scribbled:

MR. C - COFY 2 SUGERS AT 4 OCLOK
LEVI - BLAK COFY AT 11
DOK - COFY 3 SUGERS AT 5
MR. TAGERT - HOT WATR - TE WITH HUNY

She turned the paper around.

"Who's Mr. C?" he questioned.

"Mr. Coruthers. I couldn't spell his name," she replied pretending to be proud of her writing.

"You can't spell several things," Mr. Richards replied. "The writing materials will cost you."

Margaret hadn't a clue about what things cost. She'd always just signed for things she needed and her father would pay later. He quoted her a price. She didn't know if that was fair or not, but she needed the items.

"Can you deduct it from my wages?"

He opened a ledger and wrote down what she wanted. "Sign this."

She read what he wrote, signed his ledger and he handed her the materials she needed. She also asked him if he would mind correcting her spelling mistakes so she could learn from them, which he did.

"Would you care for something in the morning?" she asked before leaving.

"Tea, no sugar, at half-past six. Now get out of here, I'm busy," he huffed.

She thanked him and as she was walking out the door she heard him say, "At least he has a few brains." It was just loud enough for her to hear.

Margaret felt pleased with herself. According to Pete, a comment like that coming from Mr. Richards was high praise.

The only one she hadn't gotten an order from was the Captain. After finishing other duties she was tasked, she knocked on the door to his quarters when she didn't see him on deck.

"Come!" he shouted.

She entered and saw the Captain and Doc playing chess.

"Are you going to make a move or sit there?" asked the Captain.

"Chess is a game of patience and thought," Doc replied.

Margaret looked at the board from where she stood just behind the Captain. If Doc moved the right piece, he could win with his next move. If not, the Captain would win. When Doc started to put his hand on the Queen, Margaret cleared her throat. She figured she owed him a small token for not exposing her secret.

Doc looked up and saw Marc shaking her head no and mouth the word "rook." He removed his hand from the piece, looked again at the board and saw what she did.

"Checkmate!" Doc laughed.

"Damn! I was hoping you hadn't seen that," replied the Captain.

"First time in ten games!" Doc chuckled.

"Just pure luck." the Captain replied.

"You forget who taught you how to play in the first place," said Doc as he cleaned his spectacles and put them away.

"And you don't hesitate to remind me whether you win or lose." Then the Captain turned around and saw Marc.

"You don't play chess do you?" he asked.

The tone of his question and the look in his eye suggested that he'd suspected her of helping Doc.

"Who me?" she replied, "Checkers is my game."

"Well, maybe I'll teach you sometime," he said with a smile. He looked at his chess partner. "Then Doc will have someone he can beat regularly."

"I'd like that, Captain. I like learning new things," Margaret replied.

Doc laughed. He had a feeling Marc could play circles around both of them.

"By the way, Marc, what is it that you wanted?" the Captain asked.

"What time would you like me to bring coffee or tea in the morning?"

"Coffee, quarter past four and hot water. Anything else?" he asked, seeing that his new cabin boy just stood there.

"No, sir, just waiting to be dismissed."

He laughed slightly. "Then your dismissed."

"Aye, sir."

Margaret left with that tingling sensation she'd felt before. There was just something about his dark eyes and his smile that sent chills through her. She kept thinking about what Nathanial had told her what love was. But no, this was just infatuation she reminded herself again.

After Marc left, the Captain shook his head and laughed.

"What do you find so funny, Todd?" ask Doc. He was only on a first name basis with the Captain when they were alone.

"It's Marc. He has an eagerness to please. I haven't seen that since Jake."

"I talked to Ben Richards just before our game. He said the boy might actually have potential. That's rare for him to say about the boys that have served this ship," Doc replied.

"There's something else about him also. I can't put my finger on it."

"Oh, how so?"

"Don't know." He hesitated a moment. "I guess it's of no importance. It's just refreshing to have a boy on this ship that does his job."

"Probably so." Doc stood. "See you at dinner."

Doc left the cabin. He'd debated with himself whether or not to tell the Captain about Marc. But now, his mind was made. The Captain needed someone to care about. He'd changed after losing Jake. Marc could fill the spot that was empty. He'd also seen a look in Marc's eyes. There was more than just an eagerness to please. If the Captain found out, so be it. It wouldn't be from him.

✳✳✳

Margaret went to her cabin to take a short nap after she'd left the Captain's quarters. She also wanted to arrange her notes on what everyone wanted in the morning. Pete was the only one who wanted nothing. He'd told her that he was too grumpy in the morning when he first got up and preferred not to be bothered.

It had been a busy first day aboard ship. She had hoped to be able to go on deck and enjoy the open sea. But such was not the case. Mrs. Sarandon had her empty the chamber pot twice more and walk her dog for a second time. She had one more major task for the day and that was helping to serve dinner at the Captain's table.

On the way to the galley, Margaret saw the three watch commanders on deck. They were dresses in their finest. Some of the men were whistling and laughing at their attire. Doug Taggart looked natural in his coat and white ruffled shirt. However, Pete and Levi looked like fish out of water. Their white ruffled shirts were yellowed with age.

"I hardly recognized you, Pete," Margaret said trying not to laugh.

"This damn monkey suit!" he exclaimed tugging at the collar. "If I didn't like that fancy bird we're eatin', I'd eat with the rest of the swabs."

Pete headed for the Captain's mess and Margaret towards the galley. Hank, the cook's assistant, served the crew while she and Orvil served at the Captain's table. It was Margaret's job to stand by and pour wine upon request. She now knew how the servants at home must have felt having to stand there and smell the delicious aroma of the family dinner. Her mouth was watering and there was nothing she could do about it.

Everyone gave compliments to the cook except Mrs. Sarandon. She said the bird was overdone and the stuffing was too dry. However, Margaret noticed the woman ate every morsel. Orvil made a gesture behind her back with his middle finger. Margaret didn't know what it meant, but it was apparent that the others did, for they tried to conceal laughter, and the Captain shot him a cold glance, but said nothing.

Margaret started to clear away dishes as the men finished.

"You may have any scraps that are left over, boy," said Mrs. Sarandon after Margaret took her plate.

Margaret painted a smile on her face. "Thank you, my lady," When she walked passed Pete, she mumbled, "Bitch — scraps my ass!"

Pete choked on his wine and started to cough.

"Are you alright, Mr. Smithers?" Mrs. Sarandon asked.

"Yes, ma'am. The wine just went down the wrong pipe," he replied.

One by one the dinner guests left until there was just the Captain, Mrs. Sarandon and Margaret collecting the dirty silver.

Laura Sarandon stood, walked behind the Captain and put her arms around his neck. "I miss us, Todd," she said in a wining tone.

Margaret felt like taking the wine bottle she'd just picked up and pouring it over her head.

Doesn't she realize that I'm still in the room?

She could feel her face starting to redden.

"Laura, you're embarrassing the boy," the Captain said.

"Oh! Is he still here?" she asked.

"Marc, you're dismissed. You can clean up later."

"Aye, sir." Margaret quickly left. She wasn't embarrassed. But what was she? Jealous? How could she be? She told herself:

No, I'm just tired and hungry.

She went to the galley, fixed a plate of stew and sat there listening to Orvil fume about Mrs. High-and-Mighty's insults to his cooking. When she went back to clean the dining room, she'd found both had gone. But to where? His cabin? Or hers?

Margaret went to her own quarters and laid down. A tear rolled down her cheek, and she quickly wiped it away. She wasn't going to cry. She had no reason. She closed her eyes to sleep and hoped she would wake in time to bring Levi his coffee before his watch started.

CHAPTER 12
"Pete"

Margaret's day started early. The sun hadn't come up yet and the ship was anchored off the port of Dover. She went to the galley and found Orvil getting the breakfast ready. He pointed out the coffee, and she poured the first two cups she needed as well as the hot water for the Captain.

Mr. Coruthers was first. She knocked on the door, and he bid her to enter. He was just buttoning his vest.

"Ahhh, hot coffee! Just what the doctor ordered." He took a sip. "How was your first day, Marc?'

"A bit chaotic for me, sir," she replied.

"Always will be when we have passengers. You'll find if you work hard, do what you're supposed to do, you might learn a thing or two about sailing."

"I'll try my best," she said with a smile.

"Carry-on then."

Margaret hadn't had a chance to speak to Mr. Coruthers since she'd been aboard, but he seemed to be a pleasant fellow. The next stop was the Captain's quarters. She hesitated before knocking. She wondered:

What if she's in there?

But she shook it off.

What if she is? It's none of my business!

So she knocked.

"Come," called a sleepy sounding voice.

She entered. "Coffee, sir."

She saw him sitting on the edge of his bed wearing just his breeches and no shirt. She'd never seen a man half-dressed before and quickly turned her back. An ingrained since of modesty instinctively came over her.

The Captain looked up. "Where're you going?" he asked.

She thought quickly. "I — I left the water outside the door, sir."

"Coffee first." He yawned and waved her over toward the bed.

Margaret took a deep breath, let it out and turned around to give him his cup. She hoped her face wasn't as red as it felt.

"Whoever invented coffee was a genius," he said, after he took his first sip. He stood and stretched.

If her face wasn't red before, it was now. He was Hercules reborn with those defined muscles. She quickly turned again to get the water. If he caught her staring at his body, he might think his new cabin boy was peculiar. She poured the water in the basin and watched as he splashed his face.

"That's better." He dried off then looked up at Marc. "Looks like the sun touched you a bit yesterday."

"I hadn't noticed." She was glad he came up with a reason for her redness, she couldn't think of one.

"I'll bet you'll be glad when our passenger leaves this morning," he said, as he lathered up with his shaving brush.

"At least there's only one." Watching a man shave was a first for her also. She had a sudden urge to find out how he felt about his former fiancé. "She's a beautiful lady."

"She is a rose, that's for sure," he replied as he started to shave.

Margaret felt her heart skip a beat.

"But..." he added as he scrapped the blade down the side of his cheek, "...you have to be careful with a rose."

Margaret thought that was a curious thing to say. "Why's that?"

He chuckled. "Now it's my turn to give you advice about women." He remembered their conversation about high society women from yesterday. "A rose is beautiful and smells sweet. But you have to be careful handling one — they have thorns. If you don't, it will prick you and draw blood. That rose pricked me several years ago, and I don't intend to let it happen again."

"I guess that makes sense." A feeling of relief washed over her.

"But, that does mean you give up enjoying what a rose has to offer," he added.

Margaret saw a lustful grin on his face and both of her questions were answered. Did he want her? No. That was a sense of relief. Did he bed her? Probably. She wasn't quite sure how she felt about that.

"You'll understand what I mean when you're older," he continued.

"Maybe." She shrugged pretending ignorance.

When the Captain finished, she took the dirty water and left. She remembered what Jax's mother had told her about men. 'Most men have two brains; the one in their head and the one between their legs. When it comes to women, they mostly think with their lower brain. They can't help it, it's their nature. A good man may generally have a moral standard. But if their lower brain is tempted by a woman who wants that man, he'll more than likely do what that brain tell him — especially a single man.' As Margaret walked down the corridor she thought:

I guess he listened to his lower brain!

***

When the sun came up, Neptune's Daughter made her way to the loading dock. After Mr. Richards returned with the purchaser to sign off on delivery and collect the bill, the process of unloading merchandise commenced.

Again, there was more pushing, pulling, carrying, and hoisting. Only this time, since she had no gloves, she'd found some scraps of canvas to tie around her hands to protect the healing blisters and prevent new ones. Her muscles still ached, but not as much. It hadn't taken long to unload since not all of the merchandise was leaving the ship. Just what was earmarked for Dover. However, more goods were expected to arrive later in the day that needed to be loaded.

It was about noon before their passengers were topside and ready to disembark. Margaret was glad to see Mrs. Sarandon go. Matilda, on the other hand, had pulled her aside and pressed a coin in her hand.

"It ain't much, Marc, but ya' treated me as if I were quality," the maid said.

But in Margaret's eyes, Matilda was quality. When she opened her hand she'd found a penny. Mrs. Sarandon didn't give her a second look. But Margaret expected no less. She thought about her mother who also never tips a servant for doing a good job.

***

It was about one o'clock and Mr. Richards had just gotten word that the merchandise they were waiting for wouldn't be there for another two hours. Except for the crew of the second watch, everyone had a two hour liberty. There were also four men who had families in Dover. They were permitted the rest of the day and night off — if someone covered their watch.

Margaret went to her quarters to retrieve her bag of coins. She needed a sheath for her knife and a needle and thread to mend her breeches that had gotten torn. Pete said he was going to lend her a sheath, but he hadn't as of yet and she didn't want to ask. She'd hoped that the meager amount of coins she had was enough to get what she wanted.

The harbor was littered with shops, street vendors and taverns. She passed a dress shop and was dying to go in, for there was an absolutely gorgeous blue gown in the window. But crew from the Neptune's Daughter where all around, and she dared not give it a second glance. There was a street vendor selling pastries and she was sorely tempted to purchase a strawberry tart, but she needed to make her other purchases first.

She found a shop that sold sundries, and most of what she was looking for was there; a needle, thread, a thimble and a pair of work gloves. But there were no sheaths. She figured she'd find one at a knife shop, but there was only an hour left to finish her shopping and get back to the ship.

Margaret was getting ready to cross the street when she heard a commotion in the alley. When she looked in that direction, she saw two boys accosting a smaller one. The smaller boy was doing his best to keep the other two at bay with a stick, but then one of the bullies grabbed him.

Remembering how she wished someone had helped her, Margaret ran down the alley and grabbed the boy that was about to hit their captive.

"Leave him be," Margaret shouted as she pulled one of the bullies away. But just as soon as she did, the boy turned and popped her in the mouth.

"Mind, yer' own business," said the boy who struck her.

He was just about her size. Margaret was tired of getting punched. Her lip was bleeding and hurt like hell. She tightened her fist and swung a hard left to the boy's nose and kicked him in the shin. The boy's nose gushed blood, and he was on the ground rubbing his leg.

When she turned around, she saw that the smaller boy had worked himself free and landed a blow to his foe's stomach and a solid right to his jaw.

"Now, get out of here if you know what's good for you!" Margaret shouted. The two bullies ran off.

"Thanks mate," said the boy. "I could have taken care of the problem myself if there'd just been one. The name's PJ, what's yours?" he said extending his hand.

"Marc," she replied. The brown haired boy was well spoken, and he seemed older than his size denoted. "What happened?"

"I'd just gotten out of school when those two attacked me. My father just arrived in town, and I was buying him a present at the tobacco shoppe. I don't get to see him much. I guess they saw I had money and wanted it. You can't be too careful these days."

Margaret wiped the blood from her lip, but it still kept bleeding. She turned and spat the blood from her mouth. Apparently, one of her teeth cut the inside of her lip as well.

"Say, that lip looks bad. Why don't you come to my house? My mother can fix it up," he said.

Margaret looked at the clock tower and saw it was getting late. "Better not. I've got to get back to work, and I can't be late. Someone there can fix it."

"Well, thanks again, Marc. Maybe we can meet again," he said with a smile.

"I'd like that, but I'm leaving tomorrow morning."

"Too bad," he sighed.

They waved good-bye and each ran in different directions. Margaret's lip was still bleeding when she got back to the ship. She wondered:

Is that all boys do is fight?

So far, she'd received a black eye, blisters, sore muscles and now a bloody lip. She wondered what else she was going to have to endure for the sake of being free from Nathanial.

"What the hell happened to you?" asked Mr. Coruthers as she boarded the ship.

"Somebody's fist! I was in a small fight," she replied.

"Again!" he laughed. "Well, I hope you upheld the honor of the ship. Did you win or lose?"

Margaret rolled her eyes. "The other boy ran off with blood gushing from his nose and a bruised shin," she replied pretending to be proud of her victory.

He gave her a healthy slap on the back. "Good show, Marc!"

Her thoughts went to what Claude said about keeping a low profile —

so much for that. "Is Doc on board?"

"He's below. Check his quarters," replied Mr. Coruthers.

Margaret wondered why it was that all men seemed to care about was whether you won or lost. It didn't seem to matter much if someone was hurt or not. She arrived at Doc's quarters and knocked.

"I'm busy!" he shouted through the door.

"Doc, it's Marc," she shouted. "I'm injured."

Margaret thought sure she heard voices. After a moment, he came to the door with a robe wrapped around him. She thought she saw a figure of a woman cross the room behind him.

"Well, what do you..." He saw her lip. "Don't tell me — another fight." Doc just shook his head. "Go down to sickbay. I'll be there in a few minutes."

Margaret had to wait about fifteen minutes before Doc came in and closed the door. "What happened?"

"Two boys were picking on another and I decided to help."

He looked at her lip and went to one of the cabinets. "Well, your heroics are going to require about three stitches." He returned with a needle and thread.

"Oh, great," she groaned.

"Did you win or lose?"

"I won," she replied in a huff. "Why is my winning or losing so important to everyone?"

"That's just the nature of men, I guess," he replied. "This is going to hurt. Bite down on this." He put a stick between her teeth. "If you want to cry, that's fine. I've seen a few men shed a tear or two at the sight of a needle."

She bit down on the stick. "You're really funny, Doc," she mumbled.

When he put the needle in she felt like her toes were going to curl back to her heels and the stick between her teeth was going to snap. She clutched the edge of the table, and if she'd had fingernails, they would have been buried in the wood. The only time she took a breath was between the stitches. But she didn't cry or groan — until he dabbed it with alcohol.

"Oh! God! That hurt!" she yelled.

"That's an appropriate curse." Doc laughed. "Tell me, is it still worth it?"

"I was asking myself that same question," she mumbled trying to keep her lip still. "And the only thing that keeps coming to mind is, this is temporary and Nathanial would have been permanent."

"You've got balls — ahmm, so to speak." He then glanced down at her breeches. "Speaking of balls, how did you manage… "

"Stuffed," she replied.

"My compliments to your tailor. The family jewels look convincingly authentic with your breeches on."

Margaret chuckled slightly and winced in pain. "Don't make me laugh, Doc, it hurts!"

He gave her a small bottle of alcohol. "Dab it twice a day to prevent infection. When it stops burning the stitches are ready to come out."

"Sorry for bothering you, Doc. I know you had company," she said as she got off the table.

"It's just my wife. She'll be there when I get back."

"I thought men with wives got leave?"

"All but me," he huffed. "I have to be here just in case someone gets a splinter in his big toe…" He glared at her. "…or gets his or her lip split. Now, if you can refrain from fighting for the rest of the day, I was in a wrestling match myself."

"Doc!" Margaret blushed.

"Marc, if you're going to live in a man's world, you're going to have to quit blushing when comments like that are made. You'll hear a lot worse — or better depending on how you think of it," he grinned and then left the room.

Margaret went to her cabin to put away the things she bought — except for the gloves. She kept them for more cargo duty that was just about to commence and went back on deck. She was hoping that the men would take pity on her because of her busted lip and let her sit out. But no such luck. She received plenty of pats on the back, a cheerio or two, and was just in time to help unload the wagon that pulled up. Another two hours of pushing, pulling, lifting and hoisting was on her agenda.

***

Later that evening, Margaret pulled a four hour watch from midnight to four in the morning. She was relieved by a crewman named Flint, who gave her boxing tips and bragged about a match he'd won against someone supposedly famous. She pretended to be impressed.

When she went down to the galley to get morning cups ready, Orvil didn't hesitate to give advice, showing her how to bob and weave. Hank even threw in a comment or two, and he rarely said anything to her.

The only coffee or tea she had to deliver that morning was for Mr.

Coruthers and Doc. The Captain and Mr. Richards had not returned and wouldn't until just before they set sail. So she went to bed.

It was noon when she woke and the Neptune's Daughter had set sail. She was just in time for the noon meal. However, because of her swollen lip, she could barely sip water from a cup much less open her mouth to put anything in it. But she was about to starve. She settled for a couple of biscuits and went topside to the bow to enjoy the sea air. This was the first time she'd really had a chance to do this. She couldn't when they had their passenger.

The wind was strong and filled the sails as Neptune's Daughter cut through the high sea. She closed her eyes and breathed in the air.

"Takin' it easy, Marc?"

Margaret looked up and saw Pete. He was clean shaven. "Pete! Is that you?" She put a hand to her sore mouth. She'd agitated her lip. "What happened to the whiskers?" she asked more carefully.

"My wife," he chuckled. "She bitches at me fer' growin' it and shaves it off when I come home." He then grinned from ear to ear. "Then she gives me a tumble between the sheets for a few hours."

"That's more information than I need to know, Pete." Margaret tried not to blush.

Pete sat down next to her. "I've got somethin' fer' ya." He handed her a brand new sheath for her knife.

"Thanks, Pete. How much do I owe you?"

"Nothin'," he replied. "Consider it me thanks."

"For what?"

"Remember the little nipper from yesterday? The one ya' got the stitches fer'?"

"PJ, I think his name was," she replied.

"Aye. Peter James Smithers," Pete said with pride. "He's my son. His mother and me wanted ta' thank ya' fer what'cha done."

"But how did you know it was me?" she asked.

Pete laughed. "Now how many red haired, poodle-headed boys name Marc, with a black eye and busted lip do ya' think there'd be in Dover?"

"Not many." She started to laugh but it pulled at her stitches. "He's a tough kid for his size."

"Aye, he's scrappy when he needs ta' be. He just turned twelve. Smart as a whip too."

"How many children do you have?" she asked.

"PJ, here in Dover, and then Kyle, ten, and Amanda, eight. They live with their mother in Southampton," he replied with a grin.

"Divorced, ay" she said sadly.

"Nope! I have two wives," he replied. "Love 'em both."

"You're a bigamist!" she exclaimed. "That's illegal! How did you end up with two wives?"

"Cathy is my first wife. She lives here. We've been married near on twenty years. We never thought we'd be blessed till PJ came. Then there's Jillian. Now, there's a story."

Margaret listened as he told how he came upon Jillian.

"PJ was just a year old then. Neptune's Daughter set sail for Southampton. We was there fer' a month, whilst the ship was bein' repaired from storm damage. There was this young woman sittin' outside her father's smoke shoppe. I thought she were a might pretty. Since I didn't have nothin' better ta' do, I sat next ta' her. She we're 'bout my age, but as we talked, I found her ta' be simple-minded. We talked and laughed and I told her 'bout Cathy and PJ. Before I left she made me promise I'd come the next day. No one ever talked ta' her 'cause of the way she was. Fer' the next week, I kept visitin' since I had no duty. Then one day her father comes out and wants ta' talk ta' me. He tells me that Jillian talks 'bout me day and night. He tells me that if I sail away and never come back, it would crush her. So he says he'd pay me ta' marry his daughter."

"Didn't you tell him you were already married?" Margaret asked.

"Aye, I did, and 'bout PJ. Then he tells me that it wouldn't matter. No one knew me there. He said he would make it so me son, PJ, would have enough money ta' go ta' school and become someone better than a ship's hand. All I had ta' do was marry his simple-minded daughter and whenever the ship came ta' Southampton, I'd have a nice home and lovin' wife ta' be with. It didn't take me long ta' think about it. The thought of PJ bein' better than me made up my mind. So, Jillian and me was married the next day. Three weeks later I sailed away. I send her letters when I can get someone ta' write one fer' me. When I came back a few months later, I found she was with child and happy as a clam. Her father kept his word all these years. That's why PJ goes ta' school and is top of his class."

"It didn't bother Jillian that you were already married?" Margaret asked.

"No — like I said, she's simple-minded. All she can understand is what she loves and who loves her back. Nothin' else makes a difference. She asks me 'bout Cathy and PJ whenever I visit."

"What about Cathy and PJ? Do they know about Jillian?"

"Yes and no," he replied with a laughed. "When I came home with more money than a man of my means should have, Cathy asked me where I got it. I told her that while I was on leave from the ship, I married a rich man's daughter, named Jillian, and he gave me the money."

"I bet she wanted to keel haul you," Margaret laughed.

"No, she laughed at me and told me that I was lyin' and I'd better tell her the truth. So I thought about it and told her a wild tale that she had to keep secret from everybody. I'd been gone fer' 'bout six months, I think. We sailed to other places after Southampton. I said I'd been shanghaied by a pirate ship. A month later, after I had earned the pirate Capt'n's trust, we sunk a ship carryin' gold from the colonies, and took it to the secret island where the pirate kept his treasure. I then told her that we was in another sea battle, but this time I pretended I was badly injured and fell off the ship. Then I swam to the other ship and snuck aboard whilst others were occupied fightin'. I told her that the ship I hid on was able ta' get away from the pirate ship and I stayed hidden till we reached port where I snuck off. After that, I went to an island close to where the pirate hid his treasure. I told her I stole a one man boat and took a good bit of the pirate's booty."

"And she believed that?" Margaret laughed.

"Not at first, until I came home from another voyage with more money."

"What did she think then?"

"Again, she asked me and I said that the father of my other wife, Jillian, gave it ta' me ta' save for when PJ was old enough ta' go ta' school. She still didn't believe me. Then she asked me why I didn't just bring all the pirate gold with me."

Margaret couldn't help but laugh at the wild tail, sore lip or not. "What did you tell her then?"

"I told her that if I brought it all in and we started livin' past what I bring home, someone might get suspicious and think I was a bloody theif and stole the money. So, I just bring home enough fer' PJ's future."

"And she believes that?"

Pete laughed. "Aye, she does. But jokin'ly, she does ask me how Jillian is ever' time I come home with extra money. I've told her 'bout my son Kyle, and my daughter, Amanda, and told her that someday they'd like to meet their half brother, Peter James."

"And she still doesn't believe you about them."

"It's been a long running joke with her. She remembers ever'thing I tell her, hopin' I'd slip up on a story I told them about my other family," he laughed. "I tell her the God fearin' truth and she doesn't believe me. But tell her the whale of all tales and she swallows the lie, hook, line, and pole!"

"Unbelievable," Margaret shook her head. She then thought about another incident. "What about Matilda? You're not planning on a third wife, are you?"

"Na, she's just a friend," he replied then grinned. "She just likes ta' be tickled once in a while, so I oblige her."

"Stop, right there!" Margaret held up a hand. "I'm too young to know about that stuff!"

Pete laughed and stood up. "If yer' done with eatin', there's work ta' be done. See the sail maker. He needs some mendin' done."

"Aye, Pete."

Margaret thought about Pete's story. He may have been a bigamist, and in her former life she would have been appalled no matter what the circumstance, but in Pete's case — it seemed to be a good thing. He married a woman who otherwise may have had no one to love and care for her except her parents. He also made it possible for his other child to make something of himself. How could she find fault with that?

CHAPTER 13
"Orvil's Plan"

Margaret had now been sailing on the Neptune's Daughter for three days, and her stitches were due to come out in another day or two according to Doc. She was relieved that the crew still hadn't seen through her disguise.

She'd also quit blushing whenever she saw the Captain without a shirt in the morning when she brought coffee. The one thing she couldn't stop doing was imagining what it would be like to touch his muscular form. She found ways of watching him without being obvious whether he was on deck or in his cabin looking over charts as she cleaned.

It didn't take her long to settle into a routine. Besides delivering coffee and running errands for the Captain, her main task was to make sure that all cabins, especially the Captain's quarters, were kept ship-shape and bristol fashion — everything neat and tidy. All metal and brass instruments as well as other fixtures throughout the ship were to be polished daily to prevent rust and corrosion.

Her most hated task was taking care of the bathing area and the "head," which was how the men referred to the ship's privy, especially in the crew's quarters. The smell was horrific, and she gagged every time she went in there. Once a day she had to flush out the trap with sea water then refill it.

There were various other tasks such as mending sail, helping the cook and duty in the crow's nest. She had climbed it initially with no problem, but her next climb, she found to be more difficult with the ship moving. However, after a few times up she was able to climb with more ease and less worry about falling.

Those were duties aboard ship while sailing. When they were docked or anchored off shore, there was loading and unloading of goods and supplies. Her muscles had finally surrendered and accepted the fact that they were going to be tortured quite often, and she no longer experienced extreme soreness as that first day.

When she was off duty, Pete taught her how to use the knife he gave her. He showed her how to hold it, where on the body to strike to just incapacitate, and for the instant kill. Throwing the knife at a target she found difficult. Pete had drawn a target on a board and each time she threw it, it would just hit the board and fall to the floor. She practiced daily, even when Pete wasn't there to instruct her.

There were also off duty times when some of the men played musical instruments and sang. Other times they were allowed to gamble. The biggest gambling event was the big race. Hank had caught two rats in the food storage room and made two, twelve foot tracks for them to run on. They put a piece of food at one end, and then let the rats go. The rat that reached the other end first was the winner.

The Captain even asked her if she'd like to learn how to play chess. Of course, she said yes. She found it difficult to make herself lose. There were many times she could have beaten him in only a few moves. When she played Doc, there were no holds barred and quite often she beat him in six moves, unless the Captain was in the room then she forced herself to lose.

All in all things went pretty well for Margaret. She'd made friends with several of the crew members. There were also others who paid little attention to her — unless it was to tell her to get the hell out of the way if she was in the wrong place at the wrong time.

***

It was the morning of her fourth day aboard and they were anchored off shore waiting for cargo duty. Today was also the day that Doc removed her stitches.

"Good as new," he said after removing the last one.

She felt around the area. "Will it leave a scar, do you think?"

Doc laughed. "Finding it hard to leave the vanity behind, are we?"

"Now Doc," she said folding her arms, "You can't tell me that men aren't vain and don't care about their looks. In my past life…"

"Which was about seven days ago," he interrupted.

She continued, ignoring his comment. "…I found that men spent more time looking at themselves in the mirror than women did."

"Very well," he laughed. "I concede your point. And no, I don't think there will be a scar."

Their conversation came to a halt when they heard the bell that signaled all hands on deck.

"Well, the Captain and Mr. Richards are back. I guess it's time for you to get to work," said Doc. "How are the muscles?"

"Actually, I think I found one!" she exclaimed She flexed her left arm.

Doc put on his spectacles and looked close. "Hmmm — physically we all have muscles, but I wouldn't brag about that one."

She hopped off the table. "You're real funny, Doc. You'd make an excellent court jester."

Doc laughed and they both headed topside.

Margaret hated off shore ports. The work was slower because they had to unload cargo onto boats or rafts and it was rowed ashore. She saw the Captain standing on the bridge.

"Men, before work begins, I have an announcement to make," he said, when everyone had gathered. "As most of you know, the Southeastern Shipping Company in Liverpool holds a special boxing competition every other year between the crews of the ships that deliver their goods. This is the year for the competition. It will be held on May 23th. If the weather holds, and we make our shipment, we'll participate."

Margaret heard cheers and whistles go up from all the men. She was happy because it was the day before her birthday. She'd be eighteen in her old life, but here on the ship, she'd be fourteen.

The Captain held up a paper. "These are the rules and requirements. As always, if the crew meets the requirement, the Neptune's Daughter will sponsor the entry fee of seventy-five pounds."

Again, cheers went up.

"But, let me say this," he added when everyone quieted down. "This is strictly voluntary. No one will be forced to participate. It's not an order. The tournament will take place in six weeks. You have until then to pick the team. Training will be on your own time and will not interfere with the business of this ship. The boats from shore will be arriving in about thirty minutes. Mr. Coruthers will read to you the requirements for a team then it's back to work."

The Captain left the bridge and headed below. The men that he passed assured him that this year it would be Neptune's Daughter that took the prize.

Margaret listened as Mr. Coruthers read the requirements.

"Each ship must choose one man to participate in each of the three divisions:

Heavy weight Division:
180 pounds to 210 pounds

Middle weight Division:
140 pounds to 170 pounds

Light weight Division:
110 pounds to 130 pounds

"Weight classification is to be strictly followed. Team member will be weighed before the competition starts, and if weight requirements are not met for each division, that team will be disqualified. There are no age or height requirements. If a team wins all three events, that team will win a prize of three-hundred pounds for their ship. Afterward, the crew of the winning team will be invited to celebrate with free food and drinks at the Ship & Shore Inn. If there is no team win for all three events, the prize will be reduced to seventy pounds per event for their ship and no celebration." Mr. Coruthers held up the notice. "This will be posted for all to read. Dismissed."

After Mr. Coruthers finished reading and left the bridge, the men started talking among themselves as the best way to proceed in selecting a team. Doug Taggart, one of the watch commanders, was asked if he'd organized the selection as he did two years ago. He agreed and addressed the men.

"After the cargo is unloaded, all off duty personnel who want to be considered for the team are to report to the cargo hold for weigh in," said the commander, and then he warned, "Any man who leaves his duty station before his watch is over will not receive his share of any prize money! Am I clear?"

"Aye, Mr. Taggart," the men called out.

Charlie nudged Margaret in the ribs. "You like ta' fight, Marc. Are ya' gonna try fer' lightweight?"

"Me!" Margaret exclaimed. "I'm just a kid! They'd use my head for a mop and the rest of my body as the handle."

Charlie laughed as he sized her up. "Ah, yer probably right. Ya' are a might scrawny."

"Are you going to try?" Margaret asked.

"I did one year," he said rubbing his chin. "I've got a glass jaw. One blow and I'm down fer' the count. I didn't make it through the first round."

They headed for the cargo bay with the rest of the men to start bringing up the goods to be loaded on rafts that were coming from shore. The process of bringing up the goods took about thirty minutes. However, loading the supplies on the rafts took considerably longer. Three hours later, the ship up anchored, and they were on their way to the next port of call, which was about two hours up the coast.

Margaret went about her duties until the end of her watch. She'd gone down to the crew's quarters to find Pete, but found no one. She then remembered that they'd probably be in the cargo hold for the weigh-in.

The men were all laughing and joking as she watched each potential team member sit in a swing that was attached to a scale. Doug Taggart was standing beside it with a pen and tablet, writing down names and weights. She saw a man sit down.

"Harvey Cheatham — 182lbs — Heavy-weight!" Mr. Taggart called out.

The men cheered and laughed as Harvey flexed his muscles and showed off. The next man sat down.

"Monty Hicks, 312 lbs." The watch commander shook his head.

"Who knows? I could get in shape in six weeks," he said as everyone laughed with him.

"Fat chance, Hicks!" he replied over the laughter. "Next!"

Margaret watched as each man got on the scales. Some were rejected and some were put in their weight classes. But then she heard someone call out her name. "What about Marc! Put him on the scales!"

The peel of laughter filled the hold, and she could feel a couple of men push her forward until she was standing before the scale. She really didn't mind being the butt of a joke since she knew she wouldn't be fighting.

"Sit down, boy!" Mr. Taggart laughed. "Marcus Allen — 101½." Sorry kid, no flyweight divisions in this tourney."

The cargo bay roared with laughter as she got out of the swing. She flexed her left muscle, just as she'd done for Doc earlier, and they laughed even harder.

First watch was the last to weigh-in. Out of the sixty man crew, forty weighed in that wanted to be considered for the team. Out of those, ten qualified for heavy-weight, twenty, qualified for middle-weight, and only one qualified for light-weight. The other nine were rejected for being too heavy. Margaret was nine and one-half pounds under weight. But they'd only put her up there as joke anyway.

It had taken two days for the men to decide who they wanted to represent them. Light weight was already decided. Jeb Stone was the only one who qualified. He was tall and lean and weighed in at 125 lbs. Except for his height his build wasn't much bigger than Margaret's.

The middle-weight class took the most time. The men decided on, Patty "Pit bull" Flint. Pit Bull was what he said his ring name was. The name fit. His short stature and muscular build reminded her of a pit bull, and he weighed in at 150 lbs.

In the heavy-weight class was Angus. Whether that was his first or last name, no one knew. He weighed in at 201 lbs. He was the most muscular man aboard and also had some ring experience.

Margaret was anxious to get to Liverpool. She'd never seen a boxing match before and was just as excited as the men were. Also, with it being her birthday, she wanted to do something special for herself to celebrate it.

Training began immediately for the combatants when they were off duty. Margaret watched as Angus went through his trained regiment; punching a heavy sack, boxing with his shadow and a variety of other exercises. The other two men were on duty.

Suddenly, one of the men came running into the room.

"A line broke! Jeb Stone just fell from the rigging!" he shouted.

Everyone left the room and headed for sickbay. He was the only one who'd qualified for the light-weight division. Without him, Neptune's Daughter couldn't enter, and that meant no prize money if they won.

Doc came out of sickbay to face more than half the crew after he'd finished with Jeb.

"Well, Doc? Will he be able to fight?" asked one of the men.

Margaret just shook her head. They didn't care how bad he was hurt, just if he would be able to compete.

"His leg is broken and so is his right wrist. Sorry, men. He'll be laid up for a while," Doc replied.

The men groaned and returned to their quarters. Margaret also decided to retire for the evening. She was just as disappointed as the men. Not because of any prize, but she would have liked to have seen the crewmen of the Neptune's Daughter at least be able to compete.

***

The off duty crewmen were either laying in their bunks or sitting at the table trying to sooth their spirits with rum.

"There goes the prize money," said Charlie as he took a swallow.

"First year Neptune's Daughter will be out of the tournament," said another man, throwing cards one by one into a hat.

Orvil had just finished cleaning up the galley and sat down. "Well, has anyone figured out how we can still enter the tournament?" he asked.

"The lightest person we have is Alvin and he'd have to lose thirty pounds to be eligible," said another.

"The only other light-weight we have is Marc…" said Charlie, taking sip of rum, "…and he's 'bout ten pounds under weight."

Orvil sat there for a moment and then he had a wild idea. "Charlie! You're a genius!"

Charlie just about choked on his rum. "'Bout what?"

The men all looked in Orvil's direction, and he motioned for them to gather round. "I've got an idea. Marc *can* be in the light-weight division."

"Did ya' forget what I said? He's underweight. And he's a scrawny kid," said Charlie.

"So we fatten him up. Ten pounds is nothing. I can put the meat on his bones and the rest of you can build the muscle," Orvil replied.

"He'll never go fer' it," said Sam, shaking his head. "Like Charlie said, he's just a kid. They'd wipe the mat with him. I don't think the Capt'n will go fer' it either."

"The Captain can't say anything if Marc says he wants to do it," said Orvil.

"But how do we make him?" asked another. "We can't threaten him, and I don't want to see him killed in the ring. He's a good kid."

"I've seen this competition a few times. Most of the light-weights aren't much bigger than Marc. If we train him earnestly, he might get banged up a bit, but at least he'll have a chance," said one of the older men. "When Angus and Flint win £125 in prize money is better than nothing if Marc loses."

Orvil stood up and paced the floor thinking. "First thing we do is ask him. We all know he'll say no. I don't blame him."

"We could ignore him," someone said.

"Not enough," Orvil replied. A moment later an idea struck him. "First of all, anything that we do can't get back to the Captain or watch commanders — especially, Pete. They'll put a stop to our plans."

Orvil began unfolding his little scheme then told them to spread the word quietly to others on duty.

"Do you think it will work?" asked Charlie, laughing at one of Orvil's wild ideas.

"I guarantee you, that in two days he'll be begging us to let him be on the team," Orvil laughed.

One of the crewmen laughed so hard he had to wipe a tear from his eye. "Orvil, you know he's going to kill you."

"No he won't." Orvil grinned. "He loves my cooking."

***

Margaret woke the next morning and began her coffee rounds. After mentally drooling over the Captain's gorgeous body, she went to the galley for breakfast. It seemed funny to her that just about everyone this morning was smiling and asking her how she felt — even the ones that never spoke to her. She thought they'd all be down in the dumps and grumpy as hell today. They totally surprised her.

When she went through the line, the men let her get in front of them. Hank even gave her a smile and an extra portion of food. Something was going on.

Have they discovered me secret? Is that why everyone is being so courteous this morning?

She walked over to the table and sat down. They were all staring at her with smiling faces and few toothless grins.

"Okay!" Margaret said. "I smell a rat. What's going on?"

"Funny you should ask that, Marc," said Orvil, as he sat across from her. "The crew would like to bestow upon you the great honor of becoming representative for the Neptune's Daughter at the tournament in the light-weight class."

Margaret stood up. "What!" she shouted. "I'll be killed. No way! No how!"

"We thought about that," said one of the crew. "We'll train ya' proper! Ya' might get a scrape here or there, but yer' used ta' that."

"No! And that's final!" she said adamantly.

"Suit yourself," Orvil shrugged. He then went about his business and the men turned to their breakfast.

Margaret was relieved that they hadn't discovered her secret, but she was terrified about going into a ring of men for a boxing match. She might be crazy for serving aboard this ship disguised as a boy, but she wasn't that crazy!

She went to reach for some pepper, but just as soon as she was about to grab the shaker, someone else grabbed it, used it and passed it down the line. When she reached for the salt, they did the same thing. When she asked them to pass it, they ignored her. She finished her breakfast and went about her polishing duties. An hour later, Orvil had sent for her and told her to meet him in the food storage room.

"Marc, there's a rat's nest somewhere in this room. I need you to unload the room and find it," Orvil said.

"I thought Hank took care of this room?" Margaret asked.

"He's down in his back. Besides, I've got him doing something else. Well, get to it. You don't have all day."

Margaret looked at the task in front of her. Barrels and barrels and sacks upon sacks. This was going to take hours. She thought about asking Charlie to help her, but he'd joined the rest of the men in ignoring her.

It took her two hours to unload the room. There was no nest and she'd only seen one rat and instinctively jumped back. She quickly picked up a sack and tried to throw it at the beast, but she missed and it ran out through a whole in the floor. The first time she'd seen a rat aboard, it scared the life from her and she eeked out a girlish squeal. She considered herself fortunate that no one had been around.

Margaret looked around the room and shook her head. "Rat's nest my foot!" She picked up the broom and swept out the bugs and small piles that had leaked from some of the sacks where Mr. Rat had gnawed through. She mopped it and loaded it back after fixing the bags with holes in them.

Orvil came around just in time to see her put the last bag in. She was sweaty and worn out.

"All done," she said. "I didn't find a nest. Just one rat," she said leaning on a barrel.

Orvil looked around. "Hmmm — I wish you'd come and gotten me before you loaded it back. I thought I told you?"

"No, you didn't." She frowned at him. "Why?"

"I've decided to rearrange the room. I want the barrels on the other side. I'm afraid you're going to have to redo the room."

"Now wait a minute, Orvil!" she shouted. "I've spent better than four hours on this room, and you want me to take it all out and do it again!"

"You're right," he said. "I know you've got other things to do today."

Margaret breathed a sigh of relief.

"You can do it tomorrow," Orvil said as he turned to leave.

"Tomorrow!" she shouted.

Orvil grinned as he walked away, but didn't turn around. "Tomorrow!" Margaret just didn't see a rat — she smelled one.

This is retaliation!

This senseless chore and the silent treatment were not going to cause her to back down. She was not going to fight!

Margaret finished polishing below deck and started polishing the brass topside. She'd almost finished a brass rail when one of the off duty crewmen leaned on it and looked out over the water. He turned his head and spat a wad of tobacco. It stuck to her rail. She gave him a hard look.

"Sorry 'bout that, Marc," he grinned. "Wind must have caught it. I'll try not ta' let it happen again." He then walked away.

"Wind my ass!" she mumbled turning up her nose. The brown slime was disgusting, and she felt like she was going to puke. But she wiped it off and went about her business.

The rest of the day went like that. The men would do something disgusting that she'd have to clean up, and then they'd apologize as if it was an accident. The last task for her to do before supper was to clean the bathing area and the head. She fully expected the bathing area to be extra messy, but to her surprise it wasn't. But when she opened the door to the toilet, there was the most disgusting mess she had ever seen. Shit! Everywhere there was shit! On the floor — on the walls! One of the men had dysentery and it ran all down the side of the toilet where he'd missed. She needed a shovel!

"You sons-of-bitches!" she exclaimed loudly, as entered the crew's quarters. "Why did you bastards do that!"

"Do what?" asked Charlie innocently.

The men all looked at each other shrugging their shoulders as if they didn't know why Marc was so upset.

"All of you know what you did!" she yelled. "The bloody head!"

"Oh that," Sam replied, trying to hold back his laughter. "It happens occasionally. The ship tosses too much then everything splashes out."

"There's a shovel over in the corner," said one of the men playing cards.

Margaret turned around and grabbed up the shovel, cursing them under her breath. She knew what they were doing. She was not going to fight!

With that disgusting chore done, she went to the passengers bathing area and washed. She'd never felt so dirty and disgusting in all her life.

She didn't know whether to cry or be angry. But she decided to be angry because crying wouldn't do any good.

It was just about time for dinner. After she served the Captain and his commanders, she went to have her own. This time when she stood in line, no one let her in front.

"Marc, I have a special treat for you," said Orvil. There was a wide grin on his face. "Fresh meat."

Margaret held out her plate. Orvil plopped a piece of meat on, alright. It was rat! It had been skinned, except for the head, skewered on a stick and fried.

"I can't eat that!" she exclaimed.

"Why not?" Orvil asked, pretending to be insulted. "It's a delicacy in some countries. After all the hard work I did catching it, cleaning it and making it especially for you!"

"I know what you are trying to do," she shouted.

"Do what?" he replied. "The only thing I do around here is cook and no one appreciates it."

"Well, then you eat it! I've lost my appetite." Margaret slammed her plate down, grabbed a biscuit and stormed off to her cabin.

Orvil laughed after she left.

"Well, do you think it's working?" asked one of the men.

"I think it's working," laughed Charlie. "Ya' should have seen his face when he looked at the head. It was as red as his hair. Felt sorry for the bugger with that one."

"I think he wanted ta' beat the hell out of all of us on that one," laughed Sam. "And I say he'd probably got a few good licks in. His fists were clenched tight."

"One more day, and he'll change his mind. Now, all we have to do is get him mad enough to take a poke at someone," Orvil replied. "When he proves to himself that he can do more than just fight defensively, we'll have him. I think tomorrow will be the day. Who wants to volunteer to piss him off?"

"I'll do it," laughed Charlie. "I've got a glass jaw. One swing is all it will take. What do you want me to do?"

Orvil gathered everyone around and whispered his plan.

***

Margaret sat in her bunk mad as a hornet. She took her knife and threw it at the floor trying to get it to stick, but it just fell. She knew what they were doing, and she wasn't buying it. "I didn't run away from Nathanial just to die in a boxing match," she mumbled. She thought about telling the Captain or one of the commanders what they were doing to her, but if she did, and they got in trouble, it would be all the worse for her. The more she thought about it the angrier she got. The next time she threw her knife to the floor — it stuck deep!

The next morning, the ship pulled into port and was ready for the day's business. Margaret delivered the Captain's morning coffee and hot water.

"Anything else, Captain?" she ask.

The Captain noticed a difference in Marc's voice this morning. He was usually cheerful and wanted conversation. This morning he seemed cranky and anxious to leave.

"Anything wrong? You don't seem yourself today."

Her thought immediately went to yesterday.

That's an understatement!

"I'm fine," she replied. "Just got up on the wrong side of the bunk."

"Maybe a game of chess will cheer you up this afternoon," he said.

Margaret managed a smile. "Perhaps."

She left his quarters and started about her business. Orvil had reminded her this morning about rearranging the food storage room. She did that first and went for breakfast. Normally, Orvil was careful about sifting the bugs and tiny worms from the biscuits but hers were full of them. She was afraid to eat the meat he'd served her, for it might have been rat meat in disguise. So the only thing she ate was the orange. Her stomach was growling and the orange barely satisfied.

A few minutes later, all hands were called for cargo duty. It was going to be another half-day job. When she was on the rope with another crewman, it seemed that he gave her more than her share of the weight to pull.

After two hours of loading, Mr. Richards gave everyone a two hour break. The expected wagon had been delayed, and it would be that long before it would arrive. Margaret sat down to rest. Her stomach was growling, she was piss at Orvil and to top it all off — it was that time of the month!

After taking on fresh water, the Neptune's Daughter started on her way to the next port. The crew had treated Margaret the same way they did the other day; ignoring her, or messing up something, just so she'd have to clean it. She was glad when Pete ordered her up to the crow's nest. It was peaceful compared to below. There was no one to get under her skin. But soon that duty was over and it was time to do the thing that she dreaded the most — the head!

***

Sam ran down to the crew's quarters.

"Get ready! He's coming!"

Orvil was usually in the galley about this time, but he couldn't resist seeing what he hoped would happen.

"Damn! It stinks in here!" said Charlie as he dropped his breeches, ready to get caught in the act.

Margaret walked into the crew's quarters and saw the men standing or sitting around just as the other day. She went to the bathing area and that wasn't bad. Next she went to the head and hesitated before opening the door. Orvil and the rest of the off duty crewmen crept quietly to the doorway of the bathing area to see what would happen.

Margaret took a deep breath to brace herself and opened the door. She saw Charlie squatting, not over the toilet, but on the floor.

"Oops!" he said. "Can't a man shit in peace!"

Margaret couldn't keep her temper in check any longer. She was starving. She had cramps. And right now she was so pissed she could spit nails!

"Get your nasty ass out of there!" she yelled. She grabbed him by the hair and pulled him out with his breeches dangling about his knees.

"Aaaow!" Charlie hollered, "Let go!

Margaret let him go after she dragged him to the floor with him struggling to pull up his breeches, and then she kicked him!

"I knew you did this on purpose!" she shouted as she kicked him again.

The men laughed and Orvil went to grab Marc before he kicked Charlie where it really would hurt.

"Now Marc, you don't kick a man with his wick hanging out!" he laughed.

"Your's isn't!" she shouted. She turned around with clenched fists and punched Orvil in the stomach. When he bent over, she gave him a left cross to the chin and he fell back.

"Damn!" shouted Orvil, as he rubbed his jaw. Their cabin boy had totally taken him by surprise. "For a little guy, you pack a fair wallop!"

The men laughed and two of them grabbed her.

"Let go of me, you bastards! You want a fight! I'll give you one!" she shouted angrily. A tear ran down her cheek. She stopped struggling and they let go. She quickly wiped the tear away.

"That's all we wanted, Marc," said Orvil. "We just want you in the ring. You don't even have to win. But I'm telling you, you've got a hell of a left!"

Margaret was quiet for a moment. "I'll do it," she said quietly.

The men started cheering, but she shouted over their voices, "I'll do it on one condition!"

"And what's that?" Orvil asked.

"I never have to clean that nasty ass head again! Today, or any other day while I am on this ship."

The men looked at each other and started laughing as they nodded their agreement.

"Consider it done," said Charlie.

As soon as Marc gave his word, Sam ran up the steps to the main deck.

"Neptune's Daughter is back in the tournament!" he shouted for all to hear. "Marc is in!"

There were shouts and cheers from all parts of the deck and the news quickly spread throughout the ship.

Orvil patted their cabin boy one the back. "Marc, now it's time to fatten you up! You've got less than six weeks to gain nine and one-half pounds and maybe just a bit more for leeway."

"No rat!" Margaret said still angry.

Orvil laughed. "I promise — no rat."

They went to the crew's mess with the off duty men following. Margaret sat down and everyone gathered around her.

"I made this especially for you, Marc." Orvil sat a dish in front of her covered with a towel.

Margaret took a whiff. "Apple pie?"

"Not just apple pie. The best caramel apple pie you will ever eat," he said with pride. "It's my grandmother recipe."

He unveiled the caramel delight that was still warm. Margaret waited no longer. Forget the fork! Slipping her hand under the crust, she tore of a big portion and took a bite. She may have been pissed at him, but Orvil didn't lie. That pie melted in her mouth. She was so hungry she just about swallowed it whole. The crew laughed as they watch her eat.

"What's goin' on in here?" asked Pete as he burst into the room.

"Pie!" Margaret said with her mouth full.

"Marc, Capt'n wants ta' see ya," he said.

Margaret got up from the table as she finished off the last bite. Her hands were sticky. In her former life she would have used a napkin to wipe of her fingers. But this was her new life. What would a boy do? She wiped her mouth off with her hand, licked her fingers and then wiped them on her breeches.

Pete walked with Margaret for a way, as she headed to the Captain's quarters.

"So what made ya' decide ta' do it, lad?" Pete asked.

"Ship's honor," Margaret lied. She couldn't think of anything else to say.

Pete laughed and slapped her on the back. "I thought ya' had the makin's in ya'. Good lad!"

"Thank," she replied after she got her wind back.

Arriving at the Captain's quarters, Margaret knocked and he bid her enter.

"You wanted to see me, Captain?" Margaret asked.

"Thought we'd play a game," he said as he set up the pieces.

"Yes, sir." She managed a smile even though she was still somewhat angry.

They sat down and started moving pieces on the board. They were quiet for a moment until the Captain broke the silence.

"So, what did it for you?" he asked as he moved a pawn.

"Did what?" She moved her knight.

"Was it the silent treatment, the storage room, or the fried rat?" The Captain moved his rook.

Margaret looked up from her pieces. "You know about that?"

"There isn't much on this ship that I don't know about," he replied. "It's your move."

Margaret moved her bishop. "Actually, it was the combination of rat, and the head."

"Shit everywhere, 'ay," he replied nonchalantly as he moved his Queen.

"How did you know about that?" She moved a pawn.

"Experience. You were lucky. When I was your age, it was the head, and they hung me by my ankles from the mainmast and tickled my feet with a feather until I said yes." He moved his rook. "If you'd come to me I would have put a stop to the harassment."

"I thought it best to handle it myself." She moved her knight. "Check."

"Good move. Your game is improving." He moved his King out of danger. "You don't have to do this if you don't want to. I can still put a stop to it."

"Did you put a stop to your fight?" She took his Queen.

"No." He moved his knight.

"Did you win?" She took his bishop. "Check."

"Yes." He moved his King again.

"Weren't they bigger and stronger than you?" She moved her rook.

"Some were. But fighting is sometimes like playing chess. It's all in how you move, what you have to sacrifice and when you strike."

"Like this?" She moved her Queen. "Checkmate!"

The Captain laughed. "Exactly like that! Not bad. You're a quick learner."

"Do you still want to go on with the fight?" he asked.

"I promised," she sighed. "I just hope I live to tell about it."

"I think you will," he laughed. "I tell you what I'll do. I'm going to break my own rule. For the next five weeks, your only duty, besides my coffee and cargo, will be for you to learn the manly art of boxing. I'll have our best man work with you."

"You'd do that for me?"

"Captain Jacobson, my Captain, did it for me. I see no reason why I shouldn't do the same for you," he replied. "But let me tell you, it won't be easy."

"At least my odds will go up." She attempted a small laugh.

The Captain dismissed her and had her send for Pete and Patty "Pit Bull" Flint, the middle-weight competitor, to give them their orders.

***

"Ya' don't think Marc has backed out do ya'?" Flint asked Pete. "Ya' think the Capt'n is gonna order Marc not ta' fight?"

"Can't say, Flint. But if he is, why would he wanna see you too?"

They arrived at the Captain's quarters. "Aye, Capt'n, ya' wanted ta' see us?" Pete asked.

The Captain leaned up against his desk and folded his arms. "It's come to my attention that Marc has — volunteered to participate in the competition."

"I swear Capt'n," Flint began. "We didn't threaten the boy. He..."

The Captain held up his hand and Flint was quite. He turned to the watch commander. "Pete, you need to make some changes in the work detail." He looked at Flint. "I have a special detail for you. Marc needs a fighting chance. So, I want you to train him full time until the tournament. Except for cargo, that will be your only duty. Can you handle it?"

"Aye, Capt'n. I'll train 'em good, sir!" replied Flint.

"Then get to it. Training starts now."

"Aye, sir. Thank ya', Capt'n!" he replied in an excited tone and left.

The Captain turned to Pete. "Thanks for giving me the heads up, Pete."

"I knew the men was up ta' somethin'. He's a good lad, Marc is."

"I know. Keep a close eye on this boy, Pete. I don't want anything to happen to him."

"Ya' can count on me, Capt'n."

The Captain dismissed Pete. He went to the table with his charts and sat down. When he couldn't concentrate, he went to the widow of his cabin and looked out. He was worried about the boy. There was still something about him. It was like Jake all over again. But yet, still different, and he couldn't figure out what. He inwardly wished that Marc would have let him intervene, but he knew if the boy wanted to gain the respect of the other men, he couldn't do that. He had his chance, Marc needed his.

CHAPTER 14
"The Pugilist"

Margaret stood naked in front of the full length mirror that was in one of the passenger cabins. She thought to herself:

I never would have believed a woman's body could look like this?

Where once was just smooth skin, there was now bumps and ripples. The muscle she'd shown Doc some weeks earlier was nothing compared to the mountain, or at least a small hill, that she now had when she flexed her arms. Granted, she wasn't as well defined as a man, but for a woman? It was unbelievable! Her breasts weren't any larger, and for once she was glad, but they were firmer. Her stomach had always been flat, but it had been weak. Now it was hard and rippled with muscle, especially after one of Flint's training sessions.

What would mother think if she saw me now?

That though made her smile, but then she sighed:

What would a man think? What would the Captain think if he knew I was a woman?

Today was the final weigh-in before the competition tomorrow to see if she qualified for their team. She put her clothes back on and went down to the hold. For the past five weeks and five days, Flint put her through a rigorous schedule of training. When the Captain said it was going to be difficult, he understated it!

The first week was sheer torture. Six hours a day of toning her muscles. The only break in her routine was cargo duty, though not much of one. Her muscles were still being taxed.

First thing in the morning was muscle building before breakfast for two hours. She would climb a rope a few times and do chin-up on one of the beams in the hold. In another exercise, Flint would tie her ankles, hoist her up and then she would have to try and touch her toes. It took her about two weeks to even raise half-way. After that, she lay down and he would drop a five pound sack on her stomach an increase the weight each week. There were also various other toning exercises Flint would come up with. He never let up on her. There were many times she thought that if the boxing match didn't kill her, the training would.

Breakfast was next. Orvil would fill her plate with double portions of food, especially meat. She ate until she thought she was going to throw up. Flint gave her an hour and a half break afterward to let her food settle.

The next two hours were spent on endurance and balance training. He would have her jump rope, skip, run in place and practice foot work for the ring. Balance training was unusual. He had twelve bags suspended from the beam in the hold. He would swing them and she'd have to walk a line trying not to get hit by the bags. Once she could walk the line without being hit, she had to walk on a four inch by four inch wooden beam and not get hit by the bags. That was more difficult, but didn't take her long to master that. She'd had some balance training on a beam with Claude during some of her fencing lessons.

At noon, it was back with Orvil and more food, though not as much. She had a few more hours of rest to let her body recover and then she had to punch on a bag for about thirty minutes. The first day, she'd skinned her knuckles. The second day she brought her gloves.

Dinner was after that and again Orvil would fill her plate full. In the evening were the actual boxing lessons. Flint would have her memorized different combinations of punches, how to block, duck and cover-up. He started slow then built up speed. She also found out that the competitors were required to wear mufflers on their fist. That was at least some comfort. No bare knuckles.

At the end of each week they would weigh her. The first week she gained three pounds. The second week she was even. The third week, she'd gained a pound. The fourth week, she'd gained another three pounds. The end of the fifth week she'd gained one more pound for a total of eight pounds, with at least one and one half pounds to go to qualify and today was the day.

"Up you go, Marc," said Flint.

The off duty crew were all standing around waiting to see if their light-weight competitor had reached the goal. Margaret got on the scales and heard the men groan.

"109½," Flint read.

"Out again," Charlie sighed. "I thought sure we were in."

"Sorry, Marc, we tried. All that work fer' nothin'," said Flint.

Margaret was inwardly glad. She really hoped she wouldn't qualify. But again, she'd done all that work. She got off the scale and the crew started to slowly leave. Then Orvil stepped up.

"Hey! Hold up! I've got an idea." he shouted. He held a bucket of water in his hand. "We may not be licked yet. Marc, come here."

Margaret walked back and took the bucket. "What's this for?"

"Drink it up and we shall see."

"All of it!" she exclaimed. "That's a lot of water."

"Just drink," he repeated.

Margaret did as he asked. It took a few minutes, and she thought she was going to drown but she drained the bucket.

"Now, get back on the scale," he said.

Margaret shrugged and did as he asked.

"110 pounds. He qualifies!" shouted Flint, as the men cheered.

"Wait a minute!" shouted Charlie. "How can he hold all that water till tomorrow?"

Orvil laughed. "You twit! Before he leaves for the competition, he'll just drink another bucket of water and hold it until after weigh-in. Plus, no training the rest of the day — just food."

Margaret pretended she was excited. Some of them said she looked pretty good during training, and they'd bet money she'd actually win a round or two. All she wanted to do was get through the day alive and with her teeth still intact.

She went on deck and looked out into the bay where they were anchored. They'd arrived a few hours earlier. She counted fifteen ships anchored and there was another in the distance coming in.

"Are you nervous?"

Margaret saw the Captain come up beside her. "Would you think me a coward if I said I was terrified?"

"No," he said, with a smile. "Remember, I was in your same position once. Being a little afraid can be healthy. It keeps you sharp. If you went in thinking you can lick the world you'd probably get careless and let your guard down."

"If I went in with a suit of armor I wouldn't let my guard down!" she replied.

"I'll wager you'll do fine. You look fit," he said noticing an arm that was slightly more muscular than when he first came aboard.

"If Flint did anything, his training conditioned me better for cargo duty," she laughed.

"See there, terror is now replaced with laughter. If you were that terrified, you wouldn't be making jokes right now. I would say you've just got a healthy case of fear. It takes a brave man to face his fears. A coward refuses to. I don't see a coward, Marc, I see a young man facing his fear."

Margaret wanted so much to scream out that she wasn't a young man, but a young woman that wanted him. But she had to keep her mouth shut and her feelings inside. During these weeks when Flint wasn't training her, she'd played games of chess with the Captain and he'd also started teaching her about navigation. He even let her take the wheel a few times.

She broke out of her reverie and sighed. "Well, I need to go to the galley. Orvil has a pie he wants me to eat. He's hoping it might put another pound on me." She needed to leave him, before she wrapped her arms around him and gave him a big hug.

"Then bon appetite'. Get a good night's rest and don't worry," he said as she left.

Todd looked out into the bay. He was proud of how hard Marc had worked. Flint and Pete gave him regular reports and said the boy attempted all that was asked without complaint. Todd wanted to be there to watch his training, but being the position he was in, he couldn't. He hoped Marc would do well tomorrow, for the boy's own confidence. But if he lost, it didn't matter, because he knew Marc would have done his best.

His fondness for the boy was growing. It seemed more so for this boy than for Jake, and that bothered him, for they both were good boys.

Maybe it was because Jake was gone and Marc is here. That's probably the reason.

***

Margaret woke early. Today was it. They were going to check her weight one more time before her official weigh-in. She was up one half pound, probably due to the pie she ate that morning. Orvil was standing by with the bucket of water and she drank it. It brought her weight up to ten and one half pounds. She hoped she could hold it in until after the official weigh-in.

The competition was held at The Gentleman's Athletics Club of Liverpool. Several sporting events were held there, but the main sport was boxing. Three rings had been set up in the huge auditorium, and spectators' seats were ten tiers high all around the room. The first row was reserved. Margaret figured it was for the ship Captains and sponsors of the tournament.

The competitors were taken to a back section of the building where they were to be weighed and separated into their divisions. The competitors had to be there at six o'clock for the reading of the new rules and to qualify. The doors opened for spectators at eight o'clock and the competition started at nine o'clock. The only persons allowed to be with the competitors were the ship's physician and the corner man. Since Flint was competing, he couldn't be in Margaret's corner, so she asked Pete. Angus and Flint also chose a man from the crew to be in their corners.

Margaret was finally glad it was their turn to weigh in. All that water she drank was pressing to come out. The team that weighed in before theirs was disqualified. One of their members was overweight. Next Angus and Flint were weighed and easily qualified. She was next and her team mates held their breath. She had her fingers crossed that they also would be disqualified, but no such luck. She weighed 110 pounds on the nose. They qualified. Twenty-four teams in all were to compete. Each team was given a number to wear on the back of their shirt. Their team number was seventeen.

The rules were fairly simple in the elimination rounds. No wrestling, no biting, no hitting below the belt and no hitting or kicking a man when he's down. Points were awarded for the number of solid blows given and points taken away for not following the rules. There were three, 2-minute rounds, with a thirty-second rest between rounds. If you knocked out your opponent in any round, you won. The referee and two other judges decided the outcome of the match. In previous competitions, there was a referee, but there were practically no rules, no other judges and just about anything was allowed. Two men had died in the ring, in the previous competition, so the club established those new rules.

Flint pulled Margaret and Pete aside for last minute instructions. "Three things to remember," Flint said. "Don't pay any attention to what yer' opponents say — they'll lie. Second, make sure yer' muscles are warm before ya' fight, and third, kick their bloody arses!" he laughed. "I seen 'em! They ain't no bigger than you, Marc."

"You really think I have a chance?" Margaret asked. She was so nervous that she hadn't paid much attention to her competition. After her weigh-in, she had to find a public facility — all that water she drank wanted out.

"Me sister could beat the lot of 'em." Flint laughed. But then he warned, "But don't get cocky, they might get lucky."

One of the referees called for the different divisions to separate into different rooms. Margaret lined up with the rest of her opponents. Flint was right about one thing — they were all just about the same size. She guessed their ages ranged between fifteen and thirty. The referee told them that eight would automatically go to the second round and they would have to draw lots. When it was her turn to draw, she was one of the unlucky one that had to fight first. But she figured she may as well get it over with. She was also told she would fight the first match and had thirty minutes to warm up. The competition was about to start.

Margaret started her routine of loosening up and practicing her punches with Pete.

"Yer' lookin' good, lad!" Pete encouraged.

"Looking good is one thing, not getting my teeth knocked out is another," she said, as she practiced her right jab and left cross. She would then switch and box the other hand as lead.

"Look at these other blokes," he whispered. "Some of them ain't even twitched a muscle. Flint's right, ya' got a shot."

She looked around and only a few men were doing anything that resembled warming up. Even the man she was about to face was just sitting in a corner waiting.

"I hope you're right," Margaret said, as she continued to work up a sweat.

Doc entered the room and had her sit on the table that was in her area. He pulled out a jar and started to rub a clear substance on her face.

"What's that?" she asked.

"Lard. It will help you from getting cut up to badly if you get hit."

"That's comforting," she replied sarcastically. Pete was telling her she had a chance, and Doc was telling her she might get beat to a pulp.

A man entered the room an announced, "Five minutes!"

Pete helped her put on the thinly padded gloves and tied them to her wrist.

"I think I'm going to be sick," Margaret said. She could feel her stomach boiling.

"There's the bucket," Pete replied.

Margaret didn't hesitate. She grabbed the bucket and let it go.

"Feel better?" Doc asked as he handed her a towel.

"I guess." She rinsed the bile from her mouth. "Got any last minute advice?"

"Aye." Pete grinned. "Remember how ya' felt when ya' saw Charlie shit'n in the floor? Think on that fer inspiration."

"That might do it."

She couldn't help but chuckle a bit. Even though it wasn't funny at the time, it was now. She felt a bit of tension ease. She needed a good puke and something to laugh at.

The three of them headed towards one of the end rings. The auditorium was crowded. Both men and women started shouting and whistling as the competitors came out. She looked around to see if she could see any of their crew, but there were too many people. She looked where the reserved seating was to see if the Captain was there. But when she asked, she was told that the Captains were all at a meeting and only showed up for the main events that evening. In a way, she was glad he wasn't there. If she saw him, she might lose focus. She looked toward the other two rings, but neither Flint nor Angus were in the other rings.

Margaret took a deep breath. She'd said a long time ago, she wanted adventure. Well, she couldn't get any more adventurous than this. Pete separated the ropes, and she entered the ring. Her opponent entered from the opposite side. He was just a few inches taller and about the same build as she was. She figured him for a man of twenty.

There were no names announced. There was just the number on their backs to let the spectators know who to place bets on. The referee called them to the center of the ring and asked them if they understood the rules. Afterward, he sent them back to their corners, until the bell was rung to start the fight. Margaret prayed silently:

God help me!

The bell rang and the competitors met in the center of the ring. Her opponent came right out swinging. Margaret blocked his attack and saw he'd left himself wide open and made two left jabs and a right hook. He staggered back a bit, and came right back at her. Again, he tried the same thing, but this time she dodged his attack, punched him in the stomach and gave him a right cross. Margaret danced around the ring keeping her guard up, and the next time, the man was more careful with his attack.

and grazed her across the chin. He then faked with his right and caught her with his left. But Margaret came back with a solid left of her own, and he staggered back. The bell sounded for them to go to their corner.

"Not bad, Marc," Pete said, as he handed her some water to rinse her mouth out. Flint had told her not to swallow. Just rinse and spit.

"I don't know why I'm breathing so hard," she panted. "Flint worked me out harder than this."

"It's the excitement," said Doc, as he examined her face for injuries. "It makes the blood pump faster."

"Thirty-seconds is about up," Pete said. "This time take the fight ta' him. Don't wait for him ta' make the first move."

Margaret followed Pete's advice. She had thought just to defend, and attack when she saw an opening and accumulate points. But she wanted this over with. She came right out with a series of right jabs, and a left hook. When he blocked her hook, she saw his stomach was open. She landed a solid right to the stomach, and then a solid left cross to his jaw. To her astonishment, Margaret saw her opponent hit the floor. The referee backed her away and started to count. She heard both cheers and groans from the spectators.

Margaret was stunned, and listened as the referee counted to eight. Her opponent tried to get up but slumped back to the ground. The referee came to her corner and raised her hand in victory. She couldn't believe it!

"I won!" She was in a state of shock.

Pete and Doc entered the ring. "Ya' won, lad!" Pete shouted above the voices of the spectators.

Doc shook his head and scratched it in disbelief. "And by knockout no less!"

They exited the ring for the next competitors and Pete slapped her on the back as he usual did when he was happy about something. "Ya' just made me a few quid, Marc."

"You bet on me?"

"I knew ya' could do it!"

They passed two more competitors on their way to the ring as they headed back to the room. Pete went to rinse out her spit bucket, as Doc had her get up on the table and lay down on her stomach. As he massaged her muscles, he started to laugh.

"What's funny?"

"I never thought I would be giving a woman a rub down after a boxing match," he whispered.

"Shhhh! Someone will hear."

"Ahhh, they're not paying any attention. Tell me, what would your mother think?"

"I don't even want to go there." She laughed. "She would disown me. She gets embarrassed if I put too much food on my plate when we're invited to dinner parties."

Doc finished his rub down and slapped her on the rear.

"Doc!" she exclaimed.

"Ahhh, pipe down! I'm just telling you I'm done. It's normal. Rest for about thirty minutes. You've probably got about an hour, before the second round starts, and then you need to warm back up again."

Margaret lay down and thought about what she had just done:

I can do this!

She remembered what Claude had said about her fencing. He believed she would have won fencing competitions but never believed him. Flint told her she had a good chance at winning this. Pete bet on her, and if he did, the rest of the crew might. She had to win.

As each round came up, Margaret won match after match. With each time, she got more confidence in herself. Even when she got hit with a stout blow, she was able to quickly recover. She also remembered what Flint said — don't get cocky. She had to keep focused.

There was one more round to fight — the main event. Doc told her that Angus and Flint were also going to the finals. This year the two teams that had come to the final match were Neptune's Daughter and Arrow Star.

There was a two hour break in the action. The main event was to start at six o'clock. Margaret paced back and forth nervous about this next round. This time it would be five rounds instead of three. The Captain would also be there to watch her. She knew if she won, he would be proud of the boy, Marc. She also wondered how he would feel about the girl named Margaret winning and wondered if he would think any less of her for participating in this definitely male sport.

"Gettin' nervous, kid?" her opponent yelled from across the room.

Margaret turned around. Her opponent was about thirty, and like the others, wasn't much bigger that her and only slightly more muscular.

"I tell ya' what, boy," he continued. "Just lay down in the second round, and I'll go easy on ya' in the first."

Margaret was about to reply, but Pete came in, just hearing what he said.

"Pipe down ya' swab, before I pound yer' head between yer' shoulders, after the match," Pete warned.

The man shut up and sat back down in the corner.

"Don't pay him no mind," said Pete. "But ya' better be careful with him in the ring. He's a tricky one."

"How so?" she asked.

Pete had watched the other rounds to size up her opponents since the competitors were not allowed to watch the other matches.

"If he's winnin' rounds, he fights by the rules. But if he's not, twice I seen him give the other man a shot to the family jewels."

"And he still won?" she asked.

"Aye, they just take away points. But it weakened the other men enough fer' him ta' win by knocked out in the next round."

Margaret started to pace back and forth again. "I wish we can hurry up and get this over with!"

"It won't be long," Pete laughed. "Ya' done good ta'day."

"I hope I don't let the Captain and everyone else down," she said.

"Yer' here ain't ya'?" he replied. "Nobody thought ya'd do any good anyhow, but so fer ya' did. So, sit yer' arse down, before ya' were a hole in the floor."

Margaret sat down and closed her eyes. He was right. If she hadn't qualified, they wouldn't be there at all. She thought about what Pete had said about her opponent and smiled. If he punched her in the so called "jewels" he wouldn't get the reaction he'd hoped for.

The main events were about to begin. But this time, unlike the preliminary fights, the team members came out together. The team from the Arrow Star was the first team to enter the middle ring. The master of ceremonies introduced each competitor, and each man strut around the ring either shouting or flexing his muscles. Then their Captain was introduced from the reserved seats. Captain Deven Reid stood and waved to the crowd. Cheers came from half the spectators and hoots from the other half.

Next it was time for the team from Neptune's Daughter to enter the ring. Margaret could feel the excitement from the crowd as each member of her team stepped forward. Angus stepped forward and flexed the muscles in his great arms, as he strutted around the ring just as the team before them did. Flint stepped forward, raised his fist in the air and shouted, "Neptune's Daughter!" at the top of his lungs, and she saw the crew from their ship stand up and shout the same. It was then her turn to strut. What the hell was she going to do? Her muscles were tiny compared to Angus. Everyone would laugh if she flexed hers, and she didn't have a booming voice like Flint. Next her name was announced.

"Introducing! Light-weight competitor, at 110 pounds — Marcus Allen!"

Margaret stepped forward and the only thing she could think to do was bow like a gentleman, and then she raised both arms in the air with clenched fists. The crew of the Neptune's Daughter stood, cheered and called out several times, "Marc! Marc! Marc!" There were also catcalls mixed in with those cheers, but she didn't care about those.

Next, they announced the Captain.

"Introducing! The Captain of the Neptune's Daughter! Captain Todd Withers!"

The Captain stood, and Margaret saw him for the first time since the events started. She smiled both inside and out, until he sat down next to this beautiful, dark haired woman who looped her arm around his. Her heart pounded in her ears. She wished her brain would stop doing this to her. Every time she thought of him with another woman, a wave of sadness enveloped her. She had to shake this off.

They left the center of the ring and the matches started. This time, they only used one ring, one match at a time. The heavy-weight was first, then middle, then light.

Margaret had a hard time not looking over at the Captain and his lady as they talked and laughed with each other in between rounds. She was jealous and knew it for what it was. There was no denying it, and she chastised herself for feeling that way.

The heavy-weight match was soon over, and Angus won by knockout in the third round. Next was Flint. His final match went five rounds and the decision went to him. Now it was her turn.

Oh God! It's all up to me!

Her stomach felt like it had knots in it. Neptune's Daughter was two thirds of the way to winning the whole thing. When she entered the ring, she could hear the crew shout her name and clap their hands. She looked toward the Captain. Both he and his lady friend clapped for her. But, then they started talking together, and she saw her kiss him on the cheek.

Margaret closed her eyes for a moment.

Shake it off, Margaret! Get your head back into the game!

The bell sounded and both competitors came to the center of the ring. Her opponent, they called Meeks, came out jabbing. She covered up and returned shots of her own. They went back and forth, and he got a few more blows in than she did. When the bell sounded, she went to her corner.

"Are ya' all right, lad?" Pete asked, as he handed her the water.

She rinsed and spat. She couldn't help but glance toward the Captain. "I'm fine. I guess I'm nervous."

The bell sounded again for the second round and the same thing happened. She got some good blows in, but he was still in the lead. A trickle of blood ran from her nose as the bell sounded again to end the second round.

This time Doc was in her corner and stopped the bleeding.

"What's the matter with you!" he whispered. "You've fought better than this all day!"

"I don't know," she replied and shot a glance toward the Captain.

Doc was quick to pick up on it, and had a hint as to what the problem was. "Get your head out of your ass, girl," he whispered in her ear. "That's one of the Captain's sisters!"

She looked at Doc and then at the Captain and the lady. Just then she could see a resemblance. She felt a weight off her heart and before she could say anything the third round bell sounded.

Margaret felt a renewed energy and this time she was the aggressor and brought the fight to Meeks.

"What did ya' say ta' him, Doc?" Pete asked as he watched Marc land solid blows. "Whatever it was sure lit a fire under his arse!"

"I figured out the problem," Doc replied.

"What was it?"

Doc grinned. "The Captain has a pretty sister. Marc had a hard time keeping his mind off her."

Pete laughed heartily and cheered for his young friend. When the third round was over, Margaret was ahead in points.

"Two more rounds, lad. I think ya' hurt him with that last blow," Pete said. "Remember what I told ya' earlier."

Margaret spat out the rinse water. "I've already figured on it," she replied.

The bell sounded for the fourth round, and again, Margaret was leading in points. It was then that Meeks did exactly what Pete said he would do. He threw an upper cut to what he thought were his opponent's family jewels. Margaret dropped to one knee pretending to be hurt. The referee admonished Meeks for the foul. Margaret stood and bounced off her pretended injury, as she'd seen other men do on the ship when an accident happened to their privates.

The fight resumed, and she continued to make points. Once again, Meeks committed a foul. This time the referee warned him that the next time, he would declare the fight over and he would be disqualified. The bell rang and she went to her corner.

"I told ya' what he was gonna do!" Pete exclaimed. "Are ya' hurt?"

She leaned her head back against the ropes and held her crotch pretending to be in pain, making sure her opponent noticed. Then she answered Pete and gave him a wink. "Not a bit. But he doesn't know that."

Pete looked at Doc as the bell sounded for the fifth and final round.

"He must have balls of iron not ta' be affected by them blows!" Pete exclaimed.

Doc tried not to laugh. "They're made of something alright!"

Margaret got up and staggered to the center of the ring. They were even as far as rounds went. This was the deciding bout. She saw a smile on Meeks' face as she put up her fists ready for the moment when his guard was relaxed. Meeks danced about the ring throwing haphazard jabs and punches. She then found her moment! When Meeks drew back his fist to fire a finishing blow, Margaret opened up with a quick right hook to his nose, then a left cross. She totally took him by surprise. He'd expected that she was finished from the shots to groin. She kept firing rights and lefts, and blocking his attempts to counter. And then the final blow was unleashed — her left cross. That was her strongest weapon. Meeks hit the ground, but was up after the count of five, but the bell sounded for the match to be over.

Both went to their corners. The crowd in the auditorium was quiet waiting for the decision. A few moments later, the announcer entered the center ring.

"Ladies and Gentlemen! The decision is three rounds to two. The winner is Marcus Allen! Neptune's Daughter!" he yelled as he raised her hand.

Margaret was elated. She thought about all that painful torture that

Flint put her through these past weeks. Her lip and nose were bleeding, and she could feel one of her eyes starting to swell. She asked herself if it was worth it. She smiled inwardly and answered her own question:

Bloody hell — Yes!

Flint and Angus joined her in the center ring, picked her up and carried her on their shoulders. The crew of the Neptune's Daughter went wild with excitement. The auditorium's security had to restrain them from coming out on the floor to join their crewmates.

After everyone settled down, the Captain joined his team in the ring. The sponsor of the tournament put a gold medallion around each of their necks as the Captain shook their hands. When he got to Margaret, he gave her his congratulations and a wink. She couldn't help but smile from ear to ear. She could see that he was proud of her and just wished that he was proud of her as Margaret and not Marc. But she would take it!

CHAPTER 15
"Shore Leave"

After the match was over, Margaret and the other team members went back to the ship to clean up and retrieve their money pouches. Flint told her that he could take her to a place that would buy medallion for a good price if she wanted to sell it. To Flint and Angus, the only thing that hunk of gold plating meant to them was a few extra coins in there purses. To Margaret, it stood for six weeks of intense training, the black-eye and bloodied lip from the fight and a memento for an achievement of a life time! It was worth more to her than the diamond and emerals in her jewelry box at home.

Margaret left the ship with the rest of the crew from the Neptune's Daughter an arrived at the Ship and Shore Inn for dinner and drinks as winners of the tournament. It was the same type of establishment as the Ale House Tavern, only on a much grander scale. They too rented rooms by the week, day and hour.

The hotel section of the establishment had fifty bedrooms. In the lobby area, there were three large banquet rooms and two smaller ones. They had a large gaming room for guests who played billiards, cards, chess, or backgammon. The restaurant and tavern had a stage for entertainment. The décor was all nautical with elements of a ship hanging from the walls. It was definitely a place for mostly a higher class of clientele. Margaret thought that most of crew from the Neptune's Daughter seemed out of place and she definitely felt under dressed.

The ladies of the evening, or hostesses as they were called by the establishment, were elegantly dressed. They didn't hesitate to attach themselves to the crewmen as they entered the building. The women knew that the majority of them would their money pouches full from the day's wagering. It was their business to lighten the burden they carried to fill their own purses and as well as their employer's. One of the women approached Margaret, but she was quick to shoo her away. Shirley from the Ale House Tavern through her disguise — she wasn't about to get too close to any of these women.

"Are ya' daft, Marc?" laughed the crewman named Frank. "I've been with that one. She could give you a good tumble."

"I got better things to spend my money on than a girl," she replied hoping that would suffice for an answer.

"Like what?" Frank snickered.

Margaret was trying to think up something to say until Sam chimed in. "Now Frank — look at Marc here." Sam put his hand on Margaret's shoulder. "I know why he didn't go with her."

"And why's that?" Frank asked.

"It'd be to embarrassin' for the kid." Sam grinned. "He ain't grown into his wick yet. The wench would have ta' ask him where it was."

Those standing around started to cackle at her expense. Margaret was grateful for Sam's timely insult to her "manhood." It gave her an easy out from this situation. She forced a frown. "Piss off, Sam!" And then she turned her back and stormed off. When they were out of sight, she couldn't help but snicker as well.

Soon the doors to the banquet room were opened, and the men with their escorts entered and filed in line by the buffet table piled with food. Wine was served with dinner as well as ale on request. Margaret was surprised when the men didn't charge the table like hogs to a trough. But later she learned that Mr. Coruther's had warned them that if they acted like pigs, or caused trouble, the three day liberty that was planned would be revoked. So needless to say they behaved.

Praises from the crew on the team's win were abundant. Margaret received several pats on the back and was told by practically everyone that they had no doubts about *his* winning. Everyone that is except Charlie. He only had congratulations for Angus and Flint, but none for her.

Margaret was going through the service line with Orvil and they piled their plates with food. She hadn't eaten anything since that morning and was starving. They sat down at one of the tables with Charlie, but as soon as they sat down, he got up and moved.

"What's the matter with him?" Margaret asked. "He's been ignoring me."

"He's pissed," Orvil said, as he took a bite of one of the Cornish Hens. "Too dry," he commented, as he washed it down with wine. "I'd never hire their cook to work in a restaurant of mine."

"How come?" asked Margaret, ignoring his commentary.

"He won some money on you in your first few matches. Then he bet it all on you for your last fight."

"So, why is he upset?" She shrugged. "I won."

"Because when he saw that it looked like you were going to lose, he begged the gentleman he made the bet with to cancel their wager." Orvil laughed. "You should have seen him. He was down on his knees. He told this cock-in-bull story that he lost his head and wouldn't have any money left to send to his wife and four children."

"Charlie doesn't have a family," Margaret interrupted.

"But the man didn't know that. Charlie looked so pathetic the man took pity on him and gave him his money back. He thought he was pretty slick. Then in the fifth round when you came out like a hurricane and won, he was sick."

"How much money would he have won?" Margaret asked.

"Fifty pounds," Orvil laughed. "Ahhh, but he shouldn't be too pissed. He won twenty-five for the day." He took a bite of the spiced pears. "Too much spice. I think I'm definitely going to have a serious talk with their cook."

Margaret couldn't help but laugh at Orvil's comments on every bite of food he ate. He sounded like Mrs. Sarandon in that he had something negative to say about everything. However, he also finished his plate and went back for seconds. She had just finished eating when Pete came over to her table.

"Marc, come with me, Capt'n wants ta' see ya."

Margaret got up and followed him.

"Doc tells me ya' had eyes fer' the Capt'n sister," Pete said with a grin.

"He said what!" Margaret exclaimed. "I did not!"

"And ya' mean ta' tell me, his sister didn't have ya' distracted during the last fight?"

Margaret was quiet for a moment. Basically, she was the distraction but not for the reason Pete might think. "I don't know - maybe," she replied in a huff.

Pete laughed and didn't press her anymore. He opened the door to one of the smaller dining rooms. Margaret saw the Captain, his sister, Doc, Mr. Coruthers, Mr. Richards and ten other men and women sitting around a long ornate table. A huge crystal chandelier hung in the center illuminating the room.

"Ahhh! There's our young champion," said the Captain. "Come over here, Marc."

Everyone applauded as she entered the room. She gave a small bow and approached the Captain. She could feel her face getting red. When she was Margaret, she knew how to act in a crowd like this, but as Marc, she didn't have a clue.

"You wanted to see me, Captain?" she asked.

"Actually, my sister wanted to meet you," he replied. "Marc, this is my sister, Jessica Brighton, and her husband Sir Chester Brighton."

Now that Margaret could see the Captain's sister more closely, she could definitely see a family resemblance. She had the same dark hair and eyes as he did. Her complexion wasn't as dark, but she probably wasn't in the sun as much as he was. Jessica's husband looked about ten to fifteen years older than she was, but the touch of gray in his sideburns made him look distinguished.

"Pleased to meet you," Margaret said as she bowed.

"Todd, you should be ashamed of yourself for making this poor boy fight in that tournament," Jessica chastised her brother.

But it was Margaret who answered. "Oh, he didn't make me. It was my own decision." But inwardly she thought:

I was coerced by the crew.

"Jessi, if I recall, you watched me fight in that same tournament when I was his age." Todd laughed. "If memory serves me right, you cheered for my opponent."

"That's different," Jessica replied hiding a smile. "You tormented me terribly before you joined the ship. Besides, I was just fifteen at the time. It was my way of getting back at you."

"Me, torment you! Ha!" Todd gave Margaret a wink. "I was an angel in comparison to you."

"Liar!" Jessica smile. "I'm sure Sarah will agree with me. You were incorrigible!"

Chester Brighton laughed. "There they go again! Can't we put the two of you in the same room without reliving the battle between David and Goliath?"

"Never," they both said at the same time.

Everyone in the room laughed including Margaret. Their friendly banter reminded her of the arguments that she and her own brother used to have.

Jessica turned to Margaret. "Anyway, I want to apologize for distracting you this evening. Doctor Ridenhour tells me I almost caused you to lose your match." She smiled warmly.

Margaret could feel her face flush again, and she gave Doc a hard look. He just gave her the usual silly grin when he was teasing her.

"The fault is mine. I should apologize for being — fresh," Margaret replied.

"On the contrary, I'm quite flattered," Jessica said, and then she looked at her husband.. "It's been a while since I've turned a young man's head."

"Jessica, my love, you turn my head every day," Chester said. He then kissed her hand.

Jessica pretended to ignore his compliment and turned back to Margaret. "Todd tells me you're thirteen?"

"Actually, I'm fourteen tomorrow," she replied. She hadn't told anyone until now. She didn't think anyone would have cared.

"Then I would like to propose a toast," Todd said. He and everyone else raised their glasses. "To Marcus Allen, a bright boy with a hell of a left cross." Everyone laughed. "We wish you a very happy birthday tomorrow and..." then he gave Margaret a wink. "...hope your taste in women improves." He glared at his sister and again the people in the room laughed.

"Just as I said - incorrigible," Jessica raised her glass. "To Marc!"

Everyone at the table drank to her birthday. To Margaret, that was the best birthday present she could have had. She saw the same warmth in the Captain's eyes as he always had when he spoke kindly to her. She just wished she could tell him she was not a boy.

Margaret talked to several of the gentlemen in the room. Each was an avid boxing enthusiast. They all gave her advice on one thing or another for the next time she entered the ring. Margaret hoped there would never be a next time.

After leaving the Captain, Margaret decided to go to the gaming room. Doug Taggart was playing billiards with one of the other hotel guests, and a couple of the crewmen were playing cards. Most of the men went into the tavern or to one of the hotel rooms with the women. But what interested Margaret most were the chess games. Two gentlemen were playing and a few other guests were watching. There was a man making book on the outcome.

Margaret watched as they played and an elderly gentleman came up to her.

"Do you want me to explain the game to you, sonny?" he asked in whispered tones so not to disturb the players.

"Thank you, sir, but I know the game," she replied. "The way I see it, the only way out for the man with the pipe is stalemate. But, if the man with the spectacles is careful, he can avoid it and get the win."

The man making book heard what she'd said and came over. "Would you care to make a wager as to who will win?" he asked.

"The only game I'd bet on is my own," she replied confidently to the bookmaker.

The man laughed. "You think you can beat either of these men?"

Margaret shrugged, "It's possible."

"Would you be willing to play the winner?" he asked.

"Sure," she replied. "But it looks like I'll have to play both. It's a stalemate."

The two men that were playing had heard Margaret's boast.

"Sonny, I don't play for free," said the man with the spectacles. "If you want to play, you will have to put up. What's your wager?"

"I've only got five shillings," Margaret said.

The man laughed. "I don't play for less than twenty-five pounds, boy."

"Quite right," added the man with the pipe, as he was relighting it.

Doug Taggart had just finished his game of billiards and saw Marc involved in what seemed like an argument in the chess corner and decided to investigate.

"Is there a problem, Marc?" the watch commander asked.

"Not really, sir," she replied. "I was going to play these two gentlemen, but don't consider less than twenty-five pounds on a wager to play. I've only got five shillings."

Doug Taggart stood there for a moment in thought. Marc had already made his money pouch richer today. "Are you any good, Marc?"

"I'm very good," she replied with confidence.

"Which one would you like to play?" he asked.

Margaret hesitated a moment. "Both — at the same time."

There was a rumble from the spectators. Some laughed, some called her an impudent wretch, and others said it was impossible for a young boy to defeat two experienced chess masters.

The watch commander had just won two hundred pounds this evening playing pool on top of what he won on the fights. "What the hell. I'm game." He turned to the men.

"Gentleman, I'll back the boy. But what do you say we raise the stakes? I've got £200 pounds that says the boy will beat both of you."

"Are you saying, in order to win, he has to win both games? Is that your wager?" asked the man with the spectacles.

"Both games," replied Mr. Taggart.

The two gentlemen looked at each other and pulled out their money as did Doug Taggart. A second board was set up. The bookmaker had a feeling about the boy and started taking bets.

The two men sat down behind their boards and Margaret remained standing to move back and forth between the games. She drew white on one board and black on the other. It was going to be slightly more challenging, but she'd played with her father and brother like this before and won. They too were excellent chess players.

As the game started, more people had gathered to watch. The first few moves were made quickly, and then the game slowed considerably. Margaret had the advantage. The two men were indeed very good and could have played circles around the Captain and Doc, but they weren't that good. After twenty minutes of play, she'd put the man with the spectacles in check twice. The man with the pipe was attempting to maneuver into a stalemate, but Margaret wasn't about to let that happen. A few moves later, the man with the pipe went down. There was a rumbling of disbelief in the room. Five minutes after that, the man with the spectacles knocked over his King in defeat. There was applause from those who hadn't wagered and groans from those who had and lost.

The two men she played congratulated her on her game and then went to the back of the room and started conversing with two other men. While Margaret was receiving congratulations from the crowd, Doug Taggart had his eye on the four men. The two chess players may have put up a good front as gracious losers, but as they talked to the two other men, it seemed very suspicious, especially, when they nodded in their direction. A few minutes later, the two chess players went one way and the other two exited the room.

When the crowd dispersed, the bookmaker, who'd been holding the wager, gave Mr. Taggart his winnings. The watch commander in turn gave £100 from his winnings to Marc.

"For me!" she exclaimed.

The watch commander chuckled. "You just doubled my winning for the day. You should reap some of the profits for your effort." He patted her on the back. "Marc, you're a boy of hidden talents."

"Maybe one or two things." She smiled. Her talents weren't the only thing that was hidden.

Margaret had been excited over doubling the five shillings she'd bet on herself. She had basically wanted to play the game for the game itself. If Mr. Taggart had profited from it, all the better for him. She hadn't expected he'd give her part of his winnings.

The bookmaker then turned to Margaret. "Marc, my boy, you've got a good head on your shoulders. You should consider making a career as a chess player. You let me manage you, and we'd make a fortune."

"I appreciate the offer," she replied, "But I think I'll stay where I'm at."

"Pity," he sighed. "If you're ever this way again, look me up. I'm always around."

"Marc," interrupted Mr. Taggart. "I think it's time we leave. Come on, boy."

Margaret bid the bookmaker good-bye and went along with the watch commander.

"Thank you for your confidence in me, Mr. Taggart. This is the most money I've ever had," she said. She didn't actually lie about it — she never had money of her own.

"You didn't do me any harm today either," he laughed. "I'll walk you back to the ship."

"You don't have to do that, sir. It's only a few blocks," she replied.

"Sometimes a few blocks can be just as hazardous as a few miles," he advised. "But before we go, I need to see Pete and Levi for a moment. They're in the tavern. Stay here until I return."

Margaret waited just outside the tavern, while he talked to the two other commanders, and then a few moments later, they were off to the docks. She noticed that Mr. Taggart seemed on edge. "I anything wrong, sir?"

"Both of us are carrying a considerable amount of money. And a lot of people know it. It's best to be weary. That's why I didn't want you going by yourself," he replied.

With that said, Margaret also started to observe her surroundings. They had a fifteen minute walk to the ship.

"So far, so good," Margaret said, after they'd been walking for about ten minutes. "Maybe you're wrong."

"Good for us if I am. But when you've been around as long as I have, you get a gut feeling about things."

The ship was just in sight and Margaret was feeling relieved that they'd arrived safely, but when they passed an alleyway, two men came out of the shadows behind them.

"Hey, Mister," one of them said. "Have ya' got the time?"

Doug turned around and saw the two suspicious men with the chess players. "I'm afraid not," he replied.

"I do," said the other man. Then they pulled out their knives. "I think it's time ya' hand over yer' money."

"I don't think you're going to get a farthing from either of us," said Doug with a smile.

The two men laughed. "And how do ya' think yer' gonna stop us?"

"I'm not," Doug replied.

"We are!" said Levi, as he and Pete came up behind the two. They'd grabbed the two men and put the point of their own blades to their backs.

"Get Marc out'a here, Doug," said Pete. Then he smiled. "Levi and me is gonna have a little talk with these two 'bout mendin' their ways."

"Come on, Marc," said Mr. Taggart. The two picked up their pace.

"What are they going to do?" Margaret asked. "They aren't going to..."

"Kill them?" the watch commander finished. He noted the apprehension in the boy's voice. "No, don't worry about that. Pete and Levi are just going to give them some reasons why crime doesn't pay."

Margaret was relieved. She didn't want to have a killing on her conscience over money from a chess game. They made it to the dock without further incident. Two men from Neptune's Daughter were already there, waiting for the ferry to take them out to the ship.

"Aren't you going aboard, Mr. Taggart?" Margaret asked.

"No, I'm meeting a lady friend in a few minutes. Just wanted to see that you got back safely," he replied.

Doug Taggart, as well as the other commanders, knew that if anything happened to Marc, it would deeply wound their Captain. He'd had seen how Jake's death had affected him, and none of them want to see it happen again.

Margaret thanked him for his help and wished him a good evening as she boarded the ferry. A few minutes later, Pete and Levi joined Doug at the dock.

"Is it done?" Doug asked.

"It's done," said Levi.

"The lad won't have ta' worry 'bout them botherin' him whilst we're here," Pete said.

"Or anyone else, for that matter," laughed Levi. "You won't even be reading about them in the newspaper either."

"Come on. I think we need to have a little talk with our chess players about sportsmanship," said Doug, as they walked back to the Inn. "And if Marc asks, you just roughed them up a bit."

Pete and Levi looked at each other and then at Doug. "What do you mean, Doug?" Levi replied innocently.

"What else did ya' think we was gonna do?" Pete added.

"Pardon me," Doug grinned. "I didn't mean to imply anything, but I suggest you do something about the red stain shirts, before you go back to the ship. I don't think Marc will believe its from spilled wine if he sees you."

***

Margaret went aboard and started for her cabin when she ran into Doc.

"Go down to sickbay, Marc," he said. "I want to recheck your eyes."

"Can it wait till tomorrow?" she asked. "It's been a rough day."

"I think now is a good time," he replied.

Margaret sighed and followed him. She was tired, sore and emotionally drained. All she wanted to do was go to bed. The room was empty, and Margaret jumped upon the table, as Doc closed the door behind him.

"So, how long have you been in love with the Captain?" he asked as he sat down in a chair.

"I thought you were going to check my eyes?" she frowned.

"Ah, your eyes are fine," he grinned. "I just want the details."

"Who says I'm in love with the Captain!" she exclaimed. "And what's the meaning of telling him that I had an eye on his sister? That was embarrassing!"

"Marc, I'm not a fool. I know a jealous woman when I see her. And to answer your second question, the Captain also noticed that between rounds you were staring at Jessica. So come on, spill."

Margaret thought:

What the hell! I've got no one else to talk to about it except Doc. It might be good to get it off my chest.

"I don't think it's love," she said. "I think I'm just infatuated with him. The first time I met him was at the Seafarer's Ball in London."

"You mean you followed him on to this ship!" he exclaimed with a laugh.

"No!" she frowned. "I hadn't a clue who he was. He bumped into me and spilled his drink on my dress. I didn't even know his name. We only talked for a moment."

Doc scratched his chin. "I think I remember him telling me about some red head with incredible eyes and a nice set of teats." Then he looked at her. "You might have the hair and eyes, but you sure don't have the teats."

"Doc, if you think you're going to embarrass me by talking about my breasts that way, you won't," she smiled. "I've heard so much talk about teats on this ship that it doesn't faze me anymore. And to answer your question, my imitation "jewels" aren't the only thing on me that I've ever had stuffed. My mother had my dresses specially made when I quit growing topside. She thought that if I looked better equipped, I would start attracting suitors."

Doc laughed. "I guess it didn't work."

"I don't know," she said. "I overheard Nathanial say he had sabotaged my chances with other men. But anyway, why do you think I'm in love with the Captain? How can you tell the difference between love and infatuation?"

"That's the question of the ages," he replied. "But I've seen the way you look at him, when he's not looking at you. And then at the fight tonight, Mr. Green-eyed Monster of jealousy reared his head. It was written all over your face. The way I see it, you're going to have to tell him who you are and get it off your chest, or get over it."

"I can't do the first one, and the second is more difficult," she replied. "Now if you don't mind, since I've answered your questions, can I go to bed?"

"My curiosity is satisfied," he replied. "See you in the morning."

Margaret left for her cabin. She was glad she decided to talk to Doc. Even though he didn't have any real solutions to her problem, it did help. As soon as her head hit the pillow, she was out.

***

Even though they had shore leave, the crew still had duty watches to guard the ship from thieves. Margaret's watch was over at noon, and she decided to explore Liverpool in the daylight. She talked to Pete about last night, and he said she didn't have to worry about being jumped again from those men. He told her that they convinced the men to leave town. They also had a talk with the chess players, and they wouldn't be sending any more people after her either.

With her mind at ease, she walked about town. She came upon the Capitol Playhouse Dinner Theatre and read the poster:

Opening Night for Shakespeare's Antony and Cleopatra

Margaret thought to herself:

Oh! To see a play!

She needed some sort of feminine pursuit from her past after all these weeks of pretending. Dinner was at five and the play started at seven. She said to herself:

I'll do it! After all, I just won a tidy sum.

Margaret went to the theatre office to purchase her tickets for dinner and the play. The ticket master told her that if she wasn't appropriately dressed, even with tickets she wouldn't be admitted. She assured the man that she would be properly attired.

With that done, the next thing was to purchase something appropriate to wear. She'd seen a used clothing shop earlier and headed there. Time was short. She only had two hours to make her purchases, get back to the ship to clean up and head back at the theater.

Excitement about her big evening almost caused her to go to the women's section, but she caught herself and quickly altered her direction. She looked through the racks and actually found an appropriate suit of clothing made by Gaston's Modern Fashions. She couldn't help but laugh. If Gaston had seen a suit of his making in a used clothing shop, he would have fainted dead away. She purchased a pair of brown knee breeches, a white ruffled shirt, a vest, tailcoat and top hat to complete the look. She also bought shoes, stockings and more work clothes. Her old things were getting torn and worn.

She hurried back to the ship, thoroughly washed and then went into one of the passenger cabins to check out her new attire in the full length mirror. She tugged at her ruffled sleeves and thought to herself:

Not bad!

She fluffed the ruffles of her white shirt and headed topside. Margaret received all kinds of laughs and whistles.

"Will ya' look at 'im!" laughed Charlie. "It's the bloody Governor himself come for a visit!"

"Oh, so you're talking to me now," Margaret laughed.

"I'm broke," he sighed.

"I thought you won twenty-five pounds?"

"Them fancy whores are expensive," he replied. "Easy come, easy go. Speakin' of goin'. Where might ya' be off to?"

"Dinner and a play."

"What a waste of good money," he said shaking his head.

"Well, it's my birthday. I'm fourteen and practically a man, and men see plays," she replied with a shrug.

"Man, my ass!" Charlie laughed. "I'd bet that sword of yer's ain't pierced one cherry."

Margaret just rolled her eyes and ignored his comment. "I'll see you later. I don't want to be late."

She hurried off and hailed a cab. In for a penny — in for a pound. She was going in style!

Charlie watched Marc leave and saw Orvil come aboard.

"Is that who I think it was?" Orvil asked.

"Aye, that was Marc," Charlie said. "Ta'day's his birthday. And can ya' believe it! He's gonna waste all that money he won on some ol' play."

"His birthday — hmmm," Orvil said, ignoring Charlie's comments.

"I know that look." Charlie noticed Orvil's contemplative expression. "What have ya' got in mind?"

"We owe Marc a birthday celebration."

***

Margaret's cab pulled up in front of the theater just in time. People were starting to go in. She was anxious to see this play. It was in London about four months ago, but she could never fit it into her busy schedule with the prior obligations her mother had for her.

The dining room was decorated with Egyptian decor to set the mood for the play. There were pyramids, statues, a painting of the great Sphinx and replicas of Cleopatra's barge sitting on the tables as centerpieces holding flowers.

Margaret was seated by the maitre d' and handed a menu. Even though it was an Egyptian setting, the food was French, as was the language of the menu. As she was scanning through the entrees to see what she might want, someone called her name.

"Marc? Is that you?"

Margaret looked up to see the Captain's sister, Jessica Brighton.

"Yes, ma'am." Margaret put down her menu and stood.

"Don't you look the gentleman," she said with a laugh. "What are you doing here?"

"I'm celebrating my birthday. I've always wanted to see a play," she replied. That was as good as anything else she could have thought to say.

"But how can you afford it?"

"I won some money the other day," Margaret replied.

"Of course! How silly of me. You must have bet on yourself."

"Yes, ma'am." She knew she was thinking about the boxing tournament.

"Are you here by yourself?" Jessica asked.

"Yes ma'am."

"Will you please quit calling me ma'am! You make me feel like an old lady. Please, call me Jessi," she said pleasantly. "Would you care to join us?"

Margaret was hesitant. "I don't know if it would be appropriate, being that you're the Captain's sister and I'm part of his crew."

"Nonsense! Besides, no one else has to know."

Margaret thought for a moment. She was wanting some female companionship even though she couldn't act like a woman herself.

"Yes, ma' — .Jessi, I'd like that," Margaret replied.

"Then come with me. You can tell me all about my little brother's bad habits."

Margaret laughed and Jessica looped her arm around Margaret's and they joined her husband.

"Ah! Trying to steal my wife are we, young man?" Chester laughed, then stood and extended his hand.

"No sir, she shanghaied me." Margaret returned his firm handshake.

They asked Margaret about herself and why she signed aboard the ship. She told them the fictitious story that she'd told everyone else about her past. She didn't tell Jessica any stories about her brother, but she did tell her about some of her own experiences aboard the ship, including how she was coerced into the boxing tournament by the crew.

In turn, Jessica told her that she and her brother were both raised by their older sister, Sarah Jacobson, who lived in London. Their mother, along with a new baby sister, both died in childbirth when she and her brother were ten and eight. Their father died a year later from an illness.

When Margaret asked Jessica why the name Jacobson, sounded familiar, she told her that it was because the former Captain of the Neptune's Daughter was their sister, Sarah's husband. Todd had sailed as cabin boy during the summer until school was in session. Then when he became older, he was second in command until Captain Michael Jacobson retired.

Margaret was having a wonderful time. She thought Jessica was delightful and felt that under different circumstances, they could become good friends. When it was time to order dinner, she pretended that she didn't understand the menu and Chester ordered for them.

When dinner was over, they went into the auditorium to watch the play. It was everything Margaret hoped it would be, especially the ending, with Cleopatra and the asp. She couldn't help but tear up; it was such a moving scene. The play received three curtain calls. Afterward, the three of them left the theatre.

"So, how was your first play?" Jessica asked.

"I liked it well enough," Margaret replied, minimizing her actual enjoyment.

"What was your favorite part?" Jessica asked.

"The sword fighting," Margaret replied. That wasn't her favorite part, but that is probably what a boy would have like, so that's what she said.

The Brighton's cab arrived and Jessica insisted that Margaret ride with them to the dock. They said they didn't want him riding alone that time of evening. Margaret tended to agree, especially, after the incident last night.

When they arrived at the dock, Margaret thanked them and Jessica told her that she wouldn't say a word about their dining together, so she needn't be worried about propriety.

When the cab trotted off, Jessica sat back and laughed excitedly. Chester was puzzled about his wife's sudden, unexplainable jocularity.

"What so funny, dear?" he chuckled.

"Did you notice anything about my brother's cabin boy?" she laughed.

"No..." he shrugged, "...other than he was polite and well spoken for a boy of his station, he seemed fine to me."

"Marc, is not a Marc!" she exclaimed.

Chester just shook his head a bit bewildered. "Jessi, you're not making sense. Quit talking in riddles."

"Marc is a Mary, or Martha, or some other name. Marc is a girl! Her disguise is very good."

"What? That's preposterous!" It was Chester's turn to laugh. "And how do you come to that conclusion?"

"Point one," she started. "When I first saw her tonight, she was reading that French menu. So, she does know French, even though she pretended not to. Remember when she pointed out a dish on the menu and asked you what it was?"

"Yes, what of it?"

"She said that the writing on the menu looked interesting for the roasted pheasant you ordered for her, but I say, she already knew what she wanted."

"And how does that make Marc a girl?" he asked.

"As you pointed out earlier, how would an English boy of his station understand French?"

"Maybe that friend of his, Claude, taught him?" Chester grinned.

"Okay, point two. Remember at the fight, she kept staring at me."

"You're a lovely woman, my dear," Chester replied. "I don't fault *him* that."

"Thank you, darling, but that's not why she was looking at me. It was jealousy! She's in love with my brother. She didn't know that I was his sister."

Chester laughed, "And how do you draw that conclusion?"

"Because when I was telling her about Todd she hung on my every word with a great deal of interest."

"So, *he's* an attentive listener. Anymore points you have to make? I'm still not convinced."

Jessica pursed her lips. "Point three. When she talked about Laura Sarandon there was a definite dislike."

"Who doesn't dislike Laura, beside Todd?" he laughed. "Go on."

Jessica folded her arms and started tapping her foot, becoming aggravated with her husband's disbelief.

"There were tears in *her* eyes at the end of the play," Jessica huffed. "You thought the scene with the asp was a silly. If he was a boy, he would have rolled his eyes also. And besides! Why would a fourteen year old boy want to attend a play in the first place? Did you when you were a boy of fourteen?"

Chester laughed at his wife's frustration. "Ok, dear, I'm just teasing you. I believe you. You had me after point two." Then he spoke to her seriously. "We need to tell Todd. That ship is no place for a young woman."

"Nonsense, Chester. She's been on that ship for what, two months or more? She's had two street fights, plus won a boxing tournament. She knows how to fence and she's learning how to use a knife. Plus, there's something that you don't know," she said with a grin.

"And what's that?"

"Todd told me that he's developed an affection for Marc. He said he can't explain it. He said that if it wasn't for the fact that the boy lost his parents so soon, he would approach him about becoming his ward."

"Really!" Chester laughed.

"Todd needs someone in his life, besides that gold digging harlot...

"Now, Jessi!" he interrupted.

"Ok then, that brazen hussy, Laura Sarandon."

Chester just shook his head.

"Well, she is! And you know it. So, what do you say? I like Marc. I wouldn't be surprised if she is actually a girl of quality, and has runaway for some reason or another. Let Marc find a way on her own. Please, don't tell Todd," she asked sincerely.

"It would be interesting to see what happens when Todd realizes what Marc really is," Chester replied thoughtfully. "Very well, my dear, seal my lips with a kiss and I'll be silent."

Jessica put her arms around him. "I'll do more than that when we get home." She kissed him passionately.

∗∗∗

Margaret went aboard the ship and change out of her suit. The evening was the most enjoyable she'd had in months. Now to top it off, she was going to get a hot cup of tea, borrow one of the Captain's books, which he said she could do at anytime, and relax in her cabin.

As she headed for the galley, Charlie, Sam and Orvil approached her.

"There you are," said Orvil. "We were just getting ready to come get you."

"Why?" she asked. The three had silly grins on their faces."What is it this time?"

"Oh! Don't be so suspicious," Orvil replied.

"When it comes to you three, I have nothing but suspicions!"

"We're just headin' fer' the Crow's Nest," said Sam.

Margaret looked up the main mast.

"Not that, crow's nest," Charlie laughed. "The Crow's Nest is a little pub down the way."

"You all go on," Margaret replied. "I've just come back from a night out. I was going to relax in my cabin the rest of the evening."

"Sorry, Marc. You was out when the word came. We're loadin' up tomorrow and have passengers ta' boot," Charlie replied. "This is the last night in port."

"And it ain't good form ta' turn down a night out with yer' mates before we sail," said Sam.

Margaret glared at them. "I don't trust you three. You're up to something."

Orvil shrugged. "If you don't believe me, ask Levi. He's got the duty watch tonight."

"I think I will," she replied and then went to the bridge.

Margaret asked Levi if what Orvil said was true, and he confirmed their story. She was going to have her hands full. All twelve cabins were going to be occupied. The Arrow Star was full and the ship that was to take them to Southampton was a week late, so they booked passage aboard the Neptune's Daughter.

Margaret thought about turning the three down. But then she thought:

Why not? What's a couple of more hours?

She decided that since it was her birthday, she may as well make the most of it. The pub was about a five minute walk from the dock, and they talked as they walked. However, Sam went on ahead.

"How was the play?" Orvil asked.

"It had some good sword fighting. That's about it," she lied pretending indifference.

"I told ya' it was a waste of good money," Charlie said.

"I don't think it was a waste," said Orvil, "I saw a play once. It was called *Merchant of Venice*. I saw it back in Virginia about seven years ago."

Margaret was surprised that he'd seen a Shakespearian play. But before she could say anything, he added, "They actually had women playing female parts instead of men. There was this one actress that had a set of teats on her the size of cantaloupes."

Margaret thought as she laughed inwardly.

That figures!

"Hey, maybe I'll see me a play sometime," said Charlie. "Did ya' see any teats like that, Marc?"

"I didn't notice," Margaret replied.

"Just like I said," Charlie huffed. "He wasted good money."

Margaret just shook her head.

"There it is just ahead," Orvil said.

Margaret noticed the outside. The building was old, dirty and somewhat dilapidated. It was a far cry from the Ship and Shore Inn and better suited for most of the crew.

As they walked through the door, she saw half of her crewmates standing around the room. They all were clapping and shouted out a hearty, "Happy Birthday, Marc!"

It was then this slightly heavy blonde woman with stringy hair and over-done make-up came out of the crowd of men.

"Well, if it ain't the birthday boy!" she chuckled.

The woman put her arms around Margaret and gave her a kiss square on the lips before she even had a chance to object! All the men laughed and carried on as Margaret tried to break the woman's hold. She smelled like whiskey and tobacco. When she finally broke free, she instinctively wiped her mouth off. The woman was absolutely disgusting!

"I was gonna be yer' birthday present, but I guess ya' just ain't old enough yet!" The woman laughed, as did everyone else in the room.

"But I'm old enough." Charlie put his arm around her.

"And broke!" she exclaimed pushing him away. Again, the men in the room laughed.

"Happy birthday, Marc," said Orvil. He gave him a slap on the back. "We just wanted to show our appreciation for all your hard work. You helped all of us win a tidy sum."

Margaret was total surprised. "I don't know what to say!"

"Ahhh, just have some cake," Orvil said. Then he yelled to the bar man. "A pint of ginger beer for the boy!"

After the crew gave her their congratulations, they went back to their women and liquor. Margaret looked at the cake. There was no writing on it, just a huge sheet. "Did you make it?" she asked Orvil.

"Cake is my specialty," he bragged.

Margaret took a piece. "Wow! Now that is a cake!" It was the best cake she'd ever eaten. It had a certain tang to it. She asked Orvil what was in it, but he wouldn't tell her. He said it was a special recipe.

Margaret was glad she came. She was having a good time. After her third piece of cake, she was feeling quite giddy. Some of the men were throwing their knives at a dart board and she joined them. She was hitting the board fairly well until after her fourth piece of cake, and then her knife started falling to the floor.

A man came into the pub and went into a corner of the room. He tacked up some pictures on the wall, announced that he was a tattoo artist and those drawings were his specialties.

Margaret was on her fifth piece of cake. There was something about that cake. She just couldn't get enough of it. She walked over to the artist and watched as he worked on a man's arm. He was either drawing an anchor or two fish hooks. Her eyes were dizzy, and she wasn't sure which it was.

"You want one, boy?" asked the man.

Margaret took a bite of cake and looked at the pictures. She was having trouble making them out. They kept moving around.

Orvil and Charlie saw Marc over by the artist. Charlie laughed. "Look at him! He's got a snoot full!" They watched their cabin boy stagger as he looked at the pictures. "He only had one ginger beer. That wouldn't get a fly drunk!"

Orvil scratched his head. "I don't think it was the drink. I think it was the cake."

"The cake? Whoever heard of somebody gettin' drunk on cake!" Charlie exclaimed.

"It's rum cake. It was soaked with pure, undiluted, one-hundred proof rum. I used the good stuff," Orvil laughed. "I think we'd better get him back to the ship."

They walked over to the corner.

"I want that horse," Margaret said, and then took a bite of cake. "Can you catch it for me? It won't hold still."

Orvil laughed. "That's not a horse, it's a seahorse. It lives in the sea."

"Orvil, I think you've had too much to drink. Horses don't live in the sea." Margaret hiccupped.

"You're sure you want a tattoo?" Orvil asked.

"Why not? I like horses." Margaret finished the piece of cake. "It's my birthday, and I want that horse."

Margaret sat down in the chair and rolled up her sleeve. "Orvil, could you get me another piece of cake?"

"Why don't I just get ya' a pint of rum," Charlie laughed.

Margaret shook her head. "Can't drink rum. Two shots an I'd be drunker than you look. Cake will be fine."

"I ain't the one drunk," Charlie replied.

"That will be three shillings in advance," said the artist.

Margaret felt for her money pouch. "I forgot it." She looked up at Orvil. "If you buy me a horse today, I'll give you three shillings tomorrow."

"Are you sure?" he laughed.

She grinned. "A horse and a piece of cake."

Orvil couldn't resist. He gave the man three shillings and Marc another piece of cake.

They watched as the artist started drawing out the seahorse on her upper arm, and then he started using his needles to insert the color.

"Doesn't that hurt?" Charlie asked.

"Does what hurt?" Margaret asked as she leaned back in the chair and took a bite of cake.

"Never mind," Charlie chuckled.

Before the man was finished, Margaret was out. When he was done, Orvil and Charlie tried to get her to stand up, but her legs were limp.

"Out cold!" Charlie said.

"He's going to have one bad head in the morning," Orvil said trying to get their cabin boy to his feet.

Just then Pete came into the pub and saw Orvil and Charlie trying to coax Marc to stand.

"What happened ta' him!" Pete exclaimed, but before he got an answer he could smell the reason. "He's drunk! Why the hell did ya' get the lad drunk?"

"It wasn't intentional, I swear," Orvil said. "I baked the boy a rum cake for his birthday. He had one piece too many."

"Cake did this ta' him!" Pete laughed. Then he picked the boy up and put him over his shoulder. "I'll take him back ta' the ship and let Doc have a look at him."

As Pete walked down the street, Margaret opened her eyes and saw the ground and a pair of heels. "Who's got me?"

"Just me, lad," Pete laughed.

"Why have you got me?"

"Because yer' drunk."

"I am not!" She hiccupped. "I had one — something or other. I forgot. Put me down, Pete, I can walk."

"Are ya' sure?"

"I've been walking for eighteen years," she said and hiccupped again.

Pete put her down on wobbly legs. "You mean fourteen."

"No," she said as she leaned up against him. "Today's my birthday, I'm eighteen. But, shhhh, don't tell anybody," she whispered. "I'm pretending to be fourteen."

"Marc, ya've had too much cake."

Margaret laughed, "I got you there too, Pete!" Then she whispered. "My brother's name is Marcus, I'm Margaret." Then her legs collapsed and Pete caught her before she hit the ground.

"Lad, rum makes ya' loony!" But his words fell on deaf ears as he carried their cabin boy back to the ship.

"Looks like he enjoyed himself a little too much," said Doug Taggart, as Pete boarded.

"He won't in the mornin'," Pete replied. "Is Doc on board?"

"He's below." Doug nodded in that direction.

Pete woke Doc up from a sound sleep. When he opened the door, he saw Marc slung over Pete's shoulder. Doc just shook his head. "What happened to him this time?"

"He's drunker than owl shit. Orvil's cake was laced with rum," Pete replied.

"Why am I not surprised?" he sighed. "Marc told me liquor doesn't agree with him. Take him to sickbay. I'll be there directly."

Pete did as he asked and laid Marc on the table. When Doc arrived, he retrieved a bottle and a spoon from his cabinet. "Get that bucket over there in the corner. I need to get as much of that rum soaked cake out of him as I can."

Doc pinched Margaret's nose and poured a spoonful of his elixir down her throat. "It should start working in a few minutes."

"Ya' might want ta' check his arm. He got a tattoo also," Pete laughed. "He sure has some queer ideas when he's drunk."

"How so?" Doc asked, as he put a salve over the tattooed area to prevent possible infection.

"He said he was eighteen and pretending to be a boy," Pete replied.

Doc's head popped up. The door was slightly open and he quickly went to it and looked outside. No one was around.

"Did anyone else hear?" Doc asked seriously.

"No, just me." Pete lost his smile.

"Good!" Doc breathed a sigh of relief.

"Doc! Yer' not tellin' me he's…"

"I'm telling you he's, a she!"

"Ya' mean ta' tell me, he's — the lad is a lass!" Pete exclaimed.

Doc nodded his head.

"When did ya' find out?"

"The day we sailed from London."

"Then why the hell didn't ya' tell somebody!" Pete yelled.

"Keep your voice down," Doc warned. "Sit down. I'll tell you the whole story."

Doc considered he had no choice but to tell Pete the truth about their cabin boy's reasoning for being on the ship. He told him everything from how she arranged her own kidnapping, to the possibility that she was in love with the Captain. They both knew that the Captain was very fond of Marc. By telling Pete, Doc figured he could also keep a wary eye out for her. "Do you understand now why I didn't say anything?" Doc asked.

Pete shook his head. "I can't believe she fought in that bloody tournament — and won! She's got balls — ahhh," then he looked at her breeches. "She does have ball!"

Doc laughed. "They're fake. And her teats, what she has of them, are bound if you wanted to know."

"No wonder them shots to his pride didn't hurt," Pete laughed.

"Can I trust you to keep her secret?"

Pete scratched his head. "I ain't got much choice."

"I think you'd better leave," said Doc, as Margaret started to stir. "She's starting to come around. Oh, and don't let on to her you know. You need to treat her exactly the same as you did before. She's smart. She'll know something's not right. Think you can do that?"

"Doc, I never heard a word. As far as I'm concerned, he's Marc, plain and simple."

Pete left the room. He felt foolish not able to recognize Marc as being a girl. Although, it was some comfort knowing that no one else did either. But lad or lass, she saved his son from being hurt and for that he would always be grateful. But he was still irritated at his old friend.

"Wait till the next time I'm in London and see Claude!" He slammed his fist into his hand. "I'll give him a piece of my mind!"

CHAPTER 16
"The Day After"

Doc left Margaret in sickbay to sleep off her rum laced cake. When Pete left, she woke up long enough to expel the contents of her stomach into a bucket. The next morning when Doc came in, she was still sleeping with one arm hanging off the side of the bed. He couldn't resist waking her up the hard way.

SLAM! The door banged closed. Margaret's head shot up with her eyes still closed. "Oh God!" she exclaimed, as she turned over on her back and grabbed her head.

"Did you have a nice birthday yesterday?" Doc asked. He was grinning from ear to ear.

"Shhhh. Not so loud," she whispered. Even the sound of her own voice grated on her head. "I think I had a good time. The last thing I remember was throwing my knife at a dart board. Everything after that is blank. What happened to me, Doc? I feel like I was hit by a runaway wagon."

"I hate to tell you, but you're suffering from a bad hangover."

"Hangover!" she exclaimed, a bit too loudly. She softened her voice. "I only had one ginger beer. I know better than to drink more than one of anything."

"No, but you did over indulge in cake."

"Who ever heard of getting drunk on cake?" She slowly sat up and massaged her temples. Her head was pounding and there was a buzzing in her ears.

"You do, if it's rum cake," he laughed.

"I'm going to kill Orvil," she said. She licked her lips. "My mouth is dry, and it tastes like a herd of turtles ran through it."

"That's because I made you throw up all that cake last night. If you hadn't, you would probably still be drunk. You have duty in about thirty-minutes."

"Duty! Doc, that's an ugly word this morning." Margaret slowly stood up. "How much cake did I have?"

"Five or six pieces I'm told. Pete had to carry you back to the ship."

"I don't think I ever want to see another piece of cake again." Then she rubbed her arm. "Did I fall or bump into something? My arm is sore."

"Roll up your sleeve and look in the mirror over there." Doc couldn't help but be amused at Marc's first experience of the morning after a night of over indulgence.

She thought it was a strange request, but she did as he suggested. Her eyes widened and chin dropped when she saw what was there. "What did they do to me!" she exclaimed. "Orvil is dead!"

"Hold on, Marc," Doc laughed. "That wasn't Orvil's doing. That was all you. He just paid for it at your request."

Margaret stared at it for a moment. "What is it? It looks like a cross between a horse and a fish hook."

"It's called a seahorse. It's a sea creature that can be anywhere from an inch to twelve inches long depending on the species."

Margaret stared at it for a few minutes. "It's kind of cute. Maybe I won't kill him. But if my mother ever saw it, she would kill me!"

Doc looked at his watch. "Well, I'd say you'd better get going. Mr. Coruthers is on board and he'll want his morning coffee."

Margaret headed for the door, and then a thought struck her. "Doc, I didn't say anything to anyone about — you know?"

Doc shook his head and shrugged. "Not that I know of."

"I hope not," she sighed as she left sickbay.

She headed for the galley to prepare her coffee deliveries. She ran into Charlie on the steps.

"I got somethin' fer' ya, Marc." He took his hand from behind his back. "A nice piece of cake! The hair of the dog what bit ya' last night," he laughed.

"If I don't see another piece of cake, it would be too soon," she replied, as she pushed past him to go topside.

"Hey! There's cake boy!" she heard someone say.

There were several other men singing a song. Instead of singing, *What do you do with a drunken sailor*, they were singing, *What do you do with a drunken cake eater*. She also saw two men staggering around on deck with leftover pieces of cake in their hands.

A man shouted from the crow's nest. "Hey! Marc!"

She looked up.

"When Marie Antoinette said, 'Let them eat cake,' I don't think she really meant it!" He laughed, as did the others.

Margaret just shook her head. She raised her fist in the air and made the vulgar gesture with her middle finger as she'd seen the others use on occasion. She would have shouted her response, but her head hurt. The crewmen just laughed harder.

"Well, there's birthday boy!" Orvil laughed when she walked into the galley. "I have something for you."

"I swear, Orvil! If it's a piece of cake, I'll deck you!" she exclaimed.

"No, fresh out." He handed her a cup. "Drink this."

"What is it? And don't tell me it's a secret recipe. You know what the last one did," she frowned.

"Actually, it's a sure fire remedy for a hangover. Hank swears by it. It's the juice of a tomato, red pepper and a raw egg."

Margaret looked at him skeptically. "Sounds disgusting!"

"I swear, Marc," he replied. "If it doesn't make you feel better, you can deck me."

"What the hell," she replied and drank it down. "A bit slimy, but not too bad."

"Sorry about last night," Orvil said sincerely. "I didn't mean to get you drunk. I've never seen my rum cake do that to a person." He laughed. "But you do have to admit, it is pretty funny."

Margaret managed a smile. "Do me a favor. Just don't bake any more cake for a while. I have a feeling I'm going to be hearing about this for a long time!"

"It's a deal." Then he thought. "Did you see your arm this morning?"

"The seahorse? I like it," she replied. "How much do I own you? Doc said you paid for it."

"Consider it a birthday present and an apology," he replied.

They talked for a few moments about her antics of last night, and then he handed her the cups for her rounds. She couldn't believe she didn't remember anything.

The only beverages she delivered were for Mr. Coruthers, who was getting ready for his morning duties, and Levi, just going off. Neither of them made jokes about last night. But Mr. Coruthers did make mention that he'd heard about her chess game and congratulated her on the win. Levi just reminded her about making the cabins ready for passengers, and said she was going to be very busy this trip.

***

Carrying passengers on the Neptune's Daughter was rare; especially having the cabins filled. At least there wasn't much she had to do to the cabins. Even though they were empty, she took care of them on a daily basis.

Margaret felt like her head was going to come off, but a hangover was no excuse for getting out of work. It was rare that two or three men didn't have one after shore leave.

They started loading fresh supplies at seven o'clock. Every noise was like a hammer in her head. She couldn't understand why in the world someone would want to purposely get drunk, knowing they'd feel like this the next morning. None of the men had sympathy for her. They fired jokes at her whenever they had the opportunity.

It was ten o'clock and work was finally suspended temporarily until the next wagon arrived. Margaret sat down against a post and closed her eyes. Orvil's morning cocktail seemed to have a little effect, but not much.

"You look like something the cat dragged in."

"It did!" Margaret opened her eyes and saw Jax standing in front of her. He was wearing knee breeches, a white shirt and a vest. His hair was neatly pulled back, and he was eating a piece of fudge. "Jax, I almost didn't recognize you."

He tossed her a piece of fudge. "Are they working you that hard?"

"What you see before you is just a shell. The real Marc won't be alive again until tomorrow — I hope." She told him what happened last night, or at least what she was told happened. She also showed him her tattoo.

Jax laughed. "Sounds like you had a bloody good time to me. Wish I'd been there."

"If I had a good time, I sure wish I could remember all of it," she replied. "Have a seat. I'd stand up, but I can't at the moment."

Jax sat down and offered her another piece of fudge, but she declined. Her stomach was still not right.

"You're dressed well. Did a money wagon drop on you?" she asked wondering about his appearance.

"In a manner of speaking. I'm still a cabin boy on the Arrow Star. This is my uniform, or what I call it anyway. I've found that when you dress nicely, passengers pay better tips. The Arrow Star mainly carries passengers and some freight. I take care of twenty-five first class cabins. Passenger's luggage is mainly all I carry."

"Lucky you," Margaret sighed. "I do it all. This is the first trip that we'll have when the cabins will be full since I've been aboard. And I still load cargo." Besides Jax's gentlemanly appearance she noticed something else different about him. "Your manner of speaking has changed. Are you being schooled?"

Jax laughed. "I guess you could say that. There's a man aboard the Arrow Star who actually lives there. It's rare that he ever leaves the ship. Mr. Ebodiah Slaughter is his name, and he used to be a school teacher. He said that my murder of the King's English grated on his nerves. So in my spare time, he's been teaching me how to read, write and figure money. Actually, I think he's just bored and wanted something to occupy his time."

"I'd say good fortune smiled on you." Margaret managed a smile.

"The money's been good and so is the free education. But the crew is jealous of the extra money I make. They don't care for me much. How about you?"

"I'm the lowest paid on the ship, but I get along with the crew as long as I pull my weight. What are you going to do with all that money you're making?"

"I've got a plan," he said excitedly. "I figure that if I work hard and save most everything I make for the next ten or fifteen years, I can open a respectable hotel somewhere."

"Sounds like you've got your life figured out," she replied, wishing that she did.

"Say, how would you like to partner with me?" he asked.

"I appreciate the offer, but I'll have to think about it. I don't know where I'm going yet."

"Well, the offer still stands. You bring me luck. I won a tidy sum because of you at the fight. I tried to see you that night, but they wouldn't let me. I had to get back to the ship after the fight was over."

"You bet on me instead of your man?"

"I can't stand Meeks!" Jax frowned. "He's a lying, cheating, bastard and you'd better watch yourself if you ever meet him out. He said he's going to kick your ass the next time he sees you, and there won't be any referees to stop him."

Margaret saw a wagon pull up to the loading dock. "I think my break is over." She heard Pete's call.

"Marc! Move yer arse!"

She laughed. "See what I mean? Duty calls."

They stood, shook hands and bid each other farewell. Margaret was happy to see her young friend again. She was glad he had a plan. She needed one. She couldn't stay on this ship for much longer feeling like she did about the Captain. But she couldn't leave until she figured out where she wanted to go and what she wanted to do.

The wagon that had just arrived was the luggage of the passengers. Mr. Richards handed her the list, made sure she could read it correctly and then told her to stow the items in the proper cabins. Each piece of luggage was marked with the name of the person, and which cabin it was to go to.

Even though her muscles were stronger, today they were weighing her down. Everything felt heavy, except for the last two trunks that were going into cabin twelve. They almost felt like they were empty. But she was glad of that — she was dead tired. Now, the only thing left was to board the passengers, and they wouldn't be coming aboard until early in the morning.

As Margaret headed toward her cabin, she almost bumped into the Captain, who was coming around the corner. She was so tired, she never noticed he'd come aboard.

"Sorry, Captain, I didn't see you."

"Just the person I was looking for." He greeted her with a smile. "Did you have a nice birthday?"

"Please, Captain, I don't mean to be rude, but if you're going to tell me another cake joke, I think I've heard them all."

He laughed. "So I've been hearing. Actually, I thought you might like to play game of chess."

"Aye, sir." She would really rather go to bed, but she enjoyed his company as well as his looks.

She sat down behind the chessboard and played her usual game with him. He won — she lost.

"You made some very good moves." He reset the chessboard.

"I'm learning." She suppressed a yawn behind her reply.

"Hmmm." He hesitated a moment then added, "I tell you what, Marc. Let's push your learning curve a bit more. We'll play this next game for money. Let's say — one-hundred pounds?"

Margaret's senses just woke up. She'd forgotten about the chess match she played. She could feel her face turning red.

How could I have been so stupid? Of course, he would have known about that!

"You heard, did you?"

"You didn't answer my question?" He leaned back in his chair and folded his arms, hiding a smile behind his serious expression. "Are you going to play a real game with me or lose one-hundred pounds?"

She couldn't afford to lose all of her winning. "Aye, sir. I'll play."

The Captain made the first move. About three minutes later, she made the last. "Checkmate." Margaret was filled with embarrassment.

The Captain pulled out his money pouch and tossed it on the chessboard.

"I can't take your money," she said. "It wouldn't be fair."

"One thing I want to know. Why pretended you didn't know how to play?"

"For two reasons," she replied. "The first reason, when I saw you playing with Doc the first time, I helped him win. I figured I owed him for helping me with my eye." That wasn't the real reason, but it would do.

"And the second reason?" he asked.

She shrugged. "You're the Captain. I didn't know how you would react if I beat you like that. I didn't want to get on your bad side. Someone told me that it wasn't good to show off what you know."

He gave her a smile. "That might be true for some people, but not me. Just be yourself."

Then she thought:

If only I could!

"Here, take the money. I don't welch on a bet even when I know it's a foolish one. Mr. Taggart told me you played a mean game, and I know I'm not that good of a teacher."

Margaret took the money. "Thank you, Captain. I don't know what to say."

He laughed. "Say you'll quit sand bagging on me and teach me how to play like that."

"Aye, aye, sir. But can we do it another time? I'm still suffering from too much birthday cake."

"Go on, then. I'll see you in the morning."

Margaret went to her bunk. She was so glad that her workday was over. Today she felt like it had been her first. She hoped tomorrow would be better.

✷✷✷

Todd watched Marc leave. It amused him that Marc had been cheating himself all this time when they played chess. Doug Taggart told him everything that happened at the Ship and Shore Inn. He was pleased that the boy won all that money, but his heart skipped a beat when Doug told him about the men who'd attacked them. It was a relief that Marc was liked well enough by the men for them to protect him like they did. He didn't want anything to happen to this boy.

CHAPTER 17
"Passengers"

Margaret woke early that morning. The effects of the cake had worn off, and she felt as right as rain. She started to get dressed, and then remembered what Jax told her. She broke out her fancy clothes, except for her tailcoat, to make herself look more presentable. Mr. Richards had given her the list of passengers, so she could take them to their cabins when they arrived.

When she came upon deck she received laughter and whistles.

"Yer' turnin' into a regular dandy!" laughed Charlie. "Why the fancy riggin'?"

"I'm dressed this way for the passengers," she replied.

"What in blazes for!"

"None of your business."

"Boy — I think that cake did more ta' ya' than get ya' drunk!" Charlie shook his head as he walked off.

Margaret just shrugged. If she was going to make any extra money, it was best she kept it to herself. She walked down to the end of the gangplank to wait for her charges to check them in and hoped they didn't all arrive at once.

It was half past the hour of six when the first coach arrived. Two nicely dressed couples stepped off and Margaret greeted them.

"Good morning, ladies and gentleman. My name is Marcus. I'm your cabin boy. Welcome to the Neptune's Daughter."

She took their names and asked them to follow her. They were in the first two cabins. She asked them to make sure the luggage in the room was correct and then finished by saying, "I hope you have a pleasant voyage. If there's anything you need, please don't hesitate to call on me." The couples each tipped her a few pennies. She pocked her coins and went back on deck to wait for the others. She thought to herself:

Jax was right!

One coach after another arrived. She gave the same welcoming speech to each of the passengers that boarded. Seven couples checked in so far and each gave her a tip. In the next coach that arrived, four men got out, and she led them to their cabins.

"Boy, do they allow gambling on this ship?" one of the men asked as they walked.

"On occasion," she replied. "Tonight we have the races."

"Races?" he laughed. "What kind of races?"

"Rat. We now have a seven track course."

The men chuckled. "I'd like to see that!" one of the other men said. "But what we're talking about is poker."

"I'll check with someone in authority and inform you later, sir." She showed them to their rooms and they tipped her also.

The last person to check in was a woman. She was heavily veiled and walked with a cane.

"May I help you aboard, Mrs. Smith?" Margaret asked.

"No thank you, young man," the woman replied in a raspy voice. "I can manage."

The woman was quiet as Margaret slowly led her to her cabin. "You're in cabin twelve. If there is anything I can do for you, please don't hesitate to ask."

"Yes, young man, there is. I'm recovering from a serious accident. It has left my face badly damaged and it affected my throat. I'm going to reside with my son. I wish to take all my meals in my cabin and do not wish to be disturbed. My medication makes me sleep, which I need to help with my recovery."

"As you wish," Margaret replied. She felt sorry for the woman. "May I bring you some tea?"

"No thank you. Just a pitcher of water daily is all I want." The woman entered the room and closed the door.

Mrs. Smith was the only one who didn't leave Margaret a tip, but she didn't care. The poor thing wasn't dressed in fancy clothing as the others were. Margaret figured she probably needed every penny she had.

***

It was now eight o'clock. Margaret went topside to report to the Captain and Mr. Coruthers.

"All passengers present and accounted for, sirs."

"I say, Marc, you look sharp today," Mr. Coruthers said.

"So, how much money did you make today?" asked the Captain.

"Shhhh!" Margaret warned. "I don't want the rest of the crew to know I'm making extra money." She told them what her friend Jax had said.

The Captain laughed. "It's none of our business anyway."

She was about to leave, and then she thought to ask, "Oh, by the way, four men want to know if poker is allowed?"

"I know those men," Mr. Coruthers replied. "They're professional gamblers. I don't want them gambling with the crew. Some of them are hot heads. I'll arrange a few games for them."

"What about the rat races? I already told them about that."

"That's fine." Mr. Coruthers laughed. "Go on and see about your passengers."

"Aye, sir." She left.

***

The passengers kept Margaret busy all day with trips for tea and emptying chamber pots. The only passengers that used the ship's facilities were the four gamblers and possibly Mrs. Smith in cabin twelve. She asked for nothing. All Margaret had to do was knock on her door for meals. The woman told her that if she didn't answer it meant she was sleeping and to just leave the tray outside the door and she would get it later.

It was late in the evening and several couples were topside enjoying the night air. The four men were just returning from the rat races.

"I knew I should have bet on number four rat," said one of the men.

"Then why did you bet on number two?" asked one of the others.

"Because one of the crew told me that number two won the last three races and he also bet money on it."

The third man spotted Margaret. "Marc!" he called out. "Have you got anything besides ship's rum?"

"Yes sir," she replied. "But I'll have to check with Mr. Richards on price."

"Price doesn't matter," said the fourth man. "Bring us a bottle of your best sipping whiskey." He pulled out some coins and gave it to her.

She went to Mr. Richards for the key to the liquor storage room. He told her what to get and took the appropriate amount of money for the bottle. Surprisingly, she found the door unlocked when she got there. The storage room was filled with barrels of rum and ale, and boxes of

Champaign, whiskey and wines. She called out but no one answered. The only others who had keys to this room, besides Mr. Richards, were the Captain, Mr. Coruthers and Orvil. She thought that maybe Orvil had forgotten to lock it. She went to one of the boxes containing bottles of whiskey, found one already opened and took a bottle. She made sure the door was locked when she left and dropped the bottle of whiskey off to the man who ordered it and returned his change. Margaret was pleased when he gave her a shilling for her trouble.

Before she gave the key back to Mr. Richards, she went to Orvil first and asked him if he'd left the room unlocked. He said he didn't think he did, but he might have. He asked her not tell anyone, and he'd make sure it wouldn't happen again. Margaret shrugged it off and returned the key.

The next two days the weather was fine. But the third day it rained early in the morning. The sea was high and tossed the ship. Half of the passengers were nauseated, as well as a few new crewmen. The passengers in cabin three, The Dutton's, asked Margaret to get the doctor. Mrs. Dutton was ill. They were a couple in their late twenties.

"This is the fourth call I've made this morning," Doc complained as he walked down the passageway with Margaret.

"He says his wife never gets seasick, and it must be something else."

"We'll see," he replied as he knocked on the door.

When Doc was admitted, the woman told him her symptoms, and then he ejected the husband and Margaret from the room to continue his examination.

Mr. Dutton paced the floor while Margaret stayed with him.

"I hope she's alright," Mr. Dutton said in worried tones.

Margaret tried to sooth his fears. "Doctor Ridenhour is a good doctor. You don't have to worry."

"We've been married for ten years. She never gets sick!" he exclaimed.

"Do you have any children?"

"No, we weren't blessed," he replied. "But we have several nieces and nephews that my wife dotes on. We're on our way this trip to meet our newest niece. My sister had a baby about four months ago. We just received word."

Before Margaret could say another word Doc came out.

"Mr. Dutton, I'm afraid your wife is going to be sick the rest of the trip," Doc said seriously.

"Oh God! What's wrong?"

"Son, your wife has a condition."

"How serious is it?"

"It's a temporary condition. She may have it for maybe the next seven months or so."

"What is it? What can I do?"

Doc smiled. "Pick a couple of names. Could be a girl; could be a boy. Modern medicine can't predict that."

The man stood there in shock for a moment.

"Mr. Dutton! You're going to be a father!" Margaret said excitedly.

"Me! A Father!" he exclaimed still in shock.

"Well, man," said Doc. "Get in there and kiss your wife before she throws up again."

The man started to go into the room, and then turned to Margaret. "Marcus, Champaign for everyone tonight at dinner — on me!" Then he closed the door.

"Doc, you should be ashamed of yourself for teasing the man like that," she scolded.

"And spoil my fun! I love to see the expression on their faces when I break good news like that," he laughed.

Doc went back to sickbay, and Margaret went back to Mr. Richards. He figured four bottles of Champaign would take care of the guests at the Captain's table, and told her to inform Mr. Dutton that he'd collect the bill at the end of the trip.

Margaret was given the key again to retrieve the bottles. She opened the door to the storage room and found a broken bottle of whiskey on the floor. She cleaned up the mess, and then happened to think:

Why is there just one bottle broken? There should be others. One bottle couldn't have just jumped out of the box. The whole crate should have been turned over.

She looked for the crate she'd taken a bottle from a couple of days ago, but it wasn't there. Something wasn't right. She got the Champaign and headed straight for Mr. Richards.

"I think we have a thief," she told him. She informed him of what she found.

"I don't think we have a thief — I know, we have a thief," he replied. "I was going over my inventory and found a box of silver candlesticks had been opened. I counted them and there were two missing."

"You don't think it's one of the crew?" she asked.

"Anything is possible. We haven't had an incident until now, but we do have a few new men aboard. Keep an eye on the passengers. I'll inform the Captain."

By mid-day the sea had calmed and so had Mrs. Dutton's morning sickness. The other passengers as well had overcome their nausea. The news of the happy event didn't take long to spread throughout the ship. The passengers and officers were all invited to celebrate the Dutton's good news. Even Mrs. Smith said she would attend for just a few minutes, and Orvil was going to whip up something special for the party.

Mr. Dutton was so happy that he obtained special permission from the Captain for the crew to celebrate. He bought enough Champaign for each man to have one glass to drink a toast to his wonderful wife.

Everyone sitting at the Captain's table that evening was dressed in their best; even Pete and Levi broke out their yellowed, ruffled shirts. Margaret stood by with the Champaign bottles ready to fill empty glasses. When everyone was present, Mr. Dutton proposed a toast to his wife, Loretta, and their forthcoming child. Afterward they all sat down to dinner, except for Mrs. Smith. Her medication was making her tired and she said she needed to lie down.

"Poor woman," said Mrs. Mallory, the passenger in cabin one. "She came on deck one evening when my husband and I were out for a stroll. She was a victim of a fire and lost her husband."

"It's good she has children to take care of her in her hour of need," remarked Mrs. Shackleford, the passenger from cabin six.

"Speaking of children," said Mr. Cabot, from cabin nine, "What do you want, Dutton, a boy or girl?"

"I'd be happy with either one," he replied.

Everyone laughed and talked about the joys and headaches their children had caused them. The Captain listened, smiled and laughed, but didn't contribute to the conversation until Mrs. Dutton asked, "Captain Withers, do you have any children?"

"Not as of yet," he replied. Then he grinned. "I'm still looking for a wife that will put up with my mistress." He took a sip of his Champaign.

"Captain!" Mrs. Dutton exclaimed in shock.

The other women were equally incensed and the men laughed, including Mr. Dutton.

"Ronald! I'm surprised at you!" Loretta Dutton scolded her husband.

"My dear, his mistress is his ship, Neptune's Daughter," he replied.

Margaret listened quietly in the corner. When the Captain mentioned a mistress, she wasn't upset, for she'd heard Laura Sarandon refer to the ship in the same way.

Todd laughed and told them that someday he wished to have a wife and children. Margaret wondered what it would be like to be the wife of a sea captain. He'd almost never be home. Then she thought to herself:

What the hell, I'd go with him!

When dinner was over, the women gathered in Loretta Dutton's cabin to gossip. After Margaret finished cleaning up, the men stayed for an evening of poker and cigars, with the exception of the Captain and one of the passengers, Mr. Mallory.

Margaret had just finished helping Orvil in the galley and was on her way back to her cabin when Mr. Mallory pulled her aside.

"Marcus, by chance you didn't go into our room did you?" he asked.

"No, sir. Is something wrong?"

"I always mark the door of anywhere I stay when I leave my room. My marker is not in place."

"Is anything missing?" she asked concerned.

"We keep anything of value on our person. We were robbed once aboard a ship. We never bring anything valuable anymore. But, it doesn't look like anything was taken."

"I'll tell the Captain at once, sir," Margaret replied.

She immediately headed for the Captain's cabin, where she found him with Mr. Richards. She told them what the passenger had said.

"We were just discussing the problem," said the Captain. "Marc, what about the passengers? You have the most contact with them. Do you have any suspicions?"

"No sir," she replied. "Six of the couples have a vested interest in a race horse that will be running in the Southampton Derby. Then there's Mr. and Mrs. Dutton; they're visiting relatives. The four poker players are headed for a big tournament. Then there's Mrs. Smith. She rarely leaves her cabin." Margaret shook her head. "I just don't know."

"Do you suppose we have a stowaway?" Mr. Richards asked.

"It's possible," the Captain replied. He thought for a moment. "We only have one port to stop at before sailing on to Southampton. We'll reach it tomorrow. If we have a stowaway, he may try to leave the ship tomorrow with any ill-gotten goods. In the meantime, I'll have a search conducted of the ship." He turned to Margaret. "I'm afraid you'll be off of cargo duty tomorrow," he grinned. "I'm sure the passengers will want to go ashore for awhile. I need you to keep watch over their cabins to make sure they aren't broken into. I hope that doesn't hurt your feelings."

She chuckled a bit. "It breaks my heart, Captain, but I'll try to get over it."

"Have Mr. Taggart see me before you turn in," he said.

Margaret checked with her passengers to see if they needed anything before she turned in for the evening. She laid in her bunk and thought how nice it would be to do absolutely nothing but sit in the passageway tomorrow.

"That's better than shore leave!" she said to herself. She turned over and went to sleep.

***

Margaret was up early as usual. They'd pulled into port last night and were in the midst of docking. She'd asked the Captain that morning if the search had turned up anything. However, no one was found. He'd said there were two possibilities; the culprit was hiding in a crate or barrel; or it was one of the passengers. They were going to check everything they unloaded to make sure it didn't house a thief and keep a closer eye on the passengers.

Margaret bid the passengers a good afternoon ashore and stood watch in the passageway. The only passenger who didn't go ashore was Mrs. Smith. She had an aversion to being seen in public the way she was and elected to stay on the ship.

Margaret spent the first few hours of the day reading one of the Captain's books. She practiced throwing her knife and then pretended it was a sword and fenced with an imaginary opponent. It didn't take her long to get bored. Nothing to do seemed to be worse than too much to do. The minutes seemed like hours. She started doing some of the exercises Flint had showed her, as well as a little shadow boxing. But that too wore thin.

The only person she saw was Orvil, who brought her something to eat at noon, but he didn't stay. He said he had work to do. She knocked on Mrs. Smith's door to see if she needed anything, but there was no answer. Margaret figured her medication was making her sleep.

She'd thought the Captain was doing her a favor. Boy! Was she wrong! The next time she complained about cargo duty, she was going to bite her tongue.

It was finally time for the evening meal. Orvil brought her and Mrs. Smith a dinner tray. Margaret knocked on Mrs. Smith's door and announced that her dinner was there, but still no answer. She was beginning to get worried about the woman. There hadn't been a peep from her all day.

Is she even in there? I wonder if I should use my spare key and go in to check on her.

She decided she would and quickly went to her cabin to retrieve the key from her trunk. When she returned, she knocked again. When there was no answer she started to put the key in the lock, but before she could, the door opened.

"Mrs. Smith!" Margaret exclaimed in a relieved tone. "I was beginning to worry about you."

"Thank you for your concern, Marcus," she said in her raspy voice. "There have been many times I've slept the day around since my accident. If you would, please set my tray on the bed. I shall return momentarily."

Margaret watch as the woman headed toward the facility. She set her tray down and noticed the fancy silver brush, comb and mirror sitting on the dressing table. It reminded her of a time not so long ago when she used to sit at her own dressing table and brush her long red hair. Maybe one of these days she could do it again.

"Those were the only things I was able to save from the fire," said Mrs. Smith upon entering the room. "They were a gift from my late husband."

"It's good you were able to save something to remember him by," Margaret replied.

"Now if you will excuse me, I hate to be rude, but I have to remove my veil to eat, and I am still too self-conscious to let anyone see my face," said the woman politely.

"Of course," Margaret replied. "If you need anything, please don't hesitate to call." She closed the door.

Margaret felt sorry for the woman. She didn't know how she would react if her face was all scarred. She went back to the chair to eat her own dinner and could hardly wait until the passengers got back so she could do something else. Anything else!

Most of the passengers returned about nine o'clock that evening, except for the gamblers. Mr. Taggart came by and relieved her from guard duty.

"I hope we catch that thief!" Margaret exclaimed, shaking her head.

"Guard duty isn't what you thought it would be, is it?" Mr. Taggart laughed. "That will teach you to brag about getting out of cargo duty."

"I was wondering why they laughed at me," she replied. "Now I know!"

"Speaking of guard duty, anything happen?"

"I wish something had!" she exclaimed. "And before you ask, I only left my post three times. I had to piss twice and I went to get my key to Mrs. Smith's room to check on her. She hadn't been out all day and never answered when I knocked."

"Was she alright?"

"Just as I was about to open the door, she did. She said sometimes she sleeps all day."

"Interesting," he said, as he looked towards the woman's door.

"Anything wrong?" It looked like he had something on his mind.

"Nothing important," he replied. Then he smiled and put a hand on her shoulder. "Come on, boy. I know a place with a pool table that has my name on it. Let's get you some fresh air."

"Aye, sir!" she exclaimed.

Several of the crew went to the local tavern for a couple of hours of relaxation before they sailed in the morning. However, this time, Margaret made sure she stayed sober. No cake! Not even a ginger beer. No more hangovers for her!

***

The ship sailed early that morning. Margaret learned from some of the crewmen that the content of each crate or barrel was counted before unloading yesterday. In various boxes there were items missing. Mainly small things made of precious metals or things that could be sold easily for quick profits.

Guards had been posted at the gangway making sure no one got on or off who wasn't recognized. Strangers weren't allowed aboard without the permission of the watch commander an accompanied by another crewman. The crew's quarters was searched thoroughly for items, but everything was in order. The Captain was positive that the thief hadn't left the ship. But even if he had, there was no way the culprit could have gotten the pilfered items off the ship.

The Captain talked to the passengers individually. He told them, if they wished, they could keep anything of value in the ship's safe until they reached their destination. Three of the passengers had jewelry they wanted him to keep safe. The others said they preferred to manage their own valuables, but appreciated the offer.

Everything aboard the ship went on normally as they sailed on to Southampton. Straight-line winds filled the sails in their favor and they made record speed. The sea was rough and they headed in and out of rain showers. At dinner, the Captain informed everyone that they would reach Southampton sometime during the night and would dock in the morning.

Everyone was relieved. They were tired of the rocking and rolling of the ship and the mysterious thief. But so far, the only other break-in reported during the remainder of the trip was poor Mrs. Smith. Someone had stolen her silver brush, comb and mirror. The only mementos she had from her husband were gone.

When Margaret finished cleaning up after dinner, she was to report to Mr. Richards' office to help him with final inventory of Southampton goods. But, before she did, she decided to fix him a cup of tea and on the way to his quarters, she saw Mrs. Smith on deck getting some air.

"Are you done for the evening, Marcus?" she asked.

"No, not yet. I'm just bringing Mr. Richards some tea. We'll be doing inventory in the hold for part of the night."

"You're a hard working boy," she said then looked out over the railing.

Margaret bid the woman good evening and headed for the office. Mr. Richards was just locking up the safe.

"I brought you some tea, sir."

"Thank you, Marc." He blew the head of steam from his cup. "You've been a real surprise to me."

"How so?"

"I've found over the years that most of the boys we've had on this ship, except for poor Jake, do no more than what they are told. You go the extra mile as he did."

"My father told me once, you get what you give," she said with a shrug. Actually, he'd said that to her brother once when he was complaining about having to go to so many charity events when he was younger.

"Good philosophy." He took a sip of tea. "Well, come on, boy. We've got work to do."

When they reached the hold, Mr. Richards had her pull out the crates of silverware were marked for Sterling-Price Silver Emporium. They carried only the finest in dinnerware, candleholders and a variety of novelty items made of silver.

Margaret counted the cases of flatware in the crate. "There are only eleven cases, instead of the twelve. Our thief strikes again."

Mr. Richards just shook his head as he wrote in his ledger and then his pen broke. "Blasted flimsy thing! I wish someone would invent something a little sturdier." He reached into his pocket. "Marc, go to my office. Here's the key. There's an extra pen on my desk. Make sure you lock the door back."

"Aye, sir," she replied and headed off.

Margaret opened the door to his office. There was just enough light coming from the porthole to barely see the desk. She heard a noise behind her. "Damn rats! We need a cat aboard this ship," she huffed as she started to light the lamp.

Suddenly, she felt an arm go round her throat. The shock of the unexpected attack stunned her to silence, and she couldn't scream for help. But she quickly regained her senses and struggled with the man behind her before she was choked to death. Her newly acquired strength enabled her to maneuver her head enough to sink her teeth into the flesh of her attackers arm. The man cursed as she bit down. He released his hold enough for her to break free, pull out her knife and make a wild stab. She knew she hit flesh, but her attacker threw a solid punch to her face, and she fell back as the attacker fled the room.

Margaret shook her head to regain her equilibrium then ran out of the room and yelled at the top of her lungs, "CAPTAIN! PETE! SOMEBODY HELP!"

Doors opened from every room. Half-dressed men appeared in every doorway. The Captain was the first to her side. He saw that Marc's lip was bleeding.

"God! What wrong, Marc!" he exclaimed.

This was the first time tears came down her face in front of the crew. She tried to stop them, but couldn't. "I was attacked! A man was in Mr. Richards' office. I think it was the thief. He tried to strangle me," she cried.

The Captain put his arms around his crying cabin boy, and Margaret accepted them. She was so upset that she couldn't even enjoy the thing she most wanted to do — hold him. After a moment, she again regained her presence of mind and pushed away.

"I'm sorry, Captain." She quickly wiped away her tears. "I didn't mean to cry like a baby."

"You're alright," he replied. "That's the main thing."

Pete, Doc, Levi and several of the male passengers gathered around her.

"Ahhh, don't worry, 'bout it. Yer' a brave, lad," said Pete. "Did ya' get a look at 'em?"

"No," she replied, as she wiped the blood away from her lip. "But my knife got a piece of him."

"Levi. Pete," said the Captain. "See if you can find a blood trail. I want that bastard caught before anyone leaves the ship tomorrow."

"Aye, sir," replied the two men. They went back into their cabins to dress before beginning their search.

The Captain assured the passengers that everything would be fine, and they also returned to their cabins.

"Come on, Marc," Doc said. "Let's stitch up that lip — again!"

When Marc failed to come back with a pen, Mr. Richards came up from the hold to see what was taking the boy so long and ran Marc and Doc heading to sickbay. Margaret told him what happened.

"The safe wasn't broken into, was it?" Mr. Richards asked.

"I don't think so," she replied. "I think I interrupted him."

"Thank goodness," he sighed. "I don't mean to make light of your situation, Marc. But, not only are the valuables of the passengers in that safe, but so is the pay for the crew."

"Believe me, I understand," Margaret replied. That was her money in there also.

"Don't worry about inventory tonight. I'll just do it on the off-load tomorrow. Tonight, I'm babysitting the safe."

When Margaret and Doc reached sickbay, she hopped upon the table.

Doc checked her lip and shook his head. "This table has seen your butt more times than all the crewmen put together."

"I'm not in the mood for your humor tonight, Doc."

"Who's being humorous? It's a bloody damn fact! You draw trouble to yourself like dung draws flies."

"Story of my life," she sighed. "I was always getting into trouble at home as well."

"You're lucky. No stitches this time and all teeth still intact," he said.

Just then, the Captain came into the room. "How's your patient?"

"He's fine," Doc replied. "He just needs a good night's rest."

"So ordered," the Captain replied.

"Did you find him, Captain?" Margaret asked.

"No, but we found a bloody shirt wadded up in a seldom used storage closet. The blood trail ended there. I think you got him pretty good. There was a considerable amount of blood."

Margaret got down off the table.

"Come on, I'll walk you back to your cabin," the Captain said.

This time Margaret didn't complain about someone accompanying her. Since the thief was injured, he might jump out at her and try to kill her again.

The Captain noticed that Marc was quiet while they walked. "Will you be alright by yourself? Or would you like to bunk in my cabin tonight?"

Margaret was almost at a loss for words. She thought to herself:

Oh God! What a question.

Doc had ordered a good night's rest for her. How could she do that and spend the night in the room of the man she wanted to be with and couldn't?

"I'll be fine, Captain," she replied. "Thank you for your concern."

The Captain had been waiting for an opportunity to ask Marc a question. Now was as good a time as any. They stopped at her cabin door.

"Marc, when we reach London, how would you like to stay with me and become my ward?" the Captain asked warmly.

Margaret was stunned by his question. It came totally out of the blue. How could she say yes? How could she say no?

"I don't want to be a burden," Margaret replied. She didn't know what else to say.

"You are anything but a burden. You're a good boy, and I don't want you to be alone in London when we get there," he replied. "Since this ship is my main home, I stay with my sister, Sarah. She'll be glad to have you."

Now what was she going to say? Being someone's ward was only a few steps away from being adopted! She wanted to be with him but that wasn't what she had in mind. Margaret was trying to gather her thoughts on how to answer when he spoke first.

"I can see that I've surprised you. You've gone through an ordeal tonight. I'm just giving you something to think about. I know with the recent loss of your parents, I come in a very distant second. But I think it might be a comfort to them if you had someone to look after you."

"Can I think about it?" She was really stuck for an answer and thought to herself,

Margaret! You're an idot! Why don't you just tell him you're a woman

and get it over with!

As much as she wanted to tell him, the words just wouldn't come out!

"You don't have to say anything tonight. Just go to bed and get some rest. Take as long as you like to think about it. I won't press you."

She entered her cabin and closed the door. How could she sleep now? She was just getting herself deeper and deeper into a situation with the Captain. He cared about her, but not in the way she would like him to. What was she going to do now!

✳✳✳

The sun slowly started to rise, and the ship was in the process of docking. Passengers were topside anxious to disembark. Cabin by cabin, Margaret started bringing up the passengers luggage. She remembered the day she loaded it. She'd been suffering from a hangover, and each piece felt like it weighed a ton. Today, being sober, they felt much lighter, except for Mrs. Smith's trunks. She had to get help to bring them up. She didn't remember any of the trunks she'd brought down being that heavy.

Most all of the passengers thanked Margaret for her attention during the trip and told her they were glad she was alright from her ordeal last night. When she brought up their luggage, a few of them pressed a coin in her hand and a few others said they left something for her in their rooms.

Margaret saw the Captain and Mr. Taggart talking together. They left the bridge and approach the passengers who were waiting for the gangplank to be put in place.

"Ladies and Gentlemen," the Captain addressed them, "I hope your voyage wasn't too disrupted by an unwelcome guest aboard. But I am afraid I'll have to insist that we have a look in your luggage before you leave."

"This is highly irregular," said one of the gamblers.

"I do apologize for the inconvenience. But Marc's attacker wasn't found, and we suspect that one of you is the thief," he replied.

While the Captain was talking, Mr. Taggart noticed that Mrs. Smith was slowly backing away towards the seaside of the ship, but Pete and Levi were there to stop her each grabbing an arm.

"Let's start with your trunks — Mrs. Smith," said Mr. Taggart on approach.

One of the gamblers stepped forward. "Unhand that poor woman!"

"Woman?" Mr. Taggart laughed. "I think not!" He pulled away the heavy veil from her head.

Margaret, as well as the passengers gasped. It was a man!

"Have anything to say — Mrs. Smith?" the Captain asked.

The man spat at the Captain. "That's what I have to say to you and that stupid boy!" he exclaimed, as blood started to seep through his dress.

The Captain wiped away the spittle and gave Mrs. Smith a right cross that felled him to the deck. "That's for hurting the boy!"

Mr. Taggart opened the trunks and found all the stolen items. Mr. Richards looked through the trunks and acknowledged that, except for the bottles of liquor, all items seemed to be accounted for. The gambler apologized to watch commander for his abruptness and since the thief was caught, the passengers left the ship without their luggage being searched.

"Take him to the brig until the authorities arrive," ordered the Captain.

Pete and Levi hauled him away. and then Charlie approached Margaret.

"How come ya' didn't notice that Mrs. Smith were a man, Marc? You seen 'em closest."

"He had a good disguise and a good story to explain his voice," she replied.

"Well, if I were the cabin boy, I could'a spotted 'em right off!" he bragged with a snap of his fingers.

"You don't say!" Margaret laughed inwardly.

"Ya' can't put one over on ol' Charlie, no sir!" he declared. Then he slapped Margaret on the back. "Come on, Marc, we got cargo ta' unload."

CHAPTER 18
"The Storm"

There was a four day layover in Southampton. Statements had to be made with the authorities about their thief. As it turned out, Mrs. Smith, as the thief called himself, had been getting away with his piracy for several years. His disguises and identities have been many. Sometimes he dressed as a woman, sometimes it was a gentleman of quality or he'd just hire aboard a ship in one port, pilfer a few items and then leave at the next. Only he knew what his real name was.

With ship's business completed the crew had shore leave. Pete invited Margaret to stay with his family at his home in Southampton, and she gladly accepted. She was anxious to meet his second wife, Jillian, and children, Kyle and Amanda. It was just as Pete had said, Jillian was simple. She was pretty, sweet and she gave Margaret a hug when Pete introduced her.

At dinner one evening, Jillian told her daughter to quit playing with her food. When the girl continued, Jillian picked up a piece of broccoli and threw it at her. When her son started laughing, she threw a piece at him also. That started a big food fight at the table. Margaret had never seen the like. They were all laughing, throwing food and having fun. The incident of Amanda playing with her food was totally forgotten. When the food war ended, everyone cleaned up. Pete told her that dinner like this was a normal occurrence for this home.

It felt good to Margaret being in the midst of a family again, and even though her own parents forced her to flee, she still loved and missed them. She also missed her brother. He was probably home now, and she wondered if Scotty had given him the letter. But it didn't really matter. She couldn't go back, at least not until she established her own life.

After two days, Margaret told Pete she was going back to the ship. She said he needed time alone with his family before they had to leave again. Jillian gave her a hug and said she was welcome to stay anytime.

Margaret walked around the town of Southampton. She went to a used clothing shop and purchased a couple of vests. She found that by wearing one, she could do without her binding and that felt like freedom.

The last day in port, Margaret helped at the loading dock even though she was off duty for the four days. She told Levi that she didn't have anything better to do, so she may as well work. The men thought she was loony, but who were they to argue. It just made their job easier and they could get done faster.

The next morning they set sail. Margaret went about her routine as normal. There were no passengers and no stowaways. Even though she made some money from the passengers, she preferred to do without them.

The Captain started teaching her more about the ship; how to measure the speed they were traveling, more about navigation and he also let her take the helm more often when she had no duties. She also helped him try and improve his chess game. That was going to be a long process. Whenever they were together, she worried that he would bring up the question of her becoming his ward again, but he was true to his words and didn't pressed her again. She'd thought about telling Doc what he had in mind, but decided not to. He would more than likely make a joke of it, and to her, it was anything but a joke. She decided to keep that piece of information to herself.

They made stops at several small hamlets and seaports delivering and receiving cargo as they made their way to Dover. A few hours after they left the last port, the once bright sky turned dark as night. The sea became rough and tossed the ship. The man in the crow's nest came down so he could be heard. He reported that he'd seen a mass of swirling winds just off the starboard bow, and it was headed straight for them. Try as they could to avoid the storm, it seemed to be drawn to them, and they couldn't out run it.

The cries of the wind sounded like screeching harpies from Greek mythology. It was a ghostly sound. Small twisting winds danced about the ship haunting all decks. The Captain and Mr. Coruthers shouted orders to try and escape the path of the storm. But soon the orders they shouted were obliterated. The screeching had turned to roaring and the only sounds that could be heard were the wind and the waves that crashed against the ship.

By now all hands were called to duty. Several crewmen were used as runners to relay orders that had to be shouted into their ears. But the majority of the crewmen were well-seasoned and had been through many of Mother Nature's tirades. The Captain's orders were carried out, almost before he gave them. This was one of the worst storms they'd seen in years. It took three men on the helm. One of the sails was ripped away and flew around the ship like a ghost then disappeared.

Wave after wave of water hit the Neptune's Daughter. Margaret saw one of the crewmen get hit by a wave and it carried him over the side. There was nothing she or anyone else could do. He was lost. She should have felt fear, but there was no time. One of the men who'd been hired the same time as she was the only man who started to panic. But the Captain calmed his jangled nerves with a right cross, knowing that there was nothing worse aboard a ship struggling to survive than panic.

Margaret was one of the runners for a while, until Pete ordered her to go below and help with the bilge pump to rid the ship of excess water. She didn't have to be told twice. Charlie, Sam and a young crewman named Justin were working the pump with her.

"You don't think we'll sink do you?" Margaret shouted. Even below deck it was hard to hear.

"With Capt'n Withers givin' the orders," Charlie shouted, "It'll be a cold day in hell before Davy Jones puts Neptune's Daughter in his locker."

"Don't worry, Marc," said Justin. "We won't sink. It's impossible."

"And how would you know that?" asked Sam as he took his turn on the pump.

"Because my grandmother is a fortune-teller and predicted I was going to marry a beautiful girl. She's never wrong."

"And what's that got to do with the ship?" Charlie asked.

"I'm not married yet," Justin replied. "So see, Marc, we're not going to sink!"

The three laughed at the seventeen year old and continued pumping.

It seemed like they'd been down there forever, then suddenly everything got quiet. The ship became still and you could almost hear a pin drop.

"Is it over?" Margaret asked.

"I don't know," Charlie replied. "We'd better find out."

The four of them hurried topside. There was no one below to tell them what was going on. When they got there, the Captain was shouting orders.

"Work as quickly as you can, men! I don't know how much time we have," she heard him shout.

Carpenters were busy working on one of the masts that had cracked. Others were untangling line. The sails they had left hung limp. The deck was a mess with broken wood where planking had been blown off. Orvil and Hank were passing around water and handing out hardtack for the men to eat to keep up their strength.

Margaret looked at the sea around them. The water was calm but surrounding the ship was a wall of swirling wind about a mile out in all directions. They were like a tiny ship in a bottle.

Doc was topside helping with wounded men. He saw Margaret and called her over to help. The other three helped with rigging.

"What is this?" Margaret asked.

"The eye of the storm," Doc said, as he stitched up the forehead of one of the men. "This isn't over by a long shot."

"How long will it last?"

"I don't know. But we haven't seen the worst yet."

Doc moved to the next man. His thigh was slashed open to the bone. Margaret watched as Doc picked out splinters from the open wound. She'd never seen so much blood in her life, and she felt like being sick.

"Marc, hold his skin together while I stitch him up," Doc said. When she failed to come down to his side, he looked up. Her face started to lose its color. He then shouted at her, "Damn it, Marc! If you don't want this man to lose his leg, get your arse down here and help me!"

Margaret shook off her fear and did what he asked. Blood was covering her hands as she held together the torn flesh. Unwanted tears came down her cheeks though not a sound escaped her lips.

"Just look past the blood, Marc, it won't hurt you," Doc said calmly to try and sooth her fear. "Just think of his skin as a piece of canvas. You've sewn canvas before. He's unconscious so he isn't feeling a thing."

Margaret nodded but couldn't answer. She saw that Doc worked quickly to close the wound, and soon he was wrapping it with a bandage. He called two men to get the man to sickbay and strap him down before the storm hit them again.

Margaret washed her hands quickly in a bucket of water, threw it over the side and retrieved more as Doc moved to the next man. Most of the men just had minor injuries that just needed cleaning and bandaging. One man had a broken arm. A few moments later, she felt a puff of wind and saw the sails start to waver.

"Get ready, men!" the Captain shouted. "She's about to blow again. To your stations!"

"Come on, Marc," Justin said as he passed her. "Back to the pump."

They barely had time to leave the deck before the wind was roaring again. Time had disappeared. Hours had gone by, but it seemed like days. The four of them were weary from the pump. She couldn't imagine what the men topside were feeling. Then at last the winds started to quiet and the ship calmed.

"We're not in another eye, are we?" Margaret asked.

But before anyone could answer, Pete came below.

"The worse is over, men," then he laughed. "Old Neptune helped keep his Daughter afloat."

"Yer' a bundle of laughs, Pete," Charlie said as sat down.

They went topside. There was still wind, rain and a rough sea, but the monster that had swallowed them spit them out and head in the opposite direction. The forward mast was down. Most of the sails were ripped to shreds or gone. Planks from the deck were loose or missing. Line was tangled or snapped. Neptune's Daughter needed some serious repair.

As bad as the ship was, Pete said they were lucky. If they hadn't had a well trained, experienced crew and a Captain like Todd Withers, they would have been at the bottom of the sea instead of the top. They had battled the storm for seven hours as it carried them with it.

Margaret headed toward the bridge and met Mr. Coruthers on the way down.

"Marc, if I'm not back in four hours, come wake me," he said.

He looked haggard. His crisp attire from this morning was now drenched with water. His hat was gone and his hair was in disarray.

"Aye, sir, is there's anything you need?" she asked.

"Just four hours of uninterrupted sleep!" he exclaimed, then left.

Margaret continued her way up to the bridge. The Captain greeted her with his usual warm smile. He also looked exhausted.

"You seem no worse for the wear," the Captain said.

"I think I'm still numb," she replied. "Can I get you anything?"

"Not right now. See Doc. He'll need your help the most."

Then Margaret saw the Captain's shoulder. His black shirt was torn, and she saw blood on his skin. "You're bleeding, Captain. Should I get Doc?"

"It's just a scratch. See to the men. The back side of that storm was worse than the front."

"Aye, sir," she replied, then went to find Doc.

The Captain was relieved when Pete had sent Marc to the pump during the storm. He was worried about him being on deck. With his light weight, it would have been nothing for the wind to pick him up and carry him off.

He rubbed his shoulder. It was still a sore. In the midst of the storm, he felt a sharp pain as if he'd been hit by a pistol shot, then numbness. He was too busy trying to keep the ship from foundering amidst the wild winds to see what happened to him, and then they entered the eye. He felt his shoulder and found a nail buried into his skin as if hammered there. It didn't hurt until he pulled it out. Doc was busy mending the broken bodies of his men to bother him with a small puncture. Nothing seemed broken, and he could move his arm so he didn't see the point. It would heal on its own.

For the next three days it rained. Sometimes it came down in buckets, other times it just drizzled. The crew was put on two hour rotations to give them a break from the rain. The Captain and Mr. Coruthers rotated every four hours. Tarps were set up to keep the water off of the men at the helm and the men working on other repair projects. There were only three small sails intact and the wind was light. It seemed they just floated over the waves which carried them along.

Margaret was in sickbay helping Doc. They counted their losses. Two men were missing, one man died when the mast fell on him and the twelve bunks in sickbay were full.

"I'll be glad when this rain stops," Doc said, as he changed the dressing of a man who had a head wound.

Margaret was changing the bandaged of the man whose leg she helped Doc sew up. "You won't get an argument from me."

"I'm worried about everyone getting sick. Men are more afraid of the fever than they are of storms." Doc checked his watch. "If the Captain wanted you to wake him, you'd better be off."

"Doc, I know you've had your hands full, but he wasn't looking too well when he came off duty four hours ago."

"He's probably dog tired. Mr. Coruthers is also." He then chuckled. "David — I mean Mr. Coruthers, hasn't shaved in three days. He said he can't face the water in his bowl, and you know how particular he is about his looks."

Margaret laughed. "You're probably right. But I'd feel better if you took a look at him. He looked pale."

"I tell you what. I'm just finished. Everyone here is settled for now, and I was going to catch a few winks anyway. How about we both see to him," Doc grinned. "Then when he calls me an old mother hen, I can blame it on you."

"Fair enough," she laughed.

Doc picked up his bag just in case. When they got to the Captain's door there was no answer when they knocked.

"He's probably dead on his ass," Doc said.

Margaret knocked again. "Captain! It's Marc! You wanted me to wake you!" But there was still no answer.

Now Doc was beginning to worry. The Captain was normally a light sleeper. "Go ahead an open the door."

Margaret turned the knob but she could only open the door about three inches.

"It's blocked!"

She pushed a little harder and was able to just see inside. What she saw sent chills through her. The Captain's arm was stretched across the doorway.

"Doc! Help me push. The Captain's on the floor!"

They both pushed hard and were able to open it wide enough for Margaret to squeeze through and pull him out of the way. Doc bent down.

"Todd! Wake up!" he said as he slapped his cheeks lightly. Then he felt his forehead. "He has a fever."

"He's shivering!" Margaret was worried.

"Help me get him in bed." Between the two of them, they were able to accomplish the task. "We need to get those wet clothes off him. You get his breeches. I'll tend to his shirt."

"Ahmm, Doc," Margaret hesitated for a moment. "I don't know if I should…"

"Damn it, Marc! This is no time to be prudish. Just take the damn breeches off! It's not as if you haven't seen a man's rooster before. There are about sixty of them swinging aboard this ship and you can't tell me you haven't seen a few."

He was right, she'd seen her share. But this was different. She unlaced his breeches but pulled a blanket over his privates before taking them off.

Doc shook his head. "Women!" He removed the Captain's shirt. "What the hell! How did he get this?" There was a festering sore on his shoulder. It was red, bruised and oozed puss. "It's infected."

"The day of the big storm he said he scratched himself," Margaret replied. "I didn't think anything of it."

"It was more than a scratch. I need you to get Mr. Coruthers. Tell him the Captain needs to see him in his quarters. But don't tell anyone about the Captain's condition," he said seriously. "Then I need you to go to the galley and tell Orvil you need some maggots."

Margaret gave him a funny look. "You're kidding."

"No, I'm not. Now hurry!"

Margaret went to the bridge first and then to the galley. Orvil was busy filling his barrel with fresh rainwater.

"Orvil, Doc sent me here for maggots," she said, expecting some smart remark about the cleanliness of his galley.

"They're over there," he said, pointing to the cabinet.

That was a surprising answer. "You mean you actually keep maggots here?"

"I don't, Doc does," he replied, as he dumped another bucket.

"Why does he keep maggots?"

Orvil stopped for a moment. "I made the mistake of asking him that once, and I'll never do it again!"

"Why?"

"Because, he told me. And you thought cleaning a pheasant was disgusting? Ha! That's nothing compared to what he uses those nasty things for. So I don't want to know. Now, if you don't mind, collect your maggots and leave. I'm busy."

Orvil was definitely cranky today. So was everyone. Between the storm, the rain and the damaged ship, everyone was on edges. She collected the disgusting bugs and hurried back to the Captain's quarters. Mr. Coruthers was there.

"How long do you think he'll be down, Doc?" Mr. Coruthers asked.

Margaret handed Doc the jar.

"Thanks, Marc," Doc said. Then he returned to the question at hand. "I can take care of the infected area fairly quickly. But the fever is what I'm worried about."

"Is it contagious?" Margaret asked.

"No, this was brought on by the infection, too much rain, and not enough sleep," Doc replied. "If the fever breaks, I'll have him up in a few days."

"If it doesn't break?" Margaret asked.

"He could die," Doc said bluntly.

"I'll need to inform the other commanders," said David Coruthers. "I need sleep myself. As edgy as the crew is now, if both of us are down, we'll have a problem on our hands. We'll need to tell the crew something."

"I don't know. Tell them he broke something. I'll leave that to you. Right now, I've got to fix his wound."

Doc pulled a patch, glue and tweezers from his bag. Then he opened the jar of maggots and started to put them in his wound.

"What are you doing?" Margaret shouted, grabbing his arm.

"Marc, who's the doctor — you or me? Now, if you'll give my arm back, these nasty little creatures can do the work they do so well. They eat infected tissue and leave the healthy untouched."

Margaret let go and both she and Mr. Coruthers watched as he inserted the nasty, squiggling, white wormy things.

"I think I know what you can tell the crew, Mr. Coruthers," Margaret said as she turned up her nose.

"I think I know where you're going, Marc," he replied. "And it will definitely keep everyone out of here. Doc, that's disgusting!"

Doc smiled as he sealed in his medical miracle workers. "In a day or two, these little buggers will be fat and happy and the Captain's shoulder will be well on its way to healing."

On that note, Mr. Coruthers left. He decided to tell the crew the partial truth that the Captain had an infected wound in his shoulder, and he had to lay still for several days. He also exaggerated the amount of maggots Doc had to use to heal the wound.

Margaret was worried about the Captain. Even under the blankets he was shivering. "I wish we had a fireplace on this ship." Margaret put a compress to his feverish forehead.

"I wish we had a whore on the ship," Doc replied seriously.

"Doc!" Margaret frowned at him.

"Oh! Get your mind out of the gutter, Marc. He needs heat. The best source of heat is the human body, and I can guarantee you that none of the men will be willing to jump into bed next to him."

Margaret saw the Captain move his head and mumble something.

"I couldn't understand what he said. Is he waking up?" she hoped.

"No, he'll probably have some delirium for a while until his fever breaks. He could say or do just about anything. He may even try to get up, but don't let him."

"And how will I do that? I'm stronger than I was when I first came aboard, but not that strong."

"I don't know. Maybe a good left," he replied. "Now, I need you to get some fresh water, something to eat and anything you need to from your cabin then come back here. I don't want you to leave until he's better. And except for Mr. Coruthers, let no one else in."

Margaret acknowledged his instructions and retrieved the things she needed. News of the Captain's injury had already spread throughout the ship. One of the crewmen stopped her and asked how bad he was. She gave him an over exaggerated, gory description of the wound, and then told him how she saw the squirming maggots eating his flesh. She told him she'd puked several times when she saw it. At hearing Margaret's embellishment, the man went to the side of the ship and puked himself.

When Margaret returned, Doc walked to the door. "I'll check him in the morning." Then he had an afterthought. "Oh, Marc, if you have any ideas on how to keep the Captain warm, don't hesitate doing it. His life might depend on it. But make sure you lock the door."

Doc's meaning wasn't lost on her. She dipped her rag in the metal pan of water that she had next to his bed to cool his forehead. She could tell he was dreaming about something. He moved his head back and forth, mumbled something and then would be still.

Margaret paced the cabin. It was just about nightfall. She was struggling with her feminine morality, and her love of the Captain about doing as Doc had suggested. She went to the door to make sure it was locked and then stood by his bed. There he was, laying there so handsome and so ill. She started taking off her clothing and thought:

What if he wakes up?

She had already thrown her blanket on top of his to try and add extra warmth. Soon she stood naked before his bed. She had to do this. She didn't want him to die!

Without another moment's hesitation she crawled beneath the blanket beside him. It was a few moments before she could get up enough nerve to put her naked body next to his and put her arm across his chest, careful to avoid the maggot area.

She lay very still for a few moments. She had only touched his naked chest once, but that was in a moment of high anxiety when he comforted her from the attack of the thief. His chest felt smooth and muscular, as she massaged him to try and warm his body. She slowly snuggled a bit closer. She moved one of her legs across his and inadvertently touched his…

"Oh, Lord! Forgive me!" she whispered out loud, as she quickly rolled away from him and covered her face with her hands.

She may have seen a few, but she'd never touched one!

Margaret, get over it. This is a medical necessity. Remember what Doc said, the skin is just a piece of canvas.

Margaret shook her head and again rolled next to him and started rubbing his body to warm him.

Canvas — you're just touching canvas. Oh, bloody hell! What a piece of canvas!

Margaret continued rubbing his body, careful to avoid his family jewels. Well, maybe she touched them once or twice, maybe by accident, she told herself.

She started to fall asleep with her body practically lying on top of his. She started to dream. She dreamt that she was married to the Captain. She dreamed about the ceremony aboard the ship. Her parents were there telling her how glad they were that she ran away and married such a wonderful man, and how wrong they'd been. Her brother was there telling her that he would have helped her runaway to find this man.

Next she dreamed she was experiencing her wedding night. She was holding her Captain husband, and he was stroking her hair and kissing her. She dreamed that he had rolled on top of her and started kissing her more passionately. He whispered in her ear. "Ah, Laura!"

Suddenly, Margaret's eyes flew open. "Laura!" she repeated.

It wasn't a dream! The Captain was on top of her. He was stroking her hair and kissing her neck. She wondered if he was awake, or in delirium. His lips went to hers and she thought:

Oh, what the hell!

She kissed him back. His kisses were gentle at first and then they became more passionate as she held him close to her. She'd felt sensations in her body she'd never felt before.

Margaret had a thought:

If he isn't warm now, he isn't going to be!

She felt like she was on fire! As his kisses became more passionate, so did hers, and then she felt something else! It — was as hard as a rock and twice the size, if not more!

Oh, God! I'm about to get a wedding night!

Several thoughts quickly went through her mind all at once. She really wanted to know what it was like, and she felt as hot as a fired cannon. Those were her first thoughts. Her second thought:

Curiosity killed the cat, but satisfaction brought him back.

Third thought:

We aren't married. What if I got pregnant?

Final though:

What if I became the Captain's personal whore and he never married me?

She made her decision. Reaching for the metal pan that was beside the bed, she grabbed it and hit him hard on the back of the head. The Captain fell quickly back to sleep on her breast. She could feel his sweating forehead. His fever had broken, but hers hadn't!

She turned him over on his back, quickly got out of bed and put her clothes on. She refilled the pan with water and wiped his sweating brow. After a while, he stopped sweating. She felt his forehead and it was cool. "Thank God!" she prayed aloud. He was sleeping comfortably.

There was a large chair in the corner by the Captain's bookshelf. Margaret took her pillow and blanket and curled up to sleep. She too was dog tired.

Margaret woke the next morning with a knock at the door. But just as she was about to get up and open it, the Captain answered.

"Come!" His forearm was draped over his eyes as he lay there.

Margaret quickly opened the door.

"Well, the dead speaks," Doc said as he walked in.

"What are you talking about?" the Captain asked groggily.

"For the past twenty-four or more hours, you've looked more like a corpse."

The Captain sat up. "Oh God! My head is killing me!"

"Your head?" Doc laughed. "Your shoulder is the problem."

"Will you explain what happened to me? And why am I naked?"

Doc walked over to his bed side to check his wound. "Still another day," he said as he replaced the bandage. "Marc and I found you soaking wet, face down on the floor. You had a fever and an infected shoulder. We put you to bed, which is where you're going to stay for another day."

"I've got a damaged ship to take care of, Doc." He saw Marc standing by the door. "Marc, get my breeches."

"Marc, stay right there!" Doc ordered. "Captain, you're not going anywhere."

"We'll see about that!" He tried to stand, but got dizzy and sat back down. "Damn my head hurts! I've got a goose egg back there," he said as he rubbed the spot.

Doc checked it out. He knew he had checked his head for injuries before he left the other night. Then he looked back at Margaret. The look on her face told part of the story. Her face was red, and he knew she must have walloped him last night. He was dying to find out what happened.

"All the more reason for you to stay in bed. Everything is under control for the moment. It's stopped raining, and the sun is trying to come out."

"You've convinced me. But at least give me my breeches."

Margaret did as he requested, but before she could turn around the blanket was off and she got an eye full.

"I started to have the best dream last night," the Captain said as he pulled on his pants. "I was in bed with this woman…"

"I'll get your coffee, Captain," Margaret said, wanting to escape the room.

"Wait a moment, Marc." Doc grinned at her. "I'll come with you when the Captain finishes his story. Stay and listen it might be interesting."

Margaret felt like taking that pan to Doc's head.

"What did she look like?" Doc asked.

"Her face was a bit hazy, but she was passionate!" The Captain laid back and put an arm behind his head.

"Really!" Doc grinned from ear to ear and looked back at Margaret.

"Makes me hard just thinking about it. It was the most realistic dream I've ever had! I think I called out Laura's name, but my dream woman was a hell of a lot more passionate than she ever was."

Doc laughed as he shot a glance at Margaret. "What happened next?"

Margaret could feel her face. All she wanted to do was crawl under something and hide. But she dared not move.

"I was about to consummate my dream then everything went dark."

"How disappointing," Doc sighed.

"Tell me about it!" The Captain just shook his head.

Doc stood, his curiosity now satisfied. "Well, come along Marc. I've got other patients to see."

Margaret told the Captain she'd be back with his breakfast and left with Doc.

"Before you open your mouth, Doc," Margaret whispered harshly. "I found a way to keep him warm, and it almost got out of hand. So I don't want to hear another blasted word about it!"

"I wasn't going to say a word, Marc," Doc said innocently.

As Margaret headed for the galley, she heard Doc cackling down the corridor.

CHAPTER 19
"Jordan"

The rain finally quit, and the crew worked diligently on temporary repairs until they could get to port. Everyone was relieved to see the Captain back on the bridge. The storm had blown them about a hundred miles off course. As it stood now, they had limited sails. Most of the canvas had been blown away. The wind had died down to a light breeze that barely filled the sails they did have to get them anywhere. There was talk of lowering the two remaining long boats left to them after the storm and pulling the ship into a wind.

After that night in the Captain's bed, Margaret felt that everyone knew about it. She knew that Doc wouldn't have said anything, but she felt guilty all the same. When she was assigned duty in the crow's nest it was welcomed — she didn't feel like every eye on the ship was staring at her and it eased her mind.

She was enjoying the sunshine and the open space of the sea. As she looked toward the port side of the ship, her open sea suddenly became crowded. There was a ship off in the distance. It was no bigger than a dot on the horizon, but it was a ship.

"Ship, Ahoy!" she shouted. "Port side amidships!" She climbed down.

"Be she ship? Or be she whale?" said Charlie, as he and Sam laughed.

Margaret sneered at him. "Charlie — why don't you go squat on a belaying pin!"

"Ohhh! That hurts just thinkin' 'bout it, Marc." Sam said as he rubbed his backside, and then he added with a laugh, "But Charlie might like it."

Margaret shook her head, shot them a vulgar gesture and headed toward the bridge. The last time she spotted something that she thought to be a ship, turned out to be a giant sperm whale. The crew teased her for a few days.

"I'm sure it's a ship this time, Captain," Margaret said with confidence.

"Well, let's see what we can see." He took his glass and scanned the horizon. "It's a ship alright. She's under full sail and headed straight for us." He watched a few moments more. "She looks French," he said calmly.

"Orders, Captain?" Mr. Coruthers asked.

"Put the men on alert. Have the cannons ready to bear just in case. We're like ducks in a pond as we are now."

Mr. Coruthers gave the orders. The guns were prepared and weapons distributed among the crew. Margaret was handed a cutlass. It wasn't her blade of choice, but Claude had often trained her in the use of the different blades over the years. She was nervous but ready. Then the Captain gave her orders.

"Marc, go below," he said, as he watch the ship grow larger in his glass.

"But sir…" One stern look from him was all she needed. It was an order. "Aye, Captain," she replied. She didn't know whether to be disappointed or relieved and headed for sickbay to inform Doc what was going on.

***

"Ship off the starboard beam," shouted the man from the Antoinette's crow's nest.

The mate scanned the water before them, and then handed the glass to the Capitaine. "She's sitting low in the water with cargo, Capitaine. Shall we take her?"

"She's a bit of a mess. They must have been through the storm we missed," replied the Capitaine. "She's an easy mark, but we need a doctor for Jordan. If they have one, I don't want to take the chance on him getting killed. Hoist up the signal flag for a parley. If they don't have a doctor, then we'll relieve them of their cargo."

"Oui! Capitaine!"

"Bye the way," added the Capitaine. "Do we have anyone aboard who speaks English?"

"Just Jordan, sir."

"Hmm. This is going to be difficult if no one there speaks French. If Jordan is awake, and able, try and get a translation for what we need and learn it!"

"Oui Capitaine, immediately!" replied his subordinate.

***

"She wants to talk," said Captain Withers, seeing a flag being raised.

"I don't trust them Frenchies," said Pete. "Could be a trap."

"Nevertheless, until they start something, we can't afford to. Have the men keep their weapons out of sight until we know for sure."

"Aye, sir," said Pete. He started to turn, but the Captain stopped him with question.

"Pete, do we have anyone who speaks French?"

"No one I know of, unless ya' wanna' order a pint of ale," Pete replied.

"Hmmm. I don't think that will help."

The ship closed in and started to slowly come along side. Margaret came just to the top of the steps to see and hear what was going on. The Captain ordered her below, but he didn't say how far below he wanted her.

"Bonjour! Qui parle en Français?" called the Capitaine of the Antoinette.

The man speaking was formally dressed in what looked like a blue military uniform. Margaret could tell that his long, curly black hair was a wig, which was topped with a blue hat, sporting a long white plume. His black moustache was thin and twisted at the ends. She figured him to be the Captain.

"Does anyone speak English?" Captain Withers called back. He then turned to David Coruthers. "This will be an interesting parley if we can't communicate."

Margaret was tempted to come to the Captain's aid, but then thought better about it. Something in the back of her mind said to keep quiet until she was really needed.

"Je m'appelle Capitaine Jon-Pierre L'Orange!" shouted the Captain of the Antoinette. He made a formal bow with hat in hand.

"Well, at least we know his name." Then the Captain shouted back, "I'm Captain Todd Withers! What do you want?"

A man on the other ship came forward to speak.

"Capitaine! Do —you — 'ave — a —Doc-tor?"

The man's words were slow and rehearsed.

"Oui!" the Captain Withers shouted back. He knew at least that much French.

"Si' vous plait! Need —Doc-tor!" shouted the other man.

"Get Doc up here," the Captain ordered.

A few moments later, Doc was brought topside.

"They say they need you, Doc. It's your call," said the Captain.

"May as well," he shrugged. Then he had a thought. "If you don't mind, I'd like to take Marc. I may need him as a runner for something, and he knows where everything is in sickbay."

The Captain hesitated. But before he could answer, Margaret was soon by Doc's side.

"I thought I told you to go below?" the Captain asked.

"I did. But you didn't say how far below," Margaret replied with a grin.

"Very well," the Captain replied, as he gave his cabin boy a hard look.

The Captain motioned for the other ship to come closer. They linked the ships together and lashed planks down so Doc and Marc could cross over.

"Merci! Docteur..." said Captain L'Orange, as he prompted for names.

"Doctor Ridenhour." Doc pointed to himself. "Marcus, my assistant," he pointed to Margaret.

"Suivre moi," said Capitaine L'Orange.

"I wish I knew what he was saying," Doc said.

"He wants us to follow," Margaret replied.

"You speak French? Why the hell didn't you say something earlier?" Doc asked. He kept his voice calm as not to draw to much attention to their conversation.

"Sometimes it's best to keep what you know quiet," Margaret replied. "If they don't know I speak French, I might learn something."

"You've got a point."

Capitaine L'Orange brought them to a large cabin. There was a young man lying in the bed. But that was just at a distance. When they drew nearer, they could definitely tell that this was a young woman.

"I wonder why she's dressed as a man?" Margaret pondered. "Her features are definitely too lovely for her to disguise."

The young woman had dark, wavy hair and beautiful sky blue eyes. Her ample breast could never be flattened enough to hide. There was no way this woman could pass for a man.

"I guess she has her reasons — like you have yours," Doc said quietly.

"Jordan, c'est le Docteur!" The Captain spoke softly and lovingly, as he put his hand to the young woman's forehead.

"Merci, ma père!" the girl said in pain.

"He told her, the Doctor is here, and she said thank you to her father," Margaret translated.

"I gathered that," Doc replied. "I know one or two words."

Capitaine L'Orange motioned for Doc and Margaret to come forward.

"I wish you could tell me where it hurt," Doc said, as he put his hand to her forehead. "It would make things easier."

"The pain is here, Doctor," Jordan answered him, pointing to her lower abdomen. "If I try to sit up, the pain it is terrible."

Doc's eyes widened in surprise, and then he sighed in relief. He continued his examination and asked her various questions about her pain. When he pressed on the lower right side, she winced.

"I was afraid of that," Doc said, as he finished his examination.

"What is wrong with me?" Jordan asked.

"I'm afraid it's your appendix. If it doesn't come out, you'll die. Please tell your father I'll have to remove it."

Jordan closed her eyes for a moment and then explained to her father the problem. Margaret translated in whispered tones to Doc.

"Qu'est ce que mauvais, Jordan?" asked her father. (*What is wrong Jordan?*)

"J'ai besoin de la chirurgie," she replied. (*I need surgery.*)

Capitaine L'Orange paced back and forth. "How can I have some stranger gut you like a fish!" he shouted in French.

Suddenly, Jordan curled up in pain and Doc pushed her father out of the way.

"Marc!" Doc exclaimed. "You're going to have to translate for me now. Tell him that if I don't operate now, she will surely die!"

Margaret turned to the Capitaine.

"Le Capitaine L'Orange, Le médecin a dit s'il ne fait pas l'opération maintenant. Elle certainement mourra!" Margaret translated passionately, what Doc told her.

The Capitaine's eyes widened in surprise. "You speak French!"

"That doesn't matter!" Margaret replied. "Your daughter does. What's your answer? Doc needs to do it now!"

"Yes! Yes! Whatever he needs, do it!"

"Ok Doc," Margaret said, "He said yes."

Doc needed surgical supplies and wanted to know if this ship had an equipped sickbay. Margaret translated and found out that their surgeon died a month ago and as far as he knew, it was fully equipped. While they moved Jordan to the sickbay, Margaret informed Captain Withers what was going on.

When she returned, she translated all the labels on the medicines they had, and located all the instruments he needed to perform the operation. After Margaret helped get the young woman undressed, under the watchful eye of her father, Doc sent them both out of the room so he could begin. Margaret kept the French Captain company.

"Don't worry about her, she's in good hands," Margaret said to ease his mind.

"I can't help but worry. She's my only child," he said, as he paced. Then he stopped and looked at Margaret. "Tell me, how is it that you did not translate for your Capitaine?"

"Because I'm just the cabin boy. He didn't know and I didn't say."

The Capitaine looked at her from the corner of his eye. "But I think differently. I believe your Capitaine to be a shrewd man. Maybe he sent you here to gather information secretly."

"My Captain is a smart man, but it was my idea to gather information. But it seems that my plan failed out of necessity," she replied with a grin.

The Capitaine just smiled and shook his head. He didn't speak again until after the surgery was over. Then at last, Doc came out of the room.

"How is she, Doc?" Margaret asked for both of them, and then translated.

"She's doing fine," Doc said with a smile. "We got to it just in time. It was on the verge of rupturing. If that would have happened, there would have been nothing anyone could do. Tell him not to sail off for a few days. I'll have to check on her to make sure there's no infection and then I'll have to remove her stitches. "

Margaret translated. The Capitaine crossed himself and gave his brief thanks to the Almighty and went inside. A crewman escorted them topside and Doc had Margaret tell the man that he would be back in a few hours to check her when she woke.

Captain Withers as well as the rest of the crew anxiously awaited for their return. "So, who was sick?"

"The Capitaine's daughter," Doc replied. "Her appendix was on the verge of rupturing."

"How is she?" the Captain asked.

"Doing fine," Doc replied. "If Marc hadn't been there to translate, we might have had problems."

The Captain folded his arms and frowned at Margaret. "And why the hell didn't you tell me you could speak French?"

Margaret folded her arms and frowned back. "Because you didn't ask! You sent me below before I could tell you — sir."

"Aye, Capt'n, ya' did," Pete agreed.

"I did, didn't I," he replied, scratching the back of his head. "Tell me. Is there anything else important I should know about you?"

Margaret shrugged and shook her head. "Not that I know of."

"Go on about your duties then," the Captain said.

"Aye, sir."

Margaret went to the galley to help with the crew's meals.

"So, what's the Frenchie's daughter look like?" Charlie asked as he went through the line.

All the men were looking at her waiting for a response. She knew what they wanted to hear.

"I tell you what. Think of the prettiest woman you've ever seen. Jordan would make them look like crow bate," Margaret replied, faking the lustful look the men get when they talk about women.

"What about her teats?" Sam asked. "Little or big?"

"They're the size of cannon balls!" Margaret grabbed her imitation groin. "Makes me hard just to think about them."

"They say you helped Doc," Orvil said. "Did he let you see her naked?"

"No, damn it! He threw me out." Margaret pretended disappointment.

Some of the men laughed and some patted her on the back. She told them what they wanted to hear, and then went about the business of serving dinner.

A few hours later, Levi came to Margaret's quarters and said the Captain wanted to see her on deck.

"Aye, sir? You wanted to see me?" Margaret asked.

"What the bloody hell is he saying?" asked the Captain, frustrated over the language barrier.

Margaret asked Capitaine L'Orange what he wanted, and he replied, "Le Capitaine Withers! Donne une autorisation pour venir à bord?".

"He's asking permission to come aboard," Margaret translated.

"Granted," the Captain replied.

"L'autorisation a accordé!" shouted Margaret.

Capitaine L'Orange had Margaret convey his thanks for saving his daughter's life, and then to relay to the doctor that Jordan was now awake if he would like to accompany him back to the ship. The French Captain also told her, to tell Captain Withers that he recognized their need for sails and they had some extra canvas that he was welcome to.

Captain Withers graciously accepted with many thanks, and had Marc to convey his wishes for the speedy recovery for his daughter.

The next day, Doc and Margaret went back to the Antoinette. Jordan had requested that Marc accompany the doctor when he came to examine her. After Doc was finished and told Jordan everything was looking good, he went back to the ship, leaving Margaret behind. Jordan turned to the crewman left to guard her and ordered him out of the room.

"You wanted to see me?" Margaret asked, in French. Even though Jordan could speak English fairly well, she wasn't comfortable with it.

"Oui, first I wanted to thank you for your help. If you had not known my language, I might have died."

"I'm just glad we could help," Margaret replied.

"Second, I wanted to answer your question."

Margaret was puzzled. "What question?"

"Why I dress as a man." Jordan grinned.

"I didn't know you heard that." Margaret blushed.

"I dress as a man because it is easier to command in men's clothing. I've never known women's garments. I don't really want to. My father gave me a boy's name and has treated me as he would a son these many years. I know, no other way and neither did he."

"What about your mother? Didn't she have any influence?"

"My mother hated my father. She told me that he kidnapped her, and I was the product of his continual rape. She was English and spoke no French. So that is partly how I learned both languages. When I was eight years old, she finally escaped the ship and left me with my father."

Margaret was astounded by her bluntness and horrified by her story.

"What did your father say about what she told you?"

"My father said it was true, for the most part, but he didn't rape her. He said he loved my mother the moment he set eyes on her. He gave her everything she wanted, except for her freedom. Over the years with my father, she learned the language. She threatened that one day she would escape and take me away with her. My father told her that if she took me, he would hunt her down and killed her like a dog."

"That's terrible!"

"Not so much," Jordan shrugged. "I would have never gone with my mother anyway. She never wanted me. I think she didn't escape. I think my father tired of her and just let her leave. He's the one who raised and loved me." She hesitated a moment, to let her guest absorb what she had just said. "Now, I have a question for you? Why do you dress as a boy?"

"You heard that too," Margaret replied with a sighed.

"You hide your gender well. I would have never guessed unless I heard."

"Are you going to tell?"

"Not if you tell me the truth, as I have told you. I've not even told my father," Jordan replied.

Margaret sighed:

Another person to know my secret.

She sat down and told her the whole story, including how she fought in the boxing tournament.

Jordan laughed. "You are a very funny person, Margaret, to put yourself through all that just to escape marriage."

"It feels strange for someone to call me by my given name. I haven't heard it in months. But, I'd rather you call me Marc, just in case someone might be listening."

"As you wish," Jordan replied.

Then her father came in and Margaret stood.

"How is my daughter today?" Capitaine L'Orange bent over and kissed Jordan on the forehead.

"You can't be rid of me so easily, Capitaine L'Orange," Jordan said. "One day I will be Capitaine of the Antoinette!"

"So, when do you plan your mutiny?" he asked folding his arms.

"Time will tell," she replied, trying to look serious.

"And who will follow you? These men are loyal to me."

"Ahhh, but are you sure?"

He laughed. "Now I know you're better." The Capitaine turned to Margaret. "Boy, I think it's time for you to leave. Jordan needs her rest."

"Oui, Capitaine L'Orange," Margaret replied.

"Marc, can you come tomorrow? I'd love a good chess game," Jordan asked.

"If it's alright with my Captain," she replied.

When Margaret left, Jordan turned toward her father.

"When we are able to leave, Father," she said in low tones. "I want that boy."

"What on Earth for?" he laughed. "He's English!"

"He thinks I'm lovely," Jordan said with a smile, repeating a comment she overheard Margaret say before her surgery.

Capitaine L'Orange folded his arms. "What were you two talking about? He's just a boy. What would you do with him? Besides, I thought you told me you loved Phillip Jacard?"

"I do. But he'll never approach me. I think he's afraid of what you might do to him."

"I approve of Phillip. I don't see the problem?" her father shrugged.

"The problem is I'm not sure exactly how he feels about me. I think he loves me. I see it in his eyes, but he says nothing."

"What if I speak with him?"

"That wouldn't do either. He'd think it's an order, and our relationship would never float."

"So where does this boy fit in?"

"Marc is older than you think. He's actually eighteen; one year younger than me. For some reason, he keeps his true age a secret. I plan on using Marc to make Phillip jealous," she said with a grin.

"I don't think their Capitaine wants to part with him. I saw a fondness in his eyes — like a father for a son."

Jordan laughed and shrugged her shoulders. "So? We kidnap him before we leave. Just like you did my mother."

"How will you be assured of his cooperation?"

"Oh, he'll cooperate. Remember, Father, I am a L'Orange. I have my ways."

Capitaine L'Orange laughed heartily. "Like father, like daughter. How can I say no? Now, lie down and rest. I'll make a plan."

***

Whenever Margaret was off duty, she went to the Antoinette daily with Doc and stayed for a few hours afterward. It was the third day and Margaret had just come back from the other ship.

"Hey, Marc!" Charlie called. "Do any cherry pricking today?"

The two men standing on guard by the planks laughed and elbowed each other. One of them replied, "Now Charlie, ya' know Marc don't know where ta' find cherries."

Margaret knew they weren't talking about fruit. She grinned. "I know exactly where to find cherries." She put her hand in a sack that was hanging over her shoulder and grabbed a handful. "See! I've tasted more cherries than you'll ever dream of!"

She threw them at Charlie and the two men standing guard. Some of the men had been teasing Margaret about bedding Jordan, and when she told her new friend about it, Jordan said they had just acquired a barrel full of cherries and gave her some.

"I guess he does know where ta' find cherries!" said one of the men, as he laughed and picked up the precious pieces of fruit.

Margaret enjoyed her time with Jordan. They talked about men, about women and played chess. Margaret found her to be formidable chess player.

On the fourth day, Margaret helped Jordan walk about the deck to get some fresh air. She almost slipped but Margaret caught her. From the Neptune's Daughter it looked like an embrace. Since the men knew that none of the French crew spoke English on the Antoinette, one of them called out, "Don't take her on deck, Marc! It will cause an international incident!" Margaret knew that voice to be Orvil's.

She apologized for her crewmate, but Jordan just laughed. Actually, she'd slipped on purpose where Phillip could see. The look on his face told her that he too thought they'd embraced. He didn't look happy about it. Her plan started to unfold.

On their last day together, Capitaine L'Orange invited Captain Withers, Doc, and Marc aboard to celebration Jordan's recovery. They accepted and with Jordan and Marc to translate, the evening was very entertaining.

Capitaine L'Orange told Captain Withers that his main business was the transport of documents or goods for the government to ambassadors in other countries. He told them that before Jordan's illness, they were on their way to India and they were leaving after dinner tonight.

When dinner ended, Jordan asked permission from both captains if she could see the Neptune's Daughter before they sailed. She also said she wanted to see Marc's boxing medallion. Permission was granted and Jordan crossed over with them. Margaret gave her the tour. She could see the eyes of the men pop when Jordan passed them hanging on to her arm.

The last place to see was Margaret's small cabin. She told Jordan it wasn't much, but it afforded her much needed privacy away from the crew's quarters. She showed Jordan her medal, and when Margaret wasn't looking, Jordan tossed an envelope to her bunk addressed to Captain Withers.

Afterward, Margaret escorted Jordan back to her own ship. One of the Antoinette's crew said that Capitaine L'Orange was below and wanted to give Marc one final farewell before they left. But, just as soon as Margaret started down the steps of the passageway, she felt a sharp pain and the lights went out. She fell to the floor.

Jordan quickly ran back on deck. It was dark and there was no moon. One of the crew from the Antoinette had put on one of the Capitaine's wigs that had been cut down to resemble Margaret's hair. He was the same height and build. They walked to the plank that connected the two ships.

Jordan called over to the two men standing by the plank on the other side.

"Gentleman, if you please," she said sweetly. "I would like to say good-bye to Marc privately."

The two men laughed and when Jordan whispered something into her crewman's ear, he raised his hand and made the same vulgar gesture that Jordan had seen Margaret make whenever she wanted to express her feelings her crew.

"All right, Marc!" laughed one of the men on guard. "Kiss the hell out of her!" They walked to the other side of the ship.

With the two men gone and no one else in sight, the crewman quickly crossed over with Jordan shouting her good-byes. The impersonator waved to the two men that had given them privacy, and he quickly headed toward the front of the ship, lowered himself over the side and down the anchor chain. As soon as he was back aboard the Antoinette and the planks removed, the ship sailed into the night with their captive.

***

It was four o'clock in the morning and the Neptune's Daughter was ready to set sail. Even with the missing mast, the extra sails they'd received from Capitaine L'Orange would help them make port in half the time it would have taken them without.

Todd was surprised that Marc hadn't brought his morning coffee. If he was anything, it was punctual. He thought about knocking on his cabin boy's door to wake him, but decided to let him sleep for a change.

"Good Morning, Captain," said David Coruthers.

"And I hope it stays that way, David," Todd said looking up at the sky. The clouds were looking dark. "Are we ready to up anchor?"

"On your orders!"

"Then let's get going. I want to get to Dover as soon as possible. The ship will probably be a few weeks in dry dock for permanent repairs."

David Coruthers gave the orders. The anchor was hoisted up and the sails unfurled. They were underway.

"By the way, Captain, I didn't see Marc this morning," said David.

"I didn't either. I guess he's sleeping in. I think the boy deserves to slack off for once," the Captain said with a smile.

David laughed. "You don't suppose he decided to skip off with that French girl, do you? To hear the crew talk, they looked pretty cozy. And if I may say, she was a fine looking girl."

Todd also laughed. "No, he would have said something. But I wouldn't blame him if he wanted to."

Pete approached. "Mornin', Capt'n. Have ya' seen Marc this morning? Orvil said he was gonna help with breakfast."

"I suppose he's sleeping in," the Captain said. "I didn't see any harm in it this once."

"No sir, I checked. I knocked on his door and there were no answer. And his door is locked. Ya' don't suppose them Frenchies took him?"

Todd was beginning to get worried. "Who was on duty last night?"

"Bailey and Mipps. They were posted at the planks."

The Captain sent for the two crewmen and had Pete to go and open Marc's door.

"Did Marc come back to the ship last night?" the Captain asked.

"Aye, sir," said Bailey. Then he laughed. "We gave the lad some privacy and stood on the other side of the ship to watch the planks. He wanted to kiss that pretty wench without us watching. A few minutes later, he crossed and waved good-bye to her. After that, he went to the bow to watch them sail off. Didn't see him after that."

"Are you sure it was Marc that came over? Did he say anything to you?" The Captain was definitely concerned.

"Come to think of it, no. It was dark. It looked like his hair, and he was the same size. When we laughed at him, he gestured like he usually does."

Pete came running back on deck. "Capt'n! I found this." He handed him the envelope.

Todd looked at the handwriting. It wasn't Marc's. He opened the envelope and read the contents:

Dear Capitaine Withers,

First of all, I would thank you for my life. My father and I will be eternally grateful. However, it is unfortunate that I must do what I have done.

I have borrowed your cabin boy, Marc. I know he would not have come willingly. There is another important matter in my life that I want to take care of, and only Marc can help me. Be assured he will be treated as a guest. If you wish to have him back, you may collect him in Pondicherry, India. That is, if he decides to stay there and wait for you.

Warmest Regards,
Jordan L'Orange
Post Script:

203

I struggled with another matter I have decided to call to your attention. I am a French woman and I believe in love. Marc loves you — but not as a son for a father. Marc is a woman. Ask the Doctor.

Todd crumpled the letter in his hand and grabbed the railing of the bridge. "God in heaven!" he exclaimed and then he thought,

How could I not have seen it before?

He closed his eyes and pictured Marc with long hair and feminine trimmings. There it was! That's what was so different about his cabin boy and why he struggled with his feelings. Marc was a woman and now she's been kidnapped!

David Coruthers first saw the look of hurt on his Captain's face and then it turned to one of shock. "What is it, Captain? Have they got him?"

Todd handed him the letter as he looked in the direction of India.

"Holy Mother!" David exclaimed after he read it. "I can hardly believe it!" He put his hand on the Captain's shoulder. "What do you want to do, Todd?"

"There's nothing we can do for now," he said sadly. "The ship is damaged, and we have no supplies for such a trip." He knitted his brow. "But — I don't care what it takes, I'm getting Marc back!"

"What do I tell the crew?"

"That he was kidnapped and nothing else! Marc's secret will remain intact." Todd turned his back and left the railing. "You have the bridge. Doc has some explaining to do!"

***

Margaret woke with a splitting headache. There was a lump on the back of her head. Now she knew how the Captain had felt when she'd wacked him over the head. Her senses slowly came back and she looked at her surroundings. This was Jordan's quarters.

"Good evening, my friend," Jordan said as she sat back in a chair waiting for Margaret to come around. "You've almost slept the clock around.

"Friend — my bloody ass!" Margaret exclaimed as she sat up. "Why did you hit me?"

"Sorry for that, but it was necessary. You never would have come along willingly."

"You've kidnapped me!" Margaret shot up out of the bed and headed for the door.

But Jordan was quick to grab her arm. "Don't bother looking for your ship. We've long since sailed and you're ship was in no condition to follow us."

The two women glared at each other for a moment, and then Margaret jerked her arm away and sat back down on the bed.

"Why have you done this?" Margaret's tone was sharp.

"I need your help. Your special circumstances make you perfect for what I need you to do."

"And what makes you think I'm going to help you with anything?" Margaret huffed.

"Remember, I still hold your secret. My father thinks you're a boy of eighteen. I've told him this."

"And what good does my secret do me on your ship?"

Jordan laughed. "Because, Margaret, I have pictured in my mind what you would look like dressed in feminine attire. You would appeal to my father greatly. He's partial to fiery young women and, being that I have no — stepmother this trip..." Jordan hesitated then changed her tact. "Actually, I think I might like having a baby brother or sister. How would you like to become my new stepmother? I've had several over the years."

"What? Oh, no. Not me!" Margaret stood. "I ran from one marriage, and I'm certainly not up to becoming a Captain's whore!"

Jordan cocked her head and mimiced a look of shock. "You mean you don't find my father handsome?"

"Of course he's handsome," Margaret exclaimed. "But he's what, forty-five?"

"See you compliment him already. He's fifty-one."

"That's not the point!" Margaret folded her arms and went to look out the large window of the cabin.

Again, Jordan laughed. "Margaret, I'm just teasing you." She then became serious. "Please help me. I'm not normally a person who begs. I promised I'd keep your secret, and I will, even if you don't help me. But let me warn you, if my father does find out you're a woman, it is a certainty he will have you."

Margaret was quiet for a moment. She was stuck. What did she have to lose by helping Jordan? She was on a strange ship, bound for a strange country and needed at least one person in her corner. "What do I have to do?" she sighed.

"Help me make a man jealous."

Margaret turned around abruptly. "What!" she exclaimed.

Jordan grinned. "Actually, you've already started — you just didn't know it."

There was a knock at the door. "Come!" Jordan called out.

Margaret noticed the tone of command in her voice. A man entered with a bottle of French wine.

"Set it on the table," she ordered. Jordan walked over to Margaret and put her arms around her. "Have the chef prepare something special for two. Marc and I will dine in my cabin tonight."

"Oui! Jordan!" The man left.

Jordan released her and laughed. "See? It's that simple."

"Is he the one you want to make jealous?" Margaret asked. The man she saw was short and had the face of a toad.

"Heavens no! That was just the chef's assistant. But, he's also the worst gossip on the ship. There are only a few who know you're on board. Now everyone will know, including Phillip Jacard, the man I love."

"How is it that you need help? Jordan, don't think me a puff, but you're a gorgeous woman. If I were a man, I'd want you myself."

"Sit down, let me explain. Care for some wine?"

Margaret sat back down on the bed. "Normally, I don't drink. I get drunk too easily and lose my sensibility. But hand me a glass — tonight I think I need to!"

Jordan sat next to her and poured. Margaret listened as she explained.

"Phillip has been on the ship for as long as I can remember. As a boy, he was the powder monkey. He helped with the cannons when we went into battle. Phillip is now twenty-two." Jordan smiled and then sighed. "He's Adonis himself with that blond hair and sea green eyes of his. He's also well muscled and intelligent for a seaman and now my father's second mate, where as I'm his first."

Jordan explained to Margaret that she felt the reason that Phillip didn't approach her was because he feared what her father might do. The last man who'd asked for her hand, her father personally took him up by the neck and threw him overboard. But Jordan wasn't bothered by his actions, because she didn't like the man anyway. He was only interested in the position that a marriage might gain him.

She said she had to make Phillip jealous enough to overcome his fear of her father. Using a member of the crew wouldn't do because she would have to become too personal, and they might want to take too many liberties. But with Margaret being was a woman pretending to be a man, they could do just about anything without compromising their virtues.

"So, Margaret…"

"Marc, if you please," she interrupted, holding up her glass for a fourth refill. "I'll do it." Margaret was definitely feeling the effects of the wine. Her head was starting to spin and she was feeling giddy.

Jordan sighed in relief. "Thank you, Marc."

There was a knock at the door, but before Jordan could answer, Margaret put a finger to her lips to silence her. "You want to play a game? I'll give you a — game!" She hiccupped. "Follow my lead. Bid him to come in."

"Come!" Jordan called out. She was curious as to what her obviously drunk friend was going to do. The chef's assistant brought dinner as ordered and set it on the table.

"Jordan," Margaret said in a romantic tone. "I couldn't bear the thought of being without you. You on your ship and me on another would have been unbearable. I've never felt this way about anyone."

To Jordan's total surprise, Margaret put her arms around her and kissed her on the lips. What could she do? The ship's biggest gossip was standing right there.

What the hell!

Jordan followed Margaret's lead and kissed her back. The ship's assistant quickly left.

Margaret let Jordan go and laughed. "So, was I…" She hiccupped, "… convincing?"

"What I think is you're drunk!" Jordan just shook her head.

"You know what? I think you're right."

Jordan put her arm around Margaret to help her to the table. She needed to get some food in her stomach to mix with the wine. Suddenly, her father burst through the door.

"Jordan! What's happening here?"

Both women looked at the serious expression on her father's face and started laughing. "I told you, he was the biggest gossip on the ship," said Jordan. "Sivley hasn't been gone five minutes!"

"Capitaine L'Orange," Margaret said, and then hiccupped, "My intentions toward your daughter are strictly — business! I am in love with my Captain…"

When she hesitated, Jordan took a deep breath and hoped Margaret wouldn't reveal herself.

"…my Captain's sister, Jessica!" Margaret continued.

Jordan breathed again.

The Capitaine looked in Margaret's eyes which were glazed. "Is he drunk?"

"On four glasses of wine, no less," Jordan replied.

"He may speak French, but he is certainly no Frenchman if he can't drink," the Capitaine laughed.

"You are certainly right on that, Father!"

Jordan explained to her father what had transpired, and that Marc agreed to help her. She said it would be best if Marc slept in her room for the night since he was drunk. She said she didn't want Marc to accidentally wander around the ship and fall overboard, or come upon someone who might throw him overboard.

Her Father hesitated for a moment as he watched their guest's head lower to the table. "I'll have a sack brought up for you to bundle him in for your protection. He may be out now, but I know how men can be when they get drunk," he replied.

"Thank you, Father."

He kissed her good-night and left. Jordan helped Margaret up and led her to the bed. Thirty-minutes later the sack was brought, and Jordan sewed Margaret in. She lay next to her friend and smiled.

By now, the whole ship knows about Marc, and where he's spending the night! I wonder what Phillip is thinking right now?

Jordan closed her eyes and dreamt of what it would be like to be married to Phillip Jacard.

***

Margaret woke the next morning and found herself sacked. "Why am I in a bundling bag?"

"My father didn't want you to take advantage of me when you spent the night," Jordan replied as she brushed her hair. "And you're right, you can't drink."

"I didn't do anything I'll regret, did I?" Margaret asked as Jordan cut her free.

"Do you remember kissing me?"

Margaret closed her eyes and sighed. "Vaguely, I thought I dreamt it."

"Well, it's time to get up. All hands on deck — and that means you too. I have to deal with some ship's discipline."

Margaret got up and shook her head. It wasn't as bad as the first time she'd gotten drunk, but it wasn't good either. She looked at how Jordan was dressed. She was wearing a black pair of breeches and boots. Her blue silk blouse shimmered and a black sash was wrapped around her waist. She had a whip hanging at her side and a knife in a sheath on the other hip. She wore a blue scarf around her head to match her shirt. Margaret envied the way she dressed and often wished she could have worn something similar at home on a day to day basis instead of just during fencing lessons.

As they came topside, Margaret saw the crew gathered around the main deck. Capitaine L'Orange was on the bridge looking down. His face was stern.

"Bring him forward!" the Capitaine shouted.

Two men brought another man topside with his hands tied behind his back. Jordan stepped boldly forward and circled the man.

"Tisk, tisk, Alfonse." She took her coiled whip in hand and tapped the handle on her chin. "What do you have to say for yourself?"

The man just stood there looking forward.

"You have nothing to say in your defense? Then that must mean you're guilty. You know the penalty for stealing food, especially on a voyage such as this."

"I just took a piece of cheese," the man finally said.

"Today it's a piece of cheese, tomorrow the whole wheel. Then perhaps the next day something from the Capitaine, ay?"

Margaret listened as Jordan spoke. Her tone was even, and she was calm and collected. She then turned to the rest of the crewmen.

"Gentleman! The Capitaine has given me permission for you to determine his fate. I leave it to you. Will it be banishment from the ship for a period of three days, or the whip?"

Margaret knew the punishment for stealing food. It was one of the things told to her when she boarded her own ship. Banishment meant that the prisoner would be put in a boat and towed behind the ship. That was almost certain death. The lash was another alternative.

When Jordan finished speaking, the men all started shouting, "Whip! Whip! Whip!"

Jordan turned back to the prisoner. "They say whip, Alfonse. What is your say? I will also consider your choice."

The man kept his head held high. "Whip."

"You're a good man, Alfonse. I would hate to lose you as a member of our crew. But discipline must be maintained at all time. Do you understand?"

"Oui! Jordan!" the man replied.

Jordan let her whip uncoil, whirled it around and cracked in the air. "Alfonse!" she called out. "Put out your tongue!"

The man turned sideways and did as ordered. Jordan again cracked her whip and this time stung the tip of his tongue.

"That is for the offending organ. Maybe it will learn its place!" She had the men tie him between two posts with his back towards her. She cracked her whip twice, grazing one ear then the other.

"That is so you may hear the rules and regulations of this ship with more clarity!" Again she snapped her whip and drew blood from the backs of his hands. "So your hands may learn not to steal from this ship!" She then took the whip to his back and striped him five more times. "Untie him!" she ordered. She coiled her whip and stood toe to toe with him, looking the man in the eye. "Have you learned your lesson, Alfonse?"

"Oui! Jordan!" He looked past her gaze.

"See to your wounds. You have the rest of the day and tomorrow to think about. You're confined to the brig with half-rations and water until you return to duty," she said. "Dismissed!"

"Oui, Jordan." The man went below followed by two others.

The Capitaine ordered the men back to duty and in short order the routine of the ship was back to normal.

Jordan approached Margaret. "Shall we walk? They headed toward the stern of the ship.

"How can you bring yourself to do that," Margaret asked. "…and be so evenly tempered."

"Actually, I did the man a kindness. Did you see the stripes on his back? I just broke the skin deep enough to draw blood. The man who used to dole out punishment would have laid his back open with ten lashes. The first five lashes I did entertained the crewmen so I don't have to put so many on his back. If I give them a good show, they don't lust for excessive blood and I have a better crew member to boot."

"I can see your point," Margaret replied.

Jordan saw Phillip approaching out of the corner of her eye.

"Quickly, Marc, Phillip is coming. Take my hand and kiss it," she whispered. When Margaret's hesitated she prompted again. "What's the problem? Hell! You kissed my lips last night!"

"I was drunk!" Margaret whispered harshly. She did as Jordan requested.

"What's he doing on board!" Phillip exclaimed, as he stood with arms crossed.

"And what business is that of yours?" Margaret asked.

"I wasn't addressing you — Boy!" Phillip frowned.

"If it is any of your business, Phillip, Marc is my guest," said Jordan.

"And what do you want with this — Boy?"

Margaret folded her arms and stepped forward. "I don't like your tone. I'm a guest of Capitaine L'Orange. I suggest you return to your duty. I believe dereliction of duty also calls for punishment, does it not?"

Phillip stood there for a moment, looked at Jordan's expressionless face, and then turned and left them.

Jordan let out a giggle. "I didn't think you had it in you? He's pissed!"

Margaret leaned against the rail and sighed in relief. "Neither did I!"

After that first night aboard, Margaret was given her own quarters. She looked around at the tarnished brass fixtures that the salty sea air had turned, and the bad condition of the furniture. She compared the cabins on the Antoinette to those of the Neptune's Daughter, and it made her proud of the work she did aboard her own ship.

Margaret was impressed at how Jordan commanded the attention of the men. Her leadership was not just an honorary position. She knew the workings of the entire ship. She knew how much sail for what type of sea and wind conditions and could read charts as well as the stars at night.

***

They'd now been sailing for three weeks. For the most part, the winds were good. They'd passed through one storm, but it did little damage to the ship. Margaret went to the bow to be alone. She was feeling home sick, but not for her home in England. She was home sick for Neptune's Daughter.

She missed Doc's teasing and Pete's stories about his two families. She missed Orvil's cooking. Jordan may have called their cook a chef, but he paled in comparison to Orvil. She even missed the ship's clowns, Charlie and Sam. But most of all she missed her Captain.

"I know that look." Jordan said on approach. "You're lonely aren't you?"

"I miss my friends. I've nothing to do on your ship. No one here likes me, except you and your father."

"I'm sorry for that," Jordan said sincerely. "I was hoping by now Phillip would do or say something! He's not even talking to me except to take orders."

"Things in our lives never seem to go as we expect them too," Margaret sighed.

They heard the man in the nest call down. "Ship off the starboard bow!"

Both the women headed for the bridge. Jordan stood beside her father as he scanned the horizon with his glass.

"I make it out to be Spanish," said Capitaine L'Orange.

"See any guns?" Jordan asked.

He hesitated for a few more moments. "Ha! Ha! Call all hands, Jordan! We've got a prize ship. No guns."

Jordan rang the bell. "Prepare yourselves! We've got a prize ship!"

Margaret's eyes widened. They were pirates! She pulled Jordan aside. "I thought you said you worked for the government delivering dispatches?" Her tone was harsh.

"We do," Jordan said. "We are also empowered by the government to take Spanish ships. We're not pirates. We're privateers working for France."

"I don't see what the bloody difference is?" Margaret was angry.

"If you don't know, I don't have time to tell you. So I suggest that if you don't want to participate — go below. We're going to become quite busy," Jordan said sharply.

Margaret went below to her quarters. She looked out the porthole to see what was going on. As the Antoinette closed in on its prey, a shot was fired from the cannon, and it blew a hole in the railing of the other ship. Shortly afterwards, the two ships were connected by grappling hooks. She saw men with cutlasses on the deck of the other ship. They were getting ready to repel boarders.

Margaret paced back and forth in her cabin. Her mind was racing.

What if the other ship won?

She'd become their prisoner and she didn't speak Spanish. There was also the possibility she could be killed.

What if something happened to Jordan or her father? The crew of the Antoinette would probably kill me!

"God help me. Now, I'm joining pirates," Margaret mumbled. She ran back on deck. The only thing she had to defend herself with was her knife. She saw Jordan with cutlass in hand.

"Jordan!" Margaret shouted.

Jordan looked in her direction. Then Margaret shouted in English so the others wouldn't understand.

"Throw me a bloody sword! If anything happens to you, I'm dead whichever way the tide turns."

Jordan smiled and tossed her a sword. She had a feeling Margaret wouldn't just stay below, so she had an extra just in case. "I knew you wouldn't let me down," Jordan said.

Even though the other ship tried to break free from the Antoinette's clutches, the effort was fruitless. Capitaine L'Orange led the assault on the other ship. Jordan commanded the men on theirs. The fight was waged on both ships with men crossing over from both sides. Margaret and Jordan fought back to back. This was the first time Margaret's skill with a sword had been put to the real test. Even while she fought, she was reminded of the time when she, William and Claude waged a mock battle and she pretended to be a pirate. Now she'd joined one.

As Margaret fought, she tried to just maim, not kill. But then she looked towards the bridge and saw Phillip about to be attacked from behind while he was engaged in battle with another.

"Phillip!" she called out. Margaret pulled her knife and threw it.

Phillip turned around after dispatching his foe just in time to see his would be attacker fall. He was surprise to see that it was Marc, his rival for Jordan's attention, who'd saved his life. He saw the boy was again engaged in another fight, so he retrieved Marc's knife and wiped it off. He would return it to him later.

The battle was short lived. The crew of the Antoinette was too much for the Spanish merchant ship. It's Captain surrendered and what was left of his crew were rounded up and locked in their own brig. Everything of value aboard the Spanish ship was taken. The Antoinette's crew left them just enough water and food to make the nearest port. They only wanted goods of value — not lives that were unnecessary to take. Normally they would have taken the ship as well and sold her crew, but not this time since they were on their way to India and didn't want the extra burden.

Capitaine L'Orange also didn't worry about being reported to Spain for privateering, for they always covered the name of their ship before a battle, and he removed his black wig exposing his nearly bald pate.

Margaret looked at all the devastation around her. The injured and the dead were returned to their own ships. The deck was stained red with blood. She saw severed limbs and a head lying next to its body. Margaret went to the ship's rail and retched.

Jordan came to her side. "Death and blood is a hard thing to see, but you get used to it."

Tears were starting to form in Margaret's eyes, but she quickly wiped them away. "I've seen death and blood, and that isn't what bothers me. Killing does!" she exclaimed in English. "I'm going to my quarters." She turned and went below.

Margaret slammed the door. She had blood on her clothes and blood on her hands. She'd had blood on her hands before, but that was from helping wounded men. Now she had blood on her hands because she drew it! No matter what Jordan said, killing was one thing she didn't want to get used to.

It was several hours before the Antoinette was underway again. Margaret didn't leave her quarters. She looked out the porthole and saw that the Spanish ship was sailing in the opposite direction. Jordan hadn't come to see her, and for right now she was glad. She didn't feel like talking to anyone. Then there was a knock at the door.

"Go away, Jordan! I'm in no mood for conversation right now," she shouted in English. But what returned was not Jordan's voice, and he was speaking French.

"It is Phillip Jacard! I want to talk with you."

Margaret opened the door. "What is it?" Her tone was stern.

"May I come in?"

There was nothing threatening in his voice, so she opened the door wider and stood to the side. "It's your ship." She walked over to her bed and sat down.

Phillip entered the room and closed the door. "You fought well today."

"Not by choice. Purely out of self-preservation, I assure you."

Margaret was still angry over the events of the day.

"Here! This belongs to you." Phillip handed her the knife. "I want to thank you for my life and wanted to know why you bothered?"

Margaret laughed, but not because she thought it was funny. "That's a stupid question. The man was about to kill you!"

"I only asked because I would have let them kill you."

"That's comforting." Her tone was sarcastic.

"Anyway," Phillip sighed, "I still owe you my life and I just wanted to say that I'll stay out of your way where Jordan is concerned. When we get to port, I'm going to leave the ship."

Margaret rolled her eyes.

Oh, great! All that play-acting for nothing.

"So why leave?" Margaret inquired.

"I've loved Jordan for years," Phillip replied.

"Then why haven't you done anything about it?"

"Capitaine L'Orange is very protective of Jordan. He threw the last man that asked for her hand overboard. When Jordan became sick, I decided that when she got better, I would ask the Capitaine for her hand. If he threw me overboard, so be it. I realized that if Jordan wasn't in my life, my life would have no meaning."

Margaret leaned her head back and laughed. "She kidnapped me for nothing!"

"You forget — I don't speak English!" Phillip frowned. He didn't appreciate his feelings being laughed at.

"I apologize," Margaret rephrased. "I wasn't laughing at you. I was laughing at the situation. Sit down — we need to talk."

"I don't see what more there is to talk about!" He was becoming angry.

"I know you don't see. That is exactly why we need to talk. I have no love interest in Jordan."

Phillip put his hand on his cutlass. "You mean to tell me you're just toying with her affections!"

"No," Margaret's tone was even, but she did have her knife in hand ready just in case he became violent. "I mean to tell you that Jordan is toying with yours."

"You have me confused." He dropped his hand to his side.

"Jordan kidnapped me to make you jealous. Neither of us have anything between us but a strained friendship. I just agreed to help her for my own reasons."

Phillip laughed. "That bitch! She's done nothing but insult me since you've been aboard."

"And you should also know that the Capitaine was in on the plan. Why do you think he hasn't thrown me overboard? Did you really think he'd let me, and Englishman, have a true relationship with his daughter, even though I helped save her life?"

"That did cross my mind."

"So now that you know, why don't you just come out and tell her how you feel?" Margaret asked.

Phillip started to pace the floor. "Oh, no! Not now. I might love her but after what she has put me through — it's her turn. If she wants me, she's going to have to do the asking. She can get down on one knee to me." He stormed out the door.

Margaret just shook her head

This is ridiculous!

"And everyone thinks that red-heads are stubborn. Ha!" she said aloud as she flopped down on the bed. "We have nothing on the French!"

A few hours later, there was another knock at the door. But before Margaret could answer, Jordan just walked in and flopped down in the chair.

"Won't you come in," Margaret said sarcastically. She saw the look of frustration on Jordan's face.

"I just don't understand it," Jordan complained. "After all we've done to try and make him jealous, it just hasn't worked! He approached me a while ago. It looked like he was going to say something, then he just walked off and laughed. I guess he really didn't love me after all."

Margaret hesitated in answering. It was apparent that Phillip hadn't said anything to her about their conversation earlier.

"Well! Don't you have anything to say?" Irritation laced Jordan's voice. "If you're still mad, get over it! This is what I do."

Margaret got up off the bed ignoring her last comment. "If you love him, then why the bloody hell don't you just say something?" she yelled at her. "You dress like a man. You dole out punishment to the men and order them around like other men. The only thing you don't do is piss like a man and sometime I wonder about that! So why don't you just get down on a knee and ask him — like a man!"

"You're one to talk! You do the same thing on your ship, except give the orders. Why didn't you just tell your man?"

"That's different," Margaret huffed. But after she'd said it, she wondered why it was.

"How is it different!" Jordan replied.

Margaret hesitated a moment then walked to the porthole and looked out. "You're right," she replied sadly. "If I ever see him again, I'll tell him who and what I really am, and how I feel. I'm tired of pretending."

Jordan leaned back in her chair and grinned. "Too late, I already have."

Margaret turned around quickly. "When?"

"Remember when we went to your cabin? When your back was turned, I left him a note. I told him where we were going and how to find you, if he wanted you."

"You didn't!" Margaret didn't know whether to hit her or hug her.

"I did. I considered that I was doing you a favor. You would never have told him. You would have left his ship to escape having to."

Margaret stood there in thought. She'd planned to do that very thing, and then started to laugh.

"And what do you find so funny?" Jordan snapped.

"Well, guess what? Phillip knows how you feel also. He came to my cabin to return my knife. He said he was going to leave the ship at the next port. I saved his life during the battle, and he said he wasn't going to stand in our way. So I told him what we were doing to him."

"No wonder he laughed at me," Jordan said sadly. "He didn't love me after all."

"Jordan, you kidnapped me and played all those little games for nothing!" Margaret sat down beside her. "He's loved you for years. He told me so. When he thought you were going to die, he decided to risk being thrown overboard by your father and ask him for your hand."

"He said that? You wouldn't lie to me, would you?"

"No, but now he's angry. He was going to ask you, but now he's not. If you want him, you're going to have to do the asking."

"The bastard! How can I ask him?"

Margaret shrugged. "That's what he told me. If you want him, you get down on one knee."

Jordan paced the floor trying to think of what to do. Then she stopped. "I'll do it. But how do I do it?"

Margaret thought for a moment. "Is there any women's clothing from your — acquisitions from today?"

"Yes. Why?"

"Then take me to where these items are, and I'll tell you what to do."

Jordan took Margaret to the hold where they found several trunks of women's clothing and accessories. It seemed that the Spanish ship they had captured was transporting someone's household. There was everything from clothing and jewelry to fancy furniture and a piano.

Margaret rummaged through the clothing and picked out what she thought would be the most flattering on her, and then they went to Jordan's quarters to have her put them on. The dress was blue satin, draped with black lace. The low cut bodice was a little tight for her ample breast, but it just added to the look Margaret was going for.

"I don't see how women wear these things!" Jordan complained. "All that material and hoops underneath. How would one pass through a door without getting stuck?"

"Believe me, you look beautiful!" Margaret said. "Now quit fidgeting, so I can finish your hair."

"Are you done yet?" Jordan was getting impatient, for Margaret wasn't allowing her to look in the mirror until she was finished.

"Almost," she said, as she fastened a string of pearls around Jordan's neck. "There, I'm done."

Jordan stepped in front of the mirror. "Is that me?"

Margaret laughed. That was what she had said when she first saw her transformed into a boy. "That's you, and I think you look gorgeous."

"If feel half-naked!" she exclaimed. Her chest was bunched up with too much cleavage showing, and the puffy sleeves hung half off her shoulders. "Are you sure I won't fall out of this?" she added, tugging at the bodice, trying to cover the top of her breast.

"You don't like it," Margaret sighed.

"It's not that, it's just uncomfortable. Remember, I've never worn anything like this before. My regular clothing feels better."

"I agree. But when you're fishing, you need the right bate and believe me, you'd catch a whale if you were in London."

"Well, here goes nothing," Jordan sighed. She left her quarters and ran into her father.

"Jordan!" he exclaimed. "What is this?" He'd never seen his daughter like this before. She looked beautiful.

"I'm going fishing," Jordan replied as she passed him.

Capitaine L'Orange saw Margaret standing outside his daughter's quarters.

"Marc, who goes fishing in a dress?" he shrugged.

"Ah, but you didn't ask what type of fish," Margaret grinned and gave him a wink.

He stood there for a moment in thought and then he laughed. "Would it be a species of Jacard?"

"It would be," Margaret replied. Both followed after Jordan.

Jordan stepped out on deck with head held high as normal. She looked at the faces of the men standing around. Their jaws dropped and eyes popped. Phillip had the watch and was standing by the ship's rail looking out over the sea.

"Phillip," Jordan called out in a soft voice.

He turned around and his eyes also widened. "Jordan?"

Jordan swallowed her pride. "I would like to apologize for my behavior towards you. My only excuse is that I wanted you to want me."

Phillip smiled and approached her. "So you dress up like a piece of sugar candy to tempt my eyes? Jordan, you look beautiful in anything you wear." Then he folded his arms. "I'm tired of your games." He turned around and looked back out to the sea.

Jordan felt humiliated. With head held high, she turned around and started to go below, but Margaret blocked her way.

"I brought you something just in case this didn't work." Margaret took Jordan's whip out from behind her back and grinned. "When you go fishing, you need a pole. This will have to do in place of one."

Jordan gave her a warm smile as she took the whip and wheeled around. She uncoiled the leather, whirled it around in the air and with a flick of her wrist cracked it. "Phillip!" she called. This time her voice was more commanding. He turned around quickly.

"How dare you!" she shouted cracking her whip again, and taking a few steps forward. "I am wearing this falderal just for you, and you accuse me of playing games!" The whip snapped again. She twirled it around her head and snatched Phillip around the waist, drawing him towards her. "Now, I want to know. Do you, or do you not love me?"

Phillip laughed and put his arms around her. "Now, this is the Jordan I love. I love firecrackers, not sugar-teats."

Her voice softened. "Phillip, I can't get down on my knee in this dress, but..."

Phillip put his finger to her lips. "You don't have to ask. I love you. Will you have me to be your husband?"

Jordan wrapped her arms around him and kissed him. The crew around cheered and shouted their approvals. Capitaine L'Orange stepped out on deck. He'd discretely been watching from below.

"Jordan, is this man bothering you? If he is, I'll have him cast overboard," he said, trying to keep a serious expression.

"Father, if you throw him overboard, I'm afraid I'll have to go in after him." Jordan gave him a wink.

Capitaine L'Orange folded his arms, and tapped his thumb to his chin. "Well, in that case, I guess we will just have to have a wedding. I can't just let crewman go around kissing my daughter."

Again the crew shouted their approval. The Capitaine announced that the wedding would take place in one hour, giving Phillip time to dress appropriately to match Jordan's frills.

The ship dropped anchored. The winds and the sea were calm. There was an orange glow in the sky as the sun started to drop into the sea. When the time came, the Capitaine performed the ceremony. Jordan had picked Margaret to be her Man-of-Honor, and Phillip had picked the crewman Alfonse, to be his Best Man.

The ceremony was short and simple and when it was over, a box of wine that was captured from the Spanish ship was broken out and everyone toasted and celebrated into the night. The only one not allowed wine was Margaret. Jordan made sure her glass was filled with tea for the toast. There was no telling what she would do or say if she drank.

Margaret retired to her quarters after the evening wore down. The crew warmed up to her after they found out that Jordan was just using her as bate to catch Phillip. She lay down in her bed thinking about the evening's events, and wondered what her Captain was thinking about since he now knew she was a woman. Would he come after her? Or leave her to fend for herself?

CHAPTER 20
"Stranded in Pondicherry"

After months of travel, Margaret was glad they were finally about to reach their destination. They'd stopped at a few coastal ports of Africa along the way for provisions. Water, fruit and vegetables were desperately needed. Two of the men were suffering from scurvy, and she'd had a miserable bout with dysentery.

Margaret leaned on the railing to watch the coast line as it grew larger. Jordan joined her. "Anxious for land?"

"Definitely!" Margaret exclaimed. "I've never been at sea that long before. I am anxious to feel dry land beneath my feet again."

"For me, it's almost the opposite," Jordan replied. "Land is alright for awhile, but since I was born on the water that is where I like to be."

Margaret changed the subject. Jordan and Phillip had argued for most of the day yesterday. They always argued, but they always made up. One of their arguments had been about her. Phillip was beginning to worry about her relationship with Jordan, so Margaret gave her permission to tell him her true gender if he promised to keep it a secret.

"So, have you and Phillip made up yet?"

"We fight, we make love, we fight, then we make love again!" she grinned. "I am happily married."

Margaret laughed and looked back to the horizon. She wondered if her Captain had started out after her or not. It was hard to know.

"By now, I can read your mind. I know that look," Jordan said. "What are you going to do? Stay and wait for him? Or go back to England on your own?"

Margaret sighed. "I don't know."

"I say you don't wait!" Jordan exclaimed as she lightly slapped the rail. She reached her hand out and snatched empty air. "You grab opportunity, and if she knocks, open the door. Don't wait or it might pass you by."

"But what if on the other side of that door is disaster? Trouble seems to follow me lately."

"Then have a sword in one hand and a whip in the other," Jordan laughed. "I taught you how to use one and you're fairly skilled."

"I don't have a whip," Margaret replied.

She punched Margaret lightly on the shoulder. "You know what I mean."

Margaret laughed and then added with a sigh, "I wish you were headed back to France."

"Sorry," Jordan shrugged. "We are off to the Caribbean in a week. You know you're welcome to come along."

"Thanks, but no. I'm not cut out for your line of work."

Jordan nodded. "This I know. When ever we take a ship you yell at me like a wounded banshee and then pout for a few days."

Margaret gave her a discomforting look. "You also know how I feel about that."

They'd come across two other Spanish ships that they relieved of their goods. They also spotted and English merchant ship, but out of consideration for their guest, they let it go on its way. If it hadn't been headed in the wrong direction, Margaret would have asked the Capitaine to flag it down and transfer her.

"Be that as it may, you know you have a share in the prize ships we've taken," Jordan said.

"Blood money," Margaret huffed.

"And a little bit of your blood was spilled in that last encounter. You're entitled."

Margaret rubbed her forearm. The last time they attacked a ship, she had the misfortune to get cut when she had to fend off two antagonist. Luckily, it was just a scratch and didn't require stitching.

Jordan continued. "I know you don't want it, but you'll still have your share anyway. You'll need the money until you fine a way to earn your keep in India."

Margaret just shrugged and continued to ponder her situation.

"Well, I'll leave you to your musing. I've got a ship to dock." Jordan, sensed she wanted to be alone.

As they pulled into port, Margaret could smell a variety of spices coming from the town. She could see street venders in the marketplace. The most distinctive scents in the air came from cinnamon and ginger. It was a chef's paradise of aromas.

When they went ashore, she thought she would see more of the natives of India, but Jordan said that this port was the French quarter. She saw a few Indian women, and they were dressed very colorfully. The material was just wrapped around them, instead of sewn and pieced together as European styles.

The Capitaine, Jordan, Phillip, and Margaret, got into a carriage and headed straight for the Governor's office. To Margaret's surprise, Capitaine L'Orange just walked right in without being announced. There was a man sitting at a desk and another in a chair beside it.

"Ah ha! Casper! You're looking as ugly as ever!" said Capitaine L'Orange.

The man behind the desk stood. "Jon-Pierre! You old pirate! No one has hung you yet?" He laughed and came out from behind the desk.

"Hang a L'Orange? Never!" The two men hugged and kissed each other on the cheeks.

Margaret looked at the two men. If they hadn't been wearing different clothing, they would have looked like a pair of bookends. They sported the same style of black wig and the same cut of the mustaches. Casper L'Orange was the Capitaine's identical twin brother and Governor-General of Pondicherry.

The Governor turned to Jordan. "How did you get so pretty with a father as ugly as him?"

Jordan gave him a hug and a kiss. "Because I look like you, Uncle."

"So true, so true," he laughed. He turned to his twin. "Jon-Pierre, when are you going to quit dressing my niece like a boy? She's now a beautiful woman."

But it was Jordan that answered. "Just once, Uncle. The first and only time I wore one was at my wedding." Jordan put her arm around Phillip.

The Governor congratulated the newlyweds and welcomed Phillip to the family with a kiss on both cheeks. Afterward the other introductions were made.

The man sitting by the desk was Alec Mitchell. Margaret thought him quite handsome. He had light brown hair and a kind smile. But in his dark brown eyes, she sensed a deep sadness behind them. Margaret was next to be introduced.

"Uncle, this is my friend, Marcus Allen," said Jordan.

"Marcus Allen?" Casper L'Orange thought for a moment as he tapped his temple trying to jog his thoughts. "Why does that name sound so familiar?"

Margaret's eyebrows raised in surprised.

Who would know me here in India?

"Remember, Casper, it was in the newspaper from Liverpool that I gave you last week," said Alec Mitchell.

"Ah yes — the boxing tournament. Neptune's Daughter won this year," the Governor replied.

Margaret laughed. "That was months and months ago!"

"News from France and England travels slow in these parts," Alec Mitchell replied. "Did you quit your ship?"

"No sir." Margaret looked at Jordan. "Let's just say I played a key part in Jordan's wedding. I plan on returning to my ship when I can."

After a few moments of pleasantries, the Capitaine gave his brother a sealed document, and Mr. Mitchell stood to leave. Margaret noticed that he had to stand with the help of a cane.

"Please, Alec, you may not want to leave as of yet. This notice may concern you," said the Governor.

"Is it what we thought?" Alec asked.

"It is," he replied in a huff. "Politics. I hate politics! England and France are at it again."

Jon-Pierre laughed. "Then why, brother, are you a politician?"

"I'm not. I'm a business man with a title and a little power to get things done."

Alec sighed as he leaned on his cane. "It's a shame their disputes have to touch us here"

"Well, it's a good thing you sold your properties when you did, otherwise you might have taken a big loss."

"Thanks for your concern, my friend, but I've survived these inconveniences before."

"Would you mind telling me what's going on?" asked the Jon-Pierre.

Casper frowned at his brother. "As if you don't read everything that crosses your hands before I do."

"Yes, but it's not official until you've read it," Jon-Pierre replied.

"Another trade embargo." Casper shook his head. "No English merchant ships are to be allowed in our ports."

After hearing that, Margaret pulled Jordan aside. "What about me!" she exclaimed in a whisper. "How am I going to get home?"

"Just be calm," Jordan said to ease her. "When my uncle's guest leaves, we'll ask him."

The men discussed the trade embargo for a few moments then Alec

Mitchell bid everyone farewell and slowly limped out the door.

Casper grasped the lapels of his coat and shook his head. "Alec is a good friend. I feel sorry for him. I wish I could help."

"What happened to him?" Jordan asked.

"He's raising a small son on his own. His wife was killed by a tiger three years ago. Alec tried to shoot the beast, but his gun misfired, and he was ripped from groin to knee before someone got it. He damn near died and the doctor tell him he still might. But so far he's cheated death for three years."

"What are you trying to help him with?" Margaret asked. She felt sorry for the man.

"He's going back to England. He needs a governess that knows English to tutor his son, but she also has to be willing to go back with him. The boy speaks mostly French and Tamil, the main language of the Indians around here."

"Speaking of help," Jordan said. "Marc was expecting to meet his ship here. Is that still possible?"

"If it's English, I'm afraid not," Casper said. "The only English ship allowed in or out of the area is the Arrow Star. She's carrying several French dignitaries and isn't expected back here for another three to four months."

Margaret turned and walked to the window. She closed her eyes for a moment trying not to cry. Jordan came to her side.

"Now what am I going to do?" Margaret asked.

Jordan could tell there was a lump in her throat and she was fighting to hold on to her dignity. "I'm sorry, Marc." Her words were sincere. She looked out the window and watched as Alec Mitchell carefully climbed into a carriage. An idea struck her. "Marc! Quickly, come with me!"

Before Margaret could say anything, Jordan grabbed her by the hand and pulled her along as they ran out the door.

"Where are we going?" Margaret asked.

"You'll see!" Jordan said excitedly. She shouted to the man in the carriage. "Monsieur Mitchell! Please, wait a moment!"

The man raised his hand and the coachman stopped. Jordan and Margaret ran to meet it.

"Yes, what can I do for you?" he replied.

"My Uncle has told us you have a need for a governess or should I say a tutor for your son," Jordan replied.

"Don't tell me you're applying?" he laughed. "I thought you just got married?"

"Not for me, but for my friend, Marc. He needs to get back to England and you need a teacher."

"Thank you for the offer, but I think I need more than just a ship's cabin boy," he replied politely. He turned back to his coachman and ordered him to drive on.

Jordan nudged Margaret. "Say something, Marc!" she whispered. "He's your opportunity. Grab it!"

Margaret finally overcame her loss for words. "Mr. Mitchell!" she said, this time in English. "I'm not just your average ship's boy. I'm a well educated, read, write and speak both French and English fluently. Not only can I teach your son to read and write both languages, I play piano, I'm versed in Shakespeare, I'm a chess master and I can teach him to fence," she said with enthusiasm. She folded her arms and added, "I can also do something a traditional governess wouldn't dare to do!"

"And what's that?" he asked out of curiosity.

"Climb a tree," Margaret replied with a shrug and a grin.

Alec Mitchell thought for a moment. "How old are you?"

"Eighteen," she replied, giving her true age.

He hesitated again. He'd never thought of hiring a male as a teacher. Yet, it might be a good thing. This Marc could teach his son some of the things he was no longer capable of doing himself.

"What are you asking for wages?"

Margaret and Jordan smiled at each other.

"As far as I'm concerned, a place to sleep, food to eat, a bath and paid passage to England."

Alec laughed. "You drive a hard bargain! I'll give you a trial for a week to see how things go. Can you have your things ready and be back here in an hour?"

"We'll make sure of it!" Jordan replied for her.

They went back to the office to inform Jordan's father of what had just transpired. Margaret thanked him for his hospitality, even though they kidnapped her, then she, Jordan and Phillip went back to the ship.

Margaret gathered her meager belongings. All she had were the two changes of clothing that Jordan had given her.

"I've got something for you." Jordan handed her a black leather whip. "This is just in case opportunity turns into devastation."

Margaret laughed and gave her a hug. "Jordan, even though you're a pirate, you're still my best friend."

"Privateer," she said with a laugh. "Are you ever going to understand the difference?"

"No!" Margaret pursed her lips.

"I have something for you also," said Phillip. He handed her a sack of coins. "This is your share." Then Jordan whispered something in his ear, and he gave his wife a strange look. "Are you sure?"

Jordan nodded.

"As you wish," Phillip said with a shrug. He turned back to Margaret. "This is from both of us — Margaret!" He took her in his arms, dipped her down and gave her a long, passionate kiss as Jordan stood by and laughed.

"Wow!" Margaret exclaimed when he finally released her. "I won't so easily forget that!" She looked at Jordan. "No wonder you wanted to marry him."

"That is just to remind you what it is like to be a woman," Jordan said, putting her arm around her husband.

The three of them left the ship and headed back toward the Governor's office to wait for Alec Mitchell. Margaret was both anxious and nervous. Becoming a governess is what she'd planned to do when she had enough money to leave the Neptune's Daughter and her Captain. She started to think about him again. Maybe this was just the thing she needed to get him off her mind. Jordan was right. What if her Captain didn't come for her?

CHAPTER 21
"The Captain's Dilemma"

It took the Neptune's Daughter days to limp back to port. The ship had to be in dry dock for a month, but finally she was ready. Captain Withers and Mr. Richards went to the shipping office to try and get their routing changed for this trip.

"I'm sorry, Captain," the man said. "It's impossible! There are no ships allowed in that area right now."

"I told you that my boy is there, and I need to get him back!" Todd insisted, pounding his fist on the desk.

"Listen, I'm not any happier about this embargo than you are. Pondicherry is one of my biggest suppliers of India spices and sugars. Now I'm forced to purchase elsewhere. The cost is higher and I'm forced to raise prices which upsets my customers."

"Maybe I'll just go on my own," Todd replied.

"You can't! Be reasonable, Captain. Do you want to single handedly start a war?" the man said, as he stood and leaned on his desk. "Besides, they'd blow you out of the water without the proper recognition and papers. Then where would your boy be? Plus think about the other aspect."

"What aspect?" the Captain huffed.

"You've got the best route and contract in this company. If you just left it, another ship would jump at the chance to take your spot — especially with this political headache. The Arrow Star is the only ship allowed in or out of that region, and it's on its way there now."

"He's right, Captain," Mr. Richards added. "We all want Marc back safely. But you've got to think of the rest of the crew. If we lose this route and contract, we may lose some good crewmen to other ships. Then there's the possibility that they may not get work. That storm sunk four ships and damaged three besides ours."

The Captain sat down on the edge of the desk and folded his arms. "I know your right," he sighed.

"Marc is a smart boy. More than likely, he'll find a way to book passage on the Arrow Star, or hire on as part of their crew. You also might consider that the letter you received from that woman on the Antoinette was a lie and they never went to India. We will have traveled there for nothing," Mr. Richards added.

"I'll tell you what, Captain," said the shipping manager. "As soon as this embargo is lifted, I'll let you know. I'm sure Captain Jennings on the Calcutta, will switch his India route for yours for a year. Then I'll guarantee that you'll get your route back when you return. Is it agreed?"

"I agree," the Captain said reluctantly.

"Good," the man sighed. "Now, can Mr. Richards and I get down to the details of this next shipment?"

"I'll want that guarantee for the India route trade in writing," said Mr. Richards, before they began their other business.

"If you've got things handled here, Ben," said Todd. "I'll go back to the ship."

"Aye sir," replied the paymaster.

The Captain slowly walked back to the ship. He thought about his conversation with Doc when he found out that Marc was a woman. Doc had told him that he was bound by his Hippocratic Oath not to tell. He said everything had to be normal for her own safety in dealing with the crew on a daily basis. He also said he didn't see a problem. She did her share of the load without complain. Doc also pointed out the fact that she worked harder than any boy they'd had on the ship — besides Jake. She even entered a boxing ring of all things — and won!

Todd felt guilty as hell for subjecting a woman to the things she endured. He was also embarrassed for not being able to tell the difference between a boy and a woman. But despite that, he was proud of her accomplishments. He was confused. Was his desire to have Marc back because he had an affection for the boy she pretended to be? Or was it now the woman that he wanted?

When he got back to the ship, he was approached by a few of her friends and the commanders.

"What's the word, Capt'n?" asked Pete.

"The word is trade embargo with France. Pondicherry is off limits for the time being," he replied. Then he took a deep breath and let it out. "It's back to business as usual until after this political battle is over." He addressed the commanders. "Pete, Levi, Doug! Start making preparations for taking on provisions. We'll be leaving in two days."

"Aye, sir," replied the three men.

"Damn Frenchies!" Charlie exclaimed, before he went back to his duties. "Well, all I can say is, since that pretty bitch took him, I hope Marc took the hell out of her!"

As frustrated as he was, Todd couldn't help but laugh at how funny that sounded, knowing what he knew about Marc. He recalled some of the — man to man — talks he'd had with Marc giving him advice on women. Thought about that dream he'd had when he was ill filtered in. He'd asked Doc about it, but he was as tight lipped as an oyster holding on to its pearl. Was it Marc in bed with him? He had to laugh. Why else would he have had a lump on the back of his head when Doc said there was none the night before?

He went down to his quarters to look over his charts, but he couldn't concentrate and lay his head down on the desk. But then there was a knock at the door.

He raised his head and answered. "Come!"

"Sorry ta' bother ya' Capt'n, but there's a man topside that wants ta' speak with ya," said Pete. "He says it's important."

"Show him in."

A few moments later, Pete entered with the man.

"Captain Withers?" the man asked.

"Yes," Todd extended his hand and they shook. But the man was strangely familiar. "Have we met, sir? I usually don't forget a face."

The man laughed lightly. "Not exactly. May we speak privately?" The man looked back at Pete.

The Captain dismissed the commander with a nod. "So, who are you and what can I do for you?"

"My name is Marcus. Marcus Allen Wallingham, and I think we need to talk."

CHAPTER 22
"A Temporary Life"

Margaret got into the carriage with Alec Mitchell, and then waved good-bye to Jordan and Phillip.

"I see you're punctual," Mr. Mitchell said as they road off.

"As Mr. Taggart, the watch commander of my ship says, if you're not on time, don't show up. You pay the consequences either way. Being late for your watch was one of his pet peeves," she replied. She then changed the subject. "Tell me about your son?"

Alec Mitchell could see that he may have made a good choice after all. The young man was right down to business.

"Very well," he said with a smile. "His name is Drake. He just turned seven a few days ago. He loves the sea, sailing ships and elephants."

"Elephants!" Margaret exclaimed. "I didn't know India had elephants?"

"Apparently, geography isn't on your curriculum," he laughed.

"Well, give me a book and what I don't know, we can learn together," she replied, trying to cover her inadequacy.

"Marc, I can see you and I are going to get along fine," he replied.

They continued to talk about Drake. She also learned that the boy had nightmares about tigers on occasion. He was only four when his mother was killed by one. While his family was on an outing with friends, the animal bounded into their campsite. Silvia, his wife, had run into their tent to protect their sleeping son. The tiger followed her before anyone had a chance to get their guns. She'd covered their son tightly when she found no escape so the animal couldn't get him. It mauled her to death. He said it turned on him after his gun misfired and he too would have died if another man hadn't killed it.

Margaret could sense that the subject pained him and their was a long silence and then the subject was changed.

"What business are you in?" Margaret asked.

"I had a large field of sugar cane and was the largest grower in the region of varieties of pepper," he replied.

"Sugar and spice and all that is nice," she laughed.

"That's what Silvia used to say," he replied.

Margaret felt embarrassed. "I'm sorry if I've brought up a memory."

Alec just smiled. "Don't be. Those are the good memories. They're always welcome. It's the bad ones I try to put behind me. We can't dwell in the past. We've only got the future."

Margaret nodded her agreement. That's what she needed to do — look to her future and not to her past.

"You said you *were* in sugar and pepper. Did you sell out?"

"I had no choice. The land and the business had been in my wife's family for decades. She was an only child. Silvia's mother died the year after we were married, and her father died a year after Silvia's death. Before he passed, he left everything to Drake with me as custodian. The doctor's keep telling me that they're surprised I still live. With my life in the balance, I need to make sure Drake's future is secure. So I sold everything and put it in trust until he's old enough to know what he wants to do with his life."

"Do you have family in England?" Margaret asked.

"You sure are full of questions," Alec replied with a laugh. "I feel like I'm the one being interviewed."

"It's my inner cat," she grinned. "It's always curious."

They continued on their way and this time it was Alec who asked the questions. She told him her fake history about her family life. She hated telling him the lie, especially with what happened to his. But Claude had told her, if you tell the story, make sure it's the same one, to everyone, or it may come back and bite you.

It wasn't long before they reached their destination. Alec had the coachman stop on a ridge so Margaret could have a good look at where she was going to live.

"There it is," he said with pride. "My wife designed it. It's a piece of France with a touch of India."

It was a modest villa overlooking the sea and set in the middle of a garden with colorful flowers and palms surrounding it. There was a stone fence bordering a rock ledge with an opening and a set of steps leading down to the beach.

"Your home is beautiful!" Margaret exclaimed.

"I know," he sighed. "I hate to leave it. The new owner, Taylor Hansford, is in the same bind I am — the trade embargo. He can't get here yet, and

I can't leave. Even though I no longer own it, he's asked me to stay and oversee the property. He sent a man down as foreman, but I don't trust him."

Margaret saw the concern on his face, but it quickly disappeared, and he had the coachman drive on. When they got to the house, Alec ordered his driver to go to the neighbor's house to pick up Drake.

Margaret was introduced to the small household staff, which consisted of an Indian family that had worked there for years. The houseman, Taran, and his wife, Sri, the cook, were about middle aged. Their son, Sanjay, was a strapping young man who took care of the garden and occasionally acted as chauffeur and drove the carriage. He was twenty and due to wed in a few months when his promised bride had come of age and then she too was also promised a position in the household.

Alec took Margaret on a tour of the house. Tapestries of all varieties hung on the walls, and native flowers in large vases decorated the home. The dining area and the living area were combined. The kitchen was separate. There was also a large office area where he conducted his business. But Alec said they spent most of their time on the veranda, which was in the center of a huge flower garden with a beautiful view of the sea. Upstairs were the six bedrooms. Each was tastefully decorated with a flavor of India. He showed her where she was to sleep and put her things. The household servants had a separate dwelling just off the main house.

"Well, what do you think?" Alec asked, after the grand tour. "Will you be comfortable here?"

"I think I'd rather be here than at the royal palace!" she exclaimed, "There's only one more thing I need."

"Oh? And what might that be?" He wondered what more a boy of his station in life could want.

"A bath!" In keeping with her Marc identity, she sniffed her underarm. "I'm afraid I'm causing a stench that might wilt the flowers. I haven't had a proper one in months."

Alec laughed hardily. "I think that can be arranged. I'll have Taran take you to the bath house. When you're done, we can discuss Drake's education in depth."

"Aye sir, Mr. Mitchell," Margaret said.

Again Alec laughed. "You're not aboard a ship, Marc. Just call me Alec. I'm an informal man."

"Very well, Alec, I'll see you shortly." Margaret gave him a smile and followed Taran to the bathhouse.

To Margaret's surprise, the bath house consisted of a natural hot spring and a showering area. It was surrounded by a fence for privacy and open to the sky. Stepping stones surrounded the pool. It was also landscaped with palms and flowers with water bearing statues decorating the area.

After Taran filled the overhead container of the shower with hot water from the spring, he explained its use. "Wash in shower first. When clean, use hot spring," said Taran..

"Thank you," Margaret said as he handed her a towel and soap.

He started to leave then stopped and turned back around. "Is one thing Taran and wife, Sri, would like to know?"

"Yes?"

"Why does Mademoiselle Marc pretend to be Monsieur Marc?"

Margaret's eyes widened with surprise. The man had caught her off guard. "Does Monsieur Alec know? You won't tell will you?" she asked.

"Taran not even know," he said with a laugh. "Sri tell. She know first look. She say pretty girl who dress like boy not make sense. So, she want to know. If good reason we not tell."

Margaret sighed. "I worked on a ship of men…"

But Taran raised his hand. "Taran now know," he said with a grin. "Is very good reason. I tell Sri. She will bring some of son's clothes. Yours smell not so good. You tell Monsieur Alec what you are when ready."

When he left, Margaret undressed and mumbled, "I may as well have a sign on my forehead that says girl in disguise!"

She entered the shower and pulled the chain to release the water. The shower alone made her feel human again. But when she got into the hot spring, she thought she had died and gone to heaven. She lay back and looked up into the sky as the warm bubbling waters relaxed her muscles and calmed her spirits.

A few minutes later, Sri came in with clean clothing. "Not stay long in spring. Will make fall asleep," she said. "Don't want Monsieur Marc to drown."

"I could see how one would," Margaret replied. "I feel I could take a nap now."

Sri bent down to the pool and whispered, "When Monsieur Marc decides to be pretty girl again, Sri have pretty dress."

"Thank you, Sri, but I think I'll stay Monsieur Marc for a while," she said as she reached for the towel.

Sri told her that she would wash and fix her old clothing and return it tomorrow. She left in its place, a baggy pair of white breeches, and a white tunic. They felt light, comfortable and still kept her gender hidden. That was the important thing.

Margaret joined Alec in the living area where he was waiting with a chessboard set up.

"Feel better now?" he asked.

"Much!" she exclaimed. "I see you want to test my knowledge of chess."

"No," he shrugged, "I've not had a good game in a while and just wanted to play before dinner."

Margaret sat down and they played, while discussing Drake's education. He said the boy could speak some English, but not well. That was to be her main focus. She told him that the best way to go about it was how she learned French. Unless he was speaking to the servants, or if there were guests in the house, the only language that they should speak with him should be English. Alec agreed and said it would commence tomorrow.

After Margaret defeated him for a third time, Alec stood. "I think I've been humiliated enough for one evening."

She grinned. "I told you I was good."

He chuckled. "Good is an understatement."

They heard a door slam and a young boy bounded into the room. "Drake! What have I told you about slamming doors?" Alec scolded.

"Sorry, Poppy." He then added excitedly, "Christian has a baby elephant! Can I have one —please?"

"No! Baby elephants turn into big elephants. Besides, we're going to England in a few months, remember?"

"Oh," he said with a frown.

Alec rubbed his son's head. "I've found you a teacher, Drake."

"Not an old lady with blue hair, I hope," he replied, putting his hands in his pockets. "Christian has one like that. She's always pinching my cheeks when I come over."

"Actually, he has red hair," Alec nodded toward Margaret.

"Hello, Drake, I'm Marc."

"Hello," he said, with a small wave of his hand.

Margaret could see that the boy bubbled with exuberance. He looked like a younger version of his father with his brown hair and eyes and bright smile.

"Remember that story in the newspaper about the boy who won the boxing tournament?" Alec said.

"Yes," Drake replied.

"That's him."

"Really!" Drake became excited. "I've got to tell Christian!" He started to head back toward the door.

"Not so fast young man! You've had enough Christian for today. Dinner is ready. Get cleaned up."

The boy went upstairs with Taran following behind. Several minutes later they returned and the three of them sat down to dinner.

"It smells delicious," said Margaret, looking at the stew. "What is it?"

"I think it best not to tell you until you've tasted it," Alec warned.

Just as Margaret was about to take a bite, Drake announced, in a mischievous tone, "It's snake!"

"Drake!" his father scolded.

Margaret hesitated for only a moment and then ate it. "Excellent!" she exclaimed, then took another bite. "I can definitely taste curry. I think Orvil would kill for the recipe. Orvil is the cook on my ship."

Both Alec and his son were surprised. Most of their out-of-town guests frown at eating snake.

"You like it?" Drake asked.

"I like most anything..." Margaret replied, "...except rats. Squid and octopus are not bad but the tentacles are too chewy."

"Yuck!" Drake said, turning up his nose.

Both Alec and Margaret laughed. She recounted some of her adventures at sea, and they continued talking into the evening after dinner. She even rolled up her sleeve and showed Drake her seahorse tattoo. He really became excited when she told him she was kidnapped by pirates and that is how she ended up in India.

Next they told Drake about how they were going to deal with his English lessons. He wasn't happy about it, but when Margaret told him his reward for a good days worth of English, would be a fencing lesson, he became eager.

The evening was winding down and Alec walked upstairs with his son to tuck him into bed. Margaret was on the veranda enjoying the night sky and the moonlit sea. She watched as the waves crashed against each other and the sea foam wash upon the beach. She'd never felt so content.

"You look deep in thought," Alec said, as he saw Margaret staring at the waves. "Not home sick for the sea are you?"

"No, quite the contrary," she replied. "It feels good to have my feet dry and be with a family again."

"Drake likes you. I say he'll be dreaming of pirates and ships tonight. He said when he becomes a sea captain, he's going to name his ship the Seahorse after your tattoo.

"He's a delightful boy," Margaret replied. She then added, "How come he calls you Poppy? Is that an Indian word?"

"No," Alec let out a small laugh. "When he was a baby, I tried to get him to say Papa. It turned out Poppy. My wife thought it was cute, and she encouraged him to call me that. So I've been Poppy ever since. I wouldn't change it for anything. "

Alec slowly lowered himself down in a chair. "Drake is a high-spirited boy. I think you're going to have your hands full."

Margaret could see that his leg pained him. She thought about asking him, but decided not to. He probably had enough people asking him how he felt. If he wanted to talk about it, he would. After a few more minutes of conversation, Margaret also decided to retire. It had been a long day, and school for Drake started tomorrow.

***

Two weeks went by, and Alec couldn't have been happier with Drake's progress with his English. The first day felt like a game, and at the end of it, Margaret gave him a fencing lesson with wooden swords. The second day, he decided to be stubborn and pouted when no one would answer him when he spoke French. When he asked for a fencing lesson, Margaret said no and told him he had a job to do and that was to speak English. Payment was a lesson in fencing. If he didn't do a good job, he wouldn't get paid. The next day he tried harder and she rewarded him. At the end of the second weeks, his word power had doubled.

Fencing wasn't the only thing Margaret did with Drake. They climbed trees, played games and swam in the sea. Alec watch from a chair on the beach as Drake and Marc hunted for seashells and starfish. Marc was doing things with his son that he could only dream of doing. He was envious, but he'd accepted the fact that watching was the best he could do. At least he was still alive and able to enjoy that much.

One morning, at the beginning of the third week, Alec needed to check on the pepper fields. Drake had asked if he and Marc could come along. Alec said yes and suggested that they turn it into a picnic, so Sri packed them a lunch and they headed off. Margaret drove the buggy.

Handling the reins was too much of a strain on Alec's leg.

Margaret saw rows upon rows of pepper plants as far as the eye could see. This was the first time she'd seen any of the fields.

"I've only thought about pepper being in containers. I've never really thought of where it comes from," Margaret said, as she watched the workers in the field.

"This is just a small field of white pepper. The black pepper field is much larger," replied Alec.

Suddenly, there was a commotion in the distance. There was a man running through the field towards them. Another man on horseback chased him.

"Drake! Get out of the buggy now!" Alec ordered. He called one of the workers to come and watch him. "Take me over there, Marc!"

Margaret snapped the reigns and the horses took off. The man on horseback had caught up with the running man before they'd reach them. He'd pulled out a whip and started lashing the old man.

"Brickerman!" Alec shouted angrily, as Margaret pulled the buggy to a halt. "Stop that at once!"

Alec carefully got out of the buggy and limped over to the man. Margaret stayed behind, but ready to help where she could.

"What's the meaning of this?" Alec exclaimed, as he bent down to see to the injured man.

"I caught him stealing, Mitchell," said Brickerman.

"I not steal, Monsieur Alec!" exclaimed the old Indian man. "I take only from the section of field that is my right."

"You have no right to the pepper in these fields!" Brickerman snapped. He started to raise his whip again, but Alec stepped in front of the old man.

"There's a section of these fields that all the workers have rights to. It has been an arrangement in this family for the past three generations."

"Well, that's going to change. No more stealing from these fields."

"The small amount of pepper that this man harvested doesn't compare to the number of plants you've trampled with your horse by chasing him through the fields."

Brickerman dismounted and headed toward the Indian. But again, Alec blocked his way. "Touch him and you're discharged!" Alec warned sternly.

Margaret noticed this man, Brickerman was the same height as Alec, but much more muscular.

Brickerman laughed. "You can't do that. You don't own this land anymore."

"Neither do you!" Alec shouted. "Until the owners arrive, I have full authority."

"I don't recognize your authority, you cripple!" Brickerman pushed Alec to the ground and went after the old man again.

Margaret jumped out of the buggy and ran over to help Alec.

"Are you alright?" Margaret asked as she helped him up.

"I'm fine," he replied, frustrated at his inability. "I wish you had your sword with you. Then you could help him."

"I don't have that, but I did bring something else!" she replied, then ran back to the buggy. She'd brought along her own whip for something different to entertain Drake with during their picnic. Jordan had trained her in the use of one, and out of boredom on the Antoinette, she practiced daily.

Margaret ran toward Brickerman, whirled her whip around in the air and snapped it, ripping his shirt and striping his back. Brickerman dropped his own whip from the painful sting and quickly turned around.

"How does that feel?" Margaret whirled it around again and caught him on the cheek as he bent down to regain his own whip. "Take another step towards it, and the next time I'll take an eye!" she shouted.

Alec went to stand beside Marc. "You were saying something about authority, Brickerman? Now get on your horse and get out of these fields. You've destroyed enough plants already!"

"We'll see what the owners have to say when they arrive," Brickerman huffed as he mounted.

"What matters now is the present, and I'm the authority. If I see you in these fields again, you'll be having a talk with another in authority. Governor L'Orange wouldn't look kindly on the destruction of profitable commodities."

The man turned on his horse and rode off, but this time avoiding the pepper plants. Everyone was well aware that Casper L'Orange got his share of the tax on the exports in Pondicherry, and the willful destruction of trade goods was a serious crime in his book.

"You're a man of many talents, Marc," Alec said as Margaret helped him into the buggy. "Do you have any other secret tricks?"

Margaret grinned. "Maybe one or two."

Her biggest trick would be to show him how she could change from a young man, to a young woman. But for now, she wasn't ready to show him that trick.

They went to retrieve Drake. It was all the worker could do to keep the boy from running after his father.

"Are you alright, Poppy?" the boy cried as he hugged him.

Alec wiped away his tears. "I'm fine. Now, what were we going to do today? I've forgotten with all the excitement."

"Have a picnic!" Drake replied, as he smiled through his tears.

"Well, as soon as we have a look at the black pepper, and the chili peppers, we'll have our picnic."

The rest of the day went without incident and the three of them enjoyed their picnic. Alec had asked Margaret if he could borrow her whip. That was one thing he could teach his son that didn't cause his leg pain. Margaret found that he was just as proficient with it as Jordan. She'd asked him why he didn't carry one, and he told her that there was no need. To him, it was just a toy to play with — not a device for punishment.

After touring all the fields, they headed home. Margaret said she was going to take a bath before dinner. She got a change of clothing while Taran filled the shower container. She thought that maybe tomorrow, she'd ask if they could go to town. Her clothing was getting worn and with the money she'd gotten from her share of the pirate's booty, she wanted to go shopping.

She slipped into the hot spring after her shower and thought how the day was almost perfect — except for the Brickerman incident. She was looking forward to dinner and quiet evening on the veranda with her pretend family.

***

Alec was watching Drake play with some of his toys out on the veranda, when in the distance they heard the trumpeting of an elephant. Drake was on his feet and saw a mother with its baby just at the edge of the clearing.

"Look, Poppy, Elephants!" Drake said excitedly. "Marc said he wanted to see one." He frowned. "He's always taking a bath! How come he takes one every day?"

"I guess because on a ship you rarely take one," Alec laughed.

"He's going to miss them if he doesn't hurry," Drake said.

"I tell you what. You keep an eye on them, and I'll try to hurry Marc along."

Alec got up from his chair and headed for the bathhouse. When he got there, he opened the gate and walked in.

"Marc, there are two elephants…"

His sentence was abruptly cut off, and he froze stone still. The naked form of — Marc — stood in front of him. Words stuck in his throat.

***

Margaret had just gotten out of the hot spring. She normally laid her towel down beside it, but this time she'd left it on a bench with her clothing. Suddenly, the gate sprang open and there was Alec saying something about elephants.

After a moment of shock and dumb silence, Margaret quickly went for her towel, and Alec averted his eye.

"Drake wants you to see some elephants that have come onto the property." Alec couldn't think of anything else to say. He closed the gate behind him.

"Oh God!" Margaret exclaimed, as she wrapped the towel around her and sat down on the bench. She dreaded her next meeting with Alec. After getting dressed, she left the bathhouse to face whatever it was that Alec was going to do or say to her.

***

Alec went back to the veranda with Drake.

"Is he coming?" Drake asked.

"In a minute," Alec replied as he sat back down in the chair.

What did I just see?

Marc was a woman! He wondered if his injury had taken away his senses also. Just then Marc appeared. He noticed she didn't look at him but went straight to where Drake was. He could see her face was red with embarrassment.

"See the elephants?" Drake asked. "Poppy and me rode one once."

"Poppy and I," Margaret corrected him. Then she quickly glanced at Alec.

Then Drake turned back to his father. "Poppy, do you think you and — I — can take Marc for a ride on an elephant?"

"Maybe, that depends on…" he looked at the woman before him. " — Marc."

Just then Sri came and announced dinner was ready.

"If you'll excuse me," Margaret said politely. "I've lost my appetite for the moment." She walked off the veranda and headed down toward the beach.

"What's wrong with Marc?" Drake asked. "He's always hungry."

"I think Marc has something on — his mind," Alec said. Then he smiled. "You go have dinner, and I'll talk with him."

Alec stood by the stone fence and looked down toward the beach. Marc was sitting in the sand staring into the calm waters of the sea while the gentle waves washed upon the shore trying to reach her feet. He slowly made his way down the steps and stood beside her.

"You have something you want to tell me, Marc?" Alec asked calmly.

Margaret looked up. "My name is Margaret. I'm sorry for having lied to you for all this time." She looked down and stirred the sand with her finger.

Alec started to sit down in the sand beside her, but Margaret quickly stood.

"I know it hurts you to sit low like that," she said as she stopped him.

"There's a rock over there," Alec pointed. "We can sit and talk."

They walked toward the cliff facing and sat on a large flat rock. They were both quiet for a moment, until Margaret broke the silence. She still couldn't bring herself to look him in the eye. She felt guilty and just stared out into distance. "What are you going to do?" she asked.

"Nothing," he replied evenly. "I don't see why you still thought you had to pretend to be a man when you knew I was looking for a woman to teach Drake in the first place."

"I've played this role for more than half a year," she replied honestly. I'd just met you. So I kept it up. My role as a boy on the ship was for work. My role with you and Drake was happiness. I didn't want to ruin it."

"You haven't ruined anything," Alec said and then chuckled. "You shocked the bloody hell out of me, I can tell you that. I haven't seen a naked woman since my wife."

Margaret managed a smile. "Your appearance also didn't bode well for my dignity." She then became serious. "You haven't asked me why I hired aboard a ship."

"I don't have to. That's your business. If you want to tell me, you will. But right now, I'm starved! What do you say to dinner?"

Margaret helped him up. "So, who do you want me to be, Marc, or Margaret?"

"Either one," he replied, has he touched his hand to her cheek. "I'll leave that up to you."

"I think I'll keep the Marc persona for now, for Drake's sake," she replied.

They both headed up the steps. Margaret was glad she could finally be honest with him. At dinner, she had asked him about going into town. Alec told her he was planning on doing that at the end of the week.

***

Both Margaret and Drake were looking forward to going into town. She hadn't seen much of Pondicherry and was anxious to see the Indian side. Drake had told her of snake charmers and elephants, and even though he was afraid of tigers, they had some in cages that he wasn't afraid to look at.

They went into a men's clothing shop. Drake was growing out of some of his clothing, and Margaret's were wearing out. Alec had offered to purchase hers, but she said she had her own money, and it wasn't necessary. But he did insist on paying for the noon meal and the elephant ride he'd promised Drake.

They headed back toward the French quarter as the day was winding down and stepped out of the carriage when they arrived. Alec never left town without checking with Governor L'Orange. He took Drake with him while Margaret decided to do a bit of exploring on her own. They agree to meet back at the carriage in thirty minutes.

Margaret saw a dress shop and was sorely tempted to go in, but decided not to. She was in the wrong attire. As she walked down the street, she was about to pass a tavern when a man stepped out whom she almost bumped into him.

"Pardon me, I didn't…" she started to say, and then she recognized him.

"You!" shouted the man. "You poodle-headed son-of-a-bitch!"

It was Meeks. The man she'd beaten in the boxing tournament. Before she could say a word or do anything, he pulled back his fist and took a swing at her. Luckily she was able to dodged it before it connected.

"Oh! No! Not again!" she exclaimed.

The man ignored her and took another swing. "You know how much teasing I got being beaten by a bloody whelp like you!" he shouted. "I had to leave the ship!"

Again, Margaret dodged his blow, but when the next one came she blocked it and returned one of her own. A crowd had started to gather as she defended herself against the obviously drunk Meeks. But the battle was short lived as two policemen grabbed both of them and hauled them away. Margaret tried to explain that she was just defending herself, while Meeks ranted and raved at her, saying it was all her fault. The officers took them into a building, threw them into separate cages and slammed the iron door shut.

Alec and Drake had been waiting by the carriage for about ten minutes. Alec asked the driver where Marc was, but he hadn't seen him.

"Wonder where he is?" Alec said, looking around. "He's never late."

"Maybe pirates took him again," Drake replied, looking out at the dock to see if he saw any ships sailing away.

"Excuse me, Monsieur Mitchell," said a young boy. "Are you looking for the boy that was with you?"

"Yes, do you know where he is?"

"The boy he was arrested, Monsieur.

"Arrested!" Alec exclaimed. "What the deuce for?"

"Some man tried to start a fight with him. The police took both of them."

Alec knew it would be pointless to try and get Marc out by himself, so it was back to Casper L'Orange. He was the only man who had the power to get her released. He explained as much of the situation to the Governor as he knew, then the three of them went together.

After some negotiating, Alec was allowed to see Margaret, but the official at the prison said that he'd have to spend the night. It was one of the Governor's own policies. But he also said that the drunk, Meeks, proved Marc's innocents when he tried to take another swing at the boy. But, an example had to be made and he had to spend at least one night.

Alec went with the jailor, who opened the door to Margaret's cell. She was leaning up against the wall sitting on a straw mat. He thought she'd probably be crying, but instead she just looked frustrated.

"Are you alright?" Alec asked, as he walked in. The jailor closed the door behind him and said to knock when he was done.

"Wonderful!" Margaret huffed, as she sat pouting on the floor.

Alec heard a man shout from another cell, "Poodle-headed son-of-bitch!" Then he was quiet again.

"Apparently you have an enemy," Alec said. "Who is he?"

"The man I defeated at the boxing tournament. He's still upset about it," Margaret replied. "He tried to start a rematch on the street and you can obviously see the result."

"Well, I'm afraid you'll have to spend the night," Alec said. "I was only lucky to get to see you because Casper has pull. The charges against you will be dropped in the morning."

"Why am I not surprised?" Margaret said as she stood. "I have this tendency to draw trouble to myself without even trying."

Alec went toward her and gave her a hug, then kissed her on the forehead. "I need to go. I don't want Drake left alone for long." He chuckled a bit. "Drake's worried they might hang you and wants me to break you out."

Margaret laughed. "Tell him I'll be fine and I'll see him tomorrow. I've been in worse places than this."

Alec knocked on the door and left. Margaret sat back down on the floor. That was the first time Alec had kissed her. Granted, it was just a friendly peck, but she liked it.

She thought about this situation as she looked around her cell. "Marc..." she said to herself. "I'm bloody well tired of you getting me into trouble!" She decided that when she got home, she was going to do something about it! And then she thought,

Home!

Alec Mitchell's home may not have actually been hers, but she felt content there.

***

The next morning, Alec and Drake came to pick Margaret up. She apologized to the official for the disturbance. He told her he was giving her the benefit of the doubt and was releasing her to the custody of Mr. Mitchell. But, if she got into any more trouble, the next time it would go harder on her.

"How did you sleep?" Alec asked as they drove away in the carriage.

"Not too well. The rat kept me awake for most of the night," she replied.

"You mean the man in the next cell yelled at you all night?" Alec asked.

"No, he was quiet. The rat that was in my cell," she replied.

"Did it try to bite you?" Drake asked, with his usual inquisitive enthusiasm.

Margaret grinned. "No, he kept snoring. I tried to get him to turnover, but it didn't do any good."

Alec and Drake laughed. "I see you still maintain your sense of humor."

"May as well laugh, as to cry about it," she replied. "All I know is I need a bath."

Drake huffed. "Marc, you're always taking a bath."

"Well, if I didn't, I'd smell like you!" she exclaimed, then started to tickle him.

The rest of the day was as normal. Margaret was teaching Drake his lessons, while Alec went over the books to keep them in line for the new owners. After dinner, Margaret gave Drake his fencing lesson.

She decided to wait until after Drake went to bed, before she had her bath. As she relaxed in the bubbling waters, she thought how she would love to take this spring with her when they left for England. She also thought how much she would like to feel and look like a woman again. Just as she was getting out of the spring, Sri entered with some colorful material.

"Sri think that Monsieur Marc would like to be Mademoiselle Marc tonight," she said.

Margaret raised her eye brows. "Sri, are you a mind reader? I was just thinking how nice it would be to feel feminine again."

"No, not read mind. Just see something in Monsieur Marc's eyes when look at Monsieur Alec. Sri think that Mademoiselle Marc would like to come out tonight," she replied as she help Margaret dry off.

"I think you saw wrong, Sri." Margaret blushed. "But I would like to wear a dress again and feel pretty."

Sri took the green material and wrapped it around her body exposing her tattooed shoulder and then draped another piece of material in a different shade of green over her other shoulder and fixed it in place. Seashell bracelets adorned her wrist and ankles. Sri fixed her hair and put more jewelry around her head and neck.

"Now Mademoiselle Marc look very beautiful," Sri said, as she stood back and looked her over. "I think Monsieur Alec be surprised."

Margaret wished she had a full length mirror in the bathhouse. Even though she was clothed, she still felt naked. The material was so light in weight, it was like wearing nothing.

"Well, here goes," she said, as she walked barefooted back to the veranda.

Alec's back was to Margaret when she approached. He was in the process of setting up the chessboard. Torches were lit around the veranda giving it a romantic glow.

"I'm back," Margaret said, as she stood at the entrance.

"Good! I'm determined to beat you at chess tonight," Alec said. He then turned around. His eyes widened and he dropped a chess piece to the ground. "Oh my! Who are you, and what did you do with Marc?"

"I'm Margaret Wallingham," she replied with a curtsey. "It's a pleasure to finally make your acquaintance. Marc decided that after his night in jail, he'd retire for the evening and let me take his place. He'll be back tomorrow."

"Remind me to thank him in the morning," Alec said, as he slowly walked toward her, extended his arm and escorted her to the chessboard. "You look lovely."

Margaret blushed. "It seems ages since anyone has told me that."

They played one game, in which Margaret won as usual and then they decided to take a walk.

"I think I'd like to tell you why I created Marc," she said.

"You know you don't have to."

"I know," she shrugged. "But I want to."

She told him the whole story; her forced engagement to Nathanial, her faked kidnapping to escape him and her one way feelings toward the Captain of the Neptune's Daughter.

"So now what do you think of me?" Margaret asked.

"I think you're a brave woman," he replied. "Most women would settle with what they don't want. You're a woman who knows her own mind."

"Not really," she replied, as she looked out over the sea. "I may know what I don't want, but I don't know what I do want."

"How do you feel right now?" he asked, leaning on the stone fence.

"Happy," she said giving him a smile. "Drake is a wonderful boy, and I enjoy your company greatly."

Alec gave her a smile and suddenly had an overwhelming urge to kiss her. He put his hand to her cheek then slowly brought her lips to his, in a sweet tender kiss. Margaret put her arms around him. He dropped his cane and they embraced in a deeper, more passionate kiss.

Suddenly Alec broke away. With a kiss like that, he should have felt some stirring in his crippled body, but there was nothing.

"I'm sorry," he said, as he turned and supported himself on the wall.

"Why?" She put her hand gently on his back.

"You're a passionate woman, Margaret, and I'm — half a man. I know you've told me how you feel about your Captain. I could never give you what you need."

Margaret picked up his cane and leaned it against the wall. "Alec, you say you're only half a man, but I've spent time with a lot of them, and most are not half the man you are. They only care about what their loins feel. You care with what's in your heart."

Suddenly they heard a scream coming from Drake's room.

"His nightmare is back," said Alec. "I need to go to him."

"I'll change and meet you there. I don't want to scare him dressed like this," Margaret said.

Margaret quickly ran to her room and transformed back into Marc. Alec had just reached the boy's room and was shaking him awake.

Drake cried and put his arms around his father. "It was terrible Poppy!"

"Was it the tiger again?" he asked lovingly as rocked his son.

"No, pirates took you and Marc and left me by myself," he cried.

Margaret walked over and sat down on the other side of his bed. "I had a nightmare once."

"What did you dream about?" the boy asked, wiping away his tears.

"Well, when I was on the pirate ship, I had a terrible nightmare. I dreamed that I walked up on deck wearing a dress!"

"A dress!" he exclaimed.

"Yes. Not only that, all the pirates thought I was a girl and chased after me trying to kiss me!"

Drake laughed. "That's not a scary nightmare, that's a funny one."

"Not to me!" she replied, widening her eyes. "How would you like it if some big, smelly ol' pirate with green teeth and chewing tobacco dripping out of his mouth tried to kiss you?"

"I wouldn't like it," he said, turning up his nose. "But it's still not as scary as mine!"

"Well, when you go to sleep, don't dream my dream. It was pretty scary," she said.

Alec laid his son back down and covered him up. "You want me to stay with you?"

"No, I'm getting bigger," he said as he yawned.

Margaret and Alec headed toward the door, and Drake told them both good-night.

"Thank you for your story to him. That's the fastest he's ever calmed down from a nightmare," Alec said, as he put his arm around her waist.

"What story!" she exclaimed. "I dreamt that Capitaine L'Orange chased me all around the ship, and kissing isn't what he wanted to do. I just watered it down for Drake."

They stopped just before Margaret's room. "Now what were we discussing?" she asked, as she put her arms around him.

"I think we were discussing you getting a good night's sleep. We'll talk more tomorrow evening," Alec replied, then gently kissed her.

"That sounds like a plan," she replied, as she slowly let go and went to her room.

Margaret got ready for bed. She thought about Alec's kiss. Then she compared it to the Captain's feverish passion. The Captain stirred everything in her. But Alec stirred something different. She was in love with the Captain, and with Alec, she was happy and content. Which was better? To follow an uncertain love that may bring her heartache in the long run? Or to be with a man who could make her happy and content, who had a son she adored?

***

Alec couldn't go to bed yet. There was too much on his mind. He went back downstairs and out to the veranda.

"Would Monsieur like the torches put out?" Taran asked.

"That will be fine," he replied. "There's enough moonlight."

Taran put out the torches. "Sri make Mademoiselle Marc look beautiful tonight, no?"

"Beautiful, yes!" he replied. He gave Taran a smile. "Thank her for both of us, will you?"

Taran bowed, wished him good thoughts and left.

Alec lowered himself in the chair. His leg was bothering him more and more, and it was becoming more painful when he had to relieve himself. He looked up at the blinking stars and listened to the sound of the crashing waves against the cliff. He thought about Margaret. He could never love her as he had loved his Silvia. But she was gone, and there was Drake to think about. Drake needed a mother. Margaret had a maturity beyond her eighteen years. Probably due to the experiences she'd had aboard her ship. She was not just a teacher. She played with him, but was also strict when it came to his behavior.

Alec liked Marc as the boy, but could he love Margaret the woman? Could Margaret live with the fact that they could never consummate a love relationship? Would she even want to be with a man who could die

249

at any time?

***

During the next two weeks, Margaret played at being Marc during the day, then at night she transformed back into Margaret. She had given Sri some money to buy her some Indian dresses. Sri showed her how to wrap them in different ways.

When Drake was asleep, Margaret and Alec walked together talking and laughing and sometimes they were silent. That night they just sat on the veranda and held each other as they laid in the large chaise lounge.

"You're quiet tonight," Margaret said, as he held her in his arms.

"I've got something on my mind that I want to discuss with you."

"Sounds serious," she said light heartedly, and just snuggled closer to him.

"It is serious," he replied, as he gently pulled her away from him.

"What is it? Are you feeling ill?" A concerned look crossed her face.

"No, I'm fine." He gave her a kiss of reassurance and they both sat upright.

"When we first met, you asked me if I had family back in England. I didn't answer you."

"I remember," she replied.

"My so called — family isn't trustworthy. My father left a modest amount of money to me and my older brother, Lawrence. He squandered everything our father left him. I invested mine here. If anything happens to me, Drake and his inheritance will be under his control. He's the only family member left on either side. He'd more than likely put my son in a workhouse somewhere and squander Drakes inheritance."

"Alec, don't think so negatively," Margaret replied. "I'm sure you'll be around for Drake in the many years to come."

Alec stood and stretched out his hand. "Come walk with me." He gave her a smile. They walked quietly for a few moments, until Alec finally gathered his thoughts and broke the silence. "I have a proposition for you."

Margaret thought about making a joke, but the tone in his voice and the expression on his face denoted something very serious. "What kind of proposition?"

"I wish you become my wife and Drake's mother."

Margaret was surprised. His question came so business like. "Alec, I..."

250

"Please, hear me out," he interrupted and then gently brushed back a strand of hair from her face. "I know you don't love me the way a couple should when they get married, but I do know you have a great affection and caring in your heart for me and Drake. A marriage between us could never be consummated. It's impossible for me. It would be in name only. Even though I've known you for just a little over a month, I feel that I can trust you over anyone with what is most precious to me — my son. I know you'll be good to him."

"You shouldn't talk like that, Alec!" she exclaimed. Margaret could feel tears welling in her eyes. She hated crying. But this time she couldn't do anything else but cry.

"I'm dying, Margaret," Alec said. He also started to cry. "I don't want to, but I'm getting worse. I may not even make it to England. Please, I'm not asking for me. I'm asking for my son. I'm begging…"

But Margaret put a finger to his lips. How could she say no? Jordan said to grab opportunity. This was opportunity for a measure of happiness, not only for her, but for this man whom she cared for. Also for the love of a little boy. "You don't have to beg, Alec," she said softly. "Yes, I'll marry you."

Alec drew her in his arms and held her tight. "Thank you," he whispered softly. Then he brought his lips to hers and kissed her tenderly.

When they parted, Margaret's joyful smile turned into one of concern.

"What is it?" Alec asked, noticing her expression.

"We've got a problem."

"What problem?" He was puzzled at this sudden change of emotion.

"How are we going to tell Drake I'm not a boy?"

Alec laughed, as he wiped away his tears. "Good question. Tomorrow morning, come down to breakfast in a dress. We'll see what he says."

They walked back to the house to retire for the evening. Alec escorted Margaret to her bedroom door, kissed her good-night and then went to his own room. He was relieved that Margaret said yes. He prayed fervently to God to extend his life for a few months more to prepare his son and let the boy get even closer to Margaret.

Margaret wasn't one for crying. However, tonight she buried her head in her pillow to muffle the sound. She didn't want Alec to die! He was a good and loving man, and even though she loved her Captain, she had a great affection for Alec and Drake. She didn't want Drake to be without his father. She'd marry him. Drake was a big responsibility, but she would figure out a way. She couldn't see him go to a workhouse.

The next morning, Margaret was up and dressed in one of the saris that Sri had bought for her and went downstairs for breakfast. Alec was waiting at the table.

"Well, how do you think he'll react to seeing me like this?" Margaret asked.

"We'll find out in a moment." He gave her a quick kiss.

Drake came sleepily down to the breakfast table as he normally did. Margaret and Alec looked at each other in surprise. He didn't seem to notice her.

"Drake, are you awake? Or sleep walking?" his father asked.

"I'm awake," he said as he yawned and rubbed his eyes.

"Did you sleep well last night?" Margaret asked.

"Pretty good," he said in a normal voice.

Alec laughed. "Drake, don't you notice anything different about Marc this morning?"

"She's wearing a dress," he yawned. "You're not going to wear it all day are you? I thought we'd play pirates after my lessons today. Christian wants to play too."

Margaret was surprised. "You know I'm not a boy!"

"Sri told me a couple of days after you got here. When we went swimming, I noticed you had bumps like Christian's sister has when she goes swimming. Only hers are really big. I ask Sri about it, and she said it was a secret that you were girl and not to tell. So I didn't. I like pretending Marc is a boy. It's more fun!"

Alec laughed and rolled his eyes. "Now I'm embarrassed. My seven year old son noticed and I didn't!"

After they had a good laugh about Margaret's gender, they thought it a good time to broach the other subject.

"Drake, we have something else important to tell you." Alec took Margaret's hand. "What would you think if I married Marc? She'd be your step-mother."

Drake thought intently for a moment. "Do step-mother's play pirates?" he asked seriously.

"This one does, if you continue to do well with your lessons," Margaret said trying to keep a straight face.

"Do I have to call you step-mother? Or can I still call you Marc?" he asked.

"Marc is fine," Margaret replied.

"Ok," he shrugged. "What's for breakfast?"

"Squid!" Margaret exclaimed.

"Yuck!" Drake laughed. He got up from his chair and went to Margaret's and gave her a big hug.

"This calls for a celebration," said Alec. "How about we go to town and do some shopping?" But then he noticed a serious look come over his son's face. "You don't want to go to town?"

"Yes, but what if they put Marc back in jail?" he asked.

Margaret laughed. "Oh no! Marc is staying home. Margaret is going instead! I think she needs to be introduced, but I've got one problem."

"What's that?" Alec asked.

"Nothing to wear," she shrugged. "I can't wear a sari. It's fine for our private life and the natives, but for me in town? They'd arrest me for indecent exposure."

"I think we might find something suitable," Alec replied, and then looked at his son. "And since I'm declaring this a holiday, no lessons! Son, after breakfast you can play. We'll go into town this afternoon."

Drake cheered. He practically swallowed his breakfast whole and was out the door before his father changed his mind. When Margaret and Alec were done, he took her upstairs to one of the bedrooms.

"If you look in that trunk, I think you'll find something you might like," Alec said, leaning on his cane.

Margaret bent down and opened it. She found four beautiful French style dresses. She knew they probably belonged to his dead wife.

"Are you sure you want me to wear one of these?" Margaret asked.

Alec saw the look of concern on her face. "I'm sure," he replied. "I know what you're thinking. You're worried that my seeing you in one of her dresses might bring up painful memories. I told you before — I don't put stock in things. I remember the person, not what she wore. Besides, I think Silvia would be proud to have you wear them."

Margaret stood and gave him a hug. "You don't know how special you are to me," she said.

"I think I do." He kissed her. "Now go get your bath and change. I remember how long it takes for women to get dressed," he laughed.

"Ha, ha, very funny! I'm not your typical woman." Margaret smile and headed for the door.

"Don't I know it!" he shouted after her.

They decided to be wed in two weeks. Margaret told Alec that a simple ceremony before a minister would be fine, but he wouldn't hear of it. Alec told her that he wanted no doubt in anyone's mind that they were married. If his brother decided to contest her custody of Drake, he wanted to make sure there were plenty of witnesses to corroborate the event.

That afternoon the three of them went to town. The first thing they had to do was see Casper L'Orange. Alec couldn't wait to see the look on his face when he told him the news. Margaret hoped she wouldn't be recognized. She still wanted to keep her Marc identity a secret, just in case she might need him. They told Drake to only call her Marc when she was dressed as a boy, and to call her Margaret when she was in a dress.

Alec and Margaret walked into the office with Drake in front of them. The Governor looked up from his desk.

"Alec, my friend," he said as he stood. But his eyes were on Margaret. "Where in the world did you find this tear drop from the sun?"

Margaret extended her hand, and the Governor kissed it. "You embarrass me, Governor L'Orange," Margaret said, as she put a fan before her face to cover her pretended blush.

"Casper, may I present, Mademoiselle Margaret Wallingham. She does me the honor of accepting my proposal of marriage." Alec announced then kissed her cheek. He could see the look of surprise on his friend's face.

"Marriage!" Casper laughed as he shook Alec's hand. "When? Where did you find her? How...?"

"Too many questions all at once, my friend," Alec laughed.

Contriving a story of truths and half truths they told him that she was a good friend of his and Silvia's from England, and he'd helped her escape an unwanted marriage to one Nathanial Braxton. Casper knew that Alec was apprehensive about his brother getting custody of Drake, and getting his son in the hands of someone he trusted and cared about was of great concern. They told him that besides a deep affection they had for each other, protecting Drake was the other reason why they were marrying.

"I can't believe you've kept her hidden all these weeks? Why didn't you tell me?" Casper exclaimed, disappointed that Alec didn't trust him.

"Please, don't be angry with him," Margaret said sweetly, as she took the Governor's arm. "Nathanial was supposed to be coming to India, and I was afraid he might be here. I didn't want to take the chance on him finding me. Alec was just complying with my wishes."

"I guess I can't blame him." Casper smiled. "I'd probably want to keep you a secret myself."

Next, Alec asked him if he would do them the honor of presiding over the ceremony. Casper's disappointment turned to delight, and he gladly accepted. When the Governor asked about Marc, they said he wanted to stay home. He was afraid of running into Meeks again, and didn't relish going back to jail if another fight broke out. But Casper said he wouldn't have to worry about him anymore. When Meeks went before the court, the judge recognized him as the person who'd picked his pocket. So he was going to be in jail until the embargo was over. After the judge exacted his pound of flesh from the man, he would be deported back to England.

When they left Casper's office, Alec introduced Margaret to everyone they met. He gave verbal invitations and told them to spread the word. It was going to be a causal outdoor ceremony, and anyone who wanted to come was invited.

***

The day of the wedding finally arrived. The garden was beautifully decorated, and there was enough food prepared for an army. The French pastry chef in town created the masterpiece of all wedding cakes as a gift. It was four tiers high and had a rainbow of colors and a variety of flavors.

Drake was Alec's best man, and Sri was Margaret's Matron of Honor since she knew no one else. There were over one hundred and fifty guests attending not including the natives. Alec was well liked and respected by both cultures. With all the tragedy Alec had suffered, they were glad to see that he was going to be happy again — for the time he had left. Most knew he was just living on borrowed time.

As they stood before the Governor, Margaret thought that she should have been nervous. But she wasn't. She just looked in Alec's eyes and saw love in them. She knew it wasn't that special love he'd had for his first wife. And for her, it wasn't the same love she felt for the Captain. But it was still a measure of love and affection.

The ceremony was simple and the Governor's speech of love, honor, trust and friendship seemed to have been written just for them. Soon she heard him say, "You may kiss the bride."

Alec lifted her veil and kissed her long and tenderly. All the guests laughed and clapped, and when he delayed releasing her, one of his friends shouted from the crowd, "Please, Alec! Let us celebrate your marriage before you start your wedding night!" They finally separated and laughed with the rest of the guests.

Congratulations came from everyone. They'd received several dinner invitations from the wives of Alec's friends. Margaret knew that most of

255

them were just curious about her and wanted something new to gossip about. Only two seemed genuine in wanting to be friends, and those were the invitations that Alec accepted.

Some of the guests that had met Marc inquired about him. They told them that Marc had become sick that morning, and elected to watch the festivities from the window of his room with the porcelain throne close at hand.

Alec and Margaret saw several of the guests talking to Drake. At first, they were worried that he'd accidentally let it slip about Marc and Margaret, but he played his part well. He thought of it as a big game and had fun playing it. As the evening wore on, Drake had fallen asleep, and Taran carried him to his room. It was dark when the last of the guests left. Margaret and Alec talked for a while about the guests then finally headed upstairs. They checked on Drake and found him fast asleep.

Margaret saw that Alec hesitated on which direction to go. He looked towards the room she'd been sleeping in and then toward his. She gave him a smile, took his arm and headed toward his room.

"You don't have to do this you know," Alec said, avoiding her eyes.

Margaret put her arms around his neck and kissed him. "I don't have to, I want to," she said softly.

They walked in and she closed the door. Neither of them spoke for the moment. Margaret then took off her veil and turned around so Alec could help her out of her dress. He slowly unbuttoned and unlaced her gown, and watched as all the garments fell to the floor. Margaret turned around and stood naked before him, and he gently touched her small firm breast as she started to slowly undress him. When she started to unbutton his breeches, he stopped her.

"Margaret, you may not want to. It's not a good sight to see. I don't know if I could handle your revulsion," he said, closing his eyes, trying to hold back a tear.

"There's a lot I never told you about with my time aboard the Antoinette, and during the storm while I was on the Neptune's Daughter. I've seen more horror and mangled bodies than I care to remember. Nothing about you could ever repulse me."

He released her hand and she continued. She saw what the tiger had done. His male organs were mutilated. His thigh was caved in, and it looked like a hunk of meat had been removed and the skin sewn over it.

"You don't repulse me," she said, as she gently touched the source of his anguish.

Alec put his arms around her and pressed her small, slightly muscular form next to his. "You never cease to amaze me," he said, as the lump in his throat started to ease.

They lay down together and made love with gentle touches and soft caresses. Alec could never consummate their marriage in the traditional since, but as far as Margaret was concerned, they had.

The next morning Margaret was awakened by Alec's playful exploration of her body. She giggled as she grabbed his hands and wrapped them around her. "You lecherous thing you!"

"I'm allowed to be lecherous. You're my wife — Mrs. Mitchell! And this is our honeymoon," Alec replied nibbling on her ear.

"Say that again."

"Say what?" he asked, massaging her breasts.

"My name."

"Mrs. Margaret Mitchell," he replied.

"You know what, husband?" she said, as she turned over and looked him in the eye.

He propped himself up on an elbow. "What?"

She grinned. "I'm hungry and want some breakfast."

Alec's eyes widened. "Now! You want breakfast, now!"

"Right now!" she exclaimed, as she carefully rolled him over to not cause his leg pain. "I'd like breakfast in bed. And the noon meal and dinner." Then she pressed her breasts to his chest then kissed him passionately.

"And you called me lecherous!" He laughed, as he rolled over on her. "You'd better be glad that I'm incapacitated, or you may never leave this room!"

Alec was just about to kiss her again, when they heard a knock on the door.

"Poppy! You and Marc are going to be late for breakfast!"

Alec rolled over on his back. "Oh, Drake!" he mumbled in low tones. "I was just about to have breakfast!"

Margaret laughed then put her arms around him.

"I knew there was something I forgot to do!" Alec sighed.

"What's that?"

"Have Drake spend the night with Christian." He then shouted back. "We'll be down in a minute, son!"

✶✶✶

Margaret and Alec had now been married for three weeks. During the daytime hours, she took on her Marc persona and dressed in her men's clothing to give Drake his lessons and play with him.

As Marc, she would also take Alec out to check on the pepper and sugar cane fields. He'd hired a middle-aged Indian worker, named Hadji, as foreman. He'd worked on the plantation since he was a boy, and knew all aspects of growing and harvesting the different peppers and cane. Alec was glad to once again have someone he could trust to manage the fields and workers.

Whenever they had guests or went into town, Marc would disappear and Margaret would wear her European designed clothing. But at night after Drake went to bed, she visited the hot spring, which Alec called her sanctuary. Then she wrapped one of her colorful saris in seductive ways around her body to please her husband's eyes.

***

After the first week, Alec went to his solicitor there in India to have the necessary papers drawn up to make Margaret, Drake's legal guardian and conservator of his trust and properties should anything happen to him. He also sent a letter to his solicitor in England, Tobias Underwood, to inform him of his marriage and plans for his estate once he was gone.

Alec also started teaching Margaret about managing the business. Just in case this embargo when on too long and Taylor Hansford couldn't get here before his inevitable death, she would have to know the workings and how do deal with the customers of the plantation. He found she was quick to learn and easy to teach.

Margaret was content to be Alec's wife, but she was starting to worry about him more. His pain started to increase. Sometimes it was all he could do to walk up the stairs.

Someone suggested Opium to minimize the pain. However, he'd seen some of the effect it had on others, and he refused to use it. Taran brought in a man who knew the Chinese method of alleviating pain with the use of needles. Despite the skepticism of his doctor, the treatment helped reduce the pain to a level where it was tolerable for a few days afterward.

One afternoon Margaret and Alec headed into town for some shopping and to spend the day together while Drake was playing at a friend's house. Alec was having one of his better days. They checked with Casper and found out that things were looking up with the negotiations on trade relations, and he suspected that news of the embargo being lifted could come about at anytime.

That was good news to their ears. To celebrate, they decided to attend opening night of the Shakespearian play, Romeo and Juliet, and then dined out afterward. When the play was over they walked to a café.

"I think Juliet forgot to shave this morning," Alec laughed. "I thought this was supposed to be a love tragedy, instead of a romantic comedy."

"I have to admit, that it was pretty bad. However, Romeo's part was fair," she replied.

Alec grinned. "I think I did notice you admiring his — parts."

"Alec Mitchell!" she scolded, playfully slapping him with her gloves. "You're incorrigible!"

He stopped and put his arms around her. "So encourage me."

"Alec, if you don't behave yourself, they'll throw us in jail for public displays!" She laughed then kissed him.

"Hmmm! I wonder what it would be like to make love on a prison floor?" he said before he released her.

Margaret shook her head. "You're just bad today!"

They continued walking, talking and laughing as they headed for the café, and then Margaret noticed an announcement posted.

"Look, Alec!" she said excitedly, "A fencing tournament! Ages seven through adult, all levels and it's three weeks from Saturday. Drake would love it!"

Alec saw the gleam in her eyes and laughed. "I think you mean Marc would love it. Don't you?"

"So? What if Marc is interested?" she said as she stopped and folded her arms.

"Now don't get defensive," he laughed. "If Marc, or Margaret, for that matter wants to enter, that's fine with me."

Margaret put her arms around his neck and kissed him. "Did I tell you today that I love you?"

"I don't remember?" he said, pretending forgetfulness. "Tell me again."

They were about to kiss when they heard a man laughing behind them. They released their embrace.

"I heard you got married, Mitchell."

Alec frowned and gently nudged Margaret behind him. "Brickerman! What do you want?"

"Just to tell that pretty wife of yours that I feel sorry for her being saddled with half a man like you." He laughed then turned to Margaret.

"Honey, if you need something more, I'm fully equipped."

Margaret gritted her teeth. She wasn't a person that was prone to hate, but with this man — she would make an exception.

Alec could feel her rage by the grip she had on his arm. If she kept her mouth shut, he would have been surprised. She didn't disappoint him.

"Is that how you measure yourself as a man..." she yelled, taking a step forward to stand beside Alec, "...by that speck of meat between your legs? Ha! Don't feel sorry for me, Mr. Brickerman. Feel sorry for yourself. My husband faced down a tiger trying to defend his first wife and child and lives with constant pain because of it. I've heard you couldn't even handle a boy with a whip. So who has the — stones — Mr. Brickerman!"

Brickerman's smile left his face and he glared at Alec. "You can't even control your wife's tongue, Mitchell!"

Alec grinned. "Why should I? You were addressing her. She speaks for herself."

Brickerman took a step forward, but then a voice was heard behind him.

"Is there a problem, Monsieur Alec?" asked the Indian Policeman coming out of the dark.

"You haven't heard the last from me, Mitchell," said Brickerman, as he walked off.

Alec thanked the officer for his timely arrival, and then the man went about his business.

Alec turned to Margaret. "Stones, my dear? I must say, you do have a colorful vocabulary."

Margaret put her arms around her husband. "I'm sorry for stepping in, Alec. I couldn't help myself."

Alec gave her a squeeze and kissed her on the cheek. "I don't mind. That was just your inner Marc. If I washed his mouth with soap, I still don't think it would do any good."

Margaret laughed. "He does tend to have a gutter mouth sometimes."

They continued their walk toward the café, and Margaret tried to figure out how she and her alter ego could both enter the tournament. Alec just laughed and shook his head. The encounter with Brickerman faded from their minds.

When they returned home, Margaret had her bath and looked for Alec on the veranda, but he wasn't there.

"Alec!" she called out.

"Here!" he shouted. He was by the stone fence looking out over the rough sea.

"What are you doing out here?" Margaret asked. She stood beside him and leaned against the fence.

He put his arm around her and kissed her on the temple. "I'm just musing."

"Penny for your thoughts?" she said with a smile.

"For you, they're free," he replied. "I was just thinking that I wish I could meet your mother and thank her."

"My mother!" Margaret exclaimed, as she let out a little laugh. "Thank her for what?"

"To thank her for having a marriage arranged for you. If she hadn't done that, you would have never run away to become the person you are. Jordan would never have kidnapped you and dropped you off here, and we never would have met."

Margaret thought for a moment. "When you put it that way, I guess my mother did both of us a favor." She kissed him. "When the embargo is over, we'll sail to London and you can thank her in person."

Alec looked out over the water. "It would be nice. But I don't know if I'll make it."

"Alec, please! We've talked about this. You've got to think…"

But Alec interrupted, and lifted his pant leg. "Look, Margaret, it's starting to change color."

Margaret bent down to have a closer look. His leg was starting to blacken. "When did this start?"

"A few days ago."

Margaret hadn't seen it, because Alec had gotten in bed before she did, and then in the morning, she was up and dressed before him. "Why are you just now showing me this? We need to have the doctor look at it."

"I already have," he said sadly. "The leg is dying. I asked him if amputation would help, and he said no. My body is slowly being poisoned. He said maybe a month, more or less."

"No, Alec!" she cried, as she embraced him.

Alec held her tight to comfort her. He'd already come to terms with his mortality. Telling Margaret was hard, but how and when to tell his son would be even more difficult.

When Margaret had calmed, they discussed whether or not to tell Drake. They'd decided not to. He was a happy seven year old boy, and they wanted to keep his life as routine as possible. The time would come soon enough. Margaret suggested that they forget about the fencing tournament, but Alec wouldn't hear of it. He wanted to see his son, as well as her, participate in something they liked doing.

The next day, when Margaret and Alec told Drake about the tournament, he was ecstatic. The next weeks, the boy spent most of his time practicing either with Margaret or an imaginary opponent.

During that time, Alec kept getting weaker. He had to replace his cane with crutches. His bad leg was completely unusable. Margaret suggested that they bring him a bed down in the office area, but he wouldn't hear of it. They still had friends and business men visit on occasion. He would just smile at her and tell her he wanted to lie in bed next to his beautiful wife as long as possible. When it was time for bed, they had Sanjay carry him up the steps and then back down in the morning.

***

It was now six days until the tournament. The boy knew his father was sick, but they both told him not to worry. Alec told him, that the best medicine was to see him do his very best at the tournament whether he won or lost. Drake said he was going to win for his Poppy.

That afternoon, Margaret was practicing with the boy as Alec watched from the chaise lounge and cheered them on. A man drove up in a carriage and abruptly stopped beside the garden gate and got out.

"Alec! Marc!" the man shouted excitedly. "Good news! The Arrow Star just pulled into port. The embargo was lifted three weeks ago!"

"Finally!" Alec sighed.

"Where's Margaret?" the man asked. "She needs to hear the good news."

"She's working on a project at the moment. I'll tell her later," Alec said, giving Margaret a wink.

"One more thing," the man's voice had a note of sorrow. "The new owner of your place is here also. They've asked me to tell you that they will be out here in about two hours. Everyone hates to see you leave."

"We don't like it much either, but it's necessary," Alec replied.

"We know." The man cleared his throat. "Well, I'd better be getting off. I just wanted you to know." Then he left.

"Well, I guess I'd better change," Margaret said. She went upstairs to get her clothing and headed for the bath.

Drake sat down next to his father. "Poppy, you know what I think Marc is going to miss most when we leave?"

"What?" he replied, ruffling the boy's hair.

"The bathhouse!" he laughed. "She's in there sometimes twice a day."

Alec laughed with him. "And what will you miss?"

He thought for a moment. "Elephants," he shrugged but then added with enthusiasm, "But I can hardly wait to sail on the ship!"

"Well, one day I hope you get your own ship." Alec hugged and tickled his son.

***

Two hours passed and a carriage pulled up to the gate. A man, a woman, and a boy Drake's age got out. Margaret greeted them and they headed toward the veranda where Alec waited. Margaret thought how mismatched the man and woman looked together. She was tall and beautiful. Her long auburn hair was tied back instead of put up and covered with a hat. The man was short, balding and wore spectacles. The boy definitely looked like his mother.

"Greetings, Mr. Hansford," Alec said, as he extended his hand. "Pardon me, if I don't rise. I'm a bit incapacitated."

The man shook his hand, cleared his throat and the woman stepped forward.

"Mr. Mitchell," she said, "We have a confession to make. I'm Taylor Hansford. This is Simon Boseman. He keeps my books."

Alec's eyebrows raised in astonishment. "I thought he…"

"Simon is my alter ego you might say. When I heard your property was for sale, I came to have a look. I liked what I saw, so I had Simon broker the deal using my name," she replied.

"Why would you do that?" Alec laughed.

"I've tried to buy property before on my own, but was laughed at. So, I sent Simon. He brought me the papers to look over and sign."

Both Margaret and Alec laughed.

"I hope you still plan on going through with the deal," said Taylor.

"Pardon our laughter," Margaret said. "We are all too familiar with alter egos. We know someone who has one. And yes, the deal is still going through." There was a look of relief on the woman's face.

After all introductions were made, Alec had Drake give Taylor's son, Brock, a tour. Taylor explained that her family had been in the sugar cane business for several generations, and she'd made studies on pepper. Her brother had told her that she could never make a go of it on her own, and she wanted to prove him wrong. That was one of the reasons why she bought the place.

Alex then told her that they had to discharge Brickerman, the foreman that she'd sent down. Taylor said that he'd already approached her about it when he saw her get off the ship. Brickerman told her that they allowed the workers to steal the pepper.

Alec explained the arrangements that had been set with the workers for generations, and what Brickerman had done. He also told her he hoped she would continue the tradition and keep the household servants as well.

"So you see why I let him go," Alec said. "You couldn't get a better man than Hadji, the man I hired as foreman."

"I don't blame you for releasing Mr. Brickerman. My brother is the one who actually introduced me to him. He said he knew the business, so I hire him just to establish some sort of presence for myself. I don't believe in using whips to get workers to do their jobs. I was hoping you'd stay on a while and show me the ropes, so to speak."

"We'll be staying for just as long as the Arrow Star is here," Margaret said.

"Good," Taylor sighed in relief. "That gives me about twenty days to learn all I can from you."

***

Life was hectic for the next few days. Between showing the new owner the property, introducing her to the workers and the accounting books, they had packing to do, as well as continuing to get Drake ready for the tournament.

The day of the tournament was now upon them. That morning, Alec and Margaret were arguing. Alec was determined to use his crutches and go to the tournament under his own power. Margaret wanted to bring Sanjay to carry him. Alec said it was one thing for him to be carried around his own home, but it was another to be humiliated in public. The last two times he'd tried to use his crutches, he'd fallen. They finally compromised. Alec would use his crutches and Sanjay would follow behind him just in case he needed support. With that settled, they were on their way.

When they got to the tournament site, Margaret found out that she was the only woman who'd signed up for the women's division, so it was canceled. She was disappointed but at least she could go as Marc. After they got Alec settled in the spectators section, she and Drake got ready. The boy stood watch outside an empty room while she quickly changed.

Drake's division was up first. There were ten competitors in his group. Since the boy's were so young, their instructors were allowed to be on the floor with them to give advice.

Margaret was more nervous for Drake than she was for herself. But each round Drake competed in, he won. When the final round ended, he was awarded first place.

Margaret picked him up and swung him around. He hugged her neck and whispered in her ear. "I love you, Marc!" and she whispered the same in his.

Margaret had to wait awhile before it was time for her to compete. Her division had twenty competitors. She also won round after round, until the final. She took second. But, oh well, it was her first tournament and you can't win them all. Alec and Drake were just as proud of her as if she'd won first.

The four of them left the building after Margaret changed, and they ran into Casper L'Orange.

"Good evening, my dear friends!" He looked at Drake and rubbed his head. "You did well today, my boy!"

"Thank you, sir!" Drake grinned from ear to ear.

"Where's young Marc? I don't see him with you? I wanted to tell him not to be upset at second. LeBeau, his final opponent, has won for the past five years."

Alec cleared his throat. "We were going to celebrate the victories, but Marc found another to celebrate with — if you know what I mean." Alec winked at Margaret.

"Alec! Not in front of Drake!" Margaret pretended to scold him.

Casper laughed. "Ah, young love. There is nothing like it." Then he added, "In honor of Drake's big victory, dinner is on me."

Everyone got into the carriage, and drove a few blocks down the street to the café. Of course, Casper owned it, and there was no direct money out of his pocket. Normally, they would have walked, but just walking from the arena was taxing enough on Alec. Casper asked Margaret why he didn't see her inside. She told him she was too anxious with Drake using a real weapon and couldn't bear to watch, but she was proud of him just the same. Casper understood.

When dinner was over, they bid Casper good evening, and they said they would dine together again before they left. Sanjay helped Alec into the carriage and they headed for home.

They were about a mile out of town when they saw two men riding toward them on horseback. They thought nothing of it at first and continued talking and laughing about the evening listening to Drake's accounts with the boys he was up against. But suddenly, the men were upon them. One of them grabbed the harness of the carriage to stop it, and the other man came into view with a gun in his hand. Margaret grabbed Drake to shield him from possible harm.

"Brickerman!" Alec exclaimed. "What do you want?"

"You cost me, Mitchell. I would have had a good thing here, and you spoiled it!"

"You spoiled it yourself!" Alec scolded. "Mrs. Hansford would have discharged you herself if she'd seen what kind of methods you used."

"That's your opinion!" he shouted back. "You sabotaged me."

"Brickerman, I'm warning you, let us be on our way!" demanded Alec.

Brickerman laughed. "And what can you do about it? My man has a gun on your driver, and I've got a gun on your son."

"You wouldn't dare!" Margaret exclaimed. She clutched Drake closer with one hand, and with the other, she subtly reached down toward her leg, pulled out her knife and tucked it in the ties of her dress behind her. Carrying one had become second nature to her no matter what she was wearing whenever she was away from home.

"If you want revenge, Brickerman, take me!" Alec exclaimed.

Again Brickerman laughed. "What do I want with you? The way I hear it, you're dead shortly anyway. I want your lovely wife. Let's just say I want to give her a little going away present." He glared at Margaret and motioned with is gun. "Get out of the carriage — now."

Alec reached over and held Margaret with Drake between them. "I can't let you go!" Alec whispered.

When Margaret delayed getting out of the carriage Brickerman reiterated, "Now, Margaret, or I'll shoot your husband, then your driver and have you while the boy watches."

"I'll go!" Margaret was seething. She hugged Alec and whispered in his ear, "I love you! I'll be fine."

She kissed Alec warmly then put her arms around Drake. He was crying and she tried to comfort him.

"I'm waiting, Margaret," Brickerman insisted.

"It's Mrs. Mitchell to you — you bastard!" Her tone was harsh.

"As you wish — Mrs. Mitchell," he said sarcastically, as she climbed down out of the carriage.

Brickerman's man moved his horse closer to where he could have a better bead on the driver. Sanjay dropped the reigns and didn't take his eyes off the man, waiting for a chance to attack.

Margaret walked in front of Brickerman's horse until the darkness obscured them and then he dismounted with his gun still pointed at her. Margaret stood there defiantly with her arms folded.

"Take off that dress," Brickerman demanded.

"Ha!" Margaret huffed and stood her ground. "I'll do no such thing!"

"I'll kill you if you don't!"

"Then you'll be raping a dead body. I know your type. You're going to have your way then kill us anyway. The authorities would have your head otherwise. Why should I make it easier for you?"

"I like feisty woman!" He walked toward her, put his gun to her stomach and then touched her cheek with his other hand moving it down to her breast. Suddenly, he grabbed a handful of material and ripped the front of the dress away. He threw his gun down and pulled her to him.

"Let go of me, you son-of-a-bitch!" Margaret shouted as she struggled with him. She waited for the best opportunity to retrieve her knife.

Back at the coach they heard Margaret's shouts. Brickerman's man started to laugh.

"Margaret!" Alec cried, as Drake hollered, "Mommy!" A buried memory of his birth mother's cries surfaced from his mind and caused him to call her name.

With the cries from the dark, along with Alec's and Drake's, it was enough for Brickerman's man to become distracted and for Sanjay to make his move. He leaped from the carriage and tackled the man on the horse. A shot went off, and a cry of pain went out. Sanjay got his man to the ground. After a few moments of wrestling, Sanjay snapped the man's neck.

The gun shot heard from the carriage distracted Brickerman's attention enough for Margaret to push herself away and give him a left cross. He staggered back from the shock of the blow from this small woman. That gave Margaret her chance. She pulled out her knife and threw it. Brickerman stood there for a moment and grabbed his chest. He opened his mouth, as if to say something, and then he fell dead to the ground with Margaret's knife buried in his heart.

But Margaret didn't wait to see him fall. She recognized the scream of pain. It was Alec. She ran back to the carriage and saw Sanjay trying to attend to him and the other man lying dead on the ground.

Alec was hit in the back. When he saw Sanjay jump he quickly covered Drake, and the projectile from the gun found a target.

"Sanjay! Quickly, get us back to town!" Margaret cried, as she jumped back in the carriage.

Alec was still alive. Margaret tore pieces of her dress to press to the hole in his back to try and stop the bleeding. She tried to hold him as still as possible as Sanjay drove the horses as fast as they could go.

"Hold on, Alec," Margaret cried.

Drake held his father's head in his lap and stroked his cheek. "You'll be alright, Poppy." His words staggered through his cries.

"I can't feel anything," Alec said in a calm voice.

It wasn't long before they were in town and at the doctor house. Margaret jumped from the carriage and viciously beat on the door. A light went on in an upstairs window. When he delayed coming down, Margaret got impatient, had Sanjay break down the door and carry Alec inside.

"What's the meaning of this!" the doctor shouted.

"Doctor, Alec's been shot!" Margaret cried, as she stood next to Sanjay who was holding Alec.

"Mother of God!" the doctor exclaimed, as he ran down the steps. "Put him on the bed in that room."

Sanjay put him down, and then Margaret told him to quickly find an officer, tell him what happened and then to find the Governor.

The doctor went straight to work. His wife came downstairs to comfort Margaret and Drake in the other room, and brought a basin of water for them to wash off the blood. The woman also gave Margaret a shawl to cover her almost bare chest. It wasn't long before Casper L'Orange entered the room. He sat down beside them.

"I'm so sorry, Margaret," Casper said, as he put his arm around her.

"I'm afraid for him," Margaret cried, as she held onto Drake.

Awhile later, the doctor came out of the room and pulled Margaret aside. "I'm afraid it's no good," he said. "He's lost a lot of blood."

"Is he in pain?" A lump was forming in her throat.

"No, thank the Lord," he said in a calm voice. "He's paralyzed from neck down. The ball hit his spine. I suggest you say good-bye. He's not with us much longer."

The three of them went into the room. Alec was lying on his back.

Drake when to his father and kissed him on the cheek. Alec opened his eyes and smiled. "You were a brave boy tonight, son."

"You're going to be alright, Poppy," he said, stroking his cheek.

"Remember what I told you about your first Mommy?"

"I remember," he cried.

"Well, I'm going to be doing the same thing in a little while then I won't be sick anymore. You want your Poppy to feel better don't you?" he asked as gently as he could.

"Yes," he replied, his eyes turning toward the floor.

"You're a good son, Drake. Will you give me a good-night kiss?"

Drake held him and kissed him. "I love you, Poppy," he whispered in his ear.

"I love you too, Drake. Marc is going to need you now. Will you take care of her for me?"

"I will," he said. Then he kissed him one more time and Drake put his arms around Margaret.

Casper was the next to approach. "This is not how I want to say good-bye, my friend."

"Please, the two men on the road. I don't want…"

"Say no more," Casper interrupted. "There is no question as to what happened. Your wife and servant will suffer no ill consequences."

Alec sighed in relief, and then Casper took Drake's hand and left Margaret alone with him.

Margaret bent down and kissed him. "I'm glad you're my husband."

"You know what I wish?" he asked with a grin.

"What is it, my love," she said softly.

"I wish you would lie beside me. I'd like to make love to you like the first time."

A single laugh hiccupped through her tears. "You lecherous thing you." She lay down beside him. He couldn't move his arms, so she moved them for him, and put his hand to her breast.

"And you call me lecherous," he said with a grin and then he became serious. "Thank you. I thought I would never be able to truly love another woman beside Silvia. But I have. Take care of our son."

"I will," she said, then gently kissed him and laid her head beside him.

Alec closed his eyes and took his last breath. Margaret lay there for just a moment more and cried. But in his death, she also sensed a peace in his voice. He no longer suffered with endless pain, with death teasing him on a daily basis. She felt he was happy with this death. He died protecting his son, just as Silvia had done when she died.

Margaret left the room and closed the door. She picked Drake up in her arms and told him he was with his Mommy and wasn't sick anymore. The boy cried.

"Is there anything I can do?" Casper asked.

"Could you make arrangements for me?"

Casper smiled. "Alec made them a month ago. He already knew he wasn't leaving the land he loved. But I'll make sure his wishes are carried out."

He escorted them to their carriage, and Sanjay drove them home.

CHAPTER 23
"The Arrow Star"

Margaret stood by the stone fence looking out over the sea as she and Alec had often done. It had now been fifteen days since his passing, and the Arrow Star was leaving in the morning. She thought about the day of Alec's funeral. He was buried next to his first wife, Silvia. There were so many people. So many flowers. Pondicherry must have looked like a ghost town and every flower shop empty; he was that well like and respected. She and Drake stood beside each other as the minister read the words and Governor L'Orange delivered the eulogy. Drake had put both of their fencing medals in the coffin because he said his Poppy was proud of them.

The wake was held at the house and the food was plentiful. Everyone gave their condolences and told funny stories. Some Margaret had heard and some she hadn't. There were several people that asked where Marc was. She told them that he had his moment privately with Alec and couldn't bear to see him put under. She also told them that since he was an adventurous young man, he decided to explore India and had gone off. She still wanted to keep her Marc personality a secret.

"You're deep in thought," said Taylor, coming up beside her. "I'm not intruding, am I?"

Margaret looked at her and smiled. "No, just musing."

"There's been so much happening lately that we've never really had a chance to talk." Taylor looked out over the sea. "It's beautiful here. I bet you hate to leave it."

"Yes and no," Margaret replied. Then she laughed. "I'll definitely miss the bathhouse."

"I know what you mean. I could use it twice a day, if not more."

"I did," Margaret laughed.

"You're welcome to stay here. There are plenty of rooms and our sons seem to have become friends," Taylor said sincerely.

"I thank you for the offer, but Drake and I both want to get a new start. We went to visit his father's grave this morning to say good-bye. I asked him if he wanted to stay to be close to his parents. You know what he said?"

"What?"

"He said that his Poppy wasn't in there anymore. He said Alec told him he was going to heaven with his first Mommy to grow pepper and cane for the angels, because they need it too. Then he said that they would make their home in his heart and he would know because he could feel them there when he thought about them."

Taylor wiped a tear from her eye. "I think I would have broken down if my son had ever said something like that to me."

"I almost did." Margaret smiled. "But Drake was very positive about the whole thing, so I managed to keep my composure."

Then Margaret changed the subject. "May I ask you a personal question?"

"Depends," Taylor said casually.

"What about your husband? You've never mentioned him."

"Fred! He's barely worth mentioning," Taylor huffed. "We're divorced and I'm glad to be ridden of him."

"What happened, if you don't mind me being nosey?"

"Oh, I don't mind. Our marriage was arranged. During our engagement, he was the perfect gentleman. Compliments, flowers, presents, everything a young girl wanted. He swept me off my feet. Then we got married and he changed just a few weeks later. He was going out of town more, coming in late and once I could smell a subtle hint of a woman's perfume on him. It wasn't mine. Then Brock came along. He had absolutely nothing to do with the boy, except yell at him if he did something wrong. He never acknowledged anything good he did. I finally had enough. It took me two years to prove infidelity, but it got me out," she said with a grin.

"Do you suppose he was just after your money?"

"No," she shrugged. "His family had money. He was just an — ass. Pardon my language. It just galls me to think about him."

"No offense taken." Margaret laughed. "It sounds all too familiar."

Taylor had a puzzled look on her face. "Not…"

"No, not Alec," Margaret interrupted. "I had an arrangement also. I had the same type of ass. Only I defied my parents and ran off. Under circumstances I don't want to go into, I ended up here." Margaret closed her eyes and took a deep breath. "It was a temporarily happy life."

"I wish I'd had the guts," Taylor sighed, "But then again, I wouldn't have Brock."

"I guess there are trade-offs in life," Margaret said looking out over the sea.

They talked for a few minutes about Alec and the plantation, then Taylor left Margaret to continue her thoughts.

***

The next morning, Margaret and Drake got up earlier than normal. She made a gift of the beautiful saris that she used to wear to Sri. She'd never wear them again. They'd been something private just for Alec, and she wanted to keep it that way.

They got in the carriage and headed for the dock. Casper had asked her to see him before they left. Margaret and Drake said little as they headed for town. Then Drake broke the silence.

"Margaret, can I asks you a question?"

"Sure." She gave him a smile.

"Are you always going to wear a dress now?"

Margaret laughed. "I'll have to for a while. Why do you ask?"

"Because when you are wearing a dress, you don't look like Marc. Christian's mommy said it was bad to call you Margaret because you were my new mommy. I don't know what to call you when you wear a dress."

Margaret saw the look on his face was quite serious. She smiled and put her arm around him. "I don't care what Christian's mommy said. When I dress as Marc, you can call me Marc. When I'm in a dressed, I don't mind if you call me Margaret."

But the look on his face spoke volumes. That wasn't the answer he wanted. She sensed that Drake was feeling very alone in the world now. He needed some type of family connection now that both of his parents were gone. She realized what he did want.

"But on second thought, I think Christian's mother might be right. It's not very respectful is it?"

Drake shook his head no and gave her a smile.

"Let's see," Margaret said in thought. "You had a very good mommy, so how about just calling me Mom?"

Drake thought a moment. "Mom." Then he smiled brightly. "I like it!"

"Then that's the way it will be. You call me Marc when I'm wearing breeches and Mom when I'm in a dress."

Drake gave her a hug and a kiss on the cheek. "I love you, Mom."

"I love you too, Drake." As far as Margaret was concerned, she loved Drake just as much as if she'd given birth to him.

They arrived at the dock and bid Sanjay farewell. Margaret wished him well on his upcoming marriage next month. He offered to stay with them until the Governor arrived, but she told him they'd be fine, so he drove off.

They headed to the café where Casper had told them to meet, and then Margaret heard a familiar voice from her past.

"Well, as I live and breathe! If it isn't Margaret Wallingham."

Margaret turned around. It was Nathanial.

"So this is where you got off to." He folded his arms.

"What are you doing here?" Margaret replied defensively.

"I should ask you the same question?" he snapped.

At hearing the stiffly spoken words between this man and his Mom, Drake stepped in front of her and crossed his arms. Margaret smiled inwardly, and put her hands on his shoulders.

"The name is Margaret Mitchell now," she replied proudly. "This is my son."

Nathanial raised his eyebrows then laughed. "He's a little old to yours, isn't he?"

"Nevertheless, he is," Margaret replied.

"So where's your husband? Does he know that you were promised?" Nathanial's tone was smug.

Margaret was about to answer, but Drake spoke up.

"I don't like you talking that way to my Mom. My Poppy wouldn't have either!" He kicked Nathanial in the shin and quickly put his arms around Margaret.

Margaret laughed heartily when she saw Nathanial bend over and grab his leg.

"Damn brat!" Nathanial exclaimed.

Just then Casper arrived. "Is this man annoying you, Margaret?"

"Is this old man your husband?" Nathanial asked sarcastically, as he righted himself.

"Old man!" Casper shouted, putting his hands on his hips. "Who is this upstart?"

"Remember the man I told you about? The one I was supposed to marry," Margaret replied. "Meet Nathanial Braxton."

"Ahhh, no wonder you wanted to escape him. I don't hold any blame on you for not wanting to this — rake," Casper replied.

Nathanial puffed up his chest. "I beg your pardon, sir. Apparently, you don't know who I am."

"And it's quite apparent you don't know who I am!" Casper replied.

Nathanial turned to Margaret. "So who is this, if he's not your husband, and where is he?"

"Monsieur, we do not speak harshly of the dead," Casper said, as he motioned for two officers to come forward.

"I'm sorry, Nathanial, you didn't give me a chance to introduce you to Casper L'Orange, Governor of Pondicherry," Margaret said in an innocent tone.

Then with a wave of the Governor's hand, the two officers grabbed Nathanial.

"What's the meaning of this?" he shouted.

"The meaning, Monsieur, is that we do not insult widows and orphans in Pondicherry." He then addressed the two officers. "Lock him up!"

Margaret got a sense of pleasure seeing Nathanial hauled away.

"I didn't mean for you to have him arrested," Margaret chuckled.

Casper smiled. "Oh, I'll release him before the ship sails. I just wanted to give him time to reflect on his attitude before he got back on the ship with you. And by the look on your face, I can see you enjoyed his being arrested."

"I did!" she replied.

Then Casper turned to Drake. "You were brave. I saw what you did."

"My Poppy said I had to take care of her now."

"You did it admirably." Casper laughed. "Your Poppy would be proud."

Drake smiled brightly then the three of them went for breakfast. Margaret and Casper talked about her financial situation. He gave her the proper papers for the guardianship of Drake and custodian of his estate. She told him that she was leaving the bulk of Drake's money here in India just in case there were problems with Alec's brother. Casper told her that she'd made a wise decision. His brother wouldn't be able to touch it there without proper authorization. Margaret told him she was only taking enough of the estate to cover the conditions in the will, and get them settled and live a respectable life in the house that Alec had already purchased.

When breakfast was over, Casper walked with them to the ship. He handed her a knife. "I believe this is yours. You might have need of it again."

"Thank you. A friend told me that knowing how to use one might come in handy one day," she said sadly.

"You have a wise friend."

"I also want to thank you for keeping the fact that I killed Mr. Brickerman quiet even though it was self-defense."

"As far as anyone knows, it was Sanjay who killed both men. That's what the newspapers reported anyway. He had no objections of accepting the responsibility. It just brought honor to his family's name by defending your family and your honor."

***

Margaret and Drake arrived at the ship. New passengers were just starting to board. Casper gave Margaret a kiss on both cheeks, and wished them a safe journey. He also reminded both of them that Pondicherry would always be their home and to come back for a visit. She assured him that they would, and then they headed for the gangplank.

Margaret wondered if her young friend, Jax, was still the cabin boy. Then sure enough he appeared. He was about a head taller since the last time she'd seen him and still dressed fashionably in what he liked to call his uniform. He greeted them with a big smile and formal speech.

"Good-morning. My name is Jackson Evers. I am your personal assistant aboard the Arrow Star. Anything you might need, I shall try to be available as much as possible. May I have your names please?"

Margaret wished she could blurt out, "Hey, Jax! It's me, Marc!" But she couldn't.

"Margaret and Drake Mitchell," she replied.

He looked down the list. "I see there is a third with your party?"

"No," Margaret said sadly. "He recently passed."

"I'm truly sorry, Mrs. Mitchell." His tone was sincere. "If you'll follow me, I'll show you to your stateroom."

They followed him to their cabin or stateroom as he called it. It was large and lavish. It made the cabins on Neptune's Daughter look like her small quarters. She saw their luggage at the foot of the bed. He then handed her a list.

"This is your meal schedule for the week and a list of special services we will render for just a small fee. There is also the time when I service your room. If you wish to forgo service, just put this do not disturb sign on your door," he finished, handing her another paper.

Margaret looked down the list of extra services that they charged for:

shoe shines, laundry and meals served in their cabins just to name a few. Margaret laughed inwardly. He charged for everything that she did for free on the Neptune's Daughter. "You should be a hotel manager someday."

Jax's raised his eyebrows. "Actually, that's my plan. Is there anything else I can get for you?"

"Not at the moment," she replied, then pulled a coin from her bag and handed it to him.

He was about to leave, but then turned and asked, "Have you sailed with us before? You look and sound familiar."

"I get that a lot," Margaret replied. "I've just got one of those faces, Jax. You don't mind if I call you Jax, do you?"

"Not a bit," he replied, "That's what my friends call me." He was surprised she would use that name. Jax was not your usual nickname. Most passengers called him Jack.

Before he left, Jax offered to give Drake a tour of the ship. He said he'd call for him when they were underway and everyone was settled in. Drake was elated and Margaret couldn't say no.

With all passengers aboard, the ship finally set sail. First stop was Dover, then Calais, France, and finally London. All twenty-five first class cabins were filled. Several were the representatives from both France and England, who'd been in Calcutta discussing the embargo, which they'd finally resolved. Some of them had wives and some didn't. There were fifteen women traveling with their husbands and one was pregnant. Drake was the only child aboard. Down in the lower decks, twenty-five soldiers were housed in the dorms on their way home to England from two years tour of duty in Calcutta.

Most of the passengers that Margaret met either knew Alec, or knew of him. She hadn't realized just how widely spread his name was in India, or England, for that matter. One of the passengers said that in Calcutta and in other parts of the world, they called Alec Mitchell the Pepper King of India, and his prices were the most competitive.

When Jax came for Drake to take him on a tour, Margaret went up on deck to enjoy the breeze. It felt good to be on the deck of a ship again.

"I would like to declare a truce," said a voice behind her.

Margaret didn't bother to turn around. "Depends," she replied, in an even tone. "Are you going to talk nicely, or be a smartass?"

"I'll behave," Nathanial replied. Then he added, "Your son isn't around, is he? I've got a bruise on my shin that will take a month to heal!"

"Serves you right," Margaret huffed. "So how was jail?"

Nathanial shook his head in disgust. "I don't recommend it. The stench alone should make a man go straight. You'd understand if you'd ever been in one."

Margaret couldn't help but laugh. He only spent a couple of hours in jail, she'd spent the night.

"I don't see what's so funny?" he huffed.

"Sorry, private joke. I wasn't making fun of you."

Nathanial stood next to her by the rail. "There's a big difference in you Margaret — if I may call you that."

"Only in private conversations. If we're with others, I prefer Mrs. Mitchell."

"So why did you leave?" he asked, this time in a polite manor.

She turned to face him and looked him dead in the eye. "Tell me the truth, because if you don't, I'll know it!" She folded her arms. "Did you honestly love me, or did you just want me as a wife for a bed warmer?"

Nathanial was shocked. He said there was a difference, but what a difference! The lady seemed to have disappeared and a sailor took her place. She had a confidence in her voice. Her words were bold — not to mention the attitude. He wondered what happened to the slightly outspoken, but reserved young girl.

"Come on now, you wanted this conversation, so spit it out!" Margaret exclaimed when he hesitated on answering.

Nathanial shrugged. He may as well tell her the truth. With a son in tow, he didn't want her back anyway. "I don't like to sleep in a cold bed."

"There, you have your answer as to why I left," she replied. "I overheard you talking to Robert. Now let's see," she said, tapping a finger to her chin. "I think Robert's words were, 'If I didn't think she could do you some good, I'd tell her, to tell you, to piss off!' Am I correct?"

"Something like that," Nathanial sighed.

"So have you found anyone else?"

"After you..." he started to ply her with a smooth answer, but when she gave him the eye, he just huffed and said, "Not yet."

They stood there in silence for a moment, then a thought crossed Margaret's mind and she started to laugh.

"Now why are you laughing?"

"I know the perfect woman for you, Nathanial. She's just your type." Margaret slapped her hand on the rail.

"And how would you know my type?" he exclaimed, folding his arms.

"Trust me, I know," she said sarcastically. "Are you familiar with a woman by the name of Laura Sarandon?"

"The name is slightly familiar, that's all," he shrugged.

"The two of you should get together. She's a few years younger than you, beautiful, doesn't want children, she's richer than Midas and just wants a man for sex. In fact, the more I think about it, she's practically you in a dress."

Nathanial chuckled. "So where do I find this — perfect mate?"

"Either Dover or London. She goes back and forth. But I'm sure you won't have trouble finding her."

Then she changed the subject. Margaret was curious as to what happened in her family after she was discovered missing. So she asked, and Nathanial answered.

"When William came home, I went straight away to your parents to tell them what we knew. Your father was very upset and your mother swooned, of course. When she was revived, she blamed herself. She said she should never have let you participate in all your boyish activities then you wouldn't have been out riding."

Margaret sighed. "That's my mother! Always attacking what I like to do. Didn't she have any regrets about having marriage forced on me?"

Nathanial put his hands in his pockets. "No."

Margaret glared at him. "You wouldn't lie to me, would you?"

Then Nathanial laughed. "Let me rephrase that. Not at first, anyway. But later, after receiving your letter telling them you escaped your kidnappers and weren't coming home because of it, she was regretful. Your father said it was a good thing you'd had an interest in boyish activities, otherwise you might not have escaped."

Then Margaret happened to think. "How did you know about my letter? It was several weeks before my parents would have gotten it, and you're here," she questioned.

"I got Arrow Star's schedule and had them hold my stateroom. I met up with them in Portsmouth a month later."

"Why would you do that?"

"Think about it? My fiancé was just kidnapped, and I leave the country? How do you think that would make me look? I had to stay at least until after the investigation. When your parents got your letter, I had no reason to stay." Then he grinned. "I got a lot of female sympathy after that. So actually, you probably did me a favor — if you know what I mean."

"Hmmm, I can only imagine." She wondered if he'd created anymore offspring during her absence.

They talked for a while longer. Nathanial asked her how she met and married one of the most prominent men in India, but she said it was a private matter and with his recent death, she would rather not discuss it, so he dropped the subject.

A few moments later, Drake joined her. Nathanial excused himself and left before the boy attacked his shin again. Drake asked her if he was bothering her, but she told him he just came to apologize. Then he excitedly told her that Jax introduced him to Captain Reid, and he let him take the wheel for a few moments. Margaret was glad to see a smile on the boy's face. That was the first time he'd had anything to smile about since his father's death.

***

They'd been sailing for about a week. The Arrow Star was a large elegant ship, but she was slow. They'd made a few stops along the coast of Africa for fresh fruit and water. They'd gone through a few rain showers during that time, and hit some dead air with only the waves to slowly carry them along. But eventually they found a breeze and were on their way again.

Drake was in his glory. He followed Jax around like a puppy. Drake told Jax that he wanted to be a cabin boy and learn what to do. Jax was more than happy to push off some of the work on the boy. Margaret didn't mind. She thought it would be good for him to keep busy and out of trouble. He was always asking the crew members if he could help them hoist sails, or help them fix something. A few of them laughed and let him do some simple things and others told him to get lost. He was highly disappointed when Margaret refused to let him climb the crow's nest.

Margaret enjoyed the company of most of the passengers. Nathanial more or less kept his distance. There were a few women she liked, and some she dislike because of their 'better than thou' attitudes.

There was one woman in particular, Mrs. Petula Patronis. Margaret learned that in Calcutta, if Mrs. Patronis didn't like you, you were socially ruined. Since the woman found out who she'd been married to, she attached herself to Margaret like a barnacle and tried to give her the benefit of her ultimate wisdom, especially on the proper way to raise Drake. Margaret did her best to be tolerant and would tell her, she would consider it or smile and acknowledge her statements.

On their ninth day out, Margaret, along with ten other passengers, dined with Captain Reid that evening. Mrs. Patronis and her husband were two of the guests. She asked Margaret where Drake was.

"He's dining with the crew this evening," Margaret said, as she started to load her plate with food.

Mrs. Patronis saw her overloaded plate, shook her head and then continued her topic of conversation. "Well, my dear, I know you're young and probably don't know any better, but I hardly think your late husband would approve of such a thing."

"Oh? I didn't know you knew my husband that well."

The woman cleared her throat. "I'm sorry to say, I never met him. But I knew of him and his status in world society. "

Margaret was becoming irritated with Mrs. Patronis' interfering ways, and decided to play with her. She turned to the Captain. "Captain Reid, when I obtained permission for my son to dine with the crew, I did neglect to ask you if they practiced cannibalism. They don't, do they?"

The Captain coughed then covered his mouth with a napkin to conceal his amusement. "No, ma'am. They don't."

Margaret turned back to Mrs. Patronis. "You see? Drake is perfectly safe. They don't plan to eat him." Margaret picked up her fork and knife and continued cutting her meat.

The men at the table laughed, some of the women covered their mouths with a napkin to hide their laugher, and two others, besides Mrs. Patronis, were incensed.

"Well! That's not what I meant!" Mrs. Patronis huffed. "A boy of his station shouldn't be associating with riffraff!"

Now Margaret was becoming aggravated. "Mrs. Patronis! First, don't presume to tell me what my husband would have wanted for his son," Margaret said calmly, but firm. "My definition of riff-raff, is a person who serves no purpose in life and does nothing. As I see it, the men on this ship serve a definite purpose. That's to get us home, and they work their bloody asses off doing it."

At hearing Margaret's vulgar language, Captain Reid practically choked on his wine and a few deep breaths could be heard from others.

Margaret cocked her head and continued. "Tell me Mrs. Patronis? What purpose do you serve besides trying to tell others how to run their lives? So, on this ship, who are the riffraff?" Margaret smiled and continued eating.

Mrs. Patronis stood abruptly and turned to her husband. "Come, Sedley. I feel a spell coming on!"

The little man got up and followed his wife out the door along with two of Mrs. Patronis' uppity friends. When they left, the other women snickered, and the men cackled out loud.

"How in the world did you have the courage to tell, Mrs. Busybody off? And your language!" exclaimed the pregnant women. "She's been trying to tell me how I should behave and raise my baby when it comes ever since we left Calcutta."

Margaret sighed. "It's become a bad habit of mine lately. I open my mouth and I say what I think."

"I'm afraid you're going to be in a bad way with her now when you get to London. She has influence," said another woman.

Margaret smiled. "I'm quite familiar with London society, and I can assure you, Mrs. Busybody may be a big fish in Calcutta, but she's going to a new pond; whereas, I, on the other hand, have my husband's name plus my own heritage and reputation. The Wallingham name is well respected. How much water do you think Mrs. Patronis' threats will carry in my pond?"

The women nodded their heads and agreed. A few minutes later, Mr. Patronis returned. Margaret thought she was about to be chastised, but he surprised her.

"Mrs. Mitchell," he said with a smile. "I'd like to thank you. You're the first person who's had the courage to tell my wife to mind her own business! And so boldly I might add. Now, my lovely wife..." he said sarcastically, "...has gone to bed with a headache and I can enjoy the rest of the evening playing poker with a few gentlemen instead of listening to her prattle." He then left the room and again everyone laughed. After that evening, Mrs. Patronis avoided Margaret.

***

They had now been at sea for about a month. Drake managed to talk Margaret into letting him climb up to the crow's nest. One of the crewmen had taken a liking to the boy and told her he'd tie a rope around him just in case he slipped. She was on pins and needles the whole time he was climbing and didn't leave the deck until he came down.

Margaret got up early as usual to enjoy the morning breeze while Drake slept. It was a good time to think. Should she go home to her parents first? Or seek out Alec's solicitor in London and have him take her out to their new home. Suddenly, there was a call down from the crow's nest. "Ship off the port side!"

Margaret tried to scan the horizon, but it was too far out. She moved closer towards the bridge to hear what the Captain had to say about the ship. She wondered if it was the Neptune's Daughter.

The Captain looked in the direction with his glass.

"Can you make her out, Captain?" the mate asked.

"Not yet," he replied, "Just a little closer," he continued. A few moments later, he collapsed his glass. "Blast! It's the Tarantula!" he exclaimed. "Call all hands and get those soldiers up here! I want all men armed and ready; passengers that can fight included. I swear! When we get to London, I don't give a rat's arse what they say about schedules, I'm having cannons installed!"

When Margaret heard Captain Reid order all the sail they could muster, she immediately ran down below. She knew exactly what the Tarantula was. She'd heard men on the Neptune's Daughter talk about it. It was a pirate ship that also dealt in shipping slaves from Africa. They were also white slavers who stole beautiful women off passenger ships to sell to wealthy, lecherous men as sex slaves.

Margaret went straight to her quarters. Most of the passengers were still asleep, including Drake, until she slammed the door and started digging through her trunk of clothes.

Drake sat straight up in bed. "Mom! What's wrong?"

"Get dressed, Drake!" She grabbed the clothing she was looking for and went behind the screen.

Drake watched as pieces of her dress were tossed over the screen and then she stepped out.

"Marc!" he exclaimed. "I didn't think you were going to be Marc for a while?"

"Circumstances have changed," she said, pulling on her boots. "I can't fight in a dress. We've got pirates."

"Pirates!" Drake grinned from ear to ear.

Margaret shot him a stern glance. "This is not a game, son! Now hurry. Get dressed."

Margaret had just washed the paint off her face and was tying her hair back when there was a quick knock at the door. Jax burst in the room without being asked.

"Mrs. Mitchell! There…" Jax stopped in his tracks, eyes wide and chin dropped. "Marc! Bloody hell! You're Marc!"

"Jax, please don't swear in front of Drake."

Jax paced back and forth. "You're a girl! I can't believe it! You're a bloody girl with a kid! No wonder you looked familiar."

"Settle down, Jax!" Margaret laughed. "Girl or boy, I'm still the same Marc. Now tell me something I don't know?"

Jax finally got over his shock. "We've got pirates!" he exclaimed.

"I know that! Why do you think I've changed? What are the Captain's orders?"

"The Captain wants all passengers that can fight on deck. All women…" he hesitated a moment, then continued. "All women and children are to follow me below where they can be better protected."

Margaret turned to Drake. "I want you to go with Jax."

"But I can fight!" he exclaimed.

Margaret bent down and talked to him seriously. "Playing pirates at home is one thing. This is another. These are very bad men. Remember that bad dream you had about pirates? If I don't fight, they'll take me and kill you. I lost your Poppy. I couldn't bear to lose you." Then she gave him a smile. "Besides, they need someone brave to protect the other women. Can you do that?"

"I can do that," he replied. "Can I take my sword?"

"It's packed and in the hold," she replied.

Drake grinned. "I moved them. They're in the bottom of my trunk."

Margaret rubbed his head. "You rascal!" She hugged him. "I love you."

"I hate to break up this moment," Jax said, "But I need to gather the other women."

Margaret, Jax and Drake went from door to door waking passengers and gathering everyone who couldn't fight. There were only three men that couldn't fight. They joined the women saying that they would protect them. Nathanial and the rest of the men headed topside. Margaret smiled inwardly. Nathanial didn't give her a second glance.

When the women were properly dressed, Jax led everyone to the lower deck. Margaret wanted to see where Drake was going to be. Some of the women had asked were Mrs. Mitchell was. Margaret told them that she was well trained in swordplay and was going to guard the entrance to the lower deck. She saw in their faces that a few were impressed. Others thought she was a fool. Then there was Mrs. Patronis.

"How undignified!" exclaimed the woman in a huff.

"Madam," Margaret said stiffly. "If the pirates win, and we're overrun, how dignified will you feel when they rip off your dress and have their way with you while they make your husband watch?"

Then Mr. Patronis turned towards his wife. "Petula! If I hear another derogatory word out of your mouth about that brave woman, I swear, when we get to London, I'll tell everyone about your true heritage and how your father made his fortune!"

"Sedley! You wouldn't!" she exclaimed.

"Oh, yes I would, have no doubt about it!"

Margaret couldn't help but smile, and as much as she wanted to know about the skeleton in Mrs. Patronis' closet, she had other matters to attend to.

Margaret bent down to talk to Drake. "You be brave and don't let any pirates in."

"I will, Marc," he replied, as he gripped his fencing foil.

Jax closed the door and told the women to lock it until it was safe. With that done, Margaret and Jax headed topside.

"How am I going to explain you?" Jax asked. "Everyone on this ship knows who you are. Remember the boxing tournament?"

"We'll cross that bridge when we come to it," she replied.

With the alert, she was barely given a second glance by the crewmen that she passed. As far as they knew, she was one of the passengers, and the passengers just thought of she was part of the crew.

She mingled in with the men and listened as the Captain told them what was going on. He said that if they valued their lives and those of their loved ones, they'd better fight like they've never fought before. The men of the Tarantula was notorious for killing everyone they figured had no value, either to sell for profit, or use as slave labor aboard their ship.

Bright yellow bands were passed out for everyone to tie on their arms. In the heat of battle, it would be hard to know who was friend and who was foe. She looked toward the approaching ship. Soon the Tarantula would be in range to fire cannons. Moments later, another call came from the crow's nest. "Another Ship! Off the point beam!"

"Another one!" shouted the Captain. He put his glass to eye. It was too far to make out, but they didn't have time to worry about it. A cannon shot was heard! The pirate ship had started its attack.

***

"Ship off the point beam!" shouted the man in the crow's nest.

The Captain pulled out his glass. "Maybe that's her? She's still too far to make out."

Then they heard a noise. "Is that thunder?" David Coruthers looked up into the sky. "Clear as a bell."

"Two ships off the point!" shouted the man from the crow's nest.

"That's not thunder. That's cannon fire!" Todd Withers shouted to his commander. "Pete! Have the men add as much sail as possible!"

"It's the Arrow Star, Captain!" shouted David Coruthers, as he looked through his glass. "She under attack!"

***

Margaret stood ready. The Tarantula didn't fire to sink them; that would have been a waste of valuable merchandise. They fired on the ship's rudder and the main mast to slow them down so they could board her. The first shot was out of range. The second shot took out the rudder, and the third put a hole in the side. But now the two ships were close enough for the pirates to throw their grappling hooks. Men of the Arrow Star were standing by with axes to cut the lines, but eventually the ships were connected and the pirates crossed over.

Another shout came down from the crow's nest. "Neptune's Daughter! She's coming up fast!"

Margaret quickly turned her head and looked. He *was* coming! The Captain had come for her! But her attention was quickly brought back to the problem. They were being boarded.

***

The Neptune's Daughter was coming around to the other side of the pirate ship to trap it. Between the men of the Arrow Star and Neptune's Daughter, they hoped to possibly outnumber the men aboard the Tarantula. Their forces would have to be split.

Margaret fought valiantly. She had something of great value to protect, and she posted herself by the entrance of the lower deck where Drake was. No one was going to get past her if she could help it! Her sword found one man after another, but unlike the men she battled when Jordan's ship was on the prowl, she didn't fight to maim. She fought to kill. This was kill or be killed, and she wasn't about to go down. Drake depended on her!

The Neptune's Daughter grappled on to the pirate ship and just as Captain Withers expected, their forces had to be split. The battle was now fought on both the Tarantula and the Arrow Star. Captain Withers and his crew were cutting their way through the men of the pirate ship to reach the Arrow Star where the main battle was being waged.

They too were wearing yellow armband. The shipping company had established a color for all ships just in case of this very circumstance —

one ship helping another. You didn't want to kill the wrong person.

Another man went down under Margaret's sword. She had only a short breather to look towards the pirate ship. Her heart fluttered as she saw Captain Withers and Pete coming over the side, but again her attention was brought elsewhere. This by far, was her most aggressive attacker. He had backed her away from her self-appointed post, and she bumped into someone. She glanced quickly back and saw a yellow armband, but didn't see who was wearing it. She was too busy. The man she bumped into must have known she was also a friend, because he kept his back to hers. That made it easier to fight her man. She didn't have to worry about her back being a target.

Suddenly her foil broke! Just as her opponent had the upper hand, he dropped to the ground with a knife sticking out of his back. She looked in the direction that the knife was thrown and saw Pete. He gave her a wave then he engaged in another fight.

Margaret picked up the dead man's cutlass. She turned around to see who'd been at her back just as he dispatched his man.

"Marcus!" she shouted. It was her brother.

"I'd know that mop of red hair anywhere…" he said smiling brightly, "…no matter what you are wearing, Sis!"

She wanted to throw her arms around his neck and give him a big hug. But at the moment, they both became occupied again. Then Margaret saw one of the pirates go below deck. She was still fighting back to back with her brother.

"Marcus, watch your back, I'm going after someone!"

He acknowledged her, and she dispatched her antagonist then ran below.

The man moved through the corridor opening door after door, until he found one that was locked. Margaret was just in time to see the man kick the door in. It was the room to where Drake was.

"Hey!" Margaret shouted and he turned around. He had a sword in one hand and a dagger in the other. Margaret pulled her knife from her boot. The battle was waged in the corridor. There was no room to circle. There was only back and forth. They fought for what seemed an eternity. The pirate had managed to nick her in a few places, but Margaret was quick to recover and get in a few of her own. But then he redoubled his efforts and backed her up against a bulkhead. His foil found her shoulder. He was about to do her in, when suddenly he stopped. Blood ran from the corners of his mouth as he staggered back and fell to the floor.

Margaret looked up. There stood Todd.

"Marc!" he exclaimed, as he saw the blood flowing from her shoulder. He came toward her, and put a supporting arm around her. "Are you alright," he asked gently.

"No!" she replied sarcastically then attempted a smile. "I'm bleeding, and it hurts like hell!"

Todd laughed. "Still a smart-ass. Is that anyway to talk to your Captain?"

Then Margaret saw a small face peek through the doorway, with his pint sized fencing foil in hand.

"Excuse me, Captain," Margaret said, as she went passed him.

Drake dropped his sword ran out of the room. Margaret bent down and he put his arms around her neck.

"You get back in there now," she said to him softly. "It's still not safe."

"But you're hurt," Drake cried.

Margaret wiped his tears and gave him a smile. "It's just a scratch. I'll be fine."

The Captain came up behind her. "You don't have to worry, Marc. The battle is over."

Margaret stood and turned around. "I'm sure you know that's not my true name."

"I know," he replied. "But not everyone does. With the exception of David, to the crew you're still Marc."

Drake stoodd in front of Margaret.

"And who is this brave young man?" Todd asked.

"This is Drake," she replied. "He's my son."

The Captain raised his eyebrows in surprise. He knew this boy wasn't her true son, and he was disheartened that this meant she was married. But he smiled at the boy and put out his hand.

"Drake, I'm Captain Withers."

"Marc's Captain!" he exclaimed brightly as he shook his hand.

Margaret had told Drake several stories from the Neptune's Daughter — at least the ones suitable for young ears. He'd been anxious to meet Captain Withers.

They informed the passengers that it was now safe to return to their quarters. Hesitantly, the women and the three men came out, looked around and then quickly dashed to their cabins and locked themselves in.

When the passengers cleared the corridor, Margaret saw her brother standing at the other end. He ran toward her and put his arms around her.

"You don't know how worried I've been for you, Sis," he said, when he released her.

"I'm sorry for what I put you and our parents through, but I just couldn't marry Nathanial."

"We'll talk about that later," he said. "The main thing is your safe."

"But needing medical attention," the Todd interrupted. "Let's get you back to our ship and let Doc tend to that shoulder."

Margaret introduced Marcus to his new nephew and told both he and the Captain that she'd explain later. As much as Margaret wanted to go back to her ship, she hesitated on wanting to cross over. She expressed her concerned about Drake seeing so much devastation. He'd seen enough violent death as it was already. But Todd had a remedy for that. He took off his armband, tied it around Drake's eyes and then carried him topside. Drake thought of it as another game.

Margaret looked around at all the blood, severed limbs and intestines that were oozing from the gaping wounds. This was the worst battle she'd been in. But, just as Jordan had said, you get used to it. The pirates that weren't dead surrendered after their Captain went down under Captain Reid's blade. They were being rounded up and taken to the Arrow Star's brig.

CHAPTER 24
"Reunions"

"Well, blow me!" shouted Charlie upon seeing Margaret. "If it ain't Marc! So tell me, how was she?"

"How was who?" Margaret asked, wondering what the hell he was talking about.

"The bitch that kidnapped ya', of course! How was she?" Charlie reiterated.

Margaret rolled her eyes. "I'm gone for months, and that's all you can think to say? Can't you see I'm bleeding?"

"So," he shrugged, "Yer' breathin' ain't ya'? Now, did ya' get a piece or not?"

"Sorry, Charlie," she grinned. "I don't kiss and tell."

Several of the crew gathered around and welcomed her back. They told her they were glad *he* wasn't dead. Pete came up to her and slapped her on the back and, as usual, knocked the wind from her sails.

"Ya' done good, Lad!"

"I guess," she said holding her bleeding shoulder.

"Ah, that's just a scratch," he laughed. "You'll be right as rain in a day or two."

Then Orvil approached. "Good to have you back, Marc. I need help in the galley later. Potatoes and onions, you know."

"I just got back!" Margaret exclaimed, as blood trickled down her fingers from the puncture in her shoulder. "Do you mind if I see Doc first?"

"Sure. Take your time. See you in about fifteen minutes?" He gave her a wink and a smile.

"I'll help!" Drake spoke up, even though he couldn't see who he was talking to.

"And who are you?" Orvil asked.

"I'm Drake. Assistant cabin boy," he said proudly.

Everyone laughed including the Captain. "Well, I guess I've got a new crewman."

Some of them asked who the boy was. Anticipating that question, Margaret had her brother say it was his nephew, which was the truth. After greeting her friends, the Captain ordered the men back to their duties, and they went below to see Doc.

Upon seeing her, Doc shook his head. "It figures you'd be my first patient!"

"My bum missed your table," she replied.

Doc gave her a smile. "Believe me, my table missed your bum also. Welcome back."

Doc bandaged her up and said it would be sore for a while, and not to aggravate it until it healed. But nothing was broken. He said she'd had worse. However, he told her if she didn't keep the spot clean, it might get infected, and he'd have to use the maggots. She told him she'd make sure of it!

***

The process of collecting the dead and seeing to the injured was being attended to. The injured and the dead of the Neptune's Daughter and Arrow Star were taken aboard gingerly to either be tended to, or to be given a proper burial at sea later. The dead and unconscious from the Tarantula were cast overboard without a second thought.

They checked the hold of the pirate ship and found it empty. According to some of the captured men, they were on their way back to Africa for another load of slaves when they came upon the Arrow Star and thought they had an easy mark.

Work continued cleaning both ships of the blood and body parts. Repair crews worked on the damages to the Arrow Star made by the cannons. They scavenged parts from the Tarantula to repair the rudder. During that time, Margaret along with her brother, went with the Captain to his quarters, so she could explain everything that had happened to her, from her kidnapping by Jordan, to her marriage with Alec and then about his death. Margaret was curious as to how the Captain and her brother got together.

"After Scotty gave me your letter…" her brother said, "…she told me all that transpired. I went to Claude for further information and he told me about Pete Smithers. I searched out information about him and learned he worked on the Neptune's Daughter. After that, I kept checking the docks and learned it was in dry dock at Dover. So I headed there. I knew you were in disguise, and since I didn't want to give you away, I waited around looking for a red headed boy. When none appeared, that's when I approached Captain Withers and was filled in on what had happened."

"But how were you able to head for India with the trade embargo enforce?" Margaret asked.

"When I told him about the problem," Todd said, "He told me he had some inside information about the embargo. His wife, Rochelle, had said that her father was involved with trade relation in France, and it might be possible to get special permission to proceed to India. They said that by the time we got there, the problems would more than likely be resolved anyway. So after renegotiating our contract, which the shipping agent was more than happy to do under these special circumstances, we headed off."

Margaret sighed in relief. "I can't begin to tell you how glad I was to hear that the other ship approaching us was yours."

"So, what do you want to do now?" Todd asked. "Do you want to continue on to England on the Arrow Star? Or transfer here and sail back to India. I have a contract to fulfill."

"There's no question in my mind," Margaret replied. "I want to be here."

"What about Drake?" her brother asked. "Shouldn't you get him back home as soon as possible?"

"For Drake, England is not home." Margaret looked over by the bookshelf where Drake had fallen asleep in the chair. "Besides, a ship is where he wants to be. The majority of the time we were aboard the Arrow Star, Drake followed behind Jax', their cabin boy."

Todd was glad she wanted to stay. Margaret told her brother that if he wanted to return home in her place, he could. But he said there was no chance of that. He wasn't letting her out of his sight.

Margaret went back to the Arrow Star with her brother to retrieve her things. Todd said he'd keep an eye on Drake since he was asleep then give him something to do when he woke.

Now that the battle was over, the crew of the Arrow Star recognized her as the boy from the tournament. She introduced Marcus, as Mrs. Mitchell's brother, and that Mrs. Mitchell wanted to transfer to the Neptune's Daughter.

Captain Reid said that they couldn't account for either her, or the boy after the dust of the battle had settled. Margaret handed him a note she had written, telling him that they'd already gone over. Then if he needed confirmation, all he would have to do was ask Jax, which he did. Jax escorted them to her cabin.

On their way, they ran into Nathanial. His shirt was torn and bloody. He'd just come from sickbay with several stitches in his arm.

"Marcus! What the bloody hell are you doing here?" Nathanial exclaimed. He completely ignored Margaret, who was standing beside her brother.

"I've come looking for my sister," Marcus said, folding his arms. "You know what, Nat? This is entirely your fault. If you'd stayed away from her as I told you, this would have never happened!"

Nathanial put his fists on his hips. "So tell me, what have you got against me anyway? What have I ever done to meet with your disapproval?" he huffed.

"How about the three children you've left fatherless?" Marcus replied.

Margaret's eyebrows rose as she listened. She only knew about one. She didn't know there were three! Then there was the possibly he fathered Jax, according to Jax's mother.

"They're being financially taken care of." Nathanial frowned. "How did you know about them anyway?"

Marcus laughed. "Every servant in London knows about you. The only reason that the upper levels of society don't know, is that they don't converse with the help, except to give orders." Then he warned. "And if you don't continue to keep your children up, you'll be ruined socially. I'll see to it!"

"Who says I won't!" he exclaimed. "Now if you don't mind, I've had a bad day. I'm going to my stateroom!" He pushed passed them.

Margaret laughed and shook her head. "There goes the man who said he loved me, and he didn't even recognize me!"

"He's an ass," Marcus replied, as he put his arm around his sister. They went on to gather her things.

While in her cabin, they sat down and talked for a while. They'd missed each other terribly. She told him about the boxing tournament she won. He told her that he read about it in the newspaper and thought it funny that one of the winners had his first and middle name. Then she showed him her tattoo.

"Don't you dare show that to Mother when we get home!" he laughed. "You'll send her to an early grave."

"I don't plan to unless she tries to tell me how to run my life again," Margaret replied. "I believe I've earned the right to make my own decisions."

"You've changed, Sis. I've never known you to be so outspoken."

"As Alec used to say, that's just my inner Marc. He has a tendency to speak his own mind." They both laughed. Then they became quiet for a moment.

"I'm sorry for your loss, Sis," Marcus gave her a hug.

"Both Drake and I are coming to terms with it."

"This may sound crass, because of your loss, but Mother will certainly be impressed. By now, she's probably read about your marriage in the newspaper. You married the Pepper King of India! She'll be invited to every social event for the next year. She'll be on cloud nine."

Margaret gave a sad smile. "Then she'll be reading about his death. News of tragedy seems to travel faster than good news. It's a shame I have to go through hell and back before Mother finally approves of something I did." Then she added. "Speaking of family, where's Rochelle? You didn't leave her by herself or with our parents, did you?"

"Heavens no. Leave Rochelle with Mother!" he exclaimed, then laughed. "She would divorce me for sure if I did that. She's in Calais with her parents. She understood completely why I wanted to look for you, and I had her complete support. She loves you too."

After their reunion and private conversation on the Arrow Star, Margaret and her brother went back to the Neptune's Daughter with her things. She told Jax to have the larger items in the hold go on to England and have put in storage until she came home to collect them. She then gave Jax a small sack of coins to cover the expense and a little on the side for him.

"This is a small contribution towards the start of your hotel," Margaret said.

Jax opened the sack. "You're not Marc! You're bloody St. Nicholas!" he exclaimed, as he counted out the hundred pounds she'd given him.

Margaret also gave him two letters; one to deliver to her parents, and the other to Alec's solicitor telling him the situation and approximately when she would return to England. They shook hands, and Margaret told him she'd see him around. Jax told her that when he opened his hotel someday, she would always have a free room.

It was late in the evening before everything was set in order, and the Arrow Star was underway again. Neptune's Daughter blew a few holes in the side of the Tarantula and sank her after they stripped it of everything usable. The Neptune's Daughter then sailed on toward India to fulfill their contractual obligations.

As far as the crew knew, Drake's mother went ahead to England to make things ready, and Drake wanted to be with Marc, and get to know his new uncle. No one knew what the purpose of Mr. Wallingham's presence on the ship was anyway, except that he was the reason they were able to head to India.

Margaret told the crew a partial truth — that she was hired by Alec Mitchell to teach Drake English, and when his father died, he became attached to her. Then she warned them, not to ask the boy too many questions, or she'd kick their collective asses. Drake was just coming to terms with his father's death, and she didn't want them to stir up unhappy thoughts.

When Margaret retired for the night, she snuggled up next to Drake. The boy wanted to sleep in her cabin, and she didn't want to leave him alone the first night aboard. But after that night, he would be staying with his uncle. Her cabin was much too small for the both of them.

After a few hours she woke. She had too much going through her mind to sleep. She went topside and headed towards the bow. She loved to feel the wind and spray of the sea on her face and smell the salt sea air. The splashing of the waves against the ship as it cut through the water was soothing to her mind.

"So, what do you plan on doing now?"

Margaret looked up and saw the Captain's smiling face. She still thought he was so handsome, and even though she still grieved for Alec, the Captain was still in her heart. He sat down beside her.

"I don't know," she replied with a shrug. "I've got Drake to think about."

"He seems to be a good boy," Todd said warmly.

"He is. I just hope I can do right by him."

"It seems to me you've done a lot of things right." Todd smiled at her and discretely took her hand. "Including saving my life. Remember the storm?"

Margaret was glad it was dark. She could feel her face blush. "Doc told you about that night, I guess."

"No, you just did," he laughed lightly. "He only confirmed you were a woman. I couldn't get a word out of him. That was one hell of a dream I had not to be real. I just put two and two together and came up with you. So, why did you end that night in my bed so — painfully!" he asked, rubbing the back of his head.

Margaret grinned. "Even though I dress like a boy, have a tattoo, fight, swear, spit and have more muscles than any woman I know of," she said, flexing her arm, "I'm still a lady."

Todd laughed. He was quiet for a moment, and then he spoke serious. "I know your husband just died and you and the boy need time. But I've missed you. When I found that they'd taken you, I was crushed. Then I read the part of Jordan's note that revealed what you really were and how you felt about me. I felt as if all the air had been sucked right out of me. I wanted you in my life when I thought you were a boy needing a father figure. I know you know that. I'd now like to explore the possibility of you, as a woman, being in my life. Your son as well, if you're so inclined."

Margaret looked at him and smiled. "I'd like that. But as you said, we both need some time. Alec and I had a special relationship. We both love Drake. Alec also knew how I felt about you. I think somehow he knew that one day we might find each other again. Then Drake would have both a father and a mother." Then she sighed.

"You look troubled?"

"I may also have another battle to deal with. It's a possibility that Alec's brother, Lawrence Mitchell, might want to take Drake away from me." She looked out to the sea. "I can't let that happen. Alec feared that the most. That's part of why we married. Protecting Drake from Alec's brother weighed heavily on him."

"We'll cross that bridge when we come to it. No matter what, I'll be there for you," Todd replied.

Margaret looked at him and smiled. "I guess so. You came for me."

They both sat there in the night air for a few moments in silence. Then Todd left her to her thoughts as he had the watch in a short while. Almost a year had gone by in what seemed to be a blink of an eye. Margaret wondered what the next year would bring. Her thoughts were interrupted by the sound of Pete's voice.

"Marc! What the hell do ya' think ya' are? A bloody passenger! Move yer' arse! Ya've got work ta' do."

Margaret laughed and shook her head.

Why am I thinking of next year? It will be a long time before we reach London, and this year isn't over!

She shouted back, "Aye, Pete!" and then went about her duties.

The End?

Not yet!
This adventure is continued on into the next book.
The following is the first chapter from

High Seas:

A Matter of Blood

Chapter 1

London

"EXTRA! EXTRA! Read all about it! Alec Mitchell is dead!" shouted the newsboy.

Lawrence Mitchell reined in his horse and turned his head toward the boy.

What did he say?

"EXTRA! EXTRA! Pepper King of India murdered!" the boy shouted again.

"You!" Lawrence called. "Over here!"

The boy handed him a paper after accepting the coin and continued to peddle the word. "Get your London Chronicle! Alec Mitchell is…"

Lawrence looked at the bold headline and then read the article:

Alec Mitchell, Pondicherry, India's largest pepper plantation owner, was killed by Judd Brickerman, a former employee of Mitchell's. Mitchell is survived by his wife, Margaret, and son, Drake. Brickerman was killed

297

by the Mitchell's coachman. Wife and son expected to return to London. Margaret Mitchell, daughter of Phillip and Clarice Wallingham, of London, was just recently married to....

Lawrence stopped reading at that point, put the paper in his coat pocket and galloped home as fast as his horse could carry him. Upon his arrival, he jumped off his sweating mount and ran into the house.

"Livie!" he shouted. "Olivia! Where the bloody hell are you?"

Olivia Mitchell came out of the bedroom at the top of the stairs and looked over the railing. "I'm doing what I normally do on Wednesday's. I'm changing the bed linins!" she exclaimed, brushing a strand of hair away from her eyes. "What's all the excitement?"

"He's dead! Alec is dead!"

Olivia quickly came down the steps. "Oh no, poor Alec," she sighed. "And he was just recently married. I'm sorry for your loss, Lawrence. When did it happen?"

Lawrence pulled the paper out of his pocket. Olivia couldn't read, so he read it to her.

"How horrible!" Olivia wiped a tear from her eye. She had always liked Alec.

"Woman..." Lawrence shook his head at his dim witted wife. "...don't you know what this means? We're going to be rich! There's no telling how much Alec's estate is worth. But I do know it's a bloody fortune!"

Olivia planted her fists on her hips. "Some brother you are!" she scolded. "Alec is dead, and you're happy about it! He was a good and decent man."

"Ha! If he was so good, why didn't he share his wealth with me," Lawrence argued.

"You're forgetting, my dear husband, he saved our house from your debt collectors! If it hadn't been for him, you'd be rotting in debtors prison, and me and our son would have been sold into indentured servitude to pay the debts."

Lawrence frowned at her. "I said never to bring that subject up again. Besides — he was obligated to protect the family name."

"Reputation isn't what motivated him to help us." Olivia folded her arms and looked at him out of the corner of her eye. "Aren't you forgetting about his wife and son? Alec probably left everything to them."

Lawrence paced the floor in thought. "The woman he married was that Wallingham girl."

Olivia smiled. "She seemed to be a nice girl. I met her briefly at the

Seafarer's Ball last year. She bought a quilt I made."

Olivia made a few quilts every year for the charity auction held during the Seafarer's Ball. Her brother was killed in service of the royal navy, leaving a young daughter behind. She always felt it her duty to do her part. Her thoughts were brought back to her husband's question. "So what about her?"

"The point is she's young. She may not want to be tied down with a child that's not hers. Therefore, it's possible I could still get custody of Drake and control of his fortune. Besides — she's just a woman. What does she know about handling an estate that massive?"

Olivia shook her head. "She doesn't need to know. Mr. Wallingham is a well-to-do businessman. He could advise her."

"That doesn't matter," said Lawrence as he paced. "I'm sure the money is tied to the boy. If we get the boy, we get the money."

Olivia saw a gleam in his eye. "I know that look, and I want no part of whatever you have in mind."

She started to walk back to the stairway, but Lawrence grabbed her by the arm.

"Oh, yes you will! And so will that son of yours." Lawrence glanced around. "And by the way, where is he?"

"He's your son too!" she shouted. "It would be nice if you'd let him know you cared about him once in a while. Eric's in school and won't be home for another couple of hours."

"Waste of time," Lawrence huffed. "Eric is thirteen and it's high time he started to earn his keep around here. That private school he goes to is too expensive."

"Well, you aren't the one paying for it, so you have no say. And as for the work around here, he does his share, unlike you!" Her tone was bitter.

Alec had also been Eric's means of getting an education. When he came back to England to introduce his first wife, Silvia, Olivia secretly approached him and asked for aid. Lawrence barely acknowledged his son — much less pay for an education. Alec had set up a special trust, which he put in the hands of his solicitor, Tobias Underwood. That way Lawrence couldn't touch the money or coerce her into giving it to him. That suited Olivia perfectly.

Lawrence just ignored her comment. "I'm going back to town to talk with Alec's solicitor. I want to find out what he has to say about the matter." He walked to the door, and before he exited, he turned back to his wife. "I won't be home for dinner. In fact, I won't be home until late, so don't wait up for me." He closed the door behind him.

Olivia rolled her eyes as she walked up the steps. "So what else is new!" she muttered, as she went back to the bedroom. She figured he was probably going to get drunk with some of his friends and then visit his mistress. "Better her than me!"

Olivia thought about her life with Lawrence. He used to be handsome, and his tall frame used to be well defined and muscular. But over the past several years his chest dropped to his gut and his brown hair was thinning. She wouldn't have minded that, if he was a good person. Now, she'd much rather sleep alone. To him, she was just a vessel to satisfy his urges when he wasn't with his mistress. She hated having him slobber over the top of her. He only satisfied his needs and left her with nothing.

She sat down on the bed and sighed. Olivia wished she'd listened to her father about Lawrence when he told her that the man was lazy and good for nothing. However, she let a moment of passion get out of control, and she lost her virginity as well as became pregnant by him. What else could she do? She had to marry him. Now it was too late to leave him. She had been a child of her parents' old age. Both were now dead, and she had nowhere else to go. Lawrence had frittered away the modest inheritance her father left her in a matter of weeks.

Olivia walked over to the mirror and looked at her facial features. She was only thirty-six, but she already looked past forty. Her brown hair had streaks of grey and her hands were rough from cleaning. Instead of having a maid, she was a maid in her own house. But at least she had a house that she loved and there was no debt on it.

When her father-in-law past away, Lawrence inherited enough money for the three of them to live comfortably for many years — if Lawrence had also continued to work. For a while, they had a maid to do the cleaning and someone to cook. But her poor excuse of a husband quit his employer and gambled part of his money away. The other part he invested in get rich quick schemes which floundered. Alec tried to talk his older brother into going to India with him years ago and combine their inheritance. But Lawrence laughed and told him he had no head for business.

Olivia sighed and continued with her housework. "If only you had listened to your brother, Lawrence!" she exclaimed as she vigorously fluffed a pillow. She then thought about what Lawrence said before he left and she laughed out loud. "Who doesn't have a head for business? Ha! You surely don't. If you were in control, Drake's inheritance would be gone inside of a month!"

Arabian Sea – Same day

Two weeks had passed since the Neptune's Daughter and the Arrow Star defeated the pirate ship, Tarantula, and sunk her. The Neptune's Daughter was now on its way back to India to fulfill the shipping contract.

Margaret's shoulder wound from the battle was now healed well enough for Doc to pronounce her fit for duty. Her brother, Marcus, asked her into his quarters for a serious conversation.

"Margaret, I've never known you to be this stubborn! I'm beginning to believe it's true what they say about red heads." He paced floor of his cabin.

"Keep your voice down, Marcus," she scolded quietly. "How many times do I have to remind you to call me Marc while we're on this ship?"

Marcus looked at his sister's short mop of curly red hair and shook his head. It used to be long and beautiful. Now, his green-eyed, freckle-faced sister looked more like a street urchin. She was dress like most of the crew. Her breeches were baggy, the sleeves on her shirt were ragged, exposing that vulgar seahorse tattoo she sported on her arm and the vest she wore effectively covered up any sign that she had breasts. That surprised him, for he always thought she was well endowed on top. He laughed when she told him that their mother had her dresses enhanced for just that appearance. Marcus walked to the porthole and looked out.

"Why do insist on continuing with this charade? You look like my brother instead of my sister."

She stood beside him and leaned against the wall. "Because the crew would treat me differently."

He faced her and put a hand on her shoulder. "Neither the Captain or I would let anything happen to you."

Margaret rolled her eyes. "I'm not worried that they would do me harm." She walked back to the chair and flopped down. "I have several friends on this ship..."

"Friends!" he interrupted, frustration laced in his voice. "They tease you constantly. What kind of friends call you cake boy? What does that mean anyway?"

Margaret laughed. "It's a private joke."

She remembered her birthday. The crew had given her a party at a tavern called the Crow's Nest. She'd gotten drunk from Orvil's rum cake which was how she ended up with a tattoo. To this day, her memory was still vague about events of that night.

"If they were truly your friends, they won't change toward you," Marcus pleaded.

"Ohhh, yes they would!" she insisted. "Mr. Coruthers has already started treating me differently. I was slacking on a task I was helping Charlie with other day. He gave Charlie a dressing down, but not me."

"It's a matter of quality — he knows who you are."

"No — it's a matter of gender. He knows I'm a woman. If I were a man, he would have jumped on me with both feet whether I was quality or not. Doug Taggart, one of the watch commanders, is a gentleman. I've seen Mr. Coruthers tongue lash him with a vengeance. So don't tell me it's quality where this ship is concerned. I know better."

Marcus sat down beside her. "Very well, what about Drake? You have a responsibility toward him. What kind of example are you setting?"

"Now you're starting to sound like Mother!" she huffed.

Marcus laughed. "You don't have to be insulting."

They both laughed and Margaret continued her defense. "I feel I'm being very responsible. Drake likes me as Marc, because I can play with him and teach him things a woman wouldn't normally do."

"Such as?"

"Fight with a sword, throw a knife..." she hesitated a moment then added, "...spit for distance." She watched Marcus roll his eyes and continued. "When I'm dressed properly as his mother, he loves that too. So as I see it, he has the best of both worlds."

"I still don't like it."

"Think about it, Marcus. I have to continue this charade. Say I did expose my true identity. How would it look in the eyes of society if it were known that I served on a ship of men for over a year? And then what about the boxing tournament I won in Liverpool? People would put two and two together." She pointed to her tattoo. "Shall we forget about this? The men on this ship gossip just as much as women do."

Marcus stood and threw his hands up in the air. "I give up!" He sighed. "I concede your points. If you want to swab decks and load heavy cargo, who am I to stop you."

She gave him a smile. "Cheer up, Marcus. When we reach Dover, Marc is going to resign from the ship, and Margaret will come aboard to rejoin her son and brother for passage to London. Now if you'll excuse me, I have duties."

Marcus grinned. "Well, since it's your intention to continue as a servant aboard this ship…" He sat down in a chair and stretched out his leg. "…help me off with my boots. They are in need of a good polish."

"Certainly, Mr. Wallingham. I'll be happy to be of service. However, there's a small fee for that type of personal service."

"I saw that list." He pretended outrage. "Piracy! Shear piracy!"

"Oh, did I neglect to tell you that I was a member of a pirate's crew for a while?" she said as she walked toward the door.

"Ohhh! Get out of here before I forget you're my sister and turn you over my knee for a sound thrashing!"

She laughed as she closed the door behind her. Margaret loved her brother dearly, and he'd always been protective of her. His concern was appreciated, but her experiences over the past year had changed her. She was in control of her own destiny, and no one was going to dictate how she lived her life if she could help it.

Margaret went about her duties. She was tasked to mend canvas, so she gathered her materials and went to the bow to do her work and think. She thought about the conversation with her brother. Mr. Coruthers wasn't the only one who'd changed toward her. The Captain had also. Before he found out she was a woman, when she brought him his coffee in the morning, he was half-awake, unshaven and without a shirt. Now he was completely dressed, hair neat and not a hint of stubble on his face. They used to carry on conversations with ease in the morning — they were currently strained.

She decided to do something about it. If they were going to explore a relationship, things had to get back to normal. She had a good idea how she was going to do it, but it would have to wait until tomorrow.

***

Margaret woke earlier than normal. Quietly, she opened the door to the Captain's quarters and peeked in. He was still asleep. She went in and took one of the chairs by the chess table and straddled it next his bed. She propped her chin on the back and stared at him. Herculean is how she thought about him. He was ruggedly handsome, with his coal black hair and sun-bronzed, muscular form.

She closed her eyes for a moment and thought about the night of passion in his bed. It still embarrassed her to think about it. She had been in his bed to keep him warm and help rid him of the fever he suffered from. In his delirium, he started kissing her. She still felt badly about hitting him over the head with that metal pan. But it was a necessity. Kissing almost turned into something else.

Shaking herself from past memories, she opened her eyes and saw the Captain gone from his bed. She turned her head and met another pair of eyes staring into hers. The Captain was straddled across another chair beside her.

She smiled. "I must have dozed off."

"I don't remember giving you permission to enter my cabin," he said, mocking a serious attitude..

"I didn't ask."

"Then why are you here?"

"To talk."

"About what?"

"Me."

He grinned. "Sounds like a fascinating subject."

"Why did you keep my secret from the crew?" she asked seriously.

"That's an obvious question. Just in case we found you, I didn't want things to change for you." He smiled. "I don't have the words to tell you how glad I am we found you." But when he reached over to touch her cheek, she grabbed his hand gentle and put it back down on the chair.

"Then why is it you're treating me differently?"

Todd was puzzled. "How am I doing that?" He stood and returned his chair back by the chess table as did Margaret.

"This is how I am used to seeing you in the morning when I bring you coffee — bleary-eyed, half-dressed and hair mussed. How is that the same?"

He folded his arms suppressing the urge to laugh. "So you enjoy seeing half-naked men, do you?"

Margaret put her hands on her hips. "That's not the point!" Although in her thoughts, he was right. She loved looking at his body.

"You're right, I admit it," he sighed. "I guess I just wanted to present myself as a gentleman in your eyes."

"Do you think I'm a lady?"

Todd shrugged. "Of course. Why wouldn't I?"

"Look at me." She turned around in a complete circle. "I'm dressed like the rest of your crew. So, if attire denotes whether you're a lady or a gentleman, what does mine make me?"

"I see you're point." He put his hands on her shoulders. "I guess I just wanted to make things more comfortable for you. I still feel guilty about what I put you through aboard this ship."

Margaret took his hands from her shoulders and held them. "You didn't put me through anything. I could have left this ship anytime I wanted to. And I don't think I'm any worse for the wear. In fact, I even think it's prioritized my thinking about things."

He shook his head. "Margaret, you amaze me."

"Marc, if you please," she grinned. "When I'm dressed like this, I'm your cabin boy who brings you coffee in the morning and then tends to other duties aboard this ship. I just had the same argument with my brother yesterday. When we get to Dover, Marc is going ashore to stay and Margaret is boarding to return to London with Drake."

Todd laughed. "I offer you comfort and you take hardship."

"I've always had comfort and never really appreciated it until I came aboard this ship. A little hardship makes you appreciated the comfort when it comes your way."

Todd nodded. "Very well then — Marc." He plastered a stern look on his face. "Next time you enter your captain's quarters without knocking I'll have you flogged. Is that understood?"

She mocked his expression. "Understood, sir."

Todd put his hands on his hips. "Now where the bloody hell is my coffee?"

"I'll be back shortly." She headed toward the door and then turned around. "Oh, by the way, could you tell Mr. Coruthers to treat me as he used to as well?"

"Aye, aye, Marc." He gave her a salute. "Any other orders for the day?"

Margaret laughed. "No, that will be all — sir."

Todd watched her leave and then started to get ready for his day. He wanted to kiss her, but she subtly let him know she wasn't ready yet. There was plenty of time — a lifetime, as a matter of fact. When she was ready for a relationship between them, she would let him know.

After Margaret's talk with the Captain, things got back to normal. She tested Mr. Coruthers by slacking on an assigned task, and he called her down for it. But when he passed her, he gave her a subtle wink. He was playing a part, but that was fine. The crew heard him chastise her and that's what was important. If he showed her any favoritism the crew would notice, and it would put her in a bad way with them.

***

Neptune's Daughter pulled into its first port of call at Bombay. There were only six ports they need to make stops at before heading back home. In conversation with Captain Devan Reid of the Arrow Star, they learned he'd already picked up the contracted cargo in the area around the Bay of Bengal while the trade embargo with France was in force since his ship was the only one allowed in the area. That meant they would be able to head for home at least two months earlier than expected.

Margaret was down by the loading dock with the crew on cargo duty. Marcus was leaning on the ship's rail watching and laughing at her.

"Having fun — Marc?" he shouted down to her.

She wiped the sweat from her brow and looked up. "You should try it —Mr. Wallingham!" she shouted back. "If I were a betting man, I'd bet you wouldn't last the day before collapsing."

Marcus grinned. "Is that a challenge — boy?"

"I believe it is — Sir." She watched him take off his coat.

Sam nudged her in the ribs. "Are ya' daft, Marc! Talkin' to a passenger like that? It'll be yer' arse if Pete heard ya'."

"I know what I'm doing," she assured him.

Marcus came down the gangplank and stood beside her. So, what's your wager?"

Margaret thought for a moment. "I'll polish your boots free for a month against that fancy vest you're wearing."

"Done!" Marcus put out his hand to shake on the deal.

Margaret felt mischievous, so she spat on her palm and gripped his hand. It was all she could do to hold back her laughter at seeing the disgusted expressed on her brother's face.

"What do I do first?" he asked.

"See Pete," she shrugged. "He's the watch commander in charge. I'll take you to him."

Margaret took her brother to Pete and explained the situation.

"Are ya' sure, Mr. Wallingham? It's gonna be a long day ta'day," Pete warned.

"I'm sure," Marcus replied.

"Suit yer'self. We've got plenty of help topside. I'll take ya' ta' Levi. He's in charge of the storage hold."

Pete took him below deck. He knew exactly who Mr. Wallingham was. Marc — was his sister. He knew that the Captain and Mr. Coruthers were now aware of her charade, but no one, except Doc, was aware that he knew. Marc didn't even know.

Pete had heard Marc challenge her brother and laughed inwardly. He could have left the man on the dock to work in the fresh air, but decided to take him to the hold — the worst place to be on what was shaping up to be a hot day. He wanted to give his young friend an edge over her brother.

Pete told Levi that Mr. Wallingham was bored and wanted something to do. Levi shrugged and put him to work. But when their passenger wasn't looking, Pete pulled Levi aside and whispered, "Work the hell out of him, Levi. Marc bet him he wouldn't last the day."

Levi laughed. "If the man wants to work, work is what the gentleman will get."

It was noon before anyone had a break in their day. The bell sounded for the noon meal. Marcus could barely get his legs to climb the ladder from the hold. When he reached the deck, he saw Margaret leaning against the rail with a grin on her face. He walked to the railing and stood beside her.

"Have fun, brother?" she asked so as not to be heard. His hair was plastered to the side of his face and his clothing was drenched with sweat.

"No — since you asked. My muscles have declared mutiny on me, and my blisters have blisters." He sniffed the air. "I think that awful stench I smell is emanating from me."

Margaret laughed. That was exactly how she felt her first day aboard. "And the day isn't over with yet."

"Don't remind me!" he exclaimed. "Aren't you sore?"

"Not much. It's been a while since I've had cargo duty. But I've tried to keep my muscles in shape for it — just in case I came back to the ship." She flexed the muscle in her arm. "You want to call off the challenge?"

"And have you show me up? I don't think so. You'd never let me live it down."

Charlie and Sam were watching Marc with Mr. Wallingham.

"Will ya' look at those two," said Charlie. "By the looks of 'em, they could almost be brothers. They kind'a look alike."

"Who knows," Sam shrugged. "They might be. Maybe Marc's mother was diddled by Mr. Wallingham's father. Marc said his mother worked as a ladies maid."

"Could be," Charlie replied. "Well, come on, I'm starved!"

Marcus made it through the day — but barely. He'd gained a new respect for his little sister if that was what she had to endure on a daily basis. Though he won the wager, he called their bet a draw. He was exhausted. Instead of having dinner, he went to see Doc for liniment and went straight to bed.

Other Books and Stories By:

Michele L. Hinton

Novels

High Seas: The Cabin Boy
High Seas: A Matter of Blood
The Sin-Eater's Daughter

Children's Books

Princess Courtney and the Magic Suit
Humpty Dumpty: A Fractured Tale

Short Stories & Poetry

Tales with a Twist & Tales Totally Twisted
Michael Smith
Joshua Pennwrite: Ghostwriter

Beauregard Blue
(A children's book written by
Betty J. Rees, Michele's mother)

Made in the USA
Columbia, SC
01 July 2024